Stash

Stash

David Klein

Broadway Books

New York

BROADWAY

Copyright © 2010 by David Klein

Published in the United States by Broadway Books, an imprint of the Crown Publishing Group, a division of Random House, Inc., New York.
www.crownpublishing.com

BROADWAY BOOKS and the Broadway Books colophon are trademarks of Random House, Inc.

Grateful acknowledgment is made to Cotillion Music, Inc., for permission to use an excerpt from "I Got You Babe," words and music by Sonny Bono, copyright © 1965 (renewed) Cotillion Music, Inc., and Chris-Marc Music. All rights administered by Cotillion Music, Inc. All rights reserved.

Library of Congress Cataloging-in-Publication Data

Klein, David (David Matthew)
Stash / by David Klein.
p.   cm.
1. Rich people—Fiction.   2. Suburban life—Fiction.   3. Drug abuse—Fiction.   4. Interpersonal relations—Fiction.
5. Psychological fiction.   I. Title.

PS3611.L4435S73 2010
813'.6—dc22

                                        2009052594
ISBN 978-0-307-71681-1

Printed in the United States of America

10 9 8 7 6 5 4 3 2 1

First Edition

To my family: Harriet, Julia, and Owen,

who are always there for me

Acknowledgments

I'd like to thank early readers of this novel for their encouragement and feedback: Caroline Barrett, Aurora DeMarco, Robert Jaffe, and Phyllis Jaffe. Stephen Maher advised me on legal and criminal matters. David Haar offered insight into the pharmaceutical industry. Sam Russem and Fred Edmunds inspired elements in this story. Michael Neff of the Algonkian Writer Conferences helped me position the novel. I learned how PTAs function from the folks at Elsmere Elementary School. I relied on the wonderful book *Story* by Robert McKee to help shape later drafts. Owen and Julia taught me how children speak and think. And, of course, this book would not exist without the support and efforts of my agent, Loretta Weingel-Fidel; my publisher, Diane Salvatore of Broadway Books; and my editor, Lorraine Glennon. Most important, thank you to my wife, Harriet, who has stayed by my side every step of the way.

part 1

She Took a Hit

I'm Here to See Jude

Gwen arranged to meet Jude at ten, after dropping the kids at their morning camps. She'd already delivered Nate to Nature's Workshop, and now drove her daughter to the pool. It was Nora's last day of swim camp and Gwen had baked a tray of cupcakes, vanilla with whipped cream frosting and red, white, and blue sprinkles left over from July 4th.

Nora balanced the tray on her lap in the backseat, snitching frosting edges under the plastic wrap. Two cupcakes were missing, eaten by Nora and Nate in the car, wrappers discarded on the floor, crumbs flattened into the seats.

"Honey, will you be able to carry the tray if I drop you off in front?"

Nora hesitated. "I might spill them."

"Not if you're careful."

"Will you do it?"

Because she was anxious to get downtown, Gwen almost snapped back at Nora about being old enough for this small responsibility. But she reminded herself that Nora was only seven, a loving, intelligent girl, tall and strong and for the most part capable, yet fearful of small things going wrong—such as dropping a tray of cupcakes. You had to accept your children were people, with their own quirks and limitations as well as talent and potential. Once you realized you couldn't mold them into robotic perfection, you could do a much better job parenting; for instance, by carrying the cupcakes for your daughter who was afraid of spilling them.

"Okay, sweetie. You carry your towel and backpack and I'll carry the tray."

Gwen parked in the drop-off zone in front of the pool complex, navigating a place between the other cars coming and going.

"Mom, you're not supposed to park here, it's for drop-off only," Nora told her.

"It's just for a minute—you want me to carry the cupcakes, don't you?"

"You might get a ticket."

Nobody issued tickets at the Morrissey town pool.

Gwen lifted the tray from Nora's lap and waited while her daughter located her flip-flops, centered her backpack on her shoulders, got out of the car without her towel, and climbed back in to retrieve it after Gwen reminded her.

"Come on, honey," Gwen urged her.

"I'm not late."

"Mommy has a lot to do today," Gwen said. "Remember, you're going home with Abby. Mrs. Fitzgerald will drive you and I'll come get you this afternoon."

"And then we're going up to the lake?"

"As soon as Daddy gets home."

"I can't wait to swim in the lake."

And Gwen couldn't wait for the getaway with her husband and family. Four entire days at their house on Tear Lake, which they'd hardly been to this season because of camp schedules and Brian's work. Four days of rest, relaxation, and love.

They walked to the entrance where Nora stopped to remove her backpack and look through two zipped compartments to find her pool ID card. Gwen explained to the desk attendant that she was just delivering cupcakes for her daughter's camp party.

The party consisted of two picnic tables pinned with paper table-cloths on a grassy area between the kids' pool and the big pool. A breeze flapped the sides of the cloths and rippled the surface of the water. Not a great day for swimming, not for Gwen anyway, who liked hot weather and warm water. The pools would close for the season in another week, right after Labor Day.

She found a spot for the cupcakes on one of the tables and spent a few minutes thanking the instructors—college kids home for the summer, heading back to school this weekend—and when she turned to leave she was waylaid first by Carly Eller asking Gwen which teacher Nora got for third grade, and then by Heather John who reminded Gwen about their annual open house on Sunday, one of the few adults-only social gatherings among their circle. Gwen apologized for having to miss out. If they were in town it would have been fun to go; the Johns played great music and hosted a karaoke contest that commenced after everyone had spent an hour or two loosening up at the patio bar.

"You won't be there to defend your karaoke crown," Heather said.

Last year, Gwen and Brian were voted karaoke king and queen for their Sonny and Cher duet, "I've Got You Babe." In a silly rush of sentimentality, Gwen had felt tears when she sang, "So let them say your hair's too long, 'cause I don't care, with you I can't go wrong," and Brian, sporting a fresh haircut, had answered, "Then put your little hand in mind, there ain't no hill or mountain we can't climb." In her acceptance speech, margarita in hand, Gwen had reminded everyone she'd played the role of Maria in her high school's production of *West Side Story*, sans the painted-on Hispanic tan that Natalie Wood sported in the movie version.

"Some other lucky talent will have to go home the winner this year," Gwen said. Using talent in its loosest meaning.

"We'll miss you guys," Heather said.

A last check with Nora. Did she have the gift cards for her instructors? Her goggles? Hairbrush? Love you, sweetie. A final hug and Gwen made her way back to the car, stopping once to dig a stone from her sandal, then driving downtown to meet Jude.

In the car she called Brian. He didn't pick up—no surprise. Whenever he planned time off work, the few days leading up to it were crazy. She knew he had a big presentation today. When she got his voice mail she said, "Hi love, just wanted to wish you good luck again in your meeting. I dropped off the kids and am running errands, then going home to pack. I can't wait for the weekend. Love you." Then she added, "Call me if you need anything."

She parked in a metered spot across the street from Gull. She checked herself in the rearview mirror and played with the flip in her hair, without success, then touched up her lips. She found two quarters in her purse to feed the meter, which gave her thirty minutes.

A neon sign with blue lettering hung perpendicular from the transom over the door to the restaurant, with the L's in Gull tipped to the side to resemble a bird's wingspan. A pair of real gulls, up from the river, circled overhead, screeching.

Gwen expected the restaurant to be empty—it didn't open for lunch until 11:30—but she was greeted at the hostess stand by a short, dark woman with bangles running up and down both wrists.

"Do you want to fill out an application?"

"Excuse me?"

"Are you applying for the cocktail waitress job?"

"Oh, no. I'm here to see Jude."

"Who should I say is asking?"

"Gwen Raine. He's expecting me."

"Why don't you wait in the bar?" the hostess suggested. "I'll find him for you." She reached for the phone next to the reservation book.

Gwen sat in the bar. Three women occupied other tables. They all appeared to be in their early twenties, long hair, each wearing at least one article of black clothing—miniskirt, cami with bra, spandex T-shirt—each with dark lipstick and piercings. They all displayed a degree of cleavage.

The women were filling out job applications. Could Gwen really have been mistaken for a potential cocktail waitress? How could she—with her Eileen Fisher tee and khaki slacks and sandals—even if she had carefully picked out her clothes this morning and spent an extra minute in front of the mirror before coming in? And with the real giveaway: her crow's-feet ticking off time like the markings of a clock around her eyes.

Gwen had worked in a bar once, but that was almost nine years ago, during law school. She never finished law school, even the first year, but she'd had a blast working in the bar. It's where she first met Jude, who hired her, and later, Brian, who married her.

The woman at the table closest to Gwen tore her job application and shoved the pieces in her handbag. She was the one with the miniskirt, and when she stood, Gwen got a look at her trim, tanned legs all the way up to where her skirt just covered the curve of her butt. Not an inky vein or cellulite crease in sight. I was like that, Gwen thought, two kids ago, sigh, although she never wore her hem that high.

The woman who ripped her application left the restaurant, averting her face from the hostess.

A moment later, Jude appeared from the dining area. He approached Gwen's table, his pace slow and unhurried. Gwen remembered that even on the busiest nights at the Patriot, Jude never rushed around, appearing calm and poised amid the chaos of the dinner crunch.

She stood and hugged him briefly, catching a drift of the same cologne he'd worn when she worked for him. Whether it was Armani or Old Spice, she didn't know: it was Jude. She'd recognized the scent a few times over the years, on a stranger standing nearby or walking past her; every time it reminded her of Jude, and every time she looked around expecting to see him.

"You must have had a great summer, you're so tan," he said.

"A lot of pool time with the kids. One of the advantages of being a full-time mom."

Gray flecks streaked Jude's hair, along the temples and sideburns. He wore what Brian called an executive cut—trimmed, parted, gelled into place. Except Jude had these long straight sideburns that tapered below the ear. On someone else they would have been a mistake.

"I'm sorry I'm a few minutes late. I had to get my daughter settled at her swim camp."

Jude waved off her comment. "It's fine. Can I get you a drink? Glass of wine? A Bloody Mary?" He motioned to the bar.

"I'd have to take a nap, and it's not even noon yet."

The two remaining job applicants looked up, unsure whether Gwen had cut ahead of them in the interview line.

"Coffee then?"

"Coffee sounds good."

"We'll go to my office." On the way through the dining room Jude stopped at a dish station where a fresh pot of coffee sat on a burner. He lifted two cups down from the shelf and poured.

"You must be asking hard questions on your job application," Gwen said. "I saw one woman tear hers up and walk out."

"We get a lot of response to our ads but it's hard to find anyone who really wants to work. You ready to come back?"

"Your hostess thought so."

"In your case I'll waive the application."

"I'm sure it would be fun, only now I'm in bed every night by eleven—about the same time the bars get busy."

Jude smiled. "So much for the good old days. Let's see, coffee black, right?"

She nodded.

Jude carried both cups. They passed double doors with port-hole windows and Gwen glimpsed the kitchen where two cooks performed prep work while listening to music.

At the end of the corridor they climbed a staircase, traversed a hallway, and ended up in Jude's office, which provided a second-floor view of the river, passing slow and gray in the direction of New York City. Jude settled behind a glass desk that held nothing except a laptop. There wasn't a surface in Gwen's house that clean, despite her constantly picking up and putting away. The credenza behind him was a different story, brimming with papers and folders and books—everything from novels to business books to cookbooks. Another shelf unit to the side held a stereo dock and a pile of restaurant magazines.

Gwen sat in a chair opposite the desk, holding her cup. She didn't want to set it on the pristine desktop, although Jude had put his down. She turned to check that Jude had closed the door. This part made her tense, and she listened for footsteps, voices, anything to indicate someone approaching.

"You can relax, there's no one else up here," Jude told her.

"I'm fine," Gwen said, her face heating. Was she that obvious? She sat up straighter, set her shoulders back.

"How are Brian and the kids?"

"They're great. We're going away this afternoon for a mini-vacation, so thank you for seeing me today. We have a house in the Adirondacks now. Tear Lake. I don't think we had it last time I saw you."

"No kidding? I have a place up that way, too, just an old cabin; it was in Claire's family for years. I'm also heading north this weekend because Dana's starting her freshman year at St. Lawrence."

"Wow, that's right. Be sure to tell her I said hi. I mean, if you want to. She probably doesn't remember me."

There was a photograph of Jude and his daughter next to the stereo on the bookshelf. They wore skis. Their arms and ski poles were tangled around each other. It looked like a recent picture, Dana tall but still much shorter than Jude, with dark straight hair flowing from underneath a ski hat. Her wide smile showed off dazzling teeth, the mark on her eye just a shadow from this camera angle.

"I've been thinking about you since last time," Jude said. "I was wondering when you would call again."

She had visited Jude for the same purpose over the winter, and then in April when she had to come downtown to serve jury duty. Gwen didn't get picked for a jury, but she stopped at Gull and had lunch with Jude one day that week. Otherwise, she hadn't seen him the past nine years, and although she didn't respond to Jude's comment that he'd been thinking of her, she had thought about him a few times as well. Not about their brief relationship years ago, but about Jude's life now. She wondered if he was the only unmarried man she knew, which didn't say much about the diversity of her circle. He was the only one who didn't have the look of married men, like they were part of a whole, and when on their own came off as incomplete or inadequate, as if they hadn't dressed quite right or had gotten a bad haircut. Gwen also knew how married men looked at her, as if conducting a compare and contrast study: How did this woman stack up to my wife? Was she better looking, younger, smarter, thinner? Or just different— which may be the best attribute of all? With Jude looking at her right now, she sensed his appraisal was based more on a clean slate than a weighted scale: Is she desirable? A question that carried no qualifying conditions, just an eye of the beholder. A question whose answer made her fidgety. A question she'd rather not address because she also wondered if she might be rekindling a friendship with Jude, if such a friendship were allowed, no matter how casual—a married woman having an unmarried male friend, who also happened to be a former lover. Not against the law, but likely against the rules. She doubted Brian would welcome the news without suspicion.

"I thought you and Brian were coming in for dinner some night," Jude said.

"We haven't been out in months, he's been so busy with work, but we will."

A few seconds ticked off. "Or just come by yourself," Jude said. "We'll have lunch again."

Gwen looked at the clock on Jude's bookshelf. Ten minutes left on the meter.

"I meant some other time," he added. "When it's not business."

"Okay."

"You don't have to call ahead, just show up. That day you came in, it was a nice surprise."

Another thing about having a male friend: it would probably be okay if he was unattractive or unavailable, but in Jude's case the *un-* didn't apply. It definitely applied in her case, though, at least the unavailable part. She was firmly married, entrenched, and fulfilled in her life and role as mother, wife, and volunteer. Her days of messing up relationships were distant memories, played out by her younger, less mature, and more experimental self.

Gwen reached into her purse and handed Jude a white business envelope, the flap unsealed. "I really appreciate this," Gwen said.

"You're one person I'm happy to make a call for."

"Five hundred, right?" She was nervous and sure her voice betrayed her, although the risk seemed so low here with Jude.

"That's perfect." Jude placed the envelope on his laptop keyboard without looking in it. He opened a desk drawer and took out a brown paper lunch bag and set it in front of Gwen.

"Do you want to try it first?"

The question surprised her; he hadn't asked her this last time. It was tempting, like the old days at the Patriot, but was Jude going to join her or leave her solo? Would she get stoned with him now upstairs in his office? That wasn't a good idea.

"Actually, I'd better go," Gwen said. "I have to get packed for the weekend."

Jude shrugged his shoulders. She put the bag in her purse.

"I should get your number," Jude said. He unsnapped a phone from his belt. "You have mine, I should have yours—in case it's me who needs a small favor next time."

"Oh, sure, of course." She gave him her cell number and he keyed it into his phone.

Then Jude stood up. "Have a great trip, Gwen. Come see me when you get back. You don't have to wait until you run out."

He walked her downstairs and through the dining room, out to the bar and hostess area. A new applicant sat at one of the bar tables, filling in blanks.

"Oh, and one more thing," Jude said, leaning close and lowering his voice. "Don't tell anyone. I'm only doing this for you."

"I promise," Gwen said.

"I don't want anyone getting the wrong idea."

He pushed open the door for her. He followed Gwen outside and they were alone on the sidewalk in front. She turned for the good-bye hug but Jude reached for her, touched her chin and cheek, leaned in, and kissed her. Time slipped for the second or two that his lips found and pressed against hers, then pulled back and were gone. She hadn't seen it coming. Her breathing halted, heart drummed. She stepped back and turned without meeting his eyes and walked quickly to her car. By the time she dared a look, he'd gone back inside.

A Few Minutes to Relax

Gwen drove along Route 157, the road curving in and out along the ridgeline of the escarpment, until she came to the start of the Indian Falls trail in Thacher Park. She turned into the lot and parked in back where there were no cars.

That kiss. What was that kiss about. He'd caught her 100 percent off guard, although now that she thought about it, Jude definitely had been flirting with her. Thinking about her since he'd last seen her, he said. Suggesting she come back again for lunch, alone. Asking her to visit him when she returned to town. That was his nature, she knew, and there was nothing wrong with getting a few strokes, as long as she let it pass, which she did, as long as she didn't stroke back, which she didn't. But then he kissed her at the end and ruined it all.

Now she wouldn't be able to visit Jude again, for any reason.

It was just a kiss, one she likely misinterpreted, and she should put behind her, the sooner the better. This was her chance to relax. She had four hours of alone time before retrieving the kids from Marlene's, and only a few more errands on her list. Jude had included a sheaf of rolling papers in the lunch bag, which also contained a plastic baggie holding four pungent, sticky, egg-sized buds with frosted purple hairs around the edges. Gwen held the bag to her nose and breathed in. Wow. She broke a piece off one of the buds and crumpled it inside the bag, then pinched the loose flakes between her fingers to roll a thin joint she put into a stringed clutch along with her phone. She tucked the bag of remaining buds in the seat pocket behind her. She hung the purse over her shoulder and carried her sweater and found a remote picnic table along the fence near the edge of the cliff. The sun shone but a breeze blew and the air felt a few degrees cooler up here than in the valley.

From the ridge in the park Gwen looked out across the valley, the few taller buildings downtown poking up in the distance like toy blocks stuck in the ground. The sky blazed blue and she could make out the swells of the Adirondack foothills on the northern horizon.

She lit the joint and took a few hits and lay back on the plank top of the picnic table and let the sun warm her face. She closed her eyes. Hummed deep in her throat. Wet her lips. Four days at the lake house, just her and Brian and the kids. Hiking, swimming, canoe rides, fires at night. That's how she imagined it would be: their family nested and spending every minute together. She and Brian had bought the house when Brian's company was acquired, his stock tripled in value, and he received a bonus for staying on. But they'd hardly been up there because Brian had been too busy with work, long hours, traveling for days at a time. She thought of this trip as promoting a new lifestyle—less hectic, more simple. Breakfast and dinner as a family. No television. A bottle of wine on the couch with Brian after the kids were in bed, a little pot to relax. A lot of lovemaking. When was the last time they did that. Hugging. There would have to be a lot of hugging and holding, among all of them. Cuddling with the kids. They were still young and delicious and wanted to touch her. Nora would hold hands with her all day. Nate had stopped nursing but still wrapped himself around her, would curl in her arms and press his face against her like a baby.

A few more hours and they'd be going.

Gwen wasn't a stoner. She didn't laze around all day with a bong by her side and the TV and stereo both on, too mellow to get off the couch to wash the dishes or get dressed. She didn't order take-out day after day. She'd known plenty of people who did live like that—mostly when she was in college or working at the Patriot—but even back then Gwen didn't fit the profile. She would take a puff or two off someone's joint or pipe and stayed away from other drugs, stuck with wine as her drink of choice unless a bartender knew how to make a good margarita.

She was sixteen the first time she got high, in her junior year, hanging around the park after school with her friends one day, when a joint appeared in someone's hand. It got passed around and ended up with her boyfriend, Mark, a senior. She watched him take a long deep inhale and hold it, like he knew what he was doing. He offered it, and Gwen took the smallest poke. It came around again and this time she inhaled deeper. The next thing you know she and Mark were goofing around on the kids' playground, pumping on the swings, playing chase on the jungle gym. It was a cold November day and they had the playground to themselves. Later, before leaving the park, she made out with Mark. The past month they'd been moving closer and closer to doing it, rubbing through their clothes, hands in each other's pants, and that Saturday night she went to Mark's house when his parents were out. He'd gotten a big joint for them to smoke. She had sex for the first time and it wasn't painful or scary like she'd been made to believe but exciting and sensual—maybe quicker than she'd expected, but they did it a few times and she felt happy and full.

A few months later Mark broke up with her because she'd gone with someone else to the movies. He was too proprietary and she didn't protest much. However, he'd been her source for pot and now she stopped smoking, didn't think of it again until college when suddenly everyone had it. Gwen got high at parties and on weekends—but not before or instead of classes or as a daily ritual like some of her suitemates did. If she happened to be going out with a guy who liked to get high, she'd join him. She loved to have sex when stoned; it managed to be both soothing and intense at the same time. She had great orgasms.

Brian preferred vodka. Maybe once in a while if he had drunk enough he'd take a hit or two, get paranoid, and shortly thereafter pass out. Therefore, Gwen never encouraged him. He had no objections to Gwen getting high when they were dating, and then living together, and then married, although for the first seven-plus years of marriage she didn't smoke at all; up until last year she'd been either pregnant or nursing the entire time. When Nate finally weaned—Gwen was the only mother she knew nursing a four-year-old, making her a target for clucks and stares from some of the other Morrissey moms—what remained was a much less intimate routine of shuttling, entertaining, managing school schedules, cleaning up after her kids, and cooking for her family. Chores and errands and bills. She hung out with other moms, volunteered in the PTA, found babysitters on weekends so she and Brian could do more than pass each other coming and going, and overall loved her life and her husband and children and wouldn't trade any part of it, knowing how lucky she was. And one day when the kids were in school and Brian at work and her to-do list crossed off, she experienced a nostalgic craving while watching the wind blow the empty swings in her backyard. She wondered where she could get a little pot, that would be fun; she didn't know anyone like that now.

Then she thought of Jude. She had run into him over the winter when downtown with Brian and the kids for Winterfest. They had left the bonfire and jugglers at center square and were walking along Pearl Street toward the river to see the ice sculpting display when Nora announced she had to pee. When Nora needed to pee, you called all hands on deck; it was a state of emergency. A two-minute drill began to find a bathroom; otherwise she'd wet her pants. The nearest place with an open door was a restaurant called Gull, too elite-looking for family dining or kids, but they went in and three of them stood just inside the front door while Nora darted into the bathroom. Wait. Was that Jude Gates standing behind the bar? It was. The same Jude who managed the Patriot when Gwen had worked there, who hung out with her after hours, who shared his joints and poured free drinks. Jude who she had partied with and slept with and almost fell in love with, even though he had a wife in a rehab facility and a young daughter to care for. Long gone days. Young days. Days when she did not consider consequences.

Gwen checked on Nora in the restroom while the boys waited. She hadn't thought about Jude in a long time. Should she say hello? Would he remember her? Nora finished in the stall; Gwen decided she needed to pee, too. When they came out of the restroom, Jude was looking their way. He walked over and hugged her and shook hands with each of her kids and Brian. I guess he remembered her. And sure, he remembered meeting Brian when Gwen worked at the Patriot. He'd no idea they'd gotten married, or that she still lived in the area. He insisted they stay for a drink. Nora and Nate experienced virgin piña coladas for the first time. Gwen and Brian drank a quick glass of wine. Jude invited them to come back for dinner some night and try the menu of his new chef, Andrew Cole.

She and Brian never went back, but it was Jude she thought of when she wanted to find some weed.

Gwen lit the joint again and took a last hit, then snuffed it out against the table. She had enough time to walk the Indian Falls trail and still finish packing and have the car loaded and kids ready when Brian got home this afternoon.

Then her phone rang. It was Marlene.

"I'm stuck in the waiting room," Marlene said. "I haven't been in to see McGuire yet. I hate to do this, but I don't think I'm going to be on time to pick up the kids. Can you do it and drop them off, then they can spend a few hours with me?"

"Oh, I thought your appointment was at ten."

"I know, ninety minutes sitting here. It's probably not worth it."

"No, I can do it," Gwen said. She checked her watch. She'd have to leave in a few minutes, first to get Nate, then the girls.

"Sorry to throw this back at you."

"That's okay," Gwen said. "By the way, I got it."

"You did? What was it like?"

"Pretty easy; he's just an old friend who did me a favor."

"You're a lifesaver," Marlene said.

"I mean, it wasn't totally comfortable, but . . ."

"Roger and I don't know anyone else. If it wasn't for you, we wouldn't know where to begin looking."

"I won't be able to ask him again, though."

"Never mind, we'll worry about that later. We're flush now and I'm putting the kids to bed early tonight."

"I'll bring it by later when I see you."

"Thanks again, Gwen, for everything. You're a great friend."

Gwen took a few breaths to clear her head and focus. She'd have to save the trail walk for another time. She wrapped the remains of the joint in a tissue and zipped the tissue and pack of matches inside an inner pocket in her purse. She put the bag back over her shoulder, returned to her car, checked her teeth in the mirror, and drove back along Route 157, the road a series of wide switchbacks on descent, the sun bright through her windshield. She kept two hands on the wheel and the stereo on scan, hoping for a good song. She rounded a curve and suddenly a car appeared right behind her. She heard the bass of its stereo blaring and the growl of its engine. The driver edged out across the double line as if to pass, then pulled back behind her bumper.

Her heart pushed against her throat, but she maintained course and speed, stayed calm, and held the wheel firmly. She'd been in this situation before, she could handle it.

When the road straightened, the other car pulled out again and accelerated, defying the double yellow line, flashing past, windows dark as night. It cut back into the right lane and braked into the next turn, a long arcing curve with a wide cinder shoulder and a rusted guardrail on the ridge side. She must have been looking far ahead along the curve, to where the car that passed hers had disappeared around the bend and into the shade cast by a stand of roadside trees. It must be going so fast to be gone from view already. And then a new movement in the sunlight brought her focus in closer and another car was there, a different one, oncoming, right in front of her—a heartbeat from head-on.

Gwen wrenched the wheel to the right. The other car struck her rear quarter panel with a shuddering bang, sending her car into a spin. Her body pitched but her seat belt held her in place. She stared out the windshield. She felt motionless, as if the road and the shoulder and the road again and now the trees moved in a slow horizontal pan in front of her while she remained in place clenching a steering wheel that would not respond.

Then the view through the windshield became mottled shades of dark. A flash of sun, shade again. Then another loud bang—and this one hurt.

A Growing Market

John Wilcox, up from the mother ship in Jersey, watched Brian, not the slides. Ryan Garcia, the CFO, and Jennifer Stallworth, legal counsel, sat back in their chairs, nodding as Brian clicked through his presentation. Seated at the far end of the table, Teresa Mascetti kept watch on the reactions in the room. She'd helped Brian with the presentation and knew it as well as he did; the few times he veered from his prepared talking points he could see her inhale and get this stricken look on her face, as if he'd whispered something dirty in her ear.

Brian stood to the side in front of the room and clicked a remote to move through the slides.

"The target market is growing with no end in sight," Brian said, as his next slide came up, a bar chart showing the increasing weight of American adults over the past ten years, with ten-year projections added on. In place of simple colored bars to show the data, Brian had found a graphic of a belt, with the buckle in the middle representing median weight and the length of the belt growing longer with each successive year as average weight increased.

Teresa drew a breath. Brian wondered if he'd offended her. He'd added that slide just this morning, although it wasn't necessary. Everyone in the room knew the market situation.

"Looks like my belt," Wilcox said, patting his waistline. He was a thick, powerful man with a voice that carried like thunder over distance, a throwback sales executive who landed big contracts with hospitals and HMOs over golf, meals, and cigars. "What do you think, Jennifer? Will that belt graphic work for our revenue chart in the annual report?"

Everyone at the table chuckled.

Home run. After eliciting the reaction he had hoped for with the depiction of the belt, Brian moved quickly past the slide.

The purpose of his presentation was to promote and defend the business case for Caladon Pharmaceuticals to seek FDA approval for Zuprone as a weight-loss drug, a strategy Brian recommended and expected the executive team to support. Zuprone already was approved and marketed as an antianxiety drug, which in itself covered a broad and vague range of indications. The problem was that Zuprone had captured only a minor share in the crowded antianxiety market. There were lots of "me too" competitors, and Zuprone was one of them. Yet, even at the time of launch, evidence existed of the weight-loss benefits. Over the past three years, active off-label prescribing of Zuprone for weight loss had increased the drug's sales and profitability, and over the past six months, since Wilcox came aboard via the acquisition and immediately assigned Brian the mission of educating more physicians about the weight-loss benefits of Zuprone, sales had soared.

Seeking FDA approval for a second therapeutic indication could be cost prohibitive. Zuprone had already been through years of development and clinical trials for its original intent; repeating the process for weight loss would add significant costs to the drug's balance sheet. But Brian's projections pointed to increased profit because the second indication—obesity—*was* a growing market with no end in sight, as his clever belt slide indicated. Caladon could use the same manufacturing process and facility, and simply package, name, and market the drug differently for weight loss—

once the application was submitted, clinical trials conducted, and FDA approval granted.

"The anecdotal evidence looks good in terms of number of prescriptions already written," Garcia said. "But two things: One, we can't go back and track these patients and call that a clinical study. And two, how much is our marketing responsible for the bump in number of prescriptions for obesity?"

"What about the research at UCSF, that guy McLellan?" Wilcox said. "We've been hosting a seminar that references his study."

"It's not the same thing," said Jennifer Stallworth. "Research studies are not controlled clinical trials. They're simply data points to help make our own decision whether to move forward or not. The patients who've been prescribed off-label have had none of the usual safeguards or controls in place. Though there is a chance some of the prescription history data can be transferred to trials."

"I don't want to be accused of human experimentation if we try to co-opt the existing data," Garcia said.

"I wouldn't worry about that," Stallworth said. "*Richardson v. Miller* set precedents there. As long as the physician was seeking optimal treatment and the drug use was customary—even if off-label—it wouldn't be considered experimentation."

"If we start using anecdotal data about all this off-label prescribing, someone at the FDA might start wondering about the volume and how we built momentum," Garcia said.

Brian stepped in to regain control. "Regardless of anecdotal data, we have to conduct every stage of trial for FDA approval. And I've projected the costs of clinical trials . . ." He quickly forwarded a few slides to a table of data.

Wilcox grunted. Everyone turned to look at him.

"When is Stephen coming?" Wilcox said. Stephen Jeffries was the medical director of Pherogenix. He'd been a founder of the company now owned by Caladon.

"He's out this week," Teresa said. "On vacation."

Brian winced; Wilcox shook his head. Vacation was a sensitive topic with Wilcox, anyone's vacation; he didn't believe in them. And it was a particularly sensitive subject today. Wilcox had wanted to postpone today's meeting until Monday, but Brian stated he'd be unavailable because he was taking a long-planned, although short, vacation.

Surprisingly, Wilcox had shrugged off the scheduling conflict during a phone call with Brian. "You probably deserve it," he said. "We'll come up as planned on Friday."

You bet he deserved the vacation. Although sometimes Brian wondered what was the point. In the end you didn't work any less or reduce your stress. He'd put in almost double time trying to pull this presentation together the last few weeks, missing dinner with his family almost every night and weekend outings to the pool. And when he got back from vacation, even if he stayed in touch through e-mail and voice mail while gone, he'd be in deep weeds again.

But in this case the vacation days would be worth the price he'd pay at work. If ever he needed time with Gwen, he needed it now. With the hours he'd been working, it was like he and Gwen were living in separate, parallel worlds, catching glimpses of each other but rarely connecting. He understood now the old phrase about two ships passing in the night. This would be Brian's first time off in over a year and also the first time they'd spend more than a weekend at the lake house. They'd hardly gotten to enjoy it: a fully furnished custom house with a wraparound porch on Tear Lake, close to the road on one side, but with 150 feet of lake-front and a dock on the other. It was a luxurious second home with tall tinted windows and a view of America's wilderness. The crazy thing is that between the stock and the bonus, paying for it wasn't that much of a stretch. What a windfall the acquisition had been, with Brian the first to admit that luck, and not just ambition and hard work, had played a big role in his financial situation today.

He had started his career at Pherogenix, a start-up drug company that had been fishing medical schools to fill positions and found Brian in his fourth year. Stephen Jeffries recruited hard, offering to help pay down his school loans as a kind of signing bonus. At first Brian resisted; he had visions of becoming an MD and working a few years in war and poverty zones, making a difference for the underprivileged before settling into private practice. He'd scratched and clawed his way through four years of medical school—if he gave it up and joined Pherogenix he'd not complete his residency and never get licensed.

Then everything changed. Gwen got pregnant and Brian realized the difference he wanted to make in people's lives was actually in one life: Gwen's. He accepted a good salary and what he considered a boatload of stock from Pherogenix to help coordinate clinical trials for their new antianxiety drug, Zuprone. He was too busy to think about medical school again, and he never looked back. Seven years later, Caladon Pharmaceuticals grabbed Pherogenix when Zuprone showed potential. Since then Brian had been tracking data and surveying physicians who prescribed Zuprone. He'd been the first to notice the trend in off-label prescribing for weight loss. And while it was illegal for a manufacturer to promote a drug for off-label use, Wilcox jumped on the market opportunity and recruited Brian to educate more physicians and Caladon's sales reps about the latest in obesity treatments, including Zuprone and its full range of therapeutic benefits.

Business case aside, Brian's role in the advancement of Zuprone was a key reason he favored the FDA application. The focus would turn to new clinical trials and the drug approval process

while taking any attention away from Caladon's marketing practices on behalf of Zuprone. Brian executed that marketing under
the watchful eye of the company's attorneys, but pharmaceutical
promotion had more gray than a stormy sky. Plus you never knew
which overseeing agency or righteous physician or disgruntled
employee might start making a fuss, and with Brian on the front
lines of marketing and business development, he could quickly
become a target if the finger-pointing started.

"Since Stephen's not here let's just move on," Wilcox said. "You
were going to tell us about the competition."

In fact, Brian hadn't been about to address the competition,
but he now flicked forward another half-dozen slides and began
speaking.

"There's Orlistat, now available over the counter . . ."

"The oily discharge drug," Wilcox interjected. "Talk about
shooting yourself in the foot—or the ass."

Another round of obligatory chuckles.

"Yet a projected $1.5 billion in annual sales, despite the side
effects," Brian added. "And Rimonabant, which blocks CB1 re-
ceptors, suppressing appetite."

"It's sold as Accomplia in Europe, rejected by the FDA here,"
Teresa said. "Linked to an increased risk for suicide."

"And Meridia is still out there," said Brian.

"But none of these drugs have met expectations, with sales flat-
tening after an initial market surge," the CFO, Ryan Garcia,
pointed out.

"Zuprone works differently," Brian said. "Because it's primarily
an anxiety drug, it doesn't have the same side effects, although at
the higher doses generally prescribed for weight loss . . ."

"Let's see the market data for the others," Wilcox cut in.

It was Brian's experience that Wilcox didn't care much about competitive sales figures. Give him and his team a few talking points about competitive drugs and they were set to go. Of course, competitive research was part of any business case, and in this case it was the weak part of Brian's presentation. He hadn't the time to dig into the reams of research Teresa had gathered for him, instead taking a calculated risk that what mattered to his audience and to Caladon overall was what Zuprone could do in the market moving forward, not what older drugs had already done.

"We're still compiling some of the data," Brian said.

"I'm more concerned about drawing the FDA's attention to Zuprone's marketing efforts," Jennifer said. "And that's the first thing Stephen's going to ask about."

Brian was about to respond to Jennifer when Shelly Pearson, the receptionist, knocked at the conference room door and leaned in.

"Pardon me—I'm sorry. A call came through the switchboard for Brian." She spoke to the room in general, then turned her attention to Brian. You could see the anxious look in her eyes. "It's your wife, she said it's an emergency."

Brian blinked, vaguely aware that everyone had turned to look at him, but their faces became blurry and far away, part of the background.

What kind of emergency? The kids. Was it Nate or Nora? Or both.

He reached for his phone on the side table where he had placed it with his notebook. He had turned off the ringer for the meeting; there were three new messages on it.

"She said to call her cell phone," Shelly added.

"Excuse me," he said. He started for the door. Someone stood up. Wilcox or Garcia. Brian couldn't focus. He walked past Shelly into the hallway, hitting the speed dial for Gwen. He took a deep breath.

She answered on the second ring.

"What happened?"

Static messed the connection. Gwen said something.

"What?"

"I was in a car accident; I'm at St. Mary's. I'm not hurt—I'm a little . . ." The phone signal cleared. He heard fear in her voice.

"How are the kids?"

"They weren't with me—I was on my way to pick them up. I'm cut; they said I need stitches."

"Where?"

"St. Mary's."

"No, where are you cut?"

"Above my eyebrow. I hit my face. I mean the air bag hit me. It's not that bad, but there was a lot of blood and it was scary. It was so loud, it was terrifying."

His heart stopped thumping. "Where are the kids now?"

"They had to wait for Marlene to pick them up. But she has them now."

She coughed, then started to cry. "Brian . . ."

"I'm on my way."

"Please hurry. Please."

Teresa stood behind him now, and Wilcox. Brian turned and explained that everything was okay—mostly okay, his voice cracking. Gwen had been in a car accident and was at the hospital and he needed to leave.

"Of course," Wilcox said, creasing his brow in concern. "Is there anything we can do? How's your wife?"

"A little banged up," Brian said.

He looked at Teresa. She put a hand on his forearm. "Let us know."

Among the Cupcake Wrappers

Her face pulsed, swollen and hot, like a bad sunburn. Nose and cheeks tender. Dried blood clogged her nostrils, forcing her to breathe through her mouth. More blood stained her shirt. After the nurse had cleaned her up, Gwen asked for a mirror. A red gash capped her eyebrow.

Now she lay back on the gurney, curtains on either side dividing the treatment bays in the ER. The resident, Dr. Su, stuck the side of her temple with anesthetic before starting with the sewing kit. She heard voices and noises from behind other curtains and in the hallway, someone moaning like a cow, a steady background murmur, the hum and click of machines. Overhead lights hurt her eyes.

"Air bags can deliver a tremendous punch," Dr. Su was saying. He fingered the wound. "I've seen broken noses and missing teeth. Even a dislocated jaw. But it's better than swallowing the steering wheel, no?"

He looked like a teen refugee from a third world country, not a whisker on his face, his frame thin as a coat hanger. Gwen could see, even through the gloves, he had the long and slender hands of a model. His fingers moved with precision.

Dr. Su told her he was a resident in reconstructive plastic surgery; he'd make her look perfect again. His voice was soft, but he spoke with authority. "It will be easier if you close your eyes," he said. "That way you won't move so much."

Gwen closed her eyes. She started crying a little, tears leaking out the sides of her shut lids, crying not from the pain of the sutures along her eyebrow—although each one stung like a bee, despite the anesthetic—but because she was scared. Her legs trembled, she couldn't steady her knees. She'd never been in an accident, not even a small one. Never backed into the garage door or bumped fenders with another car in a parking lot. It had been so loud; she hadn't expected that. Like a steel door slamming in her face and reverberating through her body. Like the lid of a Dumpster crashing down. *Bang!* The entire event lasted only a few seconds, yet so much had happened. She remembered the view out her windshield when her car went sideways, how the landscape moved across her field of vision, but slowly, like a camera panning. She'd been so out of control, unable to influence any of it. She spun onto the cinder shoulder and struck the tree and that's when the air bag deployed, like a gunshot, slapping her face and collarbone, then just as quickly deflating. She sat dazed, not sure how badly she'd been hurt; she could be seconds from death or simply shaking off a slap. She didn't know—she'd never been struck in the face. Then she unbuckled her seat belt and turned off the engine. She opened her door and looked back down the road for the other car, but it wasn't there. Only a smattering of broken glass remained on the roadway. Had the other car struck her and kept going?

Then she saw the gap in the guardrail where a chunk of steel had been ripped away, the remaining edges sharp and rusted.

"Oh no, oh my God," she spluttered. Blood smeared her vision in one eye; more dribbled from her nose. She licked at it with her tongue, a metallic taste flooded her mouth.

She felt dizzy, foggy. But she had to do something, Gwen realized.

What did she have to do? Yes. Help, call for help. She was still wearing the purse around her shoulder and she reached into it for her phone. She dialed 911 and told the operator there had been an accident, she was on Route 157, yes people were injured, she was one of them—she didn't know how badly. When she hung up, nausea surged up her throat.

She should find the other car. It had gone over the edge of the ravine.

She tried to take a step in that direction but her legs quit and she collapsed to the ground with her back against the front wheel of her van. The sunlight blinked in and out from behind the canopy of leaves waving in the trees above her.

Dr. Su said, "Try to hold still, please. Almost done."

"I am trying." Then she added, "My husband is coming. He'll be here soon." Brian would hold her hand. It was an accident, that's all. Not her fault. She needed a few stitches. She would be fine.

"Just one more to go."

Gwen opened her eyes and the doctor's fingers were dancing right over her face, tying thread. "Six altogether. Luck to have an even number."

"What?"

"That's what I say. It's good luck to have an even number of sutures. I always try to do that."

"Oh, thank you," Gwen said, unsure how grateful she should be.

The nurse who had cleaned her up was back now, peering over Dr. Su's shoulder at Gwen's face. "You look good, hon. Dr. Su is very talented."

"No scar," Dr. Su said. "You'll still have exquisite eyebrows."

Other drivers had stopped across the road. One approached Gwen seated on the ground against her car and asked if she could stand. Gwen said, "Nate, I have to get Nate."

"Who's Nate? Is someone still in the car?"

She heard sirens in the distance, from the direction of town, coming up the hill. She had her phone, although there was blood on the screen and keypad. She pressed Brian's number and his voice mail picked up immediately. Next she tried Marlene and got through. Before Gwen could say a word, Marlene told her she was just walking out of the doctor's office and could pick up the kids after all.

Gwen sobbed into the phone.

The commotion increased around her. First a police cruiser arrived, then the fire rescue, a daytime disco of lights swirling around her.

A paramedic squatted next to her. Gwen was aware of activity in the distance. One of the police officers had set up flares and was directing traffic through the one open lane. Another had disappeared over the edge of the ravine where several bystanders now stood on top.

The paramedic asked her questions. Was her vision blurry? Could she turn her head from side to side? Was she injured anywhere else? Could she move her arms and legs? As he spoke he wiped away the blood near her eye and around her mouth. Gwen smelled the antiseptic on the wipe. Was she having any trouble breathing? He shone a light in her eyes.

She answered none of his questions.

When Gwen saw the stretcher being wheeled over, she got to her feet and said, "I don't need that."

"You need medical care and we need to transport you."

Gwen looked at her car. The front end was crumpled against a tree, the side near the rear caved in.

"Please, can you hold this?" The paramedic had pressed a gauze against her forehead. Gwen held it in place as she allowed herself to be helped onto the stretcher.

"I want to sit up."

The paramedic angled the stretcher into a sitting position.

"Ma'am, I'm Officer Hendricks. What's your name, please?" It was a policewoman now, uniform, pad in hand. No hat, blond hair in a ponytail. Something familiar about her.

"Gwen Raine."

"Can you tell us what happened, Ms. Raine? How the accident occurred?"

Gwen swallowed.

"The other car, it was just there," Gwen said. She looked again to where the guardrail had been ripped. There were men now in firefighting equipment, more in police uniforms. The onlookers had been shooed off.

"What does that mean, just there?"

"It came into my lane. Like the driver didn't see the curve at all."

"You say the other car crossed into your lane and struck you."

Gwen nodded. She had stayed in her own lane.

"Did you see the other driver?"

Gwen shook her head. "It happened too fast."

"Which direction were you traveling, ma'am?"

"From the park." Gwen pointed up the road.

Officer Hendricks looked in that direction, then up at the sky. "Maybe the glare," she said.

———

Dr. Su peeled off his gloves. "I'm going to write you a prescription to help with the swelling and pain. You should be fine in a few days. The bruises might take a little longer."

"Okay."

"Fine, right?" He scribbled something and handed her a slip of paper.

Fine.

The nurse said, "You can fill that here before you leave or take it to your pharmacy."

"I can go now?"

"In a few minutes," the nurse said. "We have discharge paperwork."

The curtain slid aside and the same policewoman who had interviewed her at the accident came in. She was accompanied by a square-faced man with a mustache covering his upper lip. He wore a sports jacket over a T-shirt. Behind him stood another nurse or technician, one Gwen hadn't seen before. This one held a metal briefcase.

The one with the sports jacket introduced himself as Detective William Keller and produced a folded sheet of paper from an inside pocket. It was a warrant—he read—"issued by Judge Robert Donovan of the Town of Morrissey authorizing a sample of blood from Gwen Raine following the vehicular accident on Route 157, Town of Morrissey, hamlet of Helderberg."

Dr. Su slipped away. The other nurse stood back against the curtain. The new technician moved forward, setting her case at the foot of Gwen's bed and unsnapping the latches. Gwen stared at the floor, where a dropped bloody gauze lay unnoticed.

"I wasn't drinking," Gwen said.

Her heart began to pound. She'd smoked some of the joint in the park. When was that? About two hours ago. Would that show up in a blood test?

The blood technician took out syringe, gauze pads, and rubber tourniquet.

Gwen started to protest. "The other driver crossed into my lane."

"We'll test him, too."

The tech tied the rubber band above Gwen's elbow.

Detective Keller said, "Officer Hendricks found a bag in your vehicle containing a substance that looks and smells a lot like marijuana."

The bag from Jude. She could see right where it had been—behind her in the seat pocket, stuffed in a netting next to a Spider-man action figure and Nora's American Girl books. She could see how it happened: police checking out her car, waiting for the tow truck. Hey, look what I found. What was an ounce of sticky sensimilla doing in this mom's minivan among these cupcake wrappers, toys, and books? That's not a snack food for the kids, is it? I guess when you drop out of law school the first year you miss the chapter where it says possession of marijuana is a violation of penal code 221.10, and that driving while under the influence of marijuana is a punishable offense. These moms with school schedules and camps and cooking dinner, keeping the husband happy and house presentable—it's not that they think they're above the law, but who has time to keep up with what's legal and what's not, all these sections of the penal code?

"Mrs. Raine?" Detective Keller said.

Her fingers rose to the wound along her eyebrow and stayed there, covering her eye.

"Shouldn't there be a bandage on this?" she asked, tracing the track of stitches.

"I used a spray that works like a bandage," the nurse said. "That's all you need."

The needle stuck a vein on the inside of her elbow. She winced and glanced down to watch the syringe fill.

"Do I have to?" Gwen said.

"We have a warrant, Mrs. Raine."

Is This a Daily Habit?

Neither of them said a word on the way home, until Brian turned in the driveway and Gwen let out a single, abrupt sound like a stifled laugh.

"What's so funny?"

"I'm sorry, nothing," Gwen said.

"Getting arrested is a big joke?"

"I'm just happy to be home."

He'd been composed and helpful until now—through the arrest and police station and huddle with their lawyer, Roger Fitzgerald, Marlene's husband. Yet all along he'd been working on his position: What blend of sympathy and anger should he present to her? He wasn't sure. He was so relieved that Gwen was okay, and so pissed she'd gotten stoned before driving to pick up the kids. They'd never been through anything like this.

Once inside, he pressed her. "What were you doing with an ounce of pot?"

"It wasn't all for me, half was for Marlene."

"You mean you're *dealing* it?"

"No, I'm not dealing it."

"Yet half the drugs you got busted for are going to our lawyer's wife?"

"And Roger, too. He smokes with her."

Brian sighed. "I'm having a drink. You want anything?"

She shook her head.

He got vodka and ice from the freezer, poured himself three fingers, took a stool next to her at the kitchen island. He leaned his elbows on the granite countertop.

"Where did you even *get* an ounce of pot?"

Gwen met Brian's eyes and looked away.

"From Jude again? He's your dealer?"

"He's not a dealer—he just did me a favor." Using the language Jude had: a favor between old friends.

"He likes to do you favors it seems."

"I can't just run to the store and buy it like you can a bottle of vodka."

"This morning you didn't tell me that scoring a bag of weed was on your list of errands for today."

"Am I supposed to tell you?"

"You told me you were going to the dry cleaner's. You told me you had to pick up the farm share."

Gwen said nothing.

"Did you get high with him?"

"Who?"

"Jude."

"No. What are you accusing me of?"

"You've shown an incredible lack of judgment. Don't you find that troubling?"

"I told you—Marlene was supposed to pick up the kids, but then she got delayed at the doctor's. It was an accident, Brian. There was no time to react, the other car was just there. I at least turned the wheel. If I hadn't done that, it could have been a lot worse."

"How many people were in the other car?"

"I don't know, it happened so fast."

"So we don't know who else is hurt or how badly?"

"Didn't Roger say he'd find out?"

They still hadn't heard about that. But crashing through a guardrail and down a ravine, that can't be a joyride.

"How often do you do this?" Brian asked.

"What?"

"Get high during the day, when you're with the kids. Is this a daily habit?"

"I'd never do anything to put them in danger. You know that."

Brian let it go. If anything, Gwen was overprotective of their children. She even kept a close eye when they played in the backyard. They weren't allowed to cross the street without her—and they lived on a quiet residential road. She was careful about what they ate, she limited junk food, made them wear helmets on their bikes. He couldn't question her devotion to their safety.

Gwen said, "It could have happened to you after having a few drinks when we go out."

Her mouth tightened and she swallowed. For the first time, she looked ugly to him, her face puffy and discolored, the gash over her eye a violent track of red crossed with black sutures, the rest of her thin and drained like a battered, hopeless woman from a trailer park, a druggie from the school of hard knocks. All she needed was a cigarette hanging from her lip.

Gwen moved to the couch with a cold pack they'd given her at the hospital. She opened and massaged the bag to activate it, then leaned back and rested the pack over the bridge of her nose and eyes, careful near her stitches.

"So what's Marlene going to the doctor for this time?" Brian said.

"Don't pick on her."

"I'm just asking."

"She wants to make sure she's ovulating okay. You know she's trying to get pregnant again."

"Roger said they were done."

"There are two sides to that story."

Brian nodded in agreement. "I spoke to Marlene and she's going to feed the kids dinner and drop them off later. I didn't get a chance to tell her that the drug score didn't come through."

Gwen moaned and said nothing for a minute. When Brian didn't continue, she said, "At least come hold my hand."

That's what he had done when he first saw her in the hospital: held her hand. A nurse had pointed to the curtain, the one with the uniformed police officer standing outside it, and Brian rushed in to find Gwen sitting upright in the bed, holding her forearm in the air. People loitered about the bed. He paid them no attention. He nuzzled her raised hand in both of his, then held her fingers against his cheek. He bent down and tenderly kissed her lips.

He'd battled a sick feeling in his stomach the entire way to the hospital. Gwen's voice on the phone—she was hurt more than she'd let on. The way she said "please hurry." The way she said she was scared. Something more was wrong, she was hiding the severity of her injuries. Adding to his anxiety were his own circumstances: getting pulled from a tense moment in the executive meeting he'd been planning for weeks. Gwen knew how important that meeting was to him; she wouldn't have called him out for a fender bender.

He ran a red light on his way to the hospital. She might be dead when he got there. Hadn't he let that thought cross his mind recently, just last week, when the wife of someone he knew in the lab at Pherogenix drowned in Lake George—what would life be like if Gwen died? It was only natural to ponder what could happen, how he would react, what he would do next. Contingency planning, they called it at work. Succession planning. What if the worst happened? Impossible to grasp the horror of it—the burden of caring solo for the children, his wife and soul mate gone forever, the future lonely and bleak. This is how his mind spun and plunged as he pushed the ticket button at the hospital parking lot gate, hurried through the automatic doors, approached the nurses' station.

Yet there she was, alive and beautiful and valiant. Beautiful in a wounded way. God, the surge of love and relief that flooded him. She was not dead, not about to die. The redness and swelling in her face gave her a full, flushed look, with the gash along her eyebrow a wound she'd taken in battle. Gwen had brushed against death and escaped.

"I love you," he said. "I love you so much." He held her and held back his sobs.

And then the story unfolded.

Gwen's arm was raised not to reach for him but to hold a gauze against her vein where a med tech from the police department had just sucked her blood. And that officer he'd hardly registered on his way in? She was waiting to escort his wife to the police station because Gwen was under arrest.

Hearing this turn of events, Brian delayed registering shock or anger. He simply switched modes, leaving behind the life-and-death love drama for practical detail.

You let them take your blood? Did you admit to anything?

They told me I had to.

I'm calling Roger right now.

Upon release from the hospital, Gwen rode in the back of the police cruiser. At least they didn't handcuff her. Brian took her purse and was following in his own car when Roger returned his call. Brian briefly explained that Gwen had smoked a little pot and was in a car accident. They were on the way to the police station now from the hospital.

He could see the shape of her head outlined against the back window of the police car in front of him. You see that view and wonder what murky fiend sits back there. Hard to believe that shape was his wife.

"Tell her not to say a word or submit to any tests," Roger said.

"They already took her blood before I got there."

Roger's voice stayed even. "Don't say or do anything else. Not one word. I'll meet you at the station in twenty minutes. They won't let you into the booking area so you might as well stop and get five hundred dollars in cash for bail. I'll have her out in an hour."

Roger was Brian's friend because Gwen was close friends with Marlene, and Nora was friends with the Fitzgeralds' daughter, Abby. Roger was a partner in a downtown law firm and had advised Brian and Gwen with the contract on their lake house. When Gwen was taken into police custody, Brian had no one else to call and didn't know if Roger handled this type of situation, but so far he seemed pretty sure of himself.

"Anyone injured?" Roger asked.

"Gwen banged up her face, I think on the air bag. Took a few stitches in the eyebrow."

"Single car accident?"

"No, she said someone crossed the double yellow and hit her, but I don't know what happened after that. The other car might have gone through a guardrail."

"I'll find out."

Brian turned off at the next intersection and circled back home. He kept one thousand dollars in cash in an envelope taped to the back of his dresser. Gwen knew about it, although she didn't know about the other three thousand stashed in his metal toolbox in the basement. Brian wasn't exactly sure what the money was for, other than emergency purposes. It would buy food and gas for a while if for some reason the banks shut down. It would get them across the country or out of the country. It wouldn't last long, but knowing he had the cash on hand provided comfort.

He kept the car running in the driveway while he ran upstairs. Laid across the bed in neat piles were the clothes Gwen had put out to pack for the lake, plus toiletries, books, toys for the kids. They should be on their way to the lake house right now, sharing a family sing-along in the car, goofy rhyming songs the kids liked, Brian chilled and easy because he'd slam-dunked his presentation, cleared his plate for the long weekend, and was ready for Gwen.

Brian moved the dresser to reach the envelope. He counted out five of the hundred-dollar bills, then decided to take the other five. He pushed the dresser back in place and drove to the police station.

It was late afternoon near the change of shift and the arresting officer, Sergeant Marcia Hendricks, hustled them along. She was the only woman police officer in Morrissey. Now Gwen remembered why she looked familiar. There had been a profile of her in the town's newspaper, the *Morrissey Bee,* a few months ago. The same paper that carried the town's weekly police blotter of arrests and incidents. Gwen's name could appear in next week's edition. That would be a disaster. It may not be the most widely read publication in America, but the people Gwen knew at least glanced at the *Bee* to see goings-on about town. And Gwen being arrested would qualify as a going-on in Morrissey. Mostly a progressive town, there were still rules. Morrissey might not be cultivating our next generation's leaders, but it occupied a place on the social ladder, perhaps raising the second in commands, and the town feverishly wanted to defend its place. Mothers who served as PTA vice presidents but got arrested on drug charges didn't belong in the mix.

Gwen would have to visit the editor to see what she could do to keep her name out of the paper.

She was charged with DUI and possession, fingerprinted and released on bail—a thousand dollars, not the five hundred Roger had said, due to the double charges—and told to return for court arraignment the next day at 11:00 A.M.

"On a Saturday?" Gwen asked.

"Friday's a big night for arrests," Roger explained. "There's usually a Saturday court session to prevent a backlog. But the judge tomorrow is Robert Donovan. His son plays Little League with Josh. I'll give him a call and see if I can move it to next week. It's better that way, anyway, if we have a little more time to prepare."

"We were planning on going up to the lake this weekend."

Roger looked at her. "I'll see what I can do, but I won't know until tomorrow."

So their family getaway that her husband had slaved at work to carve out time for was postponed, and now Brian sat on the couch next to Gwen, holding her hand as she had asked him to, finally breaking a long silence between them.

"I shouldn't have been so angry with you," Brian said. "It was just bad luck, it could happen to anyone, and you're right, it could have happened to me after a few drinks on a night out." He took her hand. "I'm sorry."

"Me too."

"We'll take care of this and put it behind us."

"I just feel so humiliated."

The doorbell rang and seconds later the kids ran in ahead of Roger.

"Mommy!" Nate said. "Can I see your black eye?"

Brian got up and met Roger in the hallway. He'd changed out of his suit into jeans and a T-shirt. Brian was still wearing his clothes from work, except for the tie.

"We told them their mom got a little cut on her face," Roger said. "Marlene sends her best. Says the kids ate macaroni and cheese and watched *Wallace and Gromit*."

"Thanks, I appreciate this. You want a drink?"

"Maybe a beer."

Brian went to the refrigerator and got out two beers, opening both and handing one to Roger. They walked out to the back patio. The sun had dipped below the trees and long shadows hung over them. Goldenrod bloomed in a long patch where the lawn ended.

"I've got some other news." Roger stepped closer to Brian and lowered his voice. They could hear Gwen talking to the kids inside, explaining she'd been in a car accident but was perfectly fine.

"The other driver—eighty-two-year-old guy with severe dementia. James Anderson. Lives in Niskayuna, God knows where he was going in Morrissey. Tore through the guardrail and plunged down the ravine. Died in the hospital about an hour ago."

"Jesus," Brian said.

"I know it's terrible, but I talked to the investigator and it does appear he crossed the line and hit Gwen. It's not final, the report won't be complete for a few days or a week, but it was pretty obvious just from the pattern of the glass spattering and the tire marks on the road. The blood tests aren't back yet, either, but the fact that Gwen had marijuana in her system and in her possession might complicate things."

"You mean she'll be responsible—"

"I don't mean anything yet, and we shouldn't jump to any conclusions," Roger said. "I'm just sharing with you information that I have. Everything's going to be okay."

"Gwen's going to be very upset."

"I know—we're all upset." Roger finished the last swallows of his beer. "I'd better go. I'll call you in the morning and let you know what I find out about the arraignment."

"Roger, wait a minute. Is this the right thing?" Brian asked. "I mean you representing us—not because we're friends, but . . . You know that ounce Gwen had? She said half of it was for Marlene and you."

Roger nodded. "I know, it's like being a fucking teenager again. Except it's not. The stakes always get higher. I can recommend someone else if you prefer. A colleague of mine is good with these kinds of cases."

"No, I just wanted to get that out in the open," Brian said. "I don't want you to feel obligated to do this and don't want you to get exposed if it comes to that."

"Don't worry about that. If you want me as your attorney, I'm there all the way for you."

"It's up to Gwen, but I'm sure she does."

"I think this whole thing can be cleared up quickly," Roger said. "Gwen's a model citizen, you know that. It was just a wrong place at the wrong time kind of thing. I can see this just going away."

After Roger left, Brian went back inside. He had to break the news about the other driver to Gwen. But she had gone upstairs with the kids and fallen asleep on her bed with the cold pack over her eyes. The kids sat on either side of her, silent and staring.

"Is Mommy dead?" Nate asked.

"Just sleeping, honey," Brian reassured him.

"Yes, she's just sleeping," Nora repeated, echoing her father. "She's not going to die, is she, Dad?"

"Of course not. Mom's just tired. So let's try to be quiet."

"Be quiet, Nate," Nora said.

"I am quiet," he said too loudly.

"Shhhh," said Brian.

"When will she wake up?" Nora asked.

"In the morning, probably."

"She's just sleeping."

"That's right."

"Will we go to the lake tomorrow?"

"We'll see," said Brian. "Come on, let's take a bath."

He ran water in the whirlpool tub in the master bathroom. The tub was big enough to fit them both. Brian let Nate pour the bubble powder, which meant the kids were buried in mountains of suds. He didn't bother with the soap and shampoo. They sang "Row, Row, Row Your Boat," and then Brian pretended to be a troll under the bridge while Nate and Nora played billy goats he wanted to eat.

As the tub drained, Nate started in with the numbers. "4-3-9-4-9-6-1, 4-3-9-4-9-6-1, 4-3-9-4-9-6-1, 4-3-9-4-9-6-1 . . ." He'd learned their phone number the other day and now had to repeat it a thousand times.

Brian helped the kids with their pajamas and they sat together on Nora's bed while Brian read them each a book, *Franklin Rides a Bike* for Nate and a chapter in Nora's American Girl book.

He had missed too many bedtimes recently due to late work nights and was happy tonight to perform the routine with the kids by himself. Against their fragrant hair and clean, warm bodies his stress eased like a muscle cramp fading. He shuttled back and forth between Nate's and Nora's rooms, stroking their faces, tucking them in an extra time, stealing kisses from their foreheads. Okay, Nate, you can repeat our phone number ten more times and then you have to go to sleep. Nora, I'll sing the "Nina, Nina" lullaby one more time before saying good night.

And then they were asleep, and the house quiet. Brian went downstairs to the den to log on to work and check his messages, and the comfort and love that had filled him while putting the kids to bed vanished in the time it took to download his e-mail. He scanned his new messages until he saw the one from Teresa Mascetti. He opened it.

> *Brian: I hope your wife is okay—please let me know as soon as you can.*
>
> *Just to update you on what happened after you left: No decision about the FDA application and the conversation went back and forth on whether Zuprone marketing practices would appear unethical if scrutinized closely by FDA . . . they want all documents and data collected since the new business development push began, plus a breakdown of prescriptions . . . a summarized report by Tues. Lots of work to do but we'll get it done. P.S. I put your laptop back in your office, bottom drawer of desk.*
>
> *—Teresa*

He wrote this reply:

> *Gwen is bruised but okay. Thanks for the update. Guess I'll be going into the office tomorrow to start sifting through docs.*
>
> *—Brian*

He was reading through his other e-mails when the reply came back. What was she doing working on a Friday night? Brian was surprised she didn't have other plans.

> *Oops . . . I didn't expect you'd be around this weekend and so I took most of the paperwork home with me. I can meet you at the office tomorrow if you let me know what time. Though it might be easier if you came to my place and we work on it together.*
>
> *—T*

On the Road to College

Jude watched Dana appear from behind the gas station and walk back to the van, her gait lacking its usual athletic grace.

"It was gross," she said. "I couldn't even go in, so I peed on the ground behind the back of the building."

"Hope you didn't squat in any poison ivy."

"It's just packed dirt and a bunch of tires."

Jude finished filling the tank and they got back on the road.

"How was your run this morning? Do I detect a limp?"

"My first mile was okay, but then my knee started to hurt again. I've been e-mailing back and forth with the trainer and she's going to do some tests when I'm up there."

"All that trail running this summer probably didn't help."

"Dad, it's cross-country. You're supposed to be running on trails."

Instead of Jude's Lexus, they'd taken the restaurant's van, a commercial Ford 150. They needed the van because Dana couldn't leave for college without her snow globes, desk chair, the standing lamp with the shade her friends on the track team had autographed, a minifridge, two trunks of clothing, television, three boxes of books and notebooks, the new laptop, and who knows what else.

"I got you tea," Jude said, pointing to the cups in the holders.

"I wanted a grande chai latte."

"Very funny. Be thankful for the tea, the coffee's like burnt toast." Even with three packs of sugar and two creams it tasted bitter and stale, filtering through his stomach like spent motor oil.

Last night at Gull he had thrown a party for Dana, which lasted well past the usual 2:00 A.M. closing time. His daughter had worked in his restaurants longer than any of Jude's regular employees, folding napkins when she was just four years old, arranging flower vases and filling sugar bowls at age ten, setting tables at thirteen. Throughout her senior year and over this past summer, she worked Saturday nights to earn spending money for college. Jude gave her the option and Dana chose busing tables over the more glamorous and visible hostess position. She didn't like to dress up and didn't seek the limelight, but everyone at Gull was friends with her—boss's daughter or not—and the party rocked, especially after the dining room stopped serving and Jude hung the sign on the door that said CLOSED FOR PRIVATE PARTY. Many of his staff used the open bar as a free ticket to get hammered, but not Dana. Not his good girl. Not his runner.

It pleased him to see so many people show affection and good wishes for his daughter. A few friends from school came as well—other girls on the track team whom he warned the bartender not to serve. No boys. As far as Jude knew, Dana had never had a boyfriend, although last year she'd hung around with this big kid Sean for a month or so before the boy's father was transferred to a new job in another state. Other than that, nobody. He hoped she would have told him if there had been anyone.

Jude had always encouraged her to be open about her feelings; he never hesitated to answer her questions, even the tough ones. He reminded her to say no to drugs, counseled her to be careful and mature about sex—when her time came, that is. He helped her with homework, he went to her track meets. He operated from instinct rather than expertise and wondered how many ways he must have failed. Many, he was afraid.

When she was seven, he explained to her about puberty and how her body would change. By nine, she knew the gross details about sex. Her word at the time: *gross.* He'd been fortunate in picking the right pediatrician, a woman who took a personal interest in Dana and spent time at her yearly checkups talking about women's bodies and how Dana's would change and how she might feel about it. But there were many times she could have used a mother, like the night when she was fourteen and came out of the restroom at Gull and told her father she'd gotten her period, but was having bad cramps. He took her upstairs to his office and she rested on the couch curled like a shrimp, holding her belly. He covered her with a blanket. She moaned. He didn't know what to do. She'd never complained before about pain when she got her period. Was this normal or the sign of a serious problem?

"Daddy, it hurts."

"Do you want me to call the doctor?"

"I want it to stop. Make it stop."

The emergency room—or two aspirin? He felt her forehead: no fever. She didn't have the chills. Her eyes were clear, pupils set.

He picked up the phone and called downstairs and asked Angela, the hostess, to come up to his office.

When Angela arrived she asked Dana what the pain felt like.

"A lot of pressure."

"Is your flow heavy or light?"

"It just started, so it's not that heavy."

"Poor thing," Angela said. "Sounds like menstrual cramps. Have you ever had them before?"

Dana shook her head.

"Welcome to the club. Try two ibuprofen and a warm bath, that's what I do. If the pain eases, then you'll know what it was."

She turned back to Jude. "See how easy you men have it?"

Right. Easy to be a single father with a teenage daughter. Might as well be a horse trying to parent a bird.

The challenges never ended, even with years of experience. Like now, driving on the Northway to send his daughter off to college, trying to articulate what he needed to say.

"I just want to remind you that you're going to have a lot of freedom in college. I know you'll make wise choices, but there can be a lot of distractions, too. I don't want to hear you've become the poster child for campus party girls."

The eye roll response. "I already have a lot of freedom."

"You'll be exposed to a new group of friends. I know what it's like going to college. There's lots of drinking, drugs are available."

"There's drinking and drugs everywhere, Dad. I've even seen them around Gull."

"Who? What have you seen?"

"I'm not naming names."

"No, you don't need to."

"Although who's that guy Aaron?"

"You met Aaron?"

"At the party. Well, in the kitchen anyway. He was standing in the doorway eating."

"Did he know who you were—I mean, my daughter?"

"I don't think so, but who is he?"

"A new produce supplier," Jude said, the first thing that came to his mind.

Aaron's presence at Gull last night was Jude's fault because one of the well-wishers at Dana's party had been Brandon Marks, a regular customer at Gull and a personal client of Jude's who phoned him the afternoon of the party and asked for more than Jude had on hand. He had to call Aaron to drive it down. Jude let him grab something to eat in the kitchen before heading back but didn't invite him to join the party.

Dana said, "He asked me if I wanted to smoke a bowl."

Jude slapped the steering wheel. "See, this is exactly the kind of situation you need to watch out for. A guy with a bad offer."

"He seemed harmless enough."

"That's where you're wrong. Don't let anyone pressure you to change your good judgment."

"Dad, have we had this conversation like fifty times already?"

"That's because I don't know if you're listening. I'm not saying you should turn down a beer at a party, but you don't have to be one of those students who gets roaring drunk and passes out. You don't have to be the pothead. There are plenty of other people to play that role. You can nurse a drink along, you can still have a good time."

"Have you ever seen me drunk?"

He hadn't. She was an athlete, always training. He doubted she'd ever gotten high. His daughter hadn't inherited her mother's deadly weakness for excess.

Yet he pressed on with his mission. "You're going to meet other boys, and you'll be attracted to them."

"Not that they'll be attracted to me back."

"Don't fool yourself. You're a beautiful young woman and like I said, you're going to meet new people from all over the country. It's going to be very different from high school."

She made her "yeah right" face, the one that made him feel as if she were pointing to her eye and saying, "*Hello?* Have you seen this?"

He was sorry for the mark on her face and how it had shaped her life. A darkened eye that was the first impression she made on anyone. How many people had assumed he was beating her? How often did she answer the same questions, hear the same stupid jokes? She shouldered it, mostly with dignity, although in January she was scheduled to have surgery to shut off the veins feeding it, and the doctors said the color should fade and swelling go down.

"You remember how babies get made, right?" he said. "You know to be safe."

"Dad, *please*."

"I'm just saying—be prepared, use your head. Don't rush into things."

"Why aren't you reminding me to hand in my research papers on time?"

He turned and smiled at her. "Because I know you will."

"Well, trust me, I'm not rushing into anything."

"I just want you to remember that you can tell me anything. There's nothing you need to hide from me."

"Like the same way you don't need to hide anything from me?"

Her comment came from nowhere. He didn't answer.

"At least with me out of the house you can bring your girl-friends home now. You do, don't you—try to hide them from me?"

She held her chin up when she spoke, as if challenging him, but still her cheeks flushed.

She went on before he could respond. "You did it when I was little and you still do it today. You think I don't see women com-ing in the restaurant asking for you? Do I ask where you've been all night when you stay out? Why shouldn't I hide things from you if you're going to hide them from me?"

It's true, he never brought women home. His last overnight woman had been Gwen, years ago. Technically she had been at his house as a babysitter, at least until he got home and they ended up on the couch. He remembered Dana coming downstairs and wak-ing them, asking Gwen: *Are you going to be my new mommy?* He'd never forget his daughter's face at that moment—as if she'd been thrashing in deep water about to drown and help finally had arrived. From mortal terror to sweet salvation. A look he never wanted to see again.

It wouldn't have been right to bring women home, having Dana get to know them and start thinking, wondering, yearning: Will this one be my new mom? Because none of them were going to be.

"I never brought anyone home because I wanted to protect you. I didn't want you thinking that a woman friend of mine was going to be your new mother."

"Who said I wanted a new mother? I've managed pretty well without one."

"It was different when you were younger. It would have been a natural reaction on your part."

Jude passed a double tractor trailer on a long uphill, flooring the gas pedal to give the van momentum. He said, "Do you know who I saw recently? Her name is Gwen; you probably don't remember her, but she used to work for me at the Patriot and she would help you with your homework sometimes."

"I think I remember her. Why?"

"Nothing, just thought I'd mention it. She came in the restaurant, it reminded me of when you were little."

"Are you going out with her or something?"

"No, nothing like that," Jude said. Then added, "You see, I'm not trying to hide anything; it's just that adults have personal lives, too, separate from their children."

"If we're not going to talk about your personal life, then why should we talk about mine? I'm an adult now, too. I'm eighteen." As if to emphasize her right to privacy, she put in her music earbuds and turned her gaze out the window. Conversation over.

Maybe he had pressed her too hard. Another parenting mishap. He waited a few seconds, then said, "I don't have anyone I want to bring home. The house is going to be very quiet without you around." Quiet without the daughter he had not wanted, yet the one he'd gotten anyway, the one who'd helped him stay in control of his life.

Of course he had wanted Claire to get an abortion. He'd just been through one stunning thunderclap in his life: getting married to the woman. He didn't need another. They had flown to Las Vegas to gamble, stayed at Bellagio, and burned through a ton of cash because Claire looked so hot sitting at the blackjack table and he kept paying out chips to watch her, even if she was losing. If you counted the number of cocktails consumed on the house, they might have broken even. Between the coke and the cocktails, they stayed pretty shitfaced the entire three days. Claire was the girl-friend who was both gorgeous *and* liked to party; usually the two didn't mix, not in Jude's experience. They mixed so well in this case that he married her at midnight in one of those Vegas chapels, and though he remembered it the next morning and said what a hoot, Claire told him to stop kidding around—she had a headache.

As soon as they got back home, Jude eased back on the drinking and coke and weed. Being out of control wasn't such a thrill anymore. You do crazy impulsive things, like get married. But while he eased up, Claire pressed the accelerator. It wasn't fun cleaning up her puke from his car seat or having her pass out while he was having sex with her. He didn't mind her partying but did she have to be so excessive? Did she have to raise her voice during minor disagreements when they were having dinner out? Did she have to stick her tongue down his throat when kissing him in public places?

When he tried to talk to her about it, she ridiculed him for getting stodgy overnight. "I thought I married a sexy man who liked to have a good time."

As for Jude, he didn't know what he'd married.

He focused on managing the restaurant and the niche dealing he did on the side; he selected customers and suppliers carefully, stayed low-key. He'd do a little, sell a little, risk a little, make a little. Enough to build a cushion. It was all about maintaining control. He didn't keep anything around the house because of Claire, but she would go out on the nights he was working and score something with her friends or even strangers in other bars.

When she told him she was pregnant, Jude said, "We'll get it taken care of."

"I think a baby would be nice to hold. They're really cute."

"It's not a doll, it's a human," he shot back at her. "We're not having a goddamn baby."

"It's what we need, to bring us closer together," Claire said.

"What we need is for you to get your habits under control."

"I will, sweetie, I promise. I won't put another bad thing in my body—I can't, I have a little baby growing in there." She knew she could do it, she just hadn't been motivated in the past, hadn't a reason to come clean. Now she did. Now they were going to have a baby.

He actually let himself believe that Claire would stop drinking and smoking and snorting and popping because she was pregnant. Strike that: he didn't believe it; he hoped the way a dying man hopes for a miracle cure. The miracle they got: Dana wasn't born with a bent spine or mottled brain. Yes, she had the vein problem with her eye, but at the time it seemed like a tiny birthmark, and one the doctors predicted would fade.

Then for Claire it was on and off the wagon for the next seven years. Jude didn't buy in to addiction as a disease and instead attributed Claire's problems to weakness of character. He could control and moderate himself; why couldn't she? Why couldn't she do *one* line of coke, *one* bong hit? He got her into a rehab program after she'd washed down a handful of Fioricet one night with a bottle of tequila while Dana was taking a bath and Jude was at work. Dana had called for her mother to drain the bath and got no response; she discovered Claire on the floor in her room.

Claire insisted she wasn't trying to kill herself, she just had a terrible headache and didn't think she'd be able to sleep, so she took something and lost track of how much. But she agreed to a three-month stay at a rehab clinic two hours away in White Plains. One night while there she tried to hang herself with a coat hanger in a maintenance closet left unlocked. That was the trip to the emergency room the night Gwen babysat for Dana. Jude knew by then the clinic was a waste of money and time—Claire was an incurable addict. He was raising a daughter by himself. He privately regretted that Claire's coat hanger episode hadn't succeeded, but a month later Claire disappeared from the clinic, managing to escape by getting one of the night orderlies to lead her out a locked back door in exchange for a blow job. She could be anywhere now. She could be dead, hopefully.

They arrived on campus in Canton, an outpost of brick and stone buildings among the lowlands west of the Adirondacks and east of the St. Lawrence Seaway. Parents unloaded gear from cars and trucks and trailers parked in front of the dorms. On a grassy area surrounded by paved walkways, students played Frisbee; others sat on blankets and picnic tables. A conglomerate of music could be heard coming from many windows.

Jude parked near Robert Hall, Dana's dorm, and they shared unloading duties, shuttling back and forth from dorm to van, climbing to the second floor each time. Her roommate, Jen, had already moved in with her own supply of lamps, books, favorite mementos, and boxes. That left little room for Dana's stuff, but Jude made trip after trip to the van and piled everything inside the room. Let the girls sort it out from there.

Jen appeared just as they had finished unloading. A round-faced girl from Boston with a wide smile, she sported a nose ring and a New England accent. Dana had been corresponding with her all summer, sharing photos on Facebook, text messages, and phone calls. They greeted each other like longtime friends and Dana introduced Jude.

"Nice to meet you, Mr. Gates," Jen said. "I've been waiting and waiting for Dana to show up."

Jude was about to respond but Jen didn't allow it. She turned to Dana and started telling her about all the great things she'd done in the twenty-four hours since her parents had dropped her off; not once did she stop talking during the entire walk to the dining hall where the university was hosting a dinner for entering freshman and their parents. At any moment, Jude expected Dana to tell her new roommate to close it, but so far his daughter let it flow downstream to her, taking in everything Jen had to say, smiling and nodding in all the right places.

In the dining hall they stood in a buffet line and chose brisket of beef or broiled salmon, with salad, rice, and rolls. They filled their plates and sat at a long table with other students Jen had already met, some of them solo and others with their parents. The tables were set with cloths and cloth napkins for this event. Jude introduced himself to the parents sitting across from him, who had come from Buffalo with their son Cal. The father was a chemical engineer employed by DuPont, the mother a high school teacher, and Jude a restaurant owner. What did Jude think of this meal? A question he always got once someone knew he owned a restaurant. Very nice, he said, especially considering how many people they were serving. The salmon tasted fresh and was still moist. The engineer said that for forty-five grand a year they'd better get fresh fish, although he had chosen the beef. They agreed the campus was beautiful. Jude forgot their names. He kept looking at Dana to see how she fit in. She didn't talk much, but seemed pleased with the people around her and being part of this new group. There were Jen and Cal and three other students who were without parents. Their conversation jumped from what classes they had registered for to their hometowns to favorite bands and what sports they would play. They didn't exclude the parents who were sitting at the same table with them; they simply didn't see these people who were no longer part of their world.

Then it was 7:30 and time for Jude to go. The dorm welcome party began at 8:00.

"You want to walk me out?" he said to Dana.

She turned to Jen. "I'll meet you back at the room. Wait for me."

Jude had moved the van to the parking lot after unloading and he walked now holding his daughter's hand through the courtyard and along the path out to the parking lot behind Robert Hall.

When they reached the van, Jude said, "Do you have enough money?"

"I still have what you gave me—how could I have spent anything yet? Plus my credit card."

"Here." Jude reached into his pocket and handed Dana three one-hundred-dollar bills he'd been planning to give her. "Just some extra spending money."

She put the bills in her pocket. "Parents' weekend is only three weeks away. I'll see you then."

"Or before," Jude added. "I'm thinking of coming to Platts-burgh next weekend for the meet. That's your first one, right?"

"If my knee is okay."

"Let me know what the trainer says."

"I have to go. Jen's waiting."

"Don't worry about anything, you'll be fine."

"I think you're the one that's worried."

"You'll meet new friends, you'll fit in."

"I'm not as lame as you think I am."

"I don't think you're lame, I think you're an angel."

"Maybe a little nervous," Dana admitted.

"That's okay, it's a healthy sign, like before one of your races. A few nerves help keep you on your game." He hugged and held her for a long minute and she waited for him to let her go. Then, "Oh, wait. I almost forgot." He opened the van and got the card out of the door pocket. He also picked up his camera from the center console.

"I couldn't find the perfect one so I got you this." He handed her the envelope.

That morning, while Dana had gone out for her run, Jude went to the drugstore to pick out a card for his daughter. He had scanned the racks. There were good-bye cards but their messages were final, suggesting the recipient was moving away forever. There were generic "congratulations on your new adventure" cards. Good-luck cards. Have a great trip cards. Finally he found a "we'll miss you" card. He wasn't sure what to do about the "We" part of it, fi-nally deciding to make a joke and sign it "Your Dad and Daddy."

She looked at the envelope. "Do you want me to open it now?"

"No, no—take it with you. But hold still, I want your picture."

She cocked her head and smiled as if she were used to camera-men following her around. It was strange she could be so self-conscious about the flaw in her face yet so photogenic. He snapped the photo and viewed it in the camera's window, showing it to her.

She shrugged.

He hugged her again and stroked her hair, which still maintained a little girl's feathery texture. He'd stroked that hair ten thousand times or more over these years and he wanted to stand here and stroke it ten thousand more. Then she was walking back and he was sitting behind the wheel of the van watching until she disappeared into the dorm. In whatever ways Jude had fallen short as a father, the results were tallied and already in, and not much could be done about it now. An assault of loneliness and regret struck him on all sides and he thought he might cry but didn't, and twenty minutes later he was drumming his steering wheel to Neil Young's "Rockin' in the Free World," driving fast, his attention turned to the next order of business.

The Man Who Died

Gwen woke in the morning when the kids climbed on the bed. Nate tunneled under the blankets to get next to her, Nora wedged between her and Brian. Gwen hummed something and rolled over trying to find sleep again.

Brian took them downstairs. A few minutes later he came back with a cup of coffee and the newspaper and this time she sat up.

"How do you feel?"

Her eyebrow tugged along the stitch line but the rest of her face felt fine, not even tender to the touch.

"How do I look?" she asked.

"You're a knockout."

"You mean I look like I got knocked out?"

He smiled.

"You don't know how sick I was when you called me from the hospital," Brian said. "I thought you were dying, I thought . . . how much I love and need you, how you and the kids are everything to me."

"I feel the same way." Gwen wished she could go back to yesterday, a rushed morning with Brian getting ready for work and the kids for camp and Gwen finishing her list of errands, all of them excited about their long weekend getaway. Brian deserved it, even if she didn't.

"Daddy, the pan is smoking," Nora called up the stairs.

Brian kissed her and went back down to finish making breakfast for the kids. Gwen turned to the newspaper. A story about a murder-suicide rampage at an HMO in White Plains dominated the front section—the gun work performed by an irate employee passed over for a promotion that was given to an attractive woman, who was suspected by coworkers of having a "personal relationship" with the boss. Now the attractive woman, the boss, and the disgruntled employee all were dead.

The local section was filled with fun ideas to make the most of what's left of summer, plus safety tips for grilling and two potato salad recipes. She scanned the paper slowly, drinking her coffee, afraid to see a story about the accident. She had gotten through to the last page when she saw a small headline in the far right column, near the bottom of the page, "Niskayuna Man Dies in Accident."

> James Anderson, 82, of Niskayuna, died from injuries suffered in an automobile accident when his car struck another vehicle on Route 157 near Thacher Park and plunged down a ravine. The driver of the other vehicle, Gwen Raine, 37, of Morrissey, was treated for minor injuries at St. Mary's Hospital and released. Police are investigating the cause of the accident.

Gwen held her breath and tried to swallow, but a fist of pain clogged her throat and chest: someone had been killed in the accident. An eighty-two-year-old man was dead after colliding with her car. If she'd been a fraction of a second quicker to react—able to swerve faster or brake or speed up—could she have avoided the collision altogether? Was there something she could have done? She had been looking ahead, steering through the curve, and then the car was right there, across the line, in her face.

And now a man was dead. James Anderson. Where had he been going? Did he leave behind a wife? Were there grandchildren who had lost their grandpa?

She hunched over the paper and flipped to the obits section. His was the first name listed.

> **Anderson**—James R. of Niskayuna, died August 26 at the age of 82. Beloved husband of the late Ruth Walsh Anderson, devoted father of Walter J. Anderson and Sheila R. Anderson Birch, loving grandfather to Tyler, Lily, Connor, and Michael. Brother to the late Richard W. Anderson. U.S. Navy veteran of World War II, retired professor of psychology from Union College, longtime community member, and activist. Also survived by several nieces and nephews. Service and interment on Monday, August 29, 10:00 A.M., Niskayuna Rural Cemetery. Contributions can be made to the National Alzheimer's Association.

She looked up and Nora was at the bedroom door.

"I didn't hear you come up, sweetie. Did you have breakfast?"

"What are you reading, Mommy?"

"The newspaper."

"What about?"

"A man who died."

"Did you know him?"

"No, I didn't."

"Then how come you're crying?"

"Well, it's sad when someone dies."

"How did he die?"

"He was very old."

"Can I see?"

Gwen pointed to the obituary in the paper. Nora read out loud, holding the page a few inches in front of her face. "What does inter . . . inter . . . What's that word?"

"Interment. It means burial. He's going to be buried in a cemetery."

Nora got under the blankets with Gwen. "I'll bet you had pancakes. You smell like maple syrup."

"Yep. Are we going up to the lake today?"

"Would you like to?"

"Yeah."

"Me too. We all do. I have a few things to take care of first this morning, and maybe we can leave this afternoon."

"Daddy said we might not be able to go."

"He did? Daddy and I will talk about it."

Nora peered at Gwen's stitches.

"Do those hurt, Mommy?"

"No, not really. It hurt a little bit when I got them but not now."

"Did it feel like getting a shot?"

"It was just little pricks."

"Can I touch them?"

"Sure, if you're careful. Just use one finger."

Nora slowly moved her index finger to Gwen's eyebrow and hovered there, trembling a little, then barely touched the thread of the stitches. Her hesitant gesture was heartbreaking. Gwen's eyes filled with tears again.

"Did that hurt?" Nora asked, pulling her finger away.

"No, that was fine," Gwen said, holding Nora's hand in hers.

They were quiet for a minute, then Nora asked, "Can we go in Daddy's car?"

"I think we have to, until the van gets fixed."

"It doesn't have any cup holders in the back."

"I'm sure we can work something out," Gwen reassured her.

Nora jumped up from the bed and ran downstairs, calling, "Nate, Nate, we're going—Mommy said we're going!"

Wait, I didn't say that. Not for sure. A man has died.

Brian came upstairs.

"I was just getting up," Gwen said, rising out of bed. "Brian, did you know about James Anderson, the other driver?"

"I heard it from Roger, last night."

"Why didn't you tell me?"

"By the time I got a chance you were asleep."

Gwen shook her head. "It's so sad. I feel sick over it."

"You couldn't have prevented it," Brian reassured her. "Roger told me the investigators already determined the other driver crossed the line." He put his arms around her. "There's nothing you could have done."

"How do I know that? What if there was?"

"It's okay," he whispered. He held her tighter.

She let go of Brian. "I feel terrible," she said. "I'm going to take a shower." The spray of water would drown her thoughts, the soap would smell sweet.

"You told them we were going up to the lake?" he asked.

"I said we'd talk about it. But I don't see why we can't go this afternoon after court. I could really use it now."

Brian hesitated, then came out with it. "I know this is bad timing, but I have to go into work."

"What?" She said it too forcefully and had to back off. "I thought you had cleared this time off months ago."

"I had, but circumstances changed yesterday—I never finished the meeting and wasn't there to address some issues that came up."

"Can't you deal with it when you get back?" It couldn't hurt to ask, but if he could deal with it later, Gwen knew he would wait. Brian wouldn't go into work unless he really had to, although

Gwen didn't know much more than that. Brian didn't talk about the details of work—he claimed to be immersed in them all day long and when he got home he'd had enough, wanted to leave it behind. So Gwen got only the big picture: he disappeared from home for ten hours a day or more or for a week of travel and was paid well for it. He held the title of director. He was involved with a complicated new effort to get his company's anxiety drug Zuprone approved for weight loss. About the same level of detail he knew about her day-to-day life.

"If I had stayed at the meeting, I probably could have juggled and gotten by—but I wasn't there and others decided we needed a more detailed look at some of our data. And I'm the one who has to look at it."

"Can you bring your computer and carve out a few hours?"

"My laptop's at work, and some reports. I need to go in. I'll go right after court and be back later in the afternoon. Maybe we can still go tonight. Either way, we have to get a loaner car for you while the van's being repaired."

Gwen sighed. There was nothing she could do about it, and she was the reason he'd left the meeting in the first place.

She said, "I haven't heard the phone. Roger hasn't called about postponing the arraignment?"

"It's only nine o'clock."

"I should call him. Maybe it's better if I just go to court this morning and get it over with. Who knows what day it might be next week."

"Let's have Roger figure that out; he'll work in our best interest. I'm sure as soon as he knows anything he'll call," Brian said.

The phone rang just before ten, setting off war cries of *I'll get it I'll get it* from the kids and a race to the phone that typically ended up with one of them trampling the other and hell erupting before the third ring. Today the commotion was just background noise that Gwen let Brian deal with. She had the cordless receiver next to her and answered Roger's call to find out the court appearance had indeed been moved to next week, Tuesday at 7:00 P.M.

"But that could change, too," Roger added, and now hesitated.

"What is it?" Gwen asked.

"When I was talking to Bob Donovan this morning I concluded this Detective Keller has his ear a bit. You remember him? He was at the hospital."

"The one with the warrant."

Roger explained that the Morrissey PD had been responding to an increased number of incidents involving drugs recently—traffic accidents and stops, but also residential break-ins and situations at both the high school and middle school. There was mounting pressure to clean it up before Morrissey started getting a reputation the way some colleges did. As part of the crackdown, any arrest involving drugs of any kind, in any quantity, was carefully investigated.

"They're talking to the DA," Roger said.

"The district attorney? You said this whole thing would just go away quickly." Gwen felt a pinch in her abdomen.

"That remains the most likely scenario," Roger said. "When they see the evidence in this situation it will go back to Donovan and we'll resolve it. But still, they're looking at every case."

"Am I in trouble?"

"I don't think so. There has to be a little posturing and showmanship so everyone covers their asses and shows they're doing the right thing to combat the drug problem. And you know, there has been an increase in drugs in the schools—there is a problem."

"If that guy hadn't hit me . . ." Gwen had felt sadness for the old fellow earlier, and guilty for her own involvement. Now anger rose in her. It's true: if the old guy hadn't struck her car, this never would have happened. And then, just as before, remorse and regret filled her. She replayed the accident again, trying to conjure a different outcome. There wasn't one.

Roger said, "He was suffering from Alzheimer's. I heard he was completely lost, never should have been driving up there—or driving at all. He managed to locate the keys and just drive off. I guess he wasn't supervised very well."

"Look, I've got to take over with the kids. Brian's going into work for a few hours and the sooner he goes, the sooner he gets back and we can go up to the lake."

"Have you got a quick minute? Marlene's standing right here begging to talk to you."

Marlene got on the phone and first thing asked about Gwen's injury. Gwen assured her she was feeling fine, getting stitches wasn't as bad as she'd imagined. She had pictured it less precise, not as elegant—like sewing the stuffing into the turkey on Thanksgiving.

That got a laugh from Marlene.

"I'm so sorry about what happened," Marlene said. "I feel partly responsible because I couldn't pick up the kids and you had to drive. I didn't know you were . . . you know. You didn't say anything."

"You needed to get in to see the doctor," Gwen said. "What you're going through is important."

"Well, it turns out I'm ovulating fine. It could be something with Roger, but we might never know."

"I hope it works out."

"One way or another it will," Marlene said. "I heard Roger tell you not to worry. It's true. He'll get you out of this."

Off-Label

Two cars sat like boulders in a field of empty parking spaces. Brian doubted anyone was in the office; the cars had been left since last night, young researchers or admins sharing rides to the bars after work and not making it back, spending their Friday night getting laid or drunk or both. Who was going to be working on a summer weekend? He, for one. And it wouldn't be the first time. Brian accepted weekend, night work, and travel as part of the equation: long hours plus high pressure equal financial rewards and a comfortable life for his family. The role of provider suited Brian, traditional though it was. He felt fortunate that Gwen could be a stay-at-home mom and give her attention to the kids and volunteer work, this episode with the pot yesterday just a minor accounting error on an otherwise healthy and balanced ledger. Not every family was as fortunate as his.

It's true he no longer carried the banner of global aid and community service that had motivated him to attend medical school. His family was his community now, and he served them well. He knew the mantras: think globally, act locally, make the world better one person at a time—Gwen, Nora, Nate.

He swiped his card to unlock the door. The weekend sign-in pad sat on a table near the door, the open page blank of signatures. He had the building to himself.

His office was third from the end in a row of six offices with window views on the parking lot side and a sea of cubicles on the other. He found his laptop where Teresa had said she left it, bottom drawer of his desk.

He turned it on, then called her cell number.

"You coming in?"

"I thought we were working at my place."

"I had to get my laptop, so I came to the office."

"You mean you're going to make me get dressed?"

"That's up to you."

"I just got back from a run—I at least have to take a shower."

"Don't forget the surveys."

That flirty banter—*You're going to make me get dressed?* and *That's up to you*—had been going on the entire six months they'd worked together.

Brian was ten years or so older than Teresa, and senior to her on the company's org chart. She had been transferred up from New Jersey after the acquisition and assigned to help Brian with Zuprone market development. She didn't report directly to him; theirs was a dotted-line relationship, which meant he supervised and mentored but did not own her. She still reported to her manager at corporate, which Brian preferred.

Their banter appeared benign enough. Teresa had a reputation for chatting this way with every guy in the office. A more important safety feature—and the reason he allowed himself to flirt in the first place—was Teresa's weight. She had a pretty face and dazzling smile, but Brian felt no attraction and no inclination to do anything. He had comfortably classified Teresa in the "good personality" segment: no threat, no risk.

Until recently.

Over the six months Teresa had worked with Brian, she'd lost a lot of weight. A lot. It's a good thing he remembered what she used to look like because another few pounds and she'd be pushing knockout status and he'd have to be careful. She'd overhauled her wardrobe several times, looking better and sexier with each one, and had started wearing shorter skirts and tighter tops.

Brian suspected she dosed on Zuprone—and why not, if it worked like that? He wasn't going to ask. They'd never spoken about her weight or the shedding of it; he never acknowledged her appearance or made a comment about how she looked. That wasn't their style of banter. A part of him wished she'd stop losing weight, while another part watched fascinated as if beholding a butterfly emerging from its chrysalis.

The other part of the problem was that Brian imagined Teresa might have a thing for him beyond the harmless. Yeah, she chatted up other guys, but she worked closest with him and when you see a woman every day, even the largely unused and rusty radar of a solidly married guy with kids will detect the incoming. That's how Brian saw it: as if she'd selected him as a target to lock on to. What was the risk for her—a young, single woman from out of town? None. It wouldn't be the worst thing for her to get something going with Brian.

But it wasn't going to happen.

Brian got started with work. Because Gwen's phone call had abruptly ended his presentation, he hadn't been on hand to refocus the discussion when it got derailed, and Teresa didn't have the authority or presence to steer the meeting back to the business case of seeking approval for Zuprone as a weight-loss drug. Now he couldn't present again until all the marketing data had been analyzed and summarized, even though he didn't think it had bearing on the business case.

He resigned himself to the task and got started. He opened the spreadsheets and began reviewing the prescription history of Zuprone. A whopping 70 percent of prescriptions written over the past two years for Zuprone were off-label—for weight loss, not anxiety. That in itself wasn't the problem; some drugs on the market had an 80 percent off-label rate. The problem was whether that 70 percent could be primarily attributed to Caladon's marketing practices or simply physicians using their independent medical judgment and following customary prescribing patterns. Idealists and the FDA insisted there was a difference; an industry veteran like Wilcox would scoff.

He noticed movement outside the window and saw Teresa park her Saab next to his car. She got out, reached back in, and shut the door with her foot. She carried a leather briefcase slung over her shoulder and a coffee in each hand. He watched her walk toward the door, holding the cups out in front of her, wearing faded jeans ripped in one knee and a fitted, plunging pink cardigan that gave too much away.

A moment later she stood at his office door.

"I took the liberty of getting you a coffee."

Her hair hung flat and damp from her shower, and he could smell her floral shampoo or soap. He'd thrown on jeans and T-shirt this morning without showering or washing his face. At least he had brushed his teeth. Had he combed his hair? Too late to look now and what did it matter anyway.

She set the coffees on his desk and pulled up an extra chair beside him, then retrieved a stack of paper surveys from her briefcase. "How's everything at home? I mean with Gwen?"

"She's okay—six stitches in her eyebrow. But the situation is a little complicated."

Teresa waited, but Brian didn't go on. He shouldn't have added that part about it being complicated.

"Let's get started and set objectives," Brian said. "It's hard to know what we've got in front of us at this point."

He said there were two issues on the table: whether Caladon should seek FDA approval of Zuprone as a weight-loss drug and whether the marketing practices to date for Zuprone could be construed as illegal.

"As for seeking FDA approval, I think the business case proves out," Brian said. "My recommendation is that we move forward with the application, in expectation that the FDA focus will follow the clinical trials and not past marketing practices. It's too bad I didn't get to that conclusion in the meeting, or the favorable cost projections. And now they're clamoring for the marketing data."

"What's your feeling—do you think we've crossed the line?"

"Wilcox has been aggressive in setting direction, but legal has seen all of our programs."

"Do you think we could end up with a four-hundred-million-dollar fine like Warner-Lambert?"

"That's what we're here to avoid. Probably not that much, since Zuprone doesn't have the sales of Neurontin, but the damage to the brand name would be huge—and we would lose our jobs, of course."

"There are lots of jobs in the drug industry."

That may be true, but Brian didn't want to relocate and take one of them unless he was down to his last option.

Teresa pointed out that Caladon would never make as much money on the drug if they kept to the off-label strategy as they would if they got FDA approval.

Brian said, "We'll project the numbers and the consequences of either applying for approval or not, add some kind of summary of marketing efforts, then hand it over to Stephen and Jennifer and let the lawyers decide."

"You sure you don't want me to do this? I know you were planning on time off, your family must be waiting for you."

"And you have nothing else to do this weekend?"

"Not really," Teresa admitted. "I might drive down to New Jersey tomorrow to see my brother."

Brian shrugged. "Let's get started, then I'll take off. We want to discover, where possible, any correlation between physicians we've called on or who have attended our seminars, and the frequency and reason around their prescriptions for Zuprone."

He sorted the spreadsheet data by the number of prescriptions written by each physician, then by which physicians attended one of Caladon's educational seminars on obesity. Although they had hired independent physicians to conduct the events, the seminars could be called into question, given that Caladon paid doctors to attend and hosted them in Marco Island, Las Vegas, Steamboat Springs, and other resorts.

When Brian mentioned a physician's name from the seminar list, Teresa flipped through the paper copies of follow-up surveys they'd gotten back from seminar attendees. It was the only way to correlate physician to prescription indication—whether it was written for weight loss or anxiety—and at what rate physicians who attended the seminars wrote Zuprone prescriptions for weight loss. Only about a third of the attendees had completed surveys, enough to provide general direction perhaps but not to be statistically relevant.

When finished with the surveys, they would look at data from the sales reps about which physicians requested copies of Caladon's internal studies on Zuprone and which HMOs and health plans included Zuprone on their drug plan formularies.

Teresa sat close to him, sharing the space beneath the desk where one pair of legs belonged. Too close. Their knees touched a few times. Then elbows. Each time Brian edged back. Then Teresa leaned forward to point at something on his screen, and Brian felt her breast touch his arm. He wasn't sure. He couldn't look. But he knew what breasts felt like pressed against him. He considered moving around to the side of his desk to avoid a second occurrence. As he debated this prudish—or prudent—move, his phone rang, Gwen calling.

"How's it going?"

"Fine, I said I'd call when I was finished." What a radar on that woman.

"I'm just asking—don't be angry."

"Sorry, I'm just trying to get it done."

"You can take your time, I've decided we're not going."

"Why? I thought your appointment wasn't until Tuesday night."

"Appointment?" Gwen said. "Is someone in your office?"

"No, it's just . . . ." Why was he lying? Gwen knew he worked with Teresa, and she had met her once at the holiday party when Teresa first moved up to New York. Gwen had liked her well enough and seemed to classify her as nonthreatening, for the same reasons Brian had.

But Gwen hadn't seen Teresa since then.

"Why did you change your mind about the lake?" Brian asked.

"I'm going to the funeral."

"What funeral?"

"James Anderson," Gwen said. "It's Monday morning. We'd have to come back tomorrow night and that would give us only a day at the lake."

"I don't know if that's a good idea. Let's talk about this later when we're together."

"I think I should go."

"What about the kids—I thought you said they'd be disappointed."

"I think we're all disappointed, but it's not worth driving up there for one day. You can take an extra day next weekend and we can go then."

"I guess it's better anyway, since I have a pile of work to get through."

He finished with the call and waited for Teresa to say something. Sure enough: "Did someone die? I heard you mention a funeral."

Brian could have deflected the question—an uncle or a neighbor passed away. Or told Teresa a bleached version of events. But what came out was the whole story: Gwen getting high, the accident that wasn't her fault, arrest, death of the old man driving the other car. It was a gross violation of Brian's own personal privacy rules, and could damage his reputation if word got out around the office, yet he couldn't stop even as he heard himself speaking.

"Oh my God—you guys get high?" Surprised and pleased, as if she'd been let in on a juicy secret.

"Not *you guys,* just Gwen."

"Well, okay, that I can understand."

"What does that mean?"

"When I met your wife she struck me as pretty relaxed and easygoing. You seem more the buttoned-up type."

He probably did seem that way to her. If he was such a dud, then why did she keep flirting with him? The challenge, probably—see if she could spark up the wet one.

"Let's get back to work," Brian said.

An hour later they'd sorted most of the data and gotten the results Brian had hoped not to get. Seminar attendees were 250 percent more likely to write off-label prescriptions for Zuprone. Then there were the top three deciles of physicians the sales reps had singled out over the past two years for their tendency to write more off-label prescriptions and more prescriptions for both anxiety drugs and obesity drugs. This group, which had received twice as many sales calls from Caladon's reps, were 400 percent more likely to prescribe Zuprone for weight loss.

"What should we do?" Teresa asked. "Destroy the data?"

"And every e-mail ever written on the subject—the ones those digital forensic geeks can always dig out of your hard drive even if you've deleted them."

"I'm just kidding about destroying the data."

But her suggestion had merit, if they could pull it off. If the FDA looked into the marketing practices for Zuprone, they'd be wading into that gray area where attorneys would do battle. Wilcox, as head of sales and marketing, stood on the top rung of accountability—in terms of defining strategy and targets—but Brian held up the ladder. It was no longer just a question of losing his job. Could he be held legally liable in any way if there was a problem?

Teresa leaned for a closer look at Brian's screen. He turned his computer so she could see better, but there was her breast again. No mistaking it this time. Not just brushing his arm. A warm snug compress. He couldn't believe it. He was fretting over his role in the off-label marketing of Zuprone and she was making a move. No wonder she had invited him to work at her apartment this morning. He could feel the cluster headache coming on.

He pushed his chair back and stood up, paced back and forth in his small office. She showed no sign of anything transpiring between them.

Wow, he could fuck her if he wanted to. Then again, he could also ruin his life.

The Montreal Connection

At customs Jude showed his passport and told the agent he planned to visit a friend in Montreal for the weekend. The agent asked to see the back of the van.

"It's unlocked," Jude said.

He watched through the side mirror as the agent walked to the rear of the van and disappeared from view. The back door opened, a few seconds later it shut. The agent came back around to Jude's window.

"Okay, you're all set."

Always easier getting out of the country than back in.

In an hour he reached the heart of Montreal in a section of town called Vieux Ville near the port. The streets were narrow and one-way; Jude drove slowly and turned behind the Fontaine Hotel down a service alley that opened to a small lot where two Dumpsters and a few cars were parked. He backed the van to the loading dock. The overhead door was down. Sitting in front of it was a Vulcan sixty-inch range with eight 26,000 BTU cast iron burners and two 35,000 BTU ovens below. Jude opened one of the oven doors and peered inside. Spotless.

He entered the service door of the hotel. Garbage bags awaiting transport to the Dumpster lined the hallway. Grease slicked the damp floor. Jude stepped with caution. The hallway opened into a massive commercial kitchen where two cooks filled late-night bar and room service orders. The cooking line gleamed with new double ranges and overhead broilers, the seams not yet gunked, the stainless pure.

A dishwasher with a cigarette between his lips leaned against a tub sink. He looked at Jude but made no sign of recognition or interest.

Jude asked him where he could find Gil. He repeated himself in French. *"Ou est Gil? Ou se trouve Gil?"* The dishwasher pointed to the office around the corner from the convection ovens.

Jude knocked on the open door and entered. Gil had removed his tie and rolled his sleeves halfway to his elbows, leaving the diamond-studded cufflinks hanging loose. He was sorting cash and credit card receipts into piles on his desk.

"A good night?"

"Americans are desperate to spend before summer is over, even with the exchange rate now in our favor," Gil said. "How are you?"

He stood and shook Jude's hand, then poured them each a cognac from a bottle on a glass shelf behind his desk. Gil was short with broad shoulders and a thick, solid frame and wavy silver hair, the locks parting and returning to place as he ran his hand through them. He was one of those French Canadians with a meticulously groomed bad haircut, favoring a mullet otherwise seen only on hockey players. He also wore a Breitling on his wrist and a platinum and diamond ring on his hairy middle right finger, the skin thick and bunched on either side of the band. The watch was a specimen, but the ring too loud.

Gil opened a box and offered Jude a cigar, took one for himself. He sat back and crossed his feet on his desk. Jude sank into a leather armchair. They drank and filled the office with smoke.

"You see the range?"

"Andrew will be thrilled. We've been looking for a replacement for months. And thanks for cleaning it up."

"It's heavy, my guys will load it for you," Gil said. "You want to spend the night before driving back?"

"That's what I was hoping."

Gil sat up and opened his desk drawer, retrieving a key card he handed to Jude. "The usual. Suite 1015. Use the service elevator."

"Any word on the other?"

"On schedule," Gil said. "But the credit terms are different now that we're increasing quantity. It's COD."

"How much?"

"All of it."

Jude paused and nodded. He blew a stream of cigar smoke. "The credit terms were one of the reasons I like working with you. All that cash at once makes me edgy."

"It's the size of the order, and the variety—a lot for both of us—everyone in the chain is demanding cash."

"That's to be expected, I guess."

"Any changes?"

"No, we're good, although I might need a few days to work out cash flow."

"Once I get the inventory assembled, I'll call. You'll have twenty-four hours."

"Is this a squeeze?"

"You know I'm not trying to knock you. You hear about that big bust in New York? Demand is up. I'd be foolish not to move whenever I have opportunity. I can't sit on inventory."

Jude stood up. Gil handed him an envelope. "The paperwork for the range," he said. "I put in a receipt for the GST tax, but you'll have to pay duty at the border."

"What about the girl?"

"Still part of the deal," Gil said. "She's up there now."

That gave Jude an idea. "I have to run back out to the van for a second."

"You need a wake-up call?"

"I never oversleep."

"Suit yourself," Gil said. He stuffed his cigar deep into his jaw, went back to his piles of cash and receipts.

Jude returned to the van to retrieve his camera. He rode the service elevator to the tenth floor, located the room, and opened the door with the key.

The living area was dark but he could see the blue flicker of a television from the bedroom. He turned on a light. An overstuffed couch and two chairs surrounded a coffee table, framed Monet reproductions hung on the walls. His shoes sank into a thick pile carpet. Nothing looked disturbed.

Roxanne had not heard him come in and she started when he entered the bedroom. Her clothes lay on the floor. She wore an oversized bathrobe with the letter "F" embroidered on the lapel. She looked at him and smiled and patted the mattress for him to come over.

A young immigrant from Cambodia, Roxanne spoke halting English and spent her days cleaning hotel rooms. She liked Jude. He was taking her to the United States of America to become a citizen.

Jude heeled off his shoes and joined her on the bed. He asked her to comb her hair. She didn't understand. He got up and went into the bathroom and came back with a brush and handed it to her.

"Your hair," he said. "Straighten it up. And your face—look pretty." He showed her the camera.

She said something sharp back to him that he didn't catch, but took the brush and went into the bathroom. He watched her through the open door. She stood in front of the mirror and brushed out her hair, then started with the makeup and straightened her face.

Finished, she came back into the bedroom and smiled for him. He snapped her photograph, viewed the results in the window. He took one more.

Roxanne opened her robe and dropped it off her shoulders. "You take more?" she asked.

He looked at her, the creamy skin, the small flawless breasts. But he shook his head and sighed. "How many times do I tell you? Now go to sleep."

"You don't like Roxanne?"

Jude liked her all right, but the idea of lusting for a woman close to his daughter's age horrified him, drowning any desire he might feel. If he wanted young ones, he'd bang the cocktail waitresses at Gull, but he preferred women closer to his own age, women with experience and perspective and something to share beyond a flat stomach or firm tits.

He slept in the other bedroom.

He made it back downstairs just before six. Although he saw no one, he smelled a fresh pot of coffee in the kitchen and helped himself to a mug and went out to the loading dock. Still more night than day. His breath steamed the air. The end of August and already the mornings cold.

Jude opened the doors to the van. Gil's crew had centered the range in the cargo hold and secured it with straps front and back. The panel that served as a false floor had been nicked and he checked to make sure it hadn't come loose.

He shut the doors and finished his coffee, leaving his cup on the loading dock. Forty-five minutes later he was the second vehicle in line at lane four of the U.S. Customs Inspection, with fifteen minutes to spare before Leonard's shift ended. Jude's turn came and he pulled into the booth. Leonard Deitch looked like a soldier who'd been on watch all night. Baggy-eyed and tense, an expression left over from his Vietnam days. A sidearm in a belt holster, his turkey flesh pinched in a uniform collar too tight around his neck.

He brightened when he saw Jude.

"Didn't recognize you with the van."

"You'll see me using it sometimes," Jude said. "I've got an oven in the back."

Jude handed the paperwork along with his passport.

Leonard held them in his hand for a moment.

"Also this," Jude said, turning on his camera and showing Leonard the small viewer displaying one of the photos he had taken of Roxanne from Cambodia.

Deitch smiled and nodded. "Even better than I expected. When do I get to meet my bride?"

"I'm setting that up, I just wanted to make sure you approved first."

"Oh, most definitely. Leonard approves."

"I should be back up next week, I'll bring her then."

"Sweet thing," said Deitch, blowing the camera a kiss. "I'll see you next week."

Jude pulled away from the booth and onto the Northway. He had planned to drive straight back, and then changed his mind at the next exit. As long as he was up this way, he should check on Aaron and that part of the order. Get everything lined up properly, leave no risk unmitigated, get this deal done, do it three or four times, and take that big step toward retirement. He made the call to Aaron and said he was coming, but on the way he turned off at the sign for Tear Lake and drove the perimeter, passing her house but seeing no evidence of anyone at home. No cars parked in the drive. Window shades drawn. It had been easy to find out which house was hers—a quick call to a contact in the county clerk's office and a review of the tax rolls. He drove around the lake a second time and then stopped in the market at the Adams Station junction and bought an egg sandwich, which he ate at a picnic table in a grassy area next to the gas pumps, a good vantage point for watching the few cars come and go from the parking lot.

Pain Management

In the past week Aaron had harvested and hung to dry almost two hundred plants. Moved another two hundred in vegetative stage from the bedroom to the grow room where he'd set the light timers to twelve hours on and twelve off for the flowering stage. Started ten more trays of clones with ten more to go. Fiddled again with the mixture of nitrogen, potassium, and phosphorus and wrote down the new formula before it was forgotten on a whiteboard hanging on the wall, hoping to increase the yield. He replaced crimped sections of irrigation tubing and installed new filters on the exhaust fans.

Yesterday, a pipe leading from the propane tank to the generator developed a leak in a joint and he circumvented it with a flexible hose that snaked along the floor. The scent of gas remained faintly in the air; he did his smoking outdoors now. He replaced three burned-out lightbulbs, each six feet long. He broke two in the process, one by dropping and one by cracking the connection, and ended up picking glass shards out of plants.

Now he went outside to plant the colorful mums he'd gotten from the nursery this morning. That's what the sign advertising them had said—COLORFUL MUMS/$12.99—and he became attached to them as you would a kitten at the shelter; he had to take them home. He bought eight pots jammed with the yellow and orange flowers, each blossom its own sun melting through his foggy head. He arranged the pots on either side of the fieldstone path leading to the front porch, then moved a few to create equal spacing until satisfied with the symmetry. He walked around back to the shed for a shovel and when he got there a stand of hemlocks at the back of the property drew his attention. A gust of mountain wind jimmied their tops and Aaron watched the branches sway and the clouds drift overhead against the crisp sky until the breeze had passed and he wondered if he'd been visited by a spirit. You live like a monk in isolation and you discover that spirits do exist, like the angels your grandmother told you tales about as a child: it was all true. They visit those who live alone and far away. They had never visited him in the desert or when he lay blasted close to dying, but they visited him now, when he was more alone and farther away than he'd ever been.

Another gust came and went, the trees waving some kind of signal. When his gaze returned to eye level he forgot why he'd walked back to the shed. He'd been taking extra vikes because the past few weeks the pain had been pumping through his face like a steady bass line in a song. Phantom limb pain, it was called, each beat of his heart pinging what wasn't there, though it wasn't an arm or leg Aaron had lost. One of his doctors at Reed told him the pain was real, yet not entirely explicable. It floated out in front of him and he could almost see it when he strained his eyes downward toward the airy space his cheekbone had vacated. There were theories. One doctor said that spinal cord nerves begin firing like mad because they're not getting the usual sensory input from that part of the body, sending panicky "Are you out there?" distress signals to a ship already sunk and gone. That doctor wrote him the prescription for Vicodin. Another doctor prescribed Topomax, an antiseizure med to keep the nerves from firing—at the expense of dizziness and cognitive losses. There were different approaches to managing the pain. What worked for one man might not for another. Aaron combined them: vikes and topos, along with old standbys beer and weed. Sometimes the pain waned and other times it roared and all the time he lived in a controlled blur. He knew he had to ease off the meds if anything worthy would become of his life. He shit rocky pellets that cut his hole. He closed his eyes to keep from keeling over when his eyeballs loosened from their moorings and jiggled in their sockets. He abandoned thoughts born a moment ago and forgot tasks half completed. Like what was he doing standing out here by the toolshed.

A bell sounded inside the house and the shrill ring jolted him from his daze. Someone had turned into the driveway. Forgetting the shovel, he ran back to the cabin and got the shotgun he kept against the wall behind the front door.

The gravel drive curved downhill from the road with trees encroaching on either side, their limbs hanging low overhead. Aaron waited by the window, shotgun in hand, watching for the vehicle that had tripped the sensor to appear around the bend in the driveway. His tongue stuck to the inside of his dry mouth. His pulse sped and his face panged.

The only regular visitor was the guy who delivered propane, every other Thursday, but Aaron believed today was Sunday, maybe Monday. No other visitors allowed, one of Jude's many rules, although what friends, if Aaron had any, would visit this cabin forsaken in the wilderness?

Then the van appeared and pulled into the clearing, coming to a stop next to Aaron's truck. He tensed until he saw Jude get out, stand there and survey the property and the cabin, stare into the dense woods surrounding it. Then he came up the porch stairs.

Aaron opened the door.

"Put that thing down," Jude said. "What are you doing with a gun?"

Aaron leaned the gun against the wall just inside the door. "I wasn't expecting anyone. I thought it might be an ambush and I wanted to protect your investment."

"What's wrong with you? I just called an hour ago and said I was coming. Did you forget?"

Yeah, he must have.

"No one's going to ambush you. Besides, whoever shows up here, you don't want to be shooting them. No shooting."

"Yes, sir."

He took a closer look at Aaron's eyes. "Are you all right?"

"I just forgot, that's all."

"You having a lot of pain, is that the problem?"

"I got it under control."

"What are you taking?"

Aaron shrugged. "Not too much."

"Is the safety on?"

Aaron checked the gun and clicked the safety button back on.

"You don't need a gun here. I want you to get rid of it. It's that kind of thing that makes me wonder about you."

"You can count on me. I got all the plants harvested and drying."

"Okay." Now his tone eased. "And I appreciate you making that run for me yesterday. You get something to eat before you drove back?"

"Yes, sir."

"What else did you do there?"

"I put the bag in the walk-in and helped myself to the food on the stove. I did what you said."

"You work for me," Jude said. "That means you tell the truth."

"I know."

———

They had been on the same flight from D.C., although Aaron hadn't noticed Jude on the plane. He'd kept his head down, hat brim pulled low. After deplaning, he walked through the terminal. As he approached the exit he saw the signs before he could ID the people waving them. Big cardboard banners with hand-drawn letters: "Welcome Home" and "Support Our Troops."

For a stupid instant his heart leaped, as if the signs were for him.

A few steps closer and he read "Welcome Home Alex" and "Alex, We Love You" and "U.S. Marines." The people holding them were strangers to Aaron—women, men, children, a granny.

He picked out the marine ten yards in front him in his brown service uniform, watched him pass through the exit and get swallowed by the sign holders. Aaron glimpsed the side of the marine's flushed, beaming face, handling the attention. No obvious scars or dents in his body. No missing parts. A whole man.

Passengers from other gates crowded the terminal, making their way toward the exit. Aaron felt glances his way, people sneaking a second look. Couldn't blame them. Who doesn't crane for a view of the accident.

Two things he needed to do: shed the fatigues, get a new face. Maybe three: do something with his life, now that he still had one.

Aaron moved on to retrieve his duffel. Not until he'd collected it from the carousel did he consider how to get to Glens Falls. His half-assed plan was to move in again with his buddy, Guy, who once shared a house with Aaron and had since moved to a mobile home park and said sure, come live with him again, only now his girlfriend would be there, too.

Aaron thought of where else he could stay. Nowhere. No family. Father unknown. After raising her son alone, his mother met and married Ted the real estate flake and moved to Arizona a year before Aaron had joined the Guard. Arizona. No fucking way would Aaron step foot into a desert again as long as he lived. He'd made that promise to himself one night on patrol, if only he could get out of the sandbox alive. He was still undecided about the beach, which had sand but also water. He had an older sister, Ellen, who lived in Denmark with a scientist she had married. She didn't know he'd ever joined the Guard or started college. So it was Guy, and his girlfriend, and a tin trailer, but only for the short term. He was resourceful and something better would come along.

He secured the duffel around his shoulder and the carry-on in his left hand, lowered his hat another inch over his eyes, and considered taking a taxi. No, that would cost at least a Ben and he didn't have cash to burn. He looked at the bus schedule. He'd have to get downtown first to catch a bus going north. Just the idea of it sent a stab of pain through his face. He put both bags down and reached in his pocket for a vike. When he tilted his head back to swallow dry he saw some dude approaching him.

"You need a ride?"

At first Aaron though he was military. He stood tall with his shoulders back, hair groomed. Looked straight at Aaron's face and didn't register a change in expression. Wore a smooth leather jacket and dark pants. Polished black boots.

"I saw you on the plane, and now I see you looking at the bus schedule, so I thought I'd ask."

Sure, everyone saw him. Everyone noticed the freak. Aaron picked up his two bags again. "I have to get up near Glens Falls."

"I'm driving north, if you want. Take it or leave it."

Why not. He said, "Yeah, cool." Another guilty conscience motherfucker feeling it for a soldier sent to fight a shitty war. Or, this could be his first break to bigger things.

"I'm Jude Gates."

"Aaron Capuano, sir. Pleased to meet you." Still with the manners from the Guard.

It was cold outside the terminal and scraps of dirty snow hung on where the plows had built piles on the edges of the lot. The air felt good, clean. Gates popped the trunk as they approached his car. Aaron put his bags in and helped himself to the passenger side. Nice car, heated leather, like a jet with all the cockpit lights and navigation system.

As soon as they were on the Northway, Gates reached in his pocket and pulled out a joint, holding it up so Aaron could see.

"Do you mind?"

"What? No. I mean, go ahead." A roll of Life Savers he might have expected from this dude, but a bone?

Gates produced a lighter and fired the joint. Pungent smoke filled the cabin. He took a single hit that glowed the lit end and offered it to Aaron. "You want some?"

Fuck yeah he wanted some. There hadn't been reefer in the sand and nothing at Reed except the vikes and antiseizure shit. Aaron hadn't gotten high in almost a year, since he'd last rotated to the States. But he wondered. Was Gates one of those rich, middle-aged homos trying to lure him into a hole job? Whatever. If he tried anything, Aaron would gouge his eyes out.

He took the joint and sucked, felt like a rookie when he exploded coughing.

He took another hit without coughing this time and passed it back.

"I'm good. Help yourself," Gates said. Then he switched into the left lane and set the cruise on eighty.

Aaron smoked the joint down to a roach and held it, not sure what to do with it.

"Out the window," Gates said, opening Aaron's window for him. Aaron gave it a flick. A stab of pain struck his face and he raised a hand to cup his cheek.

"You in Washington to meet with the president?" Gates asked.

"I noticed a few soldiers in the audience during his State of the Union."

Here we go. Dude hadn't said jack until now. No questions about the war or how he got wounded, no statements about pride and bravery. No political speeches leaning left or right. But he'd been waiting for an opening.

"I was at Reed."

"I hear that place is no Hilton. Mold all over the walls."

Aaron snorted. "The walls, the toilet seats, the mattresses, you fucking name it."

He didn't want to talk but found himself telling about it. Not just the grenade that carved out a chunk of his face and ripped his buddy to pieces, leaving a spray of bloody dust in their vehicle and on the road a million miles from home, but his whole lame story. Probably because he was so stoned—that always got his heart opening. They were supposed to fix his face, put in a plate and cover it up nice and neat with some skin from his ass, but that hadn't happened yet and who knows if it ever would. He didn't think about the future; it was too much like looking for something he'd lost but didn't know where. Although he'd had a future once, had graduated from high school, and even though he didn't get a ride to a Division I hockey school, he attended a semester at Adirondack Community College. He thought he wanted to be an engineer, or an architect. The problem was money. He had to pay full tuition because he hadn't submitted his financial aid forms on time; when he finally got a loan he spent most of it on a down payment for the Yamaha FZ, which he flipped in a turn the first week. Totaled the bike, a costly mistake, but at least he walked away from it. He had credit card debt up to his eyeballs and tried one of those debt consolidation companies, which only made it worse. The idea of the Guard came from a recruiter on campus. He'd seen the commercials on TV. Who hadn't, they were airing all the time. Two weeks' commitment a year and one weekend a month and you got help to pay for college and you could become somebody and do something useful with your life. At first it was great. He proved his strength in basic while other pussies dropped out. He mastered combat maneuvers. In the winter during the ice storm his unit helped evacuate people and clear roads and transport provisions. He made a difference. Then came the call-up. He wasn't worried or afraid. He'd stand for his country.

And then.

And then he shut up. Rode in stoned silence swallowing down the same panic he'd felt while on patrol and a loneliness he didn't know existed. The pot was too strong.

At Exit 18 Gates asked him for the address. Aaron said he didn't know the number, just the road name, which Gates keyed into the navigation system and got audio turn-by-turn directions and a full-color map display. What a system—better than anything the Humvees were equipped with. Car probably had better armor, too.

"Thanks for driving me all this way," Aaron said. "I would have been fucked otherwise."

Gates found the entrance to the park and turned in. Aaron told him to stop at a group of mailboxes with names and numbers. He got out and scanned the names and found Guy's.

Gates cruised slowly down the row. It was late and no one was outside. A few of the trailers had spotlights shining into dirt patches posing as lawns. They located the right one and Gates stopped. The windows were dark. A cracked vinyl awning hung lopsided over the door.

"Hold on." Gates handed Aaron a business card with his name and phone number. "I'm sure you've got good friends here who can help you get connected again, but in case you're looking for something new I might have a position available. Some property that needs looking after. It's a bit farther north, near Adams Station, so you'd have to relocate. Rent included."

"What kind of position?"

"Like a caretaker, with benefits—like that joint you smoked."

"What do I have to do?"

"You have to be discreet. You wouldn't want to mention it to your friends."

"Discreet?"

"It means careful, unnoticed."

"I know what it means." He shoved the card in his jacket pocket.

"We can talk again if you want." Gates released the trunk but didn't get out. Aaron retrieved his bags and Gates pulled away, swinging around the perimeter of the park and accelerating hard as he got out to the main road.

Aaron rapped the aluminum door. Then again, this time on the glass. He heard noises from inside and saw someone moving and Guy came to the door wrapped in a towel.

"Jesus fucking Christ, Aaron. What the hell . . ."

Aaron stepped into the living room with his bags. The place reeked of lemon freshener masking mildew or mold, like at Reed. Guy turned on a lamp near the couch.

"I thought you said tomorrow. Shit, I could have picked you up."

"That's okay, I got a ride."

"Who is it?" a voice called from the other room.

"It's Aaron, babe. Get out here and meet Aaron."

"What—hang on, I've got to get dressed."

"Me too," Guy said to Aaron. "Let me just throw on some jeans."

Aaron sat on the couch. The springs pricked his ass. He could hear the conversation in the bedroom, the girlfriend asking where was Aaron going to sleep, how long was he going to stay, and Guy telling her to be quiet, it would all work out.

Guy came out first. He got two beers from the refrigerator and opened Aaron's for him. He looked at Aaron's face below the brim of his hat.

"You got blasted," Guy said. "Fucking Hajis. Does it still hurt?"

"Not really."

"Sorry, man. At least you're home now."

Home. "Where you working?"

"National Grid, I got a gig as a lineman, working second shift so I get all the emergencies, cars running into the poles and shit. Tonight's my night off."

Guy's girlfriend came into the room, wearing sweatpants and a too-small T-shirt. She'd put on makeup and brushed her hair. She was tall with a big ass and boobs. She'd be someone to wrestle. That was another thing he hadn't done in over a year: gotten laid. Or even kissed a girl. That was something he needed to do real soon. He'd had a girlfriend during his one semester at college, but she transferred to Boston University and stopped returning his phone calls and texts after he'd been made a regular and sent to the desert.

Guy said, "This is Rose. She goes to ACC, just like you did."

She gawked at Aaron's face, the part caved in below the eye where a chunk of his cheekbone was gone.

"Sorry I disturbed you," Aaron said.

Rose fidgeted. "That's okay, you didn't. Are you hungry? We

don't have much. There's cereal and I think some hot dogs in the refrigerator."

"I'm not too hungry."

The three of them fell silent for a moment. Finally, Rose said, "We only have one bedroom, but you can sleep on the couch."

He lived on the couch for two days and the third morning before Rose and Guy woke up he dug Jude's card out of his jacket pocket and called the number on it.

"You want to see the plants?" Aaron asked. At least that was something he could be proud of.

He led Jude inside and through the kitchen to a door that Aaron opened into a room as bright as midday sun. The windows were covered with blackout shades and the walls painted a brilliant glossy white. Rows of alternating metal halide and high-pressure sodium light fixtures beamed down on the grid of young plants rising from their nutrient-soaked trays. A three-foot-diameter ceiling fan hummed above. Aaron had researched and found out about painting the walls to reflect more of the light. He also rigged the system of chains and pulleys he used to raise and lower the lights to be the right distance from the plants as they grew.

Jude squinted from the glare, shading his eyes with one hand. He touched one of the plants, the stem thin and fragile.

"These are the new ones," Aaron said. "The last crop is drying next door."

He opened the door to what once served as a small bedroom and stood back and let Jude step in first. Clothesline spaced a foot apart crisscrossed the room. From each clothespin hung a thick bud on its stem, the tips of the flowers purple and frosty. Two fans oscillated on the floor, blowing air over the buds, like a breeze playing with laundry on the line.

"What do you think, thirty pounds?"

"I'll bet more."

Jude fingered one of the buds. Resin stuck to his fingers.

"You've got a green thumb, anyone ever tell you that?"

His mother had told him that once, when he was a kid, and he had looked at his thumb, unsure what she'd meant. He still could see how she smiled when he did that, feel how she kissed his face. He used to help her plant flowers along the fence in their back-yard. She showed him how to use a hand spade and which way to point the bulb in the dirt. He'd forgotten about gardening with his mother, never would have remembered it again if Jude hadn't mentioned a green thumb.

"I got some honey oil, too, just from cleaning off the trimming shears. You need hash?"

"I'll take some when I pick this up. When will it be ready?"

"A few more days is all it needs. It's drying good."

"I'll be back within a week, I'll let you know. And this time no shotgun."

They returned through the kitchen, which Aaron also used as his bedroom, sleeping on a bed he'd put in place of the dining table. At the foot of the bed was a wide-screen TV on a stand, wires running along the floor and out through the wall to a satel-lite dish mounted on the roof. The generator emitted a constant hum and in the background the fans flitted.

When they were outside again, Jude looked around and said, "I might need someone to drive a couple of important deliveries."

"I could do that."

"You got a passport?"

"Still got my military ID."

"You can't be fucking up on me. I heard you were getting high in the parking lot of my restaurant."

Was he? He didn't remember.

"Sorry, sir."

"Is that what you think my place of business is for?"

"No, sir."

Jude turned around and headed for his van. Aaron gave Jude the finger behind his back. Drive the big runs. Fuck that. There was nothing big about this guy and Aaron was going nowhere with him, even though he worked like a mule in this backwoods hideout and cultivated superior product, as good as any Aaron had ever seen or tasted.

Jude hesitated at the van, turned to face Aaron again.

Come on, just leave, for shit's sake. But Jude was hanging, holding back. Looking close at him, trying to make eye contact, as if on the verge of a decision.

"By the way," Jude said, "the mums look great."

It's Not Closure

Gwen parked at the end of a short single row of cars on a narrow, hilly lane in Niskayuna Rural Cemetery. Behind the gray hearse and matching limousine, she counted five other cars. She had expected more people. The obit had mentioned that James Anderson was an active community member and retired professor. Had he outlived his circle or made enemies of those he knew? Gwen would not go unnoticed here, approaching the tidy group alone and late, stepping between granite tombstones, trying to maintain a dignified posture with her heels sinking into the grass.

A dozen or so heads bowed in front of a brushed silver casket topped with cascading flowers. Gwen had memorized the names from the newspaper: son Walter, daughter Sheila. And the four grandchildren: Tyler, Lily, Connor, and Michael.

That must be the daughter, Sheila, the one dressed like a widow in black dress and veil, a man on either side supporting her, although her square frame appeared sturdy and firmly planted. That must be her husband to one side, and on the other, her brother. Next to them stood a younger woman, the lone black face among a bouquet of lilies, holding a toddler in her arms. The grandchildren were teenagers, sullen boys in ill-fitting jackets, the blue-haired girl staring off into the trees.

Gwen stood at the back of the group, a small gap between herself and the others. A few faces turned to notice her. The morning was humid and hazy. Sweat trickled beneath her dark sleeves and her forehead glistened. The stitches over her eye itched.

The priest spoke about the good and noble life of James Anderson, which should not be overshadowed by the last few difficult years.

About his reunion with God.

Gwen had no image of who lay inside this casket. She'd never seen James or even a photograph of him. There'd been no glance of his face through the windshield just before the accident, no screaming imprint in her mind. The way the light had reflected the sky on the glass, the speed of the event—it might have been an empty car that crossed her path. But it wasn't.

Now the priest sprinkled holy water on the casket. "Ashes to ashes, dust to dust . . ." And now he made his way among the mourners, flicking sprinkles of holy water from a golden nozzle onto the family. Even in the back, standing to one side, Gwen felt a few drops like the first hint of rain. Cicadas twanged in the nearby trees.

Brian had been against her attending the funeral. He questioned whether she'd be welcome at the service. After she'd spoken to him about it on the phone, he'd come home from work a few hours later in a curt, cranky mood, going so far as to call it a stupid idea.

"Whether I'm welcome or not isn't the point," Gwen insisted. They didn't often accuse each other of having stupid ideas.

"Then what is the point? Why do you want to insert yourself in this situation?"

"To pay my respects to someone who died in an accident I was involved in."

"Gwen, stop blaming yourself for what happened. He hit *you*."

"I'm not blaming myself, but I feel awful."

"Then send flowers to the family, buy a mass card."

"It's not the same thing."

"I think it will only make things harder for you."

"And I think it's the right thing to do, even if it is hard. I need to go."

"Then it's not about paying respects to the family, it's about getting closure for yourself."

Closure. She hated that word. She didn't believe in it. All those self-help articles and therapists who spoke about achieving closure after traumatic events: death, divorce, downsizing. Such chasms don't close so neat and tidy; they reveal a new path that alters the course of your life. Like the time she'd had an abortion and afterward visited a cemetery, a different one from this one, in a different city, and sat on a bench until closing at dusk when a guard on patrol approached and asked her to leave the grounds. She'd made up her mind that evening never to have another abortion, no matter what. She didn't look upon that assertion as an ending or a closure ritual; it was a life decision, one that made a big impact once Brian came along and she became pregnant again, this time with Nora.

The service ended and the group parted and moved about and the teenagers sat together under the canopy of a willow tree. The priest put an arm around James's daughter, Sheila. Gwen should approach the family, she should say something—to somebody. Express regrets, explain the reason for her presence. She was not a funeral crasher.

Before she could take initiative, one of the men peeled from the group and approached her.

"I'm Walt Anderson—James's son."

Gwen had guessed his identity correctly.

"My sister wants to know who you are."

Gwen introduced herself.

"I was the driver of the other car in the accident. I thought . . . I wanted to pay my respects. I'm very sorry for your loss."

Walt nodded. "The car my father struck. I'm sorry you had to be involved. He never should have been driving with his condition. It's kind of you to come."

Take that, Brian, I told you it was the right thing for me to be here.

"I see you didn't come through the accident unscathed," Walt said.

Gwen fingered her stitches. "Oh, this is nothing, nothing compared to . . ." Compared to a dead man.

"Who is it?" the daughter, Sheila, called out, loud enough that the others present turned their focus on Gwen.

"My father had Alzheimer's," Walt explained. "He lived with my sister—at her insistence, although it was very challenging for her."

"Walter! Who is it?"

Walt shrugged as if apologizing to Gwen. "The car keys were hidden, but he must have come across them while looking for something else, who knows what. And the next thing he's driving somewhere, who knows where. He talked a lot about the Adirondacks, where he'd grown up, but he was driving in the other direction when the accident happened."

"That must have been frightening for you, not knowing where he'd gone."

"It's like having a two-year-old," Walt said. "You don't know what they'll get into—you can't leave them alone. I should know, I have one now. That's my daughter, Mali, over there; my wife is holding her."

He motioned to the black woman and the youngster in her arms, standing apart from the others.

Gwen went through the list of grandchildren mentioned in the obituary: no Mali.

Sheila made her way over to where Gwen and Walt stood, her husband following several paces behind.

"Sheila, this is Gwen Raine. She was kind enough to come for Dad. She was driving the car that Dad struck."

Shelia flinched, as if a bug had flown into her face. "You," she said.

"I'm sorry for your loss," Gwen said. "Your brother was just mentioning that you cared for your father—I mean, that he lived with you. I'm sure it was a great comfort to him being with his family."

"You were on drugs," Shelia snapped.

Now it was Gwen's turn to flinch. "Mrs. . . ." Gwen started and stopped. She didn't remember Sheila's last name, hadn't prepared for this.

Sheila moved closer, swaying in and out of Gwen's face, like a boxer feinting.

"You were high on drugs. You struck and killed an innocent person. I know what happened. I have a friend in the Morrissey police. She told me all about it."

"Sheila, that's not what happened," Walt said.

"You should be in prison. And what do you get—all you get is a black eye."

"Sheila, please," Walt said. He tried to put an arm on his sister. She brushed him off.

"What religion are you?"

"Um, well . . ." Gwen didn't have a concise answer for the woman. She had a long and convoluted answer that she and Brian worked out with the kids, about how people have different beliefs regarding God and religion and each person has to make their own decision and right now their family was not any one particular religion by name, but their goal was to introduce their kids to . . . It was the usual agnostic plea bargain from parents who had lapsed. But Nora wanted to wear a white dress and receive her First Communion like other girls in her class. Or celebrate eight nights of Hanukkah. Or at least know more about Episcopalians, the faith both Brian and Gwen had been raised in.

"Just as I thought," Sheila said. "And you probably have young children." She crossed herself.

"Sheila, let it go," Walt said.

"Are you a mother?"

"I don't see why that matters," Gwen said, ready to fight back now.

"Oh, those poor innocent babes."

"We should get going," Walt said. "We're expected back at the house."

But Sheila would not let up. "If it weren't for God—if it weren't for the grace of God, where would I have found the strength to care for Dad every day? It's me, I'm the one who . . ." She started to cry and fought back tears with the righteous defiance of a martyr about to be stoned.

Her husband, who had yet to say a word, took her arm.

"I've got a good mind to sue you for wrongful death. I can, you know," Sheila said.

"Gwen was not at fault in the accident," Walt said. "The police have already determined that."

"What are you—defending her?" Sheila spat back.

"Please calm down."

"A drug addict and a heathen. If the police don't get you, God will." She turned to her husband. "Peter, can't I bring a lawsuit? I can, can't I?" Now looking at Gwen again.

"You can try," her husband said miserably. "Come on, now, let's go. It's time to go home."

Peter led his wife away, toward the limousine behind the hearse.

Gwen let Walt walk her back to her car.

"I'm sorry, that was embarrassing," Walt said.

Now she was sorry she had come and wished she had listened to Brian, although he'd been such a jerk about it that she couldn't have followed his advice even if she wanted to.

"For me, my father hasn't been my father for years now—he's just a shell, his mind gone—but for Sheila, he was still everything."

"It must be really hard for her," Gwen said. They had reached her car.

"You know what I said about it being like having a two-year-old? Sure there's confusion and tantrums and repetitive boredom, but calm and loving moments, too, when your baby's resting on your shoulder and the love and dependency is so deep and mutual."

Yes, Gwen remembered that feeling; she missed it often.

"It was like that with my father and Sheila. Imagine losing your two-year-old."

Gwen shook her head. "No, I can't."

He opened the car door for her. "Thank you for coming, Gwen. I appreciate it."

She got in her car and cried most of the way home, not that it provided any closure.

The Detective Joins the PTA

Allison Witherspoon, former bank vice president now constructing a second career as mom and PTA president, chaired the Morrissey East PTA meeting like a corporate CEO dazzling the shareholders. It was about strategy and results, about serving your shareholders: the students.

In her opening remarks, she made use of a laptop and a projector to show slides about last year's successful programs—book exchange, Helping Hands, new school sign, bus trip to the New York State Museum, after-school enrichment, teacher appreciation program, visiting author series, and a half-dozen others. She outlined ambitious goals for the coming school year, including three new programs.

All achievable, Allison remarked. If everyone works hard and makes their projects a priority.

She introduced the other PTA officers for the upcoming year: secretary, treasurer, vice presidents.

Allison singled out Gwen for her efforts over the summer on the new school sign, which now hung near the street for every passerby to see. Gwen had made the sign herself, chiseling the words *Morrissey East Elementary—A Place to Learn and Grow* into a desk-sized hardwood plaque that had been planed and joined by another parent volunteer. She painted the letters using three different colors and recruited a local contractor to hang the sign on a post set in a solid concrete footing. On top of this, Gwen raised the funds to pay for it.

This was Gwen's second year on the PTA, and her first as a vice president. She missed Nora's first-grade year because she'd been president of the Parents' Club at Nate's kindergarten and that had been obligation enough. She preferred the undercommit/ overdeliver model of promises to its frenzied and disappointing opposite. To her credit, she did overdeliver on her selected commitments. Last year, as school banking volunteer, she'd increased the number of student bankers more than 50 percent, by instituting a parent matching program in which parents signed a contract to match each dollar that kids banked of their own money. As a library aide, she developed recommended reading lists by compiling students' favorite books and soliciting student reviews, which she published in a binder kept in the library.

In her one year on the PTA, she had gained a reputation as a reliable parent with creative ideas, which is why Allison had approached her about becoming an officer candidate, and Gwen had accepted.

When Allison closed her remarks, applause just short of a standing ovation filled the room. What an enthusiastic bunch, Gwen thought—or at least a bunch that rallied around Allison Witherspoon's rhetoric. She must have been a consensus builder at the bank, the kind of leader who inspired others to join the cause of any project she embraced.

"You'd think she just announced world peace," Marlene leaned over and said to Gwen.

Gwen had sat in front because Allison had asked the officers to sit in the first few rows. Now Gwen turned around and scanned the room of faces. Many she knew. Almost all were women. A couple of men, one a repeat from last year, another one new. Some people in the back she couldn't see.

After Allison stepped away, the meeting broke into a refreshment reception. In front of the cookies and brownies and beverages were sign-up sheets for this year's programs.

Gwen was still in her chair when Sandy Makowski found her and took the seat that Marlene had just vacated.

"Jimmy got Mrs. Mardeki, I can't believe it," Sandy said. "I . . . What happened to your eye?"

"I was in a car accident," Gwen said.

"That looks like it hurts."

"No, it's fine now," Gwen said. The swelling had reduced and the bruising faded to a dull green that showed up only in certain light, but the stitch line stood out like railroad tracks where her eyebrow had been shaved. The stitches would come out tomorrow.

"But Mrs. Mardeki," Sandy continued. "I specifically requested a calm and structured environment for Jimmy and who does he get but Mrs. Hustle & Bustle. I was really hoping for Mrs. Quinn. Nora got Mrs. Quinn, didn't she? I'm really not happy about this at all and . . ."

Gwen interrupted her. "Marlene's son, Josh, had Mrs. Mardeki a few years ago and she said it was a great experience."

"Jimmy's not like Josh—he's very introspective and quiet."

"You should talk to Marlene," Gwen said. "She knows Mrs. Mardeki well."

Gwen could blame herself for this onslaught, and similar ones from other Morrissey moms. As a library aide, she got to know most of the teachers when they brought their classes in for library period. During the time the kids browsed the shelves, Gwen chatted with the teachers, getting to know their personalities and asking about their teaching styles and what was going on in their classrooms. She had no intention of gathering intelligence, yet other moms interrogated Gwen for everything she discovered, as if she were harboring classified information.

Sandy was still hounding her. "Do you think there's anything I can do about it? Should I ask for a change?"

For all Gwen knew, Mrs. Mardeki might be the best third-grade teacher in the world. What a mistake to have nicknamed her Mrs. Hustle & Bustle, all because she ordered her class into straight lines coming and going from the library and kept a close watch on time. Gwen should have kept that name to herself.

"Sandy, I think Mrs. Mardeki is a great teacher," Gwen said. "That hustle and bustle business is way off target. I don't know how it got started."

She had to tolerate Sandy Makowski because her husband, Richard, was the editor of the *Morrissey Bee.* Gwen had visited him at his office and explained in minimal detail about her accident and arrest and asked if he could keep her name off the police blotter. Richard, long and stooped with black-framed glasses, told Gwen he wasn't in the habit of suppressing news.

"I wouldn't want you to do that," Gwen said. "But it's not really news at all. Mostly a misunderstanding."

"You said you were arrested for possession of marijuana?"

Gwen nodded. That was one of the charges. "Sandy and I are on the PTA together. I've been a subscriber to the *Bee* ever since we moved to Morrissey."

Richard thought for a moment. He took his glasses off and bit the end of the frame. "As long as it doesn't go to trial, or become part of a larger story. If that happens, I would have to cover it. We've paid close attention to the drug issue this past year."

"I'm glad you have," Gwen said. "I think it's important."

Gwen excused herself and went over to check out the sign-up sheet for the program she was chairing this year, Helping Hands.

The sheet was fronted by the plate of brownies she had baked and a folded paper card with her name on it. Why did they have to identify the source of baked goods? The brownies had hardly been touched. The edges were ragged and the tops sunken and cracked. She'd baked them in a hurry with the help of Nate and might have forgotten or mismeasured an ingredient because she'd spent most of the time keeping Nate from spilling the bowl.

There were no signatures yet on the Helping Hands sheet—maybe that's why her brownies had been ignored. With Helping Hands, you could end up doing very little or doing a lot, depending on the fate of families in the school district. In the event someone got sick or hurt or divorced, or if someone died or a family was struck by any other plight, Helping Hands provided services for the family such as running errands, driving kids, and cooking meals.

Gwen had a disconcerting thought: What if her misdemeanor with the bag of pot had been something much worse and she faced prison time? If the guilt she felt was guilt by law? Would Helping Hands come to the aid of her family? Stricken by cancer, yes, we'll help you. Sent to prison: not sure.

As this thought crossed her mind, someone came up from behind and a hairy-knuckled hand reached in for a brownie.

"Are you sure you want one of those?" Gwen said, speaking as she turned.

"Don't tell me you baked *those* kind of brownies?"

Gwen's face drained. She stood eye to eye with the square-faced Detective William Keller of the Morrissey Police Department. Did he have some telekinetic power that sensed her thoughts of prison? What an eerie coincidence.

If she'd been bold and clever she would have said she'd left those other brownies at home, that she was a responsible parent and vice president of the PTA and would never make a mix-up like that. Instead, she moved her mouth without forming any intelligible words.

"I'm sorry, that was a bad joke," Detective Keller said. He took a bite of the brownie and a crumb clung to his mustache. "They taste much better than they look," he added. "Your eye looks a lot better too."

Gwen recovered her composure. "Are you joining the PTA?"

"My son, Andy, started first grade this year. I thought I should get involved. My wife can't because she's an ICU nurse and her shift hours change a lot."

Mustering her courage, Gwen said, "Then I hope you're signing up for Helping Hands."

"I'm going to be starting a new program," he said. "Well, not new—we're moving DARE down to the elementary grades. Send a few of the handsome young uniforms in for a poster talk about drugs and alcohol. Seems like it's already too late for some of the kids by the time they reach middle school."

"DARE?"

"Drug Abuse Resistance Education," Keller said.

"Yes, I know. That's a good idea," Gwen said, stomach tightening like a wrung rag.

"You wouldn't think so in a nice suburban community like this, but there are a lot of drugs."

"Really?"

"Maybe we should establish a program for the parents, too. A kind of refresher course."

Gwen considered excusing herself. She willed someone to interrupt them, but others in the room seemed far away and small, their conversations distant chatter carried on the wind.

"In fact, that reminds me—maybe we can step out in the hallway for a moment, Mrs. Raine. I'd like to ask you about something in private."

"What? Of course." The hallway. The execution chamber.

Detective Keller motioned for her to go first. Gwen took a last look around for someone to save her, then composed a nonchalant face and walked from the classroom into the hallway.

The noise of the classroom faded. Cork bulletin boards lined both walls, soon to be filled with student artwork and photos and school mantras. One of the boards held a collage of photographs from last year's special events—kids upon kids playing music, making art, listening to authors, eating pizza. There was a photo near one edge, partially buried by others, of Nora and two classmates holding a Morrissey East Pride poster.

"You have one or two children here?" the detective asked.

"My daughter, Nora, is in third grade and my son, Nate, is starting first grade this year."

"Whose class?"

"Mrs. Viander."

"I hear she's very good. Andy is in Miss Amico's class."

Gwen bit her lip, shifted her weight from one foot to the other. Waited.

"That remark about the brownies really was uncalled for," Detective Keller said. "I apologize for that. My wife is always warning me about my sense of humor, or lack of."

"And the refresher course for parents?"

"That's actually under consideration, or maybe a seminar for parents and their children to attend together," Keller said.

Gwen said nothing.

Keller went on. "It's pretty clear standing here talking to you that circumstances put you in the wrong place at the wrong time. What I'm saying, Mrs. Raine, is that we don't think you're a drug dealer we need to take off the streets. We don't think you're a danger to the community."

"No, I'm not." She began to relax.

"Not that anyone is condoning operating a motor vehicle while under the influence."

"That was a mistake," Gwen conceded. More than a mistake. There were a handful of fateful decisions in her life Gwen wished she could take back, and this was one of them.

"And I do understand that adults make choices within the privacy of their lives. I don't have to agree with those choices, but who would benefit from this situation getting messy? Not you or your family, certainly, or the school. It would be better for everyone if this situation just went away."

The detective smiled. He motioned with his hand as if to touch Gwen's arm, then pulled back.

"Then why did my court date get pushed out again?"

It had been moved twice, with her appearance scheduled now for next week.

"There's still some investigative work to be done, so the charges against you could change—or they could be dropped altogether."

"That would be helpful."

"Let me explain something. As I mentioned, we're starting DARE in the elementary school because studies show that the earlier kids learn how dangerous drugs can be and the more that message is reinforced, the less likely they are to try them. It's a simple equation. At the same time, there were a number of drug incidents in the middle school and high school last year and over the summer involving students. Too many. Mostly involving marijuana, but there's been prescription drugs and even some meth. It's not a good situation for the town."

"I've read about some of it."

"So you know. Break-ins are up. Vandalism is up. And what we need to find out is where the drugs are coming from."

"They're not coming from me," Gwen said.

"No, we know that."

The classroom door opened and two women came out and crossed the hall to the girls' bathroom. Detective Keller took a few more steps down the hall and Gwen followed.

"While we don't think you're a danger to the community, there are others out there who are. Do you know what I'm saying?"

"I think so."

"We'd like to know where you got that bag of marijuana."

Gwen stood still, her feet heavy on the floor.

"It would help us put together this puzzle."

"No, it was just someone—not anyone who . . ." Gwen stopped. Her comfort level sunk further.

"Think of it as being for the kids' sake."

"I should talk to my attorney about this, shouldn't I?" After what she'd admitted at the hospital, she'd been drilled by both Brian and Roger about keeping her mouth shut unless Roger advised her otherwise.

Detective Keller's shoulders slumped, as if he'd been standing at attention for too long.

"You do that, Mrs. Raine. You speak to your attorney." His voice had turned flat, having lost its previous tone of concern and confidence.

"But think of the children, that's all I'm asking. Think of protecting them, the way, for instance, Child Protective Services helps out when a parent abuses a child, or endangers a child's welfare in some way or is sent to prison. Maybe because of something to do with drugs. That's worth thinking about, isn't it?"

He turned and left her standing alone.

part 2

Side Effects

A Flawed Specimen

Less than a half mile into her workout the pain kicked in, a sharp, crushing sting on the outside of the knee every time her right foot landed. She tried to work through it but the burn got worse. She was running with the team and fell behind so quickly that no one had a chance to ask her what happened. Her teammates ahead of her rounded a bend in the campus path and disappeared beyond the maintenance building.

Dana slowed to a walk, stopped, then turned around and started walking back to the field house.

Walking didn't hurt, but that was only a tease.

She spotted her coach in the bleachers at the track. He stood when he saw her approaching and she fought the desire to cry. She'd already fought it and won twice this week, once waking up during the night suffering from homesickness and missing her father and friends, and the second time a delayed reaction about an hour after a guy she was talking with from the lacrosse team looked at her eye and asked who she'd been in a fight with, a comment she'd heard a million times that wouldn't normally faze her. Now here was yet another reason to cry—a knee injury that could prevent her from running this weekend in the first cross-country meet of her collegiate career, the Plattsburgh Cardinal Classic. But she held her tears back.

"The knee flaring up again?" her coach asked.

She nodded. "Every stride. It feels okay when I first start out, then as soon as I'm warmed up it starts to hurt."

"You've tried icing, stretching, and didn't you say you rested it for a week over the summer?"

"Yeah, it was good for about two days once I started running again. Then it came back."

Coach went inside with her and they consulted with the trainer, Sarah Sullivan, who held the university's record time in cross-country from her student days, a record Dana dreamed of breaking during her four years here. She told Dana to stand with her knees slightly bent and she massaged with two fingers the bony protrusion on the outside of the knee. "Is this where you feel it?"

Dana winced. "Yeah."

Sarah stood back and looked at her frame. "You're bowlegged and a pronator, and you started training harder on off-road hilly surfaces over the summer."

Dana nodded.

"Coach, you know it and I know it and I think Dana here knows it. Classic case of ITBS."

The trainer was correct: Dana did know it. Iliotibial band syndrome, the official tongue-twisting name for ITBS. When she first started feeling the pain about a month ago, she researched on the Internet and e-mailed back and forth with Sarah Sullivan at St. Lawrence. The trainer suspected ITBS then and was confirming it now. She'd suggested the regimen of icing and stretching and resting, and Dana had followed the advice exactly, even though it was tedious to sit with ice on her knee four times a day and go through the stretching routine, and taking a week off from running put her through a withdrawal that made her almost physically ill.

Until this past summer she never had suffered a running injury, and she'd been racing competitively for ten years. At age eight, when she started running, she placed second in the Morrissey Mile, a race for kids that coincided with the Morrissey 5K for adults on the weekend after Labor Day. For her finish, she received a trophy, cheap and garish, with a sprinting, faceless gold woman perched atop a molded plastic tower painted to look like marble. She loved the hardware, and wanted more.

Prior to that first race, Dana had thought of herself as woefully inadequate—a motherless, disfigured child among a sea of classmates all who had mothers and unmarred faces. Now, suddenly, she had an identity: she was a runner. Now she had a passion and skill that gave her substance. She could beat them all, or most of them.

During School's Out, the program for elementary-grade students requiring supervision after school because their parents worked, Dana ran every day on the decrepit cinder track circling the playing fields. In middle school she joined the track team and ran the 800 and one mile. In high school, she was one of two freshman girls who made the varsity track team. She sprinted the first leg of the 4x400 relay and also ran the mile. Thanks to genetics, she developed an ideal physique for a runner: long legs like her father combined with a shorter torso, and a thin frame. Small breasts, which did not sway or bounce when she ran.

She gave herself over to running, where she felt confident and unself-conscious, unlike most of the rest of the time, when she felt exactly the opposite. She found a group of friends in her teammates, and it was due to being on the track team that she managed to meet her first and only boyfriend.

Sean Connelly was a junior transfer student. He played football in the fall and participated in track in the spring. There was a pit next to the track where the shot-putters and discus-throwers practiced, flinging their heavy loads into the playing fields beyond the bleachers.

Dana heard Sean before she saw him. He let out a frightening roar with each release. She identified the source of that primordial yell while rounding the fourth curve on the track, the one closest to the pit before the homestretch. She was training at 400-meter intervals and looked over when she heard Sean bellow, and immediately slowed down because it didn't seem like a human sound. It was more like what she'd expect from an attacking lion or a charging elephant.

Her coach chastised her for her poor interval time.

"I was distracted by that yelling from the pit."

"Are you going to be distracted when the stands are full of cheering spectators?"

Full of spectators? So far, at every track meet Dana had competed in, the stands were largely empty, occupied by a smattering of parents.

"You can run three extra intervals, maybe that will help you focus."

She'd already run ten, and had reached her bonking point, but now put in three more—all poor times—and when practice ended, she slumped over on the first row of the bleachers, too tired to stretch or drag herself into the showers.

A few minutes later, the shot-putters and discus-throwers broke practice and made their way from their pit toward the locker room. The loud one passed in front of Dana. She was so tired and irritated that she spoke up.

"Thanks a lot for getting me in trouble."

"Me?" The loud shot-putter stopped and looked at her with his eyebrows arched—one eyebrow; he was a unibrow person, with a single dark centipede of hair growing over his eyes.

"You make a lot of noise when you're throwing. I couldn't concentrate."

The shot-putter turned a blazing red and cast his eyes at the ground. Dana immediately regretted what she'd said.

"I'm sorry, I can't help it," he admitted.

She tried to soften the blow. She added, "I mean, you must put a lot of effort into your throws. It must hurt."

He looked up at her again, but wasn't going to let her off so easily. "That must hurt too—your eye."

Okay, she deserved that. "If you must know, it doesn't," Dana said.

"I think you're in my chem class."

Her usual routine after practice was to go to Gull and see her father and eat an early dinner with him. She considered asking Sean to go with her, but decided it would be better if they went someplace else. She didn't need her father getting involved. When she called him and said she was going to Christy's Diner with a friend, he asked why she didn't bring her friend to Gull.

"I feel like something different," Dana explained.

"What friend? Courtney?" Courtney was one of her teammates.

"His name is Sean. He's on the track team. Shot put and discus."

"A date?"

"It's not a date, Daddy, it's just something to eat."

But it turned out to be a date. Sean opened doors for her, he held out her chair so she could sit, he even paid for the check against her protests. He told her about his plans to earn a football scholarship and to take premed at the same time, so if he didn't have a career in the NFL he could become an orthopedic surgeon and repair other football players who were injured.

She wasn't particularly attracted to him—he wore an open collar shirt and tufts of black chest hair stuck out like a wild plant, matching the thickness of his unibrow. He also continued to sweat, although practice had ended more than an hour ago and he'd showered. His forehead glistened and he swiped away several drips coursing down his face.

Still, she went out with him again, to the movies that weekend. And then again the following week to a soccer game. Maybe she was attracted to him after all. For a big person, Sean was a surprisingly gentle kisser. His lips were soft. Once he put a hand under her shirt and touched her breasts over the material of her bra; she did the same to him, feeling a thick mane of hair on his stomach and chest. She didn't mind about the hair—her touching of Sean became more like petting an animal, and when she moved her hand over his hair he made moaning noises that sounded like precursors to the explosive howls he emitted when throwing the shot put.

He tried running with her a few times, telling her he needed to cross train to keep his body fat down, but he was too slow and lacked the stamina to keep up with her. It would be like her trying to throw the shot put with him.

Then one day, just three weeks before the start of a summer that Dana thought she would spend with her boyfriend, Sean announced that his family was moving to California as soon as the school year ended. His father had been transferred to a new job in San Jose.

The news shocked her, and she performed poorly in her last two track meets. On the day Sean moved, Dana gave him a hand job without unbuckling his pants, just by reaching down and stretching his jeans with her fist and grabbing his dick and tugging. He stared into her eyes with a grateful and loving expression, unsure what he'd done to deserve such an honor. And the moment he came all over her fingers he let out one of his trademark yells, as if he were throwing something heavy as far as he could.

She thought that having Sean as a boyfriend for a few months marked the beginning of an expansive sexual awakening and a string of boyfriends. But it ended up being the extent of her sexual and relationship experience. A few other boys asked her out, but they looked at her body, not her face. Her face, her eyes, they avoided. At least she had more time to work on her distance running, and in the end it paid off with a scholarship to St. Lawrence.

Because she'd never been injured before, Dana thought she'd been granted some kind of immunity to the bone spurs and shin splints and ankle sprains and sciatica and other pains that many competitive runners endured. Wrong again. Just another reminder, girl, you are a flawed specimen.

If it didn't get better, if she couldn't compete this season, she could be off the team and lose her scholarship.

She went to the library after practice, worked through dinner, and headed back to the dorm after dark. Overall, it had been a mixed first week of college. The running injury depressed her but she was excited about being a writing mentor and she'd signed up as a volunteer editor for *Laurentian Magazine*. She'd made new friends, although she hadn't met any potential boyfriends. Why she expected college to be any different from high school, she didn't know, maybe because there would be more guys and some of them might be open-minded and discerning about their choices, but in reality most were shallow as puddles and the frenzy among her suitemates to hook up had the one-upmanship of an arms race. She found the word *whatever* running through her mind on a regular basis. Also, *whocares*.

She was busy enough that the disappointment didn't overwhelm her. Already she had a paper due next Monday for her Women in Short Story class. At the library she checked out the only two books she could find containing critical mention of Margaret Atwood's story "Death by Landscape." In addition to the paper, she had more than one hundred pages of textbook reading for poli sci and her first meeting with her team from psychology class to discuss research experiments.

Returning to the dorm, she broke into a jog to see if her knee felt better, but it always felt fine at the start of a run, and she slowed to a walk after a few strides.

When she got back to her room she went down the hall to where her roommate, Jen, was hanging out with Mark, her new boyfriend. A rerun of *Friends* was on the TV, although no one paid much attention. Steve, who also lived on their floor but already was avoiding his roommate, was sunk in the room's one chair with his laptop. Mark and Jen sat together in the middle of Mark's bed, holding hands. Mark roomed single, which meant Dana pretty much had a single now, too, since Jen had spent the last four nights with Mark. Dana couldn't believe the speed with which Jen and Mark had become a couple.

Jen and Mark slid over to make room for Dana.

"*Friends* again?"

"It's on every night."

"You at the library?"

"I'm writing a paper on this Margaret Atwood story."

Steve looked up at Dana while continuing to type on his laptop. "I've read Atwood," he said. "*The Handmaid's Tale.*"

"That's the one everyone's read. It's not her best."

"I liked it."

"I saw the movie. It was creepy."

"How's government policy?"

"Also creepy."

"Steve's already planning significant changes to the Constitution," Mark said.

"Those would be called amendments," said Steve.

"The first one would lower the drinking age and legalize recreational drug use."

Dana liked Steve. She shared a Monday-Wednesday-Friday class with him—intro to poli sci—and twice now they'd stopped for coffee together on their way, both half asleep, Steve with bed head, Dana in whatever sweatshirt she'd slept in. He treated her like a political ally. He told her that his girlfriend back home in Syracuse was coming to visit this weekend, much to his ambivalence.

Mark said, "I'm telling you, your fake ID business will come back to haunt you, Steve. Everything from your past gets dug up when you're in an election."

"When the journalists come knocking on my door for the dirt on you, I won't tell," Dana said.

"I won't, either," Jen said. "Unless it's Anderson Cooper. He's pretty hot."

"He's old. He's got gray hair."

"It's blond."

"Gray."

"Blond-gray."

"I don't care, he's red hot."

"Yes, I've got it!" Steve said to his laptop. "There's still tickets for Grace Potter this weekend in Potsdam. Who's in?"

Mark and Jen simultaneously said, "We are."

"What about you, Dana?"

"We've got our first meet on Saturday, I can't go."

"The concert's Friday night," Jen reminded her.

"A lot you know about athletics," Steve said. "You can't go out the night before a big game."

"It's not a game, it's a meet."

"And you can't have sex the night before."

"That's just a myth."

"It's not an issue anyway."

"We'll have you home in time."

"How's your knee?"

"It's pretty sore right now."

"Well, if you can't run this weekend, then you can go with us to the concert."

"No," Dana said, "I can't go. I have a race." She left it at that. She'd be at the starting line with her team in Plattsburgh on Saturday morning. Had to be.

Tell Us Where You Got It

They had been to Roger's firm once before, when they purchased the house in Tear Lake and sought Roger's expertise on the contract. Since that time Roger had become a managing partner and moved to a corner office on the sixth floor with one window offering a view of the river and the other facing the restaurants and bars lining Pearl Street.

Roger settled them around a table and asked if they wanted coffee. Neither did. Two framed photographs guarded either corner of his desk. One of Marlene on her wedding day twelve years ago, her face smooth and smile soft, lacking lines around her cheeks and eyes, her veil framing her face. The other photo showed a close-up of Marlene and Roger with their arms around Josh and Abby, the four of them squeezed together. It looked fairly recent by the ages of the kids. The flash from the camera reflected off Roger's forehead, which had gotten higher the last couple of years.

Gwen and Roger knew more about each other than clients and attorneys should—with all of the disclosure flowing through Marlene. Roger was married to a woman who treated intimate details about their personal life like giveaways at trade shows. Anyone coming by could have some. Marlene told Gwen about everything, from the big blowouts when Roger had gone so far as to get in his car intending to leave and igniting a crying scene in the driveway, to big blow jobs she gave him, some as rewards for favors such as taking her on a clothes shopping spree, others in return for going down on her, which he did only when asked. Only after she'd showered. Yet methodically and with an attention to detail that worked for Marlene.

You're telling me more than I need to know, Gwen would say. Which would not slow Marlene in the least.

Roger and Marlene each had endured failed first marriages in their early twenties. Marlene missed graduating from college by a single three-credit course, which she had taken an incomplete in and then over the summer had driven cross-country with her boyfriend instead of writing the required paper. Roger, despite finishing near the top of his class, had taken the bar exam three times before passing. Marlene wanted another baby; Roger did not.

In return, Gwen confided in Marlene, who, like any spouse, shared with Roger. Gwen and Brian rarely yelled at each other—their fights were like high school debate team competitions, polite and structured but seething under the surface. Sex was healthy, occasionally spectacular, but not as frequent since the kids were born. How can you simply go from twice a day to twice a week or even less, and hardly notice? She'd told Marlene about a boyfriend in college who committed suicide and afterward Gwen had an abortion because she was pregnant with his child. She would have had the abortion, anyway; the boyfriend, a beautiful guitarist who'd stopped taking his meds for bipolar disorder, killed himself before Gwen could tell him about the pregnancy. Later, she married Brian *because* she was pregnant—well, not only for that reason, but up until the positive pregnancy test they'd never talked about marriage.

The personal details that Gwen and Roger knew about each other could make a professional meeting both intimate and stilted, as if they were discussing everything except what was on everyone's mind.

Now they were discussing Gwen's legal situation, the three of them huddled around the table.

"First off, you did exactly the right thing by not telling Keller anything," Roger said. "He shouldn't have been badgering you at the PTA meeting."

"So she shouldn't divulge where she got the pot from?" Brian asked.

"What I'm saying is all communication goes through me. From now on you don't say hi to Detective Keller without asking me first. Because it's getting a little complicated. I spoke with Keller yesterday and what normally might be a simple DUI has turned into a crusade for the Morrissey PD."

"What do you mean?" Gwen asked.

Roger repeated most of what Keller had told Gwen: arrests and incidents involving drugs were trending up in town; break-ins, vandalisms, and even a recent bank robbery were linked to drug users seeking money and valuables to pay for their habit. Two high school students were expelled just this past May for having quantities of prescription painkillers in their locker. A maintenance man found a bong under the middle-school field bleachers. Police and parents feared that Morrissey was getting a reputation as the drug capital of upstate.

"We all read about the high-school incident," Brian said, "but what does it have to do with Gwen? Or the bong. She had a small bag of marijuana in the car. She's on the PTA board, for God's sake. She's a mother of two kids in the schools. She's never been in trouble in her life." He looked at her and took her hand.

"All true, and I laud you for defending your wife. But the police are applying pressure in all drug arrests in the town. That's why they spoke to the DA about Gwen's case—and other cases."

"What kind of charges are they talking about?" Gwen asked.

Roger stroked his chin. "I'll temper this by saying the charge will never hold. I mean, it's outrageous." He paused.

"Come on," Brian said.

"The DA mentioned vehicular manslaughter."

Gwen stiffened in her seat.

Roger quickly added, "It's an outlandish charge, and like I said it will never hold up."

"This is absurd," Brian said. "The other driver was at fault, we all know that. Even the investigative report confirmed it. He crossed the double line and hit Gwen. If he hadn't done that, we wouldn't be sitting here today. Nothing would have happened."

"That pretty much sums it up," Roger agreed, "although the investigative report is still classified as preliminary."

"Then how do you get vehicular manslaughter out of it?" Brian said.

"It's just the way it works sometimes. You tell them what they want to know and they drop the charges—probably all charges, even the DUI—and you walk away. You don't tell them and they bring up charges of vehicular manslaughter."

Gwen began making soft percussive sounds, tears filled her eyes. Whatever resolve she'd had finally eroded. She'd been waking up every night replaying the accident, the lightning sequence, the split-second confusion, her sudden reaction. How could she be sure she'd done enough? Still, the leap between uncertainty and vehicular manslaughter crossed a wide chasm. It wasn't right.

Brian reached across the table and stroked her face, thumbed away a stream of tears. Gwen looked up and composed herself.

"I'm sorry," Roger said. "Do you want to take a break? Can I get you some water?"

Gwen shook her head. "But what's the point if the charges can't hold?" she asked.

"The point is that when they charge you with vehicular man-slaughter it becomes a big story in Morrissey—especially given all the attention to the drug problems. Front page news in the *Morrissey Bee*. Remember how eager you were to keep your name out of the police blotter after the arrest? This time Richard won't suppress the story. Everyone finds out you were high, had a bag of pot in your possession, got into an accident in which someone died, and later, when the final investigative report comes out and the charges don't hold and are dropped—by then the damage is done. Sure, there will be some sympathy for you from your friends and the more compassionate citizens, but you'll be branded with the scarlet letter. You'll be a witch living in Salem. You'll be . . ."

Gwen cut him off. "I get the picture. So what do we do?"

No one spoke. Roger waited.

Brian broke the silence. He faced Gwen and said, "It's pretty obvious."

Gwen had been thinking about Jude while Roger was speaking, recognizing the inevitable current of the conversation.

Brian turned to Roger. "That's the right thing to do, isn't it? Give up the supplier."

"There aren't a lot of other options," Roger agreed. "I hate to say it, but it's the way the system works."

"But I didn't get it from a dealer," Gwen said. "He's just a friend who did me a favor." Ratting out Jude didn't make sense. It was an act of betrayal against someone who had helped her out. She had promised him not to tell anyone.

"Is he really a friend?" Brian said, his voice rising a note. "You haven't had any other contact with him in years. Have you?"

"But he was just doing me a favor."

Brian said, "That's what drug dealers do: they make themselves available to you, they get what you ask for, they act like your friend."

"I'm telling you, he's not a drug dealer."

"Of course he's a drug dealer. He sold you drugs, didn't he? He didn't give them to you, did he? You didn't barter, did you?"

She tensed under Brian's questioning. "Stop interrogating me," she shot back.

Then Brian leveled his voice, and said flatly. "Gwen, tell Roger who it is."

Gwen turned to Roger. "Part of what I got was for you and Marlene. What if this had happened to Marlene? Or even you, Roger? Would you tell the police that I was your drug dealer?"

Roger shifted in his seat. Brian stood and walked to the window, leaned against the tall pane of glass.

Roger said, "Gwen, you can't focus on hypothetical events that could have or should have or might have happened. Just think about what has happened—has happened to you. Think about the current situation that's in front of you right now."

"I am thinking about it! And I'm thinking maybe we need a different attorney, one who would have stood up to the DA against their extortion tactics. And for my rights."

Seeing the flash of hurt in his eyes, Gwen regretted what she'd said. But she felt trapped and continued to lash out. "I mean, this is ridiculous that I'm in this situation. I should be facing a misdemeanor charge at worst."

"I'm willing to step away and recommend someone else," Roger said. "I made that offer the first day and it still holds. In fact, maybe it's the best idea. But that won't change anything. You'll still be in the same position: give up the name of your dealer or face the charges."

"Gwen, I don't think you're saying you want a different lawyer," Brian added, still looking out the window.

"I'm sorry," Gwen said. "I shouldn't have said what I did. I'm just upset. I wasn't expecting this."

"Think about our goal," Brian said. "We want this problem to go away, and this is how you make that happen. I don't see any other course of action."

"That's a good way to look at it," Roger said. He hadn't made eye contact with Gwen since she'd insulted him. "It's how you make the problem go away."

Gwen raked her hands through her hair, loosening the clip holding her bangs to the side. She fixed the clip and sighed. She exchanged a glance with Brian, and he gave her a nod of encouragement. It would be easier if he would spit out Jude's name—he knew where she'd gotten the bag—and then she could blame him for breaking the trust. But he wasn't going to let her off the hook. She had to make the decision.

Jude Gates. What did he mean to Gwen, anyway? Maybe at one time, years ago when she worked for him at the Patriot, maybe then he'd meant something to her, when she'd almost fallen in love with him.

What allegiance did she have to him now? None, really. It was more an allegiance to her self-respect. There had to be an ethical rule about this, didn't there? You don't betray your source. You don't tattle. She'd learned that as a kid. Tattling is no way to solve your problems. Wasn't that what she told Nora and Nate? No one likes a tattletale.

"Gwen?" Brian said.

"You're not bound by the oath of omerta here," Roger added. "You aren't in the Mafia. The police simply want to know your supplier for an ounce of pot."

"Think of your family," said Brian.

Of course she thought of her family; she thought of Detective Keller's veiled comment to her about Child Protective Services helping out when a parent abuses a child or is sent to prison.

Everyone Gwen knew would hear about it if she faced charges

of vehicular manslaughter, even if she were cleared. Roger was right: their dull little town newspaper would love to chew on a story like this. It might even make the local television news on a slow day. The entire community would know she had gotten high and been in an accident. She'd be asked to leave the PTA. She'd no longer be a driver for Brownie field trips. The news would filter down to children from a gossipy parent or an older sibling. Her kids would get teased, shunned—or preyed upon by whoever was dealing drugs around the schools. My God, they're babies. How can this happen? Even Brian's colleagues would find out, damaging his reputation at work.

There wasn't a choice here. Quit kidding yourself.

Roger interrupted her thoughts; he entered them. "I'll tell you right now—whatever's going through your mind, it's all true. Not only will your family be hurt and your reputation damaged, this will drag on and the legal fees will be steep, no question about it, no matter who your attorney is."

Gwen got up and went to be with Brian near the window. She took his arm. She remembered how Jude had asked for her phone number in case he was the one in need of a favor next time. Here's your favor, Jude: I'm turning you in to the police.

You shouldn't have kissed me.

Roger swiveled his chair to face them.

"So what happens if I tell?" Gwen asked.

"I go back to the DA, who has made pretty clear that all charges pending against you would be dropped."

"I mean what happens to . . ." She wasn't sure what to call him. Not dealer. Not by name, not yet. "My source," she said, afraid Brian would jump all over the term "friend."

Roger shrugged his shoulders, as if that consequence hardly concerned Gwen. "I'm no investigator, but I suppose the police will put him under surveillance," Roger said. "They'll look for evidence of crime. If, as you say, he's just a friend who did you a favor by getting someone to do him a favor, then nothing much happens. Or maybe he can lead the police to a bigger source, and so on up the ladder or across the scaffolding or wherever the trail goes."

Gwen nodded several times. Brian relaxed his arm and took her hand in his.

"To me, he's just a friend," Gwen said. There's that word again: friend. "But what if he is some kind of drug dealer—I mean, I don't know him that well. I have no idea what kind of life he really has now. What will happen then?"

"Then maybe his time is up," Roger said.

"Because of me. What if he finds out? I could be in danger. He could come after me. That's what they do, isn't it? You open your mouth and they come after you."

She pictured the possibilities, the revenge, and grew agitated, her lip starting to quiver. Would they have to move out of town? She couldn't imagine Jude hunting her down.

"That won't happen," Brian said. "No one will know it was you."

"What if I have to testify at his trial?"

"If he is a drug dealer, the police will collect a lot more evidence before making any arrest," Roger explained. "A small transaction like yours won't be on the docket. Gwen, if there was any risk to you at all, I'd counsel you otherwise."

"Sweetie, don't worry," Brian said. "Roger's right."

Roger's desk phone rang, followed a few seconds later by his cell phone. Brian saw him glance at the clock on the wall.

"Okay," Gwen finally said.

"Good," said Roger.

Brian let out a breath and squeezed her hand.

Hold on. Gwen thought of something else. "You know, I went

to James Anderson's funeral. I met his daughter and she threatened to sue me—for wrongful death of her father."

"You didn't tell me that," Brian said, letting go of her hand and turning to face her.

"If the criminal charges are dropped, will I be protected from a civil lawsuit?"

"I told you it wasn't a good idea to go to the funeral."

"You won't," said Roger. "But when there's no evidence of legal culpability, proving responsibility in a civil suit is very challenging."

"It happened to OJ," Gwen pointed out.

"After a botched criminal trial that was a media spectacle," said Roger. "I wouldn't worry about a wrongful death suit in this situation."

"But it could happen."

Roger's mouth tightened. He spoke slowly. "It could happen, whether you tell the police or not where you got the bag. But it probably won't. It's a separate issue entirely."

They stopped talking and exchanged looks in the taut silence, like three Wild West gunfighters waiting to see who would draw first. What was she delaying for? There was no other way out. No other role to play except that of a rat.

Don't think of it that way—you're a protective mother and wife. Look at your priorities. Think of your family. You're backed into a corner and there's one and only one escape hatch, so what are you waiting for?

"He's a parent, too," Gwen said. "He has a daughter starting college."

Brian and Roger waited, saying nothing.

Gwen reached into her purse. Her hand came out holding Jude's business card from Gull. She handed it to Roger.

She Had to Get It Somewhere

They stopped at Pearl Alley Bistro for an early lunch. Gwen ignored the menu, and so Brian ordered a half bottle of wine even though he had to return to work, and a salad and plate of steak frites they would share.

Gwen didn't have much to say. She kept her eyes anywhere except on Brian, watching the restaurant fill with the lunch crowd. He didn't try for her attention or distract her with banter. Some lunch date. She was upset and who wouldn't be after you've been legally extorted, and he was embarrassed at her reluctance to reveal Gates. He'd known where she'd gotten the pot—you don't surface a bag of weed and not tell your husband where it's from. But the finger-pointing responsibility belonged to Gwen. They both knew it, and Brian had waited her out.

He had never liked Jude, not from the night he first met Gwen and watched her work around the bar with a tray of drinks. He had been studying her movements and noticed the tall guy walk up to the waitress station to get his glass refilled. He remembered Gwen's body language. She leaned in when he spoke to her. She looked into his eyes. She smiled at what he said. Brian didn't know this woman yet but he felt the threat of the other man, understanding he'd have to get past him to get to her.

He was at the Patriot that night because his parents had come to town for the weekend. They arrived fifteen minutes early for their dinner reservation and the hostess escorted them to the bar where she said they could enjoy a drink while waiting for their table to be set. His father groused about this strategy to get them spending more money; his mother complained about the rigid chairs and tiny bar table. Brian had already spotted the cocktail waitress and begun plotting to ask her out.

When the waitress arrived for their drink order, Brian's mother announced they were visiting their son who was attending medical school here; she had to get in that comment about her son becoming a doctor. Gwen took the news with a glance at Brian and a neutral smile, asking what they would like to drink. The bar was busy. Brian ordered for the three of them, his eyes on Gwen.

When their table was ready, his father refused to tip the cocktail waitress because the drinks were going on their dinner bill and he said he'd tip on the total then, after subtracting the tax. His parents had a discussion about it. His mother said it wouldn't be fair because the dining room waiter would get tipped for service that the cocktail waitress provided. His father said they shared the tips. His mother wasn't so sure. Brian got up during dinner to use the restroom and found Gwen in the bar, gave her a ten-dollar bill, and apologized for forgetting to tip. "I sat over at that table," he said, pointing. She said, "Sure, I remember, you're the doctor I'll call when I get sick." He took her comment as an invitation and asked her out right then, the hottest-looking woman in the building, the best he'd seen in a long time, considering he spent most of his time studying and working with med school geeks. Why shouldn't he start with the best-looking woman and work his way down the list until someone said yes or he admitted defeat? This was one of those lucky times when he started and ended at the top of the list. Within a week they were paired up. In a month she moved in. The speed with which their relationship launched meant he had to carefully vet the conditions that got them started—what led up to, what got left behind. Was she on the rebound? Was there something weird about her? How could there not be consequential events and important people in Gwen's life that he was interrupting? Those first few weeks, whenever he came to pick up Gwen at the restaurant, Brian kept an eye on Jude. Because Brian knew. Men knew when other men had an interest in a woman.

Six months into their love affair—that's what they called it, as if it were secret or illicit even though they had moved in together after the first month—Gwen was missing too many lectures and working more hours at the Patriot trying to save money for the following year. She wasn't as enthusiastic as she'd hoped to be about law school, she admitted to Brian. She thought she'd serve as a lawyer for a civil rights or women's organization someday, in contrast to most of her classmates, who were targeting the more practical and lucrative world of corporate or criminal defense law. Everyone seemed so mercenary. The reading was dull. Classmates competitive. Yet she had no other plans or prospects, and dropping out of law school to work full-time in a bar didn't seem like a good option, so she trudged on, relying on innate intelligence to get through her classes. They were in debt, with Brian in medical school struggling with his own ideals of working for a global relief organization in some third world country, providing health care to the poor and underprivileged.

Then she got pregnant. Her period had always been erratic—twenty-five days, thirty-two days, light then heavy—and Gwen wasn't conscious of being late, only of the nausea that morning, which she attributed to being out too late the previous night and getting up before sunrise to see Brian before he left for the hospital. After he'd gone, she took a shower and a long hit off a joint and she felt better, the queasiness faded. Then the realization came upon her like a snap of her fingers. Part of it was the nausea, part the long interval it seemed since her last period. But mostly all of her awareness zoomed toward a spot deep in her abdomen, a spot the size of a pinhead, a spot that thrilled and terrified her. She felt it. She knew. She went to the drugstore, not to answer a question but to provide evidence to support her conclusion, and when Brian got back to their apartment that night, after nine o'clock, after a long day of his internal medicine clerkship and an evening in the lab, as soon as he walked through the door she cried and fell into his arms. She'd had an abortion once before, in her second year of college, and it had been harder and sadder than she'd expected, and now she didn't know what to do, didn't know how she'd gotten pregnant. They'd been using birth control, most of the time.

Brian saved her. She wasn't afraid to admit it. This was one of those times in her life when she was drowning and needed to be saved and he was the perfect person to pull her out and he did. He wanted the baby. He didn't want to be a doctor after all: more years of residency, paying back loans, dealing with managed care. The idealistic vision of giving back to the community didn't seem so ideal. He wanted to do something now—like make money, like have a baby with Gwen. The concept of chivalry drove him. He knew of a good job opportunity with this drug company, Phero-genix. One thing about Brian, he reduced everything to its simplest terms and made a fast decision.

Brian smiled to himself, and though she'd been looking at a group of businesspeople at another table, Gwen caught his expression.

"What now?"

"I was just thinking of when I first met you. That was a special night for me."

"You were bold, I'll give you that."

"It's not bold when you go after what you want."

"Need I remind you—I'm a 'who' not a 'what.'"

"Don't spoil it."

"I'm sorry." She took his hand. He poured more wine.

"So what is it with you and Jude?"

Gwen lowered her voice. "There is no 'it.' He's someone from the past. And when I wanted to get some . . . he's the only person I could think of who might be able to help me out."

"And you felt fine looking him up after all these years."

"We ran into him that day of the Winterfest, so it wasn't completely out of nowhere," Gwen said. "I was okay with it."

"Because you wanted to get pot."

"And it would be good to see him. We were friends once."

"And you've bought something from him twice now?"

"Once in the winter and this time."

"You haven't seen him otherwise?"

"I had lunch with him the week I was downtown for jury duty," Gwen admitted.

Brian nodded. Another piece of information not volunteered. "So did you ever do him?"

Gwen fingered her eyebrow. Now that the stitches were out, the tight skin itched. "That's a charming way to put it."

"You don't have to answer."

"We had a brief relationship before I met you," Gwen said.

"Did it end before you started going out with me?"

"That's what ended it."

"I thought he was married then."

"Do you want all the gory details?"

"No." It was pretty much in line with what he suspected at the time. He and Gwen had never dissected each other's past relationships, agreeing early on that the body count or details weren't necessary or desired. He leaned closer to his wife. "You were pretty protective of him in Roger's office. It seemed like there might be something more going on."

"What—then or now?"

"You tell me."

"Stop it. Why are you doing this?" She felt a strange sensation of the remnants of Jude's kiss on her lips. She wiped her mouth with her fingers. Brian sensed something, but she couldn't tell him. That wouldn't benefit anyone.

"But you've thought of him," Brian said. "He's the one you went to see when you were looking for weed."

"I told you, he's the only one I could think of. Don't make a bigger deal out of this than it is."

The kiss from Jude had not been a big deal. Nothing with Jude had been a big deal, even nine years ago, when she worked at the Patriot. Or it didn't turn out to be one, whatever Gwen might have thought at first. Jude had taken an immediate interest in her, beyond the employer-employee relationship. But not romantic. Not sexual. Not at first. He protected her, like a big brother. He wouldn't let her hang around after work if she had a class the next day. He had hired her although he knew she lied about experience, he showed flexibility with shift scheduling, and intervened when a fling she had with one of the cooks ended ugly and the guy started harassing her—making comments whenever she walked into the kitchen, showing up one night at her apartment and knocking on the windows, even slamming himself against her door trying to get in. Gwen wasn't sure if Jude fired him or he quit, but she never saw or heard from that cook again. And while Jude seemed tuned in to her personal and academic life, she knew little about him. Allegedly he had a wife, although he never talked about her and Gwen had never met her; not once had Gwen seen the woman in the Patriot. He also had a daughter, who unlike her mother did spend a lot of time at the Patriot, eating dinner in the kitchen, playing with dolls in an empty booth, eventually falling asleep on a cot in the office if the babysitter didn't show up to take her home. She was a third or fourth grader then. Gwen helped her with homework a few times and taught her to sketch faces and fold paper into a cootie catcher that told fortunes.

One night Jude had to leave the restaurant in a hurry, pulling Gwen aside and telling her his wife had been taken to the emergency room, asking if Gwen could take Dana home after her shift. So he did have a wife.

He gave her the key to his house.

After work, Gwen lifted Dana from where she slept with a stuffed dog on a cot in the office and carried the sleeping girl and her pet down to her car. She drove to the address Jude gave her and parked in the driveway in front of a big wooden Victorian house with a turret and a porch. It was a historic house, completely restored, in one of the oldest neighborhoods.

When Gwen opened the door, Dana woke, asking where her father was.

"He had to go out for a little while," Gwen explained.

"Are you my babysitter?"

"Yes, tonight I am."

"Can I have ice cream?"

"It's kind of late for ice cream," Gwen said.

She escorted Dana up to her room. Sweet and sleepy, Dana leaned against Gwen as they climbed the stairs.

"Do you want me to help with your pajamas?" Gwen asked, but Dana had found her bed and was already drifting again. Gwen decided it was okay to let the girl sleep in her clothes, easier than trying to get her undressed and dressed again. She tucked Dana in, pulling the blankets to her chin, then cinching them down a few inches. It wasn't a cold night. She looked at the girl's cheek for a few minutes, then leaned down and kissed it.

She went back downstairs and after poking around all the rooms fell asleep on the living room couch. She opened her eyes when Jude came in the front door. Her face stuck to the leather couch as she sat up; then she stood, wobbly, unsure of her environment. Had she gone out and then home with someone after work? No.

In two long strides Jude stood in front of her. He placed a hand on each of her arms. He said, "Thank you so much. You really bailed me out."

"How's your wife?" Gwen asked. "What happened to her?"

"To be honest, she's in a rehab facility right now. She was having convulsions and had to be taken to the emergency room."

"I hope she's okay. I didn't know—I wouldn't have said anything."

"No, I'm glad you asked. You're one of the few people I don't mind telling," Jude said. "How was Dana?"

"An angel—now a sleeping angel."

She wanted to hear more about Claire, but Jude didn't go on, and she didn't ask. He said he was having a glass of wine and did she want one. He chose a bottle of red from a rack on the wall and poured two glasses. With a deep exhale he sunk in next to her on the couch and handed her a glass. He looked at her as if undecided about something. Then a movement, like a tremor, passed through his eyes. She thought he might kiss her and she prepared for it, panicking about her sticky mouth, her sleepy breath. She took a quick drink of wine and swished it around her mouth.

Nothing happened. Yet she was sure he wanted to. Kiss her. And he did, finally, after they'd shared a few lines of coke, smoked a joint, and drank most of the bottle of wine, which turned out to be the recipe for Gwen to forget a little girl sleeping upstairs and a convulsive, addicted wife in the hospital. She was pretty wasted but fully into it and had sex with Jude twice on his plush leather couch. They fell asleep together covered by an afghan and Gwen opened her eyes only when someone shook her shoulder.

It was Dana, who'd heard a noise and come downstairs to get her daddy. "Are you going to be my new mommy?" she asked Gwen.

She left the house as pink dawn began to filter through the windows, head pulsing and stomach queasy.

They slept together a few more times—at her apartment—and she half expected something complicated and electrifying to start up, or maybe it already had. That churning feeling in her stomach from the first night never entirely toned down, the edge remained. But they never talked about their relationship; they gave each other no status reports; they didn't take each other's temperature. Jude didn't bring up the subject and neither did she, but those late nights when he showed up at her apartment, she always let him in and didn't ask about his wife. And then around that time she met Brian, which eliminated any chance of getting more involved with Jude, because she fell in love with Brian right away. He fit a vision of her ideal man in a way that Jude never would. She didn't tell Brian about Jude. The recent all-nighter of getting wasted and having sex with her boss, then repeating, the sense of stepping along an edge—it wasn't a talking point in a new relationship.

The waiter brought their lunch and two extra plates. Brian told the waiter to leave just the one plate in the middle and they'd share.

"Now who are you going to call?"

"What do you mean?"

"To get your supply."

She shook her head no, she wasn't going to be pulled into that conversation.

"All I'm asking is that you tell me if you do—and who it's from," Brian said.

"If I ever do, I'll let you know."

"So why were you so hesitant to give Gates's name—considering the consequences to you and your family? You owe an old boyfriend such loyalty?"

"It's called integrity, Brian. I gave him my word I wouldn't say anything."

"Did you get high with him when you picked up the pot?"

"No, and you already asked me that question. And he wasn't my boyfriend."

"So, you just smoked by yourself in the park."

"Yes."

He looked at her. Close to tears, but beautiful still—after almost nine years together and two kids and even or maybe especially now when she was upset. So she had a history of past relationships, what halfway normal person didn't? She'd clipped her hair back this morning, the way he liked it, and put on more makeup than usual and even lipstick and the diamond earrings Brian had given her when Nate was born. With the stitches out, just a thin red line remained where her eyebrow was starting to grow back. She wore a chocolate skirt paired with one of his favorite blouses, pure white with simple pearl-like buttons, sheer enough that you could see the outline of her camisole when she leaned and the fabric formed to her. One extra button open at the top showing the tiny birthmark to the left of center. Earlier, he'd wanted to punish her for withholding Jude's name for so long.

Now he wanted to make love to her. He wished he could blow off his meeting and take her to a hotel for the afternoon.

He put down his fork and reached and held her free hand.

"I know this was hard for you, I don't mean to twist it into something it's not. You did the right thing."

"I don't know if he's a drug dealer or not," Gwen admitted. "Really, how can I know what he does? But if he isn't and is just doing me a favor, then I don't want to be the person that gets him harassed. And if he is some kind of drug dealer, I don't want him knowing I snitched on him."

"He won't know."

"And his daughter, Dana. What happens to her if Jude gets in trouble?"

"There's nothing we can do about it. They have their life and we have ours."

"She's only eighteen."

"What about his wife? What happened to her?"

"Ran off years ago from a rehab facility, I think it was just after I stopped working at the Patriot. Hasn't been seen or heard from since."

Brian looked at his watch; he had to get back for his one o'clock with Jennifer Stallworth.

"So for you it was an integrity issue?"

"Weren't you taught not to be a tattletale?"

Brian nodded. "Sometimes you have no choice—or your choices aren't good and you have to pick the one that does the least damage."

"While preserving your integrity."

"If you can. If you have your priorities straight, then integrity flows from that. You make decisions based on your priorities—on what's important to you." He might as well have been talking about his situation at work, trying to discover where priorities and integrity fit in. He wanted to discuss it with Gwen, but this wasn't the right time.

"You're saying I was wrong to buy pot from Jude—or from anyone?"

Brian shook his head. "If you want it, you have to get it somewhere, and there aren't a lot of options in our circle. And if you don't know anyone, how do you go about asking? Who do you approach without risking a stain on your reputation?"

"It's definitely not college dorm days where you could follow the smell down the hall and everyone knew the resident dealer."

The waiter returned to clear. The plate was empty except for a curl of gristle Brian had trimmed off one end of the steak. Gwen had managed to eat her share.

Did they want dessert or coffee?

Before Gwen could answer Brian said no, just the check, they had to leave.

"You need to get back?" Gwen asked.

"I've got a meeting in thirty minutes. But I'd rather spend the afternoon with you in bed."

"That's a nice offer—or it could be."

But he had only enough time to walk Gwen to her car and make out for a few minutes.

Miracle Drug

Brian was on the phone with Dr. Marta Everson, whom he knew from industry conferences and Caladon's physician seminars. A short, caved-in woman with tight coils of oily hair springing from her head, Dr. Everson looked like the absentminded professor, garbed in stained clothes and eyeglasses worn askew on her nose. She promoted herself aggressively, published widely, and lectured incessantly. She contributed a monthly health column for *Female* magazine and served as an expert source of quotes for journalists working on women's health stories. You could find her speaking at medical conferences and trade shows on her favorite topics. Caladon paid her to travel to resorts and present "Trends in Obesity Treatment," an educational seminar for physicians, where she subtly spread the word about Zuprone. Onstage or in front of a room, despite her physical deficiencies, she had the dynamic presence of a Hollywood starlet. Brian believed a lot of her success as a presenter had to do with her voice, which was rich and resonant as an oboe, sexual even, in complete opposition to her appearance.

"How many patients did you say were in your study?" Brian asked.

"I'm tracking twelve patients for whom I've prescribed Zuprone for weight loss, and three are showing significant symptoms of anorexia."

Well, there you go. That's weight loss, isn't it?

He shouldn't have had the extra glass of wine at lunch with Gwen.

"How long have they been taking Zuprone?"

"Between six and eighteen months." That husky voice, making *six* sound like *sex*. Although no one would be taking Zuprone for sex, since one of its documented side effects was reduced sex drive in those treated for anxiety. Which seemed to Brian a case of piling on the anxiety, not mitigating it.

"What dosage are you prescribing?"

"120 milligrams daily."

"That's twice the recommended dosage," Brian pointed out.

"For anxiety, yes. There are no recommended doses for weight loss—it's not FDA approved for that indication."

As if she were telling him news.

"The fact is, Brian, you have a serious issue with Zuprone and you must do something about it."

"It could be a dosing issue."

"Are you a licensed physician?" Everson asked, knowing the answer. "It's common knowledge among the medical community that 120 milligrams is the weight-loss dosage. It's what I've been mentioning in the seminars."

"That's right, the seminars," Brian said. "Caladon is paying you to present at seminars twice a month."

"Not anymore they're not. I can't continue in the face of this evidence."

It wouldn't be the worst thing if Marta bowed out of the seminars, or if the series were canceled altogether. During an earlier meeting with Jennifer and Stephen, they agreed the seminars were the riskiest of the marketing practices and needed to be toned down or turned off. Brian also had issued his final recommendation that they should begin the application process with the FDA to seek approval for Zuprone. He'd hate to reverse himself on that, even though no paperwork had been filed yet.

"Did you contact Stephen?"

"Of course I called Stephen. I left him a voice mail and he never called back. I guess your medical director doesn't seem to think there's an issue. Have you had other physicians reporting problems?"

"We haven't, no problems," Brian told her. "As a matter of fact, we have several internally published studies that show no serious side effects from using Zuprone for weight loss. And these trials are scientifically based, not just anecdotal evidence."

"Are you doubting what I'm personally witnessing in my patients?"

"No, no I'm not doubting it," Brian said. "I'm just letting you know we have other studies. As you're well aware, I cannot offer them to you unless you make a request."

"I don't want your studies; I know exactly what they're for. What I want is for you to issue warnings about the dangers of prescribing Zuprone for weight loss," Everson said. "I'm treating some very sick women here." Even in her aggressive, demanding words, the throaty undertones flourished.

"I understand you're upset, Marta, but I think you need to put this in a broader perspective. You're talking about a universe of twelve patients . . ."

"Three of whom have developed anorexic symptoms. That's twenty-five percent."

". . . and no control group to compare them against. And you're dosing at 120 milligrams while our studies used 100."

"I'm giving Caladon the benefit of the doubt here. I'm giving the company a chance to correct a major problem. It's not like

I'm bringing this up for selfish reasons—I won't have the income from the seminars any longer. And I called you because I thought Brian Raine of all people would appreciate the gravity of this situation."

"I do appreciate it. I'm just as concerned as you are."

"Drug companies must be more accountable for putting people at such great risk."

"Marta, I'm sorry, we're not the ones prescribing the medication for off-label uses. That's at the discretion of physicians."

Marta snorted. "Physicians have become dependent more on drug companies than their peers for information. You know that as well as I do. What do you think those seminars are about? Physicians believe what they hear in them."

"That sounds more like an indictment of your profession than mine."

"I regret signing a speaking contract with Caladon. It makes me feel like I'm hawking potions in traveling carnivals."

You're the one who's hungry for the stage, Brian thought.

As if on cue to Brian's thoughts, Marta added, "I could get a lot of media attention on this, you know."

"I would caution you against that at this point."

"Caution me? What's that supposed to mean?"

He had to deflect her. "You're a highly respected physician, Marta, and you have an excellent reputation among your colleagues and in the media—and with Caladon, who pays you generously for the seminars. Bringing up a study that is not really a study at all but just the isolated experience of a few patients . . . Well, that could harm everyone, including you and your reputation."

Marta paused for a few seconds, then found her voice again. "Would it harm the untold number of people out there taking Zuprone for weight loss? What about them? Are you cautioning them as well? Would it harm Caladon? How much has Caladon profited from this off-label use of Zuprone?"

How much have you? Brian wanted to shoot back. He was getting nowhere. He'd stuck to the company line as best he could, but one of the attorneys or Stephen should be handling this. He wished he hadn't picked up his phone without looking at caller ID. He thought it would be Gwen calling, thanking him for lunch earlier that day, whispering something in his ear, a promise for later.

"Marta, I'll have Stephen call you back as soon as possible. He should be the one to address this with you."

"You want to abdicate, is that what you're saying?"

"Stephen's our medical director. I'm not abdicating, I'm escalating." He had to control his voice better, but Everson was getting to him now. "Can you at least give him the opportunity to speak with you before you do anything else? Don't you think that's the right thing to do, especially considering your own association with Caladon and in particular Zuprone?"

Reluctantly, Dr. Everson agreed.

"I'll get in touch with him right away," Brian said. "I'm sure you'll hear back from him within a day."

After getting Marta Everson off the phone, Brian called Stephen Jeffries's office. He had moved to the New Jersey headquarters after the acquisition of Pherogenix; he also kept an office upstate and traveled often. He got Stephen's voice mail and was routed to his assistant. When Gina answered, Brian told her he had to speak with Stephen as soon as possible.

"He's in San Jose at Pacik Labs," Gina said. "Do you have his new mobile number?"

"Could you give it to me?"

He wrote down the number.

"It's noon on the West Coast, this might be a good time to catch him," Gina said. "He's probably on his lunch run."

Stephen ran every day at noon, wearing a headset to take and make calls.

He answered his phone panting.

"I'm running through downtown San Jose, the fucking sky is brown from smog. Imagine what I'm embedding in my lungs now."

"The benefits of running outweigh it," Brian said.

"Let's hope so. What's on your mind?"

Brian explained his call with Marta Everson. Her alleged study of patients on Zuprone—all twelve of them. The symptoms of anorexia. Her demand that Caladon do something about it.

"Jesus, Hurricane Marta," Stephen said. "She left me a voice mail, I didn't pay much attention."

"Sounds like it could be a problem."

"*It* isn't a problem—*she's* a fucking problem. I've never met anyone so desperate for publicity. We never should have hired her for the seminars. Whose decision was that, yours?"

Brian didn't answer, and Stephen continued. "What do you think we should do?" He cleared his throat, and Brian heard a series of short gasps.

"Have you heard of anyone else reporting these side effects?" Brian asked.

"A handful of incidents, yes, but there are many causes of anorexia and someone with a weight problem is already predisposed to weight-related illnesses, including anorexia and bulimia. I don't think it's an issue, Brian. And I don't think it's related to Zuprone. Do you know how many prescriptions were written for Zuprone for weight loss last year?"

"One-point-two million," Brian stated.

"That's right. And next year it will be, what—double that?

Didn't you just present some figures on that to Wilcox and Garcia?"

"Of the one-point-two million prescriptions, the majority were written in the past six months," Brian said. "It may be too early for the problems Everson reported to start showing up in any significance."

"Oh, shit, I think I was supposed to turn there. You think I should try to run across the freeway?"

"Everson said she might publish her findings."

Stephen laughed. "Twelve patients? No, I can run up this ramp and avoid it. I'd never get past all those cars. Did you tell her about our own studies? You and Teresa compiled a whole library, didn't you? That was good work, really helpful for the reps."

"She's seen the reps carrying them around at the seminars. She knows what they are and doesn't want them."

"We can get her back on our side," Stephen said. "I know everybody is supercautious and our industry has a target on its backside for anyone with ammunition these days, but we can handle this correctly and it will blow over."

"I told Marta you'd get in touch with her as soon as possible, within a day. I had to tell her something."

"That's okay, I'll take care of it. Consider it off your plate. Shit, Brian, it's hard to breathe out here."

Later, getting coffee in the cafeteria, Brian saw Teresa at the vending machine. She hadn't noticed him come in and he watched her put coins into the slot and bend to retrieve her diet soda. Here was a woman whose ass had steadily diminished over the past six months, requiring several wardrobe overhauls. Lots of new clothes on that body, each change more tailored, more fitted, than the last. Brian noticed. Everyone had. There had been an increasing volume of banter and cracks among the guys about Teresa behind her back. That was one of them: "I'd like to get her from behind her back."

While her body underwent rapid transformation, her demeanor held steady. Teresa had always been outgoing and chatty, friendly to everyone at the office—both women and men, no enemies. A personality that might have been a defense mechanism for an overweight woman became offense for a slimmer one. Now men interpreted her sweetness as flirting, her chitchatting as interest. Yet Brian doubted she was seeing anyone right now, and on those weekends when she went back to New Jersey she talked about visiting her parents and brother, nothing about a boyfriend.

"Hey you," Teresa said, turning around with her can of soda. "You look a little dazed."

"A lot going on."

"Tell me about it. Are we still meeting later to put together the Zuprone training for the new reps?"

"I have to postpone," Brian said.

He debated whether to tell her about his conversations with Marta Everson and Stephen Jeffries. He didn't want to be the information source regarding serious accusations and problems about Zuprone. The upheaval in the company would be felt like an earthquake; Caladon would find itself in crisis management mode because of something Brian brought to attention.

Hopefully, Jeffries could talk Everson down from her frenzy and the situation would settle quietly.

"Have you heard any of the rumors that Zuprone can cause anorexia in those using it for weight loss?" Brian asked.

"You mean on top of the nausea, abdominal pain, diminished sex drive, and paresthesia we already know about?"

Brian smiled.

Teresa popped the tab on her can of soda. "I haven't heard."

She looked at him in a way he had not seen before and smiled just enough to show a hint of teeth, as if they shared a secret. He shifted his weight to his heels.

"Do I look anorexic to you?"

"I thought you might be taking it."

"So you've noticed a change in me?"

"Of course."

"I've seen you looking. But I don't mind; in fact, that's the whole idea in a way. Well, not the whole idea—I have health reasons to consider—but you know what I mean."

Two women came into the room and Brian stepped aside so they could get at the coffee. He started walking out and Teresa kept up beside him. They went down the hall toward Brian's office.

"I've lost twenty-five pounds in six months. That's a pound a week," Teresa said. "And I run two miles every morning before work. I think Zuprone is a miracle drug."

"What happens when you stop taking it?"

"I'm not stopping. I'm not finished losing."

"What if you can't stop when you're finished?"

"Anorexia is about having a pathological problem dealing with body image, not about taking control of your life to lose weight."

"But the drug can change components of your physiology."

"I'm not worried about it."

"You don't have any side effects?"

"I didn't say that, but I'm not anorexic. I eat healthy, I'm losing at an aggressive but not unsafe rate."

"Can I ask what dosage you're taking?"

"One twenty."

Same as what Everson prescribed her patients. "That's what your physician prescribed?"

Teresa made a face, as if Brian had said something lame.

He decided to tell her about the call from Marta Everson and her patients on Zuprone who'd developed anorexia. After recounting the story, he registered her hesitation—Teresa didn't know what to say.

"You know who Dr. Everson is, don't you?"

"Who doesn't? But I thought she was hosting some of our seminars on the West Coast."

"She is—or was."

"You said we contracted with her to make sure she was on board. Isn't she like the worst possible person to be bringing this up?"

"I passed her off to Stephen Jeffries. He said he would deal with her."

"But what do you think? Is there validity to her claims?" Teresa asked.

"I don't know. I do think we should be running more clinical trials, whether we apply for FDA approval or not."

The other thing Brian knew was that Stephen was right when he said pharmaceutical companies were targets for anyone or any group that had a gripe—legitimate or not. And with Zuprone, Caladon was coming awfully close to stepping into the sights of the FDA, consumer watch groups, and now even physicians. The off-label prescribing of Zuprone for weight loss was not in itself a problem, since doctors were free to use their medical judgment to prescribe any FDA drug for any indication, but Brian believed Caladon's marketing practices for Zuprone—many of which he implemented under direction from Wilcox—to be right on the crumbly edge, although the company's squad of lawyers rubber-stamped most activities. Such as the unpublished internal studies that the reps could let physicians know existed in case anyone wanted to request a copy. Such as dividing physicians into deciles based on their prescription history and focusing rep visits on the top tiers that would deliver the greatest results. Or hosting consumer weight-loss blogs and websites underwritten by the company. Or bundling Zuprone with Caladon's more mainstream drugs into the take-it-or-leave-it formularies offered to health plans. And, most of all, the "independent" educational seminars hosted by doctors paid by Caladon.

All standard pharmaceutical loophole practices, just legitimate enough to keep whistle-blowers doubtful and regulators at bay.

But if Marta Everson makes a stink, then suddenly it all might start to smell.

Hopefully, Stephen could control her.

A Sweet Deal

Jude counted twenty-seven of twenty-nine tables occupied, plus every stool in the bar taken. They'd serve a hundred dinners tonight, maybe a hundred and twenty if the late crowd trickled in when the Rep Theater let out. Another solid Saturday, but even on weekdays they'd do fifty while in other restaurants the staff stared out windows and took turns sneaking away to get stoned.

Andrew deserved the credit for Gull's success. Jude's management of the dining room and service staff was akin to making the trains run on time; Andrew's skill was inventing a train and laying tracks in the first place.

On the wall behind the hostess desk hung a framed review from *Table* magazine with a picture of Andrew Cole. The headline read "Old Town, New Delight." The photographer wanted Jude in the shot, too, but Jude had declined, preferring not to have his picture taken. Besides, everyone knew that chefs were trendy, not managers. Let Andrew be the star. He created the most interesting and varied menu in town while keeping food costs under control. When he ordered ducks, every scrap of meat got used: breast of duck, duck and goat cheese ravioli, a few of the bones roasted for the stock. A house favorite was a duck confit salad with grilled radicchio, which Jude's companion was devouring now, along with a third Manhattan, straight up.

His name: Daryl Sweet. Known to all as Da Da Sweet, ever

since his NFL playing days, because of his reputation for taunting the competition across the line of scrimmage about their mothers, saying he fucked or was going to fuck their mama. He'd goaded plenty of offensive linemen into false starts and personal foul penalties over the years. A clever teammate came up with the nickname Da Da. As in "Da Da goin' to do yo' Ma Ma." Juvenile, locker-room stuff, but it stuck.

Sweet stood Jude's height at over six feet but weighed forty or so more pounds, mostly ropy muscle wrapping his neck, chest, arms, and legs. He still carried the intimidating body of a former NFL linebacker, first four seasons with the Giants, last three with the Bills, until injuries finished him. A torn Achilles tendon, which cost him an entire season, a dislocated elbow, a broken collarbone, spasms in the back. Two or three concussions. Plus the strains and cracks and contusions and bruises that don't make the injury report. Talented, high motor, mean streak, nose for the ball, but brittle—that was the scouting report and legacy on Daryl Sweet. Arthritis already creaked his body, and he moved slowly now.

But Da Da knew going in that short, brutal, and violent defined NFL careers. He'd been smart enough to stash away some of the millions he'd made instead of blowing it all on bling and cars and dope. He'd invested in a business and now his name graced a half-dozen health clubs around the New York City area and two upstate with more planned. Sweet Fitness catered to high school, college, and club team athletes, offering custom strength-and-conditioning training programs for any competitive sport. He had contracts with a few minor-league hockey and baseball teams and one indoor football team to be their official training facility. He was planning further expansion and considering franchising his brand.

Tonight, he was finalizing negotiations to become Jude's newest, and largest ever, client. He was looking for a safe, reliable source for performance enhancement—steroids, HGH, and speed, but also coke, GHB, X, and weed. There's the natural runner's high, and then there's the chemist's high. Even some athletes like the additional boost after a hard workout; some work out hard just to party hard.

Jude had been introduced to Sweet through a Yonkers city councilman who also served on the board of a chamber of commerce Da Da had recently joined after opening a club there. The councilman was an occasional customer of Jude's, purchasing a variety of prescription drugs for his extended family through Jude's online pharmacy. At first, Jude had been reluctant about Sweet; he held back, but Da Da made clear what he wanted and displayed good business instincts. Sweet knew the language of risk and margins, he understood channels, he knew enough math to negotiate. Jude had left their last meeting with an agreement, and tonight they would finish the details over dinner at Gull.

"How's your salad?"

"I could eat three of these. But I'm trying to shed a few. Can't be Fat Albert if I'm promoting fitness."

"Andrew's menu is very healthy," Jude said. "Everything is fresh, and he calculates calories in each dish."

Jude had ordered the Bibb lettuce salad with Hudson Valley blue cheese and glazed pecans. They shared a bottle of Russian River Valley pinot noir, which Sweet sipped between Manhattans.

"You kidding, right, about this being a . . . What did you call it? Proof of concept," Sweet said. "I don't like no jokes when it's business."

"We have to see how it goes. The first time I'll supply the product directly, and if everything goes smoothly and we're both satisfied we can set up an online mail-order pharmacy that will handle all the prescription products. The street gear will continue to be direct, with delivery to your preferred destination. But only if the first deal works as planned."

"You can't just give a taste and cut me off, it don't work that way."

Was Sweet questioning Jude's business model or making a vague threat? He said, "One deal at a time. It's the only way I work with new clients and larger transactions."

"So I'd be a big customer for you?"

He shouldn't have said that part about larger deals. "You'd be an important customer," Jude clarified. "You know, like any business, it's all about the customer."

Sweet laughed. "Tell that to those gangbangers and greaseballs in the city. They don't give a fat nigger's ass about treating a customer right."

"That's why you came to me, for the service you deserve."

Despite his anxiety over this new client, in many ways Jude sympathized with Sweet and his reluctance to work through the drug gangs. Jude had managed to stay under the radar of the usual murderous distribution channels, meticulously carving out a niche for his business. He built his client list over the years, never selling product to anyone he didn't research first, and staying away from street users. His only direct sales were higher end. His profitable clients included a United States congressman and his cronies, the CEO of a software company, an entire network of restaurants and clubs in the region (but not his own; no fishing off the company pier), and select individuals who purchased and resold. Establishing the business in this manner took longer and he sacrificed income, especially in the early years, but by being careful and avoiding the trap of greed, his brains still occupied his head and not some shallow woodsy grave or the inside of his car windshield. He owned an unregistered Jericho 941 semicompact

9 millimeter, an Israeli model you rarely see, which he seldom carried and had never fired. He backed down in disagreements over money or product and subsequently removed that client or supplier from his list. After he had met Gil at a National Restaurant Association show six years ago, sourcing through Canada proved to be an astute business decision, and although border security had tightened over the past few years, he now scheduled border crossings for specific dates and times when his pal Leonard Deitch manned booth number four.

His Montreal connection didn't offer the volumes or rates that larger organized drug operations needed, and Gil took a hard line regarding cash up front on this deal for Sweet that required such an array of product, but it was a perfect fit for Jude's niche and kept him from having to deal with the gangbangers and greaseballs in New York City that Sweet referred to.

Yet here a dude sat across from him, black as squid ink, about to buy a larger volume and more variety than Jude had ever dealt, which required a level of risk he'd never before shouldered.

And therein lay the dilemma. Jude was looking to reduce his risk—in fact, retire from the business altogether, but first he needed to be more financially secure. Although his daughter had a partial scholarship to St. Lawrence, Jude still needed to write checks for tens of thousands of dollars over the next four years. Plus he needed to stash away more funds for his own retirement, pad Dana's trust fund, pay off the Florida place, and finance a second restaurant he and Andrew wanted to open.

Working this deal a few times with Sweet would get it done, but the risk/reward ratio intensified. He couldn't afford to get careless; he couldn't sell so much as an ounce of pot to the wrong person. As careful as you are about whom you do business with, at some point you simply have to accept the risk, knowing that luck played its own indifferent role. And no one's luck held out forever.

Jude returned his focus to the table. He reached for the bottle of pinot and filled Sweet's glass.

"When you retired from football, did you ever think about just staying retired?"

"What do you mean retired? I was thirty years old. I had a whole life ahead of me."

"Well, I'm sure you made enough money to last, if you wanted to live a modest life."

"Da Da don't live a modest life. Da Da makes a splash everywhere he goes. You know what I'm saying? I'm keeping my foot on the pedal until I'm dead. No retirement. What about you?"

"My daughter started college this year."

Sweet flashed a smile. He may not have blinged his teeth, but his mouth had more white caps than the Jersey shore. "College ain't cheap. Besides, I never heard of nobody retiring from this business, except in the usual way."

Sweet was right. The usual way would be getting killed or sent to prison. That's why Jude needed a smooth transition, a soft landing. If he got out, his clients would have to find a new supplier, and his own suppliers would need new distributors. There could be some angry, desperate people left with or without inventory, which could lead to a dangerous situation for him. He'd do his best to divest and make everyone comfortable; if Sweet ended up a trusted partner, Jude would introduce him to his pharmacist and his Montreal connections, although the French Canadians threw the word *nigger* around like it was still back-of-the-bus days.

"You have the down payment with you?" Jude asked.

"I don't like the cash-up-front part. I never done it that way."

"I don't have the liquidity to float it, not at these quantities," Jude said.

"You better not fuck me over."

"I can't do anything about the terms—at least for this first time. If you want a smaller order, I can do that, but price per goes up, of course. Or you can work COD with your city connections."

Sweet frowned, as if he'd just thought of a new problem.

"I got it. Down in the car with my man."

"I'll send someone out to pick it up," Jude said. "Does your guy need something to eat?"

"He's fine."

"I can send something out."

Sweet shook his head. "So Friday night, right?"

"That's when I get it. By the time I get back it will be Saturday."

"Get back from where?"

Jude smiled at Sweet's question, but his heart rushed a few beats. As if Jude would tell him. "I'll deliver to you on Saturday afternoon."

"You be with my money for too long a time. If you get it Friday night, I want it first thing Saturday morning."

Sweet had to posture and get tough about every little detail that didn't fit his vision. A few hours here or there. Everything a hassle. Is this someone he wanted to get into a business relationship with?

Think of the objective, Jude reminded himself. You're doing this for Dana, making sure she has a good safety net. You're doing this to retire sooner.

"I can't do any earlier than the afternoon. I have to make a few stops to get everything together. What about by three?"

"You not there by three, I'll think you've run off with my money. I don't like any . . . what do you call them? Chinks in the plan."

"I'm a businessman, Daryl, just like you. Where am I going to run, and more importantly, why would I run? Why would I sit on all this inventory when I have you waiting to buy it?"

"Just so long as we know. And it's Da Da, not Daryl. I ain't been called Daryl since I came out of Florida State."

"Fine. Da Da, then. We can set up the pharmacy anytime. Your customers can order online, even pay with credit cards."

"After I distribute the samples and get some demand."

Their waiter brought coffee and set down cream and a bowl of sugar.

"Can I offer you dessert?"

"Don't tempt me."

"This is Simon," Jude said, introducing the waiter to Sweet. "This is Da Da Sweet."

"I know who you are. Pleased to meet you," said Simon.

"We're going to pass on dessert," Jude said to Simon, "but I want you to go outside and pick up a package from Mr. Sweet's driver. He's waiting in his car."

"Black Navigator," Sweet said, reaching for his phone. "I'll tell him you're coming."

"Navigator," Simon repeated.

"Use the rear door," Jude said. "And Simon, on your way out, could you send Vicki over here?"

Simon nodded and left.

"You seen the IFL at all?" Sweet asked.

Jude shook his head. Now that they'd come to an agreement, he'd had enough of Sweet and wanted to excuse himself.

"International Fight League. This shit's the hottest sport going. You haven't seen it?"

"No."

"I'm sponsoring some fighters. Maybe I'll get a team someday. It's about one step up from dog fighting—except it's legal, no one talks about cruelty because it's humans and not animals. Taking over from boxing. When you come down, we'll go into the city for a match."

"Sounds great. I'd love to see it." He'd find a way to get out of it.

Vicki, the hostess tonight, came to their table. They had stopped seating people, and Vicki's only tasks now were finalizing the count and tidying up around the hostess stand. About this time she usually planted herself on a stool and started drinking, surveying the bar for anyone of interest.

Jude introduced her to Da Da. Vicki wore a strapless black dress that showed her smooth tan shoulders and squeezed her small breasts into a respectable cleavage, between them a rose tat inked like a target into her skin.

"Please sit, and say hello to Da Da Sweet," Jude said to her. He turned to Sweet. "If you'll excuse me."

Sweet stood when Jude did and shook his hand. "Soon, bro."

Please, not *bro,* don't call me that. At least the handshake was normal.

Walking back toward the kitchen, Jude ran into Andrew, who stood with his arms folded across a clean chef's jacket he'd put on to walk the dining room.

"Look at her," Andrew said. "Sitting down like that."

"Who? Vicki? The dining room's closed. I asked her to come over."

Andrew shook his head. "I've been thinking we should let her go. She's a half hour late for every shift."

"Is that the only problem?"

"Isn't that enough? The dining room opens and we don't have a hostess to seat people."

"Move her start time up a half hour and she'll be on time. So it costs a few extra bucks a week."

Andrew considered this.

"She's good at VIP entertainment," Jude added.

Vicki had cozied up to Sweet. He slid his drink to her and she tried it and licked her lips. Sweet's teeth blazed, his eyes roaming Vicki's dress.

"New customer?" Andrew asked.

"Mr. Big."

Andrew made a clicking sound with his teeth. He knew about Jude's other business, although he didn't participate except to take his points.

Simon approached, carrying four dinner plates in his arm. "I put it in the safe," he said.

"Okay, thanks."

Simon motioned to table eighteen across the dining room. "Guy over there wants to speak with you."

"Me?" said Andrew.

"Jude. He said he needed to see the manager."

Simon delivered his plates to another table. Jude walked toward eighteen, a couple out for dinner, looked like a special occasion, dressed in their nice clothes. Sports coat and tie for him, sleeveless dress and gold necklace for her. Usually if Jude was called to a table of unknowns it was to field a complaint—prices, a weak drink, an overdone steak.

"Hi, how are you," Jude said. He introduced himself, offered his hand, the guy first. "I'm Jude Gates."

"This is our first time here. We just wanted to tell you how great our dinner was." The guy shook, but no name back. The wife shook, too, hands dry as hay.

"I loved my halibut," the woman said. "It was so tender." She was prettier up close, tired but sexy, as if she'd been through it but could go another lap around. They both had that look.

"Andrew—the chef—he's really outstanding," Jude said. "I was just telling someone else that he creates both a healthy and tasty menu."

"Our waiter was very nice, too."

"And my drink," the guy said, draining his glass and clinking the cubes. "It's nice to find a place that puts a real shot in."

"I'll have your waiter bring another—on me," Jude said.

"Honey, maybe you'd better not," his wife said.

The husband narrowed his eyes at her, then shrugged.

"I'm glad you're having a good time." He tried to get a bead on these two—what did they want? Something.

"I saw you talking with that fella over there—he looks familiar, like a celebrity or someone," the man said. "I can't quite place him."

He meant Sweet.

Jude said, "He gets that a lot. I don't know if it's because he's big or has nice teeth."

"I think we've seen him in a movie," said the woman. "Is he an actor?"

"You're right, I think he's an actor," the man said.

"What movie? Was it *Rocky*?"

"Sweetheart, that was thirty years ago. That guy would have been a little baby. Now who is he?"

"I really can't tell you," Jude said. "I have to respect his privacy, of course."

"Oh no, we won't bother him, we just wanted to know."

"I didn't mean *Rocky. Pulp Fiction.*"

"No, that was—who was that in *Pulp Fiction*?"

"I know, Samuel L. Jackson."

"That's not Samuel L. Jackson, is it? I don't think so."

Jude cut in. "It was nice to meet you," he said. "Enjoy the rest of the evening."

Rocky. He went upstairs to his office and opened the safe and took out the package from Sweet that Simon had retrieved, an oversized and overstuffed manila envelope taped at the seams. He ripped away one corner and counted the wrappers of one-hundred-dollar bills. They were all there, many of the bills old and wrinkled, as if collected from many sources. That's the way he liked it. Between this cash and his own he'd have enough for Gil. This deal was a green light.

Stakeout

Patty loved when Bill took her to dinner; she'd gone out earlier that day and bought a new dress for the occasion, maroon and sleeveless, showing off the arms she'd toned teaching a sculpting class at the gym on Saturday mornings. And a place like Gull—she oohed and ahhed over it. Usually they went to Chili's or Olive Garden.

Bill ordered a scotch and soda. Patty got a martini and right away turned frisky. She slid over to his side of the booth and sat close, put her hand in his lap.

The move gave her a better view, too. Gates was having dinner at a nearby table with a big black guy. Keller pointed Jude out to his wife.

"He's cute," Patty said.

"You ever seen him before, around town?"

She shook her head no. Keller had already filled her in about the woman he'd arrested after an accident, and how they'd found a bag of marijuana in her car. With all the recent drug incidents going on in Morrissey, Keller had gotten the DA to threaten tougher charges even though the accident and other driver's death had not been her fault. That way, he could press the woman hard for her supplier, and the strategy had worked. He now knew it was that handsome guy sitting right over there.

"Her kids go to Morrissey East, she's got a first grader," Keller said.

"Not in Andy's class?"

"No."

"The parents, for God's sake. No wonder children are getting in trouble."

Not that Patty was shocked. She knew what went on. Pedophiles strolling near elementary schools. Drug dealers selling to middle-school students. Three years ago, a teenager bludgeoned his father to death, the first murder in Morrissey in five years. That involved drugs, too—the kid high on something, trying to get at his old man's cash.

"She says it was just a friend doing her a favor, and she may be right," Keller said. "But until you follow the breadcrumbs you don't know."

When Gwen Raine's attorney called with the name, Keller kept the info close. He planned to check it before getting the state boys involved, in case there was nothing to it. Why get caught up in turf wars with other departments if you don't have to? But Keller had another reason for doing the first leg: his personal interest in anyone who might be dealing in his town. He considered it his responsibility to clean up Morrissey, using whatever tactics were necessary. He had run everything he could on Jude Gates, which these days was a lot more than it used to be. Married, age forty-four, one daughter, Dana, age eighteen, freshman at St. Lawrence University. Residence in Loudonville, adjacent to Morrissey, upscale but not obscene. Partner with Andrew Cole in an LLC named Upstate Dining Company. Co-owner of Gull for the past six years, before that managed a restaurant called the Patriot. Drove a 2009 Lexus GS300, license plate 468-DEL. Clean driving record. U.S. passport, used eight times in the past twelve months at two different border crossings into Canada, could be of interest. No priors, no convictions. A regular guy, except he worked in the restaurant industry, a known conduit for drug trafficking. Mexican dishwashers, African porters, they worked sixty hours a week in the kitchens and lived ten to a tiny house and moved product for their cartel uncle or cousin back home. Keller had never known of a restaurant that didn't have some level of drug trade. The bartender, one of the waiters, a cook—somebody was on point, supplying the rest of the place. Usually not the owner. It would be counterproductive to have your employees stoned on the job.

Their waiter was a young kid with good manners. He talked up the halibut and Patty ordered it. New York strip steak for Keller, leave off the shiitake mushrooms. You couldn't just get a salad. You had to get a baby Bibb salad or a spinach and pancetta salad or field greens and roasted peppers salad. They decided to share the Bibb lettuce salad.

Another drink for my wife, and I'll take another scotch. Officially, he wasn't working tonight.

There wasn't much to see. Gates got up a couple times and went into the kitchen. Once he went up front to the bar for a few minutes. He stopped at a table here and there and said a few words. The staff was busy and focused. Looked like any other restaurant, Jude like any other owner.

But who was that big guy Gates sat down with? He looked familiar, or maybe just out of place.

Their dinners came, and Keller had to admit it was the best steak he'd eaten in a long time. Perfectly cooked with a pink center.

"How's your fish?" he asked his wife.

"Melts in my mouth," Patty said. "You should take me on stakeouts more often."

"I wouldn't call this a stakeout."

"What do you think? He doesn't look suspicious to me."

"Let's have a chat with him," Keller said. When the waiter came back, Keller asked if he could speak with the manager.

When Gates came over, it was like having a conversation with the customer service rep at a bank. Gates smiled, pleased to have them at Gull, asked about their dinners. Keller tried but couldn't get the name of the black guy. And then Patty made that comment about *Rocky*. It was brilliant, but Gates didn't fall for it.

When their check came, Keller asked the waiter about the other guest.

"That's Da Da Sweet, used to play in the NFL."

"I thought I recognized him."

"Linebacker for the Giants."

"Is he a friend of your boss?"

The waiter shrugged. "I haven't seen him here before. But I heard he's opening a new health club in town. The River Rats are going to train there."

"Maybe you could teach a class there," Keller said to his wife.

When they left, a few people were standing at the corner of the building, smoking. With no smoking allowed inside anymore, patrons had to step outside with their cigarettes. Across the street was parked a monster black Lincoln Navigator with dark tinted windows. Hard to know if anyone sat inside. Ten to one it belonged to Sweet. Keller repeated the plate number to himself three times. Then he led Patty down the alley to the back of the restaurant. There were spaces for a few cars, one of them Gates's Lexus. Also an Explorer, an Audi, and a commercial Ford van. He jotted down the makes and plates, added the info on the

Navigator to his notebook. He lifted the lid to the Dumpster and peered inside.

The back door opened and a worker with a white apron stepped outside. He stared at Keller and his wife and lit a cigarette.

Keller motioned with his fingers to his lips that he wanted a smoke. The apron shrugged and fished out his pack.

Keller lowered his voice. "We're looking for something else to smoke."

The apron looked at him, then at Patty.

He'd be pegged as a cop if Patty wasn't with him. She was perfect cover.

"Like what?"

"Like whatever we can get," Keller said. "It's our anniversary and we want to celebrate," he added.

The apron guy raised his cigarette and shook his head.

"Try the Tight Spot on Dove."

"Yeah, I know it."

Keller had seen enough. Not anything of substance, but enough to come back and take a second look sometime.

"Let's go," he said to Patty.

"You want me to drive?"

"What for?"

"You've had a lot to drink. You seem a little wobbly."

"Christ, woman, get in the car."

We Used to Get High

Marlene and Abby stopped by with the produce share from their community farm. A lot of corn still, along with broccoli, beets, a few twisted carrots. Gwen would make a beet salad for herself and Brian for dinner; Nora and Nate would eat corn and carrots with their pasta. Marlene also brought a tub of chili for Gwen to deliver to the Harrisons. Two days ago, Celeste Harrison fell down her basement stairs and broke her leg in two places. She had three children at Morrissey East and an ex-husband who lived in Philadelphia. Celeste's sister from Albany was staying with her, and Gwen arranged to have the five Helping Hands volunteers take turns making dinner for the Harrison family until Celeste recovered. She had created a schedule and e-mailed it to her volunteers. Gwen had made lasagna last night; Marlene's turn was today. Gwen would deliver the dinner later.

She put the produce box and tub of chili in the kitchen, then made coffee and sat with Marlene on the patio in the lounge chairs under the pergola. Shafts of sunlight filtered through the vines Brian had planted when they moved in, which after seven years had wiggled up and over the support posts and onto the overhead slats to provide shade cover in the summer.

"It's such a gorgeous day, I can't believe summer is over," Gwen said.

"Are you kidding? I'm so glad school starts tomorrow. Since swimming ended all Abby says is how bored she is."

"We've had a great summer—except for the accident thing. I love that Nora and Nate still want to do things with me, and that's not going to last forever. Brian's brother has two teenagers who want nothing to do with him."

"By the time they're teenagers, parents don't want much to do with their kids, either. I think humans are wired that way."

Gwen believed it but couldn't imagine it. She and Nora and Nate had done so much together this summer: swimming, hikes, farm visits, bike rides, tie-dyeing T-shirts, planting flowers. They stuck together like a team. The moody teen years still seemed far away, although Gwen knew they would arrive in an eyeblink.

Abby joined Nora and Nate for a popcorn snack in the tower of the swing set. Gwen could hear them playing Cave Times, a made-up game consisting of grunting instead of speaking, and eating without using hands.

"Look at them, they're like animals," Marlene said.

"I actually don't mind playing that game when they ask," Gwen admitted.

Marlene smiled. "We used to get high for this."

Sometimes they took turns sneaking to the garden shed or basement to light the pipe. Afterward, engaging the kids on their level was fun and easy, playing make-believe games with silly rules or baking cookies or having water fights. Cave Times had been Gwen's invention, at least the sign language and grunting part. The kids added eating out of bowls without hands or silverware.

"That won't be happening anytime soon," Gwen said.

Marlene sipped her coffee. "It was so unfair what you've been put through. Although Roger said it's just how the system works, you having to give up the name of your friend."

Gwen wondered if Roger had told Marlene the name of her friend. Hopefully, he had respected client/attorney confidentiality, but husband/wife intimacy might have trumped it.

"I can't imagine having to hand *your* name over to the police if someone asked me where I got a bag of pot," Marlene said. "It would be terrible, I couldn't do it."

"That's funny, because I asked Roger what he would tell the police if he'd been the one arrested."

Marlene didn't respond. Gwen had said something wrong. Marlene was taking some measurement of friendship and loyalty and didn't like the results. Gwen added, "He told me I can't deal with hypothetical situations when the real problem is staring me in the face. Which I suppose is true."

"You didn't have a choice," Marlene said. "You did the right thing."

"They basically backed me into a corner. Neither option felt right—giving up the name or dealing with the charges."

"At least now it will all go away," Marlene said.

Gwen nodded. "Yes, that's why I did it."

Gwen went inside and brought out the coffee and refilled both their cups.

"I wish I knew where to get something now," Marlene said. She flipped her hand, as if chasing a fly. "But I guess I shouldn't be doing anything if I'm trying to get pregnant. Not that it's going to happen. We have sex only if I initiate it. I'm ovulating fine, but Roger refuses to have any testing done. He says our two children are proof enough he's firing live ammo."

"What is it with guys and the weapon metaphors?"

Marlene laughed. "Did I tell you I once saw Richard Makowski take a hit off a joint at Heather's party?" Marlene said. "Maybe I could ask him."

"The editor of the *Bee*? I went to see him to keep my name out of the police blotter. I wouldn't have taken him for someone who gets high."

"I can't ask anybody I don't know well."

"And I'm never asking anybody again," Gwen said.

"You said you couldn't go back to your friend?"

"Are you kidding? After what I just did?"

"I mean before this happened. You said you couldn't go back to him again."

"It got a little complicated," Gwen said. "I used to go out with him, years ago, just before I met Brian. When I went to see him, he . . . I think it's unresolved for him."

Marlene leaned forward in her chair, interested. "What about you?"

"Me?" Gwen paused. "I feel awful for giving his name."

The Shot

After another painful day on the track, Dana sat on the training table with an ice pack on her knee. Her coach and the trainer stood next to her.

"The next course of treatment would be a cortisone shot, if we want to go that route," Sarah said. "The only other thing to do is stay off it, for at least a month."

"The season will be practically over," Dana said. "And I'll be completely out of shape by then."

"Injuries are part of any sport, and the hardest part to deal with."

"I want to race this weekend."

"It's the cortisone then," Sarah said. "What do you think, Coach?"

"We could use her in Plattsburgh." He turned to Dana. "And I think you've got great potential for Rookie of the Year."

"Frank's in the building today. We could get it done this afternoon. If it works, there's a chance you can run this weekend. If you don't get it, there's no chance."

Dr. Frank Collard was the consulting orthopedist for the Saints athletic teams. He administered the shots, set the bones, performed the surgeries—the kind of doctor that her former boyfriend Sean Connelly had wanted to become, if he didn't make it as a football player. Dana had seen Dr. Collard around the athletic facilities but had never spoken to him.

"Is there any reason not to get it?" Dana asked.

"It doesn't always work," Sarah said. "And it is a steroid, so you have to take it seriously. The most common side effect is called steroid flare. The cortisone crystallizes and it hurts for a few days, but that doesn't happen often."

"Am I allowed to have it?"

"You mean is it within the rules? Sure. But the effect of a cortisone shot is inconclusive. It definitely masks the pain, whether it helps or hinders the healing process is not as clear."

She didn't hesitate: "I have to run this weekend. I really want to."

She waited around the training room for an hour to see Dr. Collard. When he arrived, he explained that the iliotibial band was a strip of tendon that wrapped around the outside of the knee and connected to the tibia. When it gets inflamed, it rubs against the bone and causes pain. The cortisone would help reduce inflammation and hopefully she could be back on the track in a few days.

He injected the cortisone directly into Dana's joint, and she snapped her jaw shut from the burn.

"That's it," he told her. "Take tomorrow and Thursday off, then test it on Friday."

She returned to the locker room and showered, staying under the spray for a long time and muting all sounds except the water falling over her face.

When she was dressed and heading to the library for an evening of study, her phone rang.

"Hi, Daddy, what's up?"

"Just checking. How are you?"

"I might not be able to race this weekend because of my knee. I've got ITBS in my tendon."

"I thought that was irritable bowel syndrome."

"That's not funny. I said ITBS. It stands for 'iliotibial band syndrome.'"

"I'm sorry; that hurts just hearing the name. It's the same thing that bothered you over the summer?"

"I got a cortisone shot today, so I might be okay in a couple of days."

"Does that help with the pain?"

"It's supposed to."

"Let me know how you feel, because I want to come to your meet."

There was a pause, then Dana said what she'd been rehearsing to say the next time she spoke to her father. "I'm sorry I said what I did about you being able to bring your women home now. I was just mad because you keep asking me the same stuff about drugs and sex."

"I know, I can't help it, I'm your father."

"I can take care of myself." Although she couldn't take care of one small tendon on her knee; if she had no control over that, could she really take care of the rest of herself?

"I miss you, Dana. It's good to hear your voice."

"I miss you too."

"Call and let me know about the track meet. I hope the cortisone shot works."

First-Grade Breakfast

It was one of those mornings if you breathed near Nora a firestorm ignited. She couldn't find the pants she wanted to wear and threw a full body fit. The zipper stuck on her backpack. She could see much better today than yesterday and didn't need glasses. Really. I promise. I don't need to go to the optometrist appointment.

"Wear your yellow pants," Gwen suggested.

"They have a stain."

"Did you put them in the laundry?"

"I want to wear a skort."

"Then wear it. Just get dressed. We have to leave soon or we'll be late for the breakfast. And stop flapping around like the world is ending."

"I don't want to go. It's a bunch of first graders."

"You have to go because no one is here to get you on the bus."

"Daddy can."

"Daddy's coming with us—just like he came to your school breakfast when you were in first grade."

Nate worried about being late. Mom—it's 7:47. It's 7:48.

Everyone bagged their own breakfast. The school provided coffee for parents, juice for kids, and doughnut holes to share, which Gwen had to pick up at Dunkin' Donuts now that she had been named room parent in Mrs. Viander's first-grade class.

Gwen sliced bagels and spread cream cheese, packed bananas and grapes.

"Mom, it's 7:52!"

"Nora, are you ready?"

"Mommy, Nora's crying!"

"Let me finish up here and bring the kids," Brian said, taking the knife from her. "You go ahead and set up at school."

She couldn't grab the keys fast enough and bolt. She had gone to bed tense, woke up the same way—and the feeling had spread like a virus to her kids. Instead of making love last night as Gwen had hoped, she and Brian had argued. He'd been coming home late every night from work, a noncommittal expression on his face, as if walking into a hotel of strangers and not his home of waiting loved ones. When she asked what was wrong, he explained in a slow, patient voice that a lot was going on at work.

Did he want to talk about it?

Not really, he'd been talking about it all day.

This wasn't like Brian. Although he didn't get into work details with her, she was his most trusted counsel when a problem came up. Two years ago they'd spent weeks discussing whether he should accept the transfer offer to business development. Now he didn't want her opinion.

"I know there's a lot of pressure on you," Gwen said. "And I appreciate what you do for our family. But you seem so stressed. You're working all hours and coming home late and—"

He interrupted her. "That's why it's called work, Gwen."

"Don't talk down to me."

"I'm just telling you it's part of the package. If you want to live in Morrissey and own a house on a lake in the Adirondacks, and have the luxury of staying home with your friend Mary Jane—"

"I was waiting for that one. You should leave your job if it's making you this mean," Gwen said.

"I'm sorry, that was out of line."

Still, she fumed. There would be no love again tonight, and at this point she didn't care.

"Mary Jane," she repeated. "No one calls it that."

She picked up two box carafes of coffee—regular and decaf—and three boxes of Munchkins, then hurried to school.

In the cafeteria, Mrs. Viander helped her set up the coffee and put out the cream, sugar, and napkins. Gwen opened the doughnut boxes, resisted the sparkling glazed ones. First graders from two classes and their parents trickled in. Gwen saw Amy Hellman sitting with her daughter. Amy had sold Gwen and Brian their house in Morrissey six years ago. When she saw Gwen approach, she got up from her chair and smiled. She wore a fitted gray suit with a red blouse and stood poised and confident like an executive on the rise.

Gwen asked how real estate was going.

"In a few select cities it's booming, in most of the country it's flat or down, and here in Morrissey it continues a steady but slow growth trend," Amy said. "We're a desirable community. Are you planning on selling, or buying?"

"Actually, I was thinking of getting my real estate license. Going back to work."

"That's a great idea, Gwen! You'd be perfect. I remember when we were looking at houses together—you noticed all the things that are important to buyers. And of course with your personality. Everyone trusts you."

"I don't know if I'm much of a salesperson."

Amy brushed off the comment with a *bah* sound. "I'll let you in on a secret. Houses sell themselves. All you have to do is speak for them."

"The buyers?"

"No, the houses. You speak for the houses because they can't speak for themselves."

Gwen tried to decode this. "Don't I have to take a course to get my license?"

"A forty-five-hour course. You could do it five consecutive Saturdays or get it all done in one week. You can even take some of it online. You need a broker to sponsor you, though. I could do that."

"Wow, that would be great." Gwen could see herself showing prospective buyers houses around Morrissey. She wouldn't be aggressive; she'd try to match buyers to the right house. She'd speak for the house, like Amy mentioned. Let its personality channel through her. She'd get to see the inside of a lot of houses, maybe pick up decorating ideas.

"There's going to be a lot of opportunity with the Vista Tech Park opening next year—more people moving up from downstate, people moving from adjacent towns. You should call me at the office."

"I will. Thanks," said Gwen.

She'd never felt compelled to pursue a career once the children were born, had not let the lack of professional achievement interfere with personal fulfillment. She was satisfied being a mom, helping in the school, spending the time with her children. Unsusceptible to the "having it all" syndrome that preyed on many women she knew. Yet maybe it was time to get a part-time job to take the pressure off her husband. She had graduated from college and finished most of a year of law school, although that was a long time ago. What skills did she have? What contribution to family finances could she make compared with the income Brian wheelbarreled home? A little. A gesture. Selling real estate in her spare time could help. She should do it.

The lift in her spirits from this idea lasted the time it took to turn and see Detective Keller with his wife and their son. Gwen knew that running into him was a possibility, had hoped it wouldn't happen, yet also had prepared for it. But rather than lurk and stare and avoid from the other side of the cafeteria, Gwen walked up to them.

She had never met Mrs. Keller, a thin woman with bags under her eyes and heavy lids on top. Attractive, but tired, like she'd been working too hard. The boy a miniature of his father: square head and a stocky frame, needed a better haircut.

Keller introduced his wife, Patty, and son, Andy.

"This is Gwen Raine. She has a son in first grade."

Patty threw Gwen a smile as fake as play money, revealing a small chip in one of her front top teeth. She knew all about Gwen. Of course the detective shared the gossip with his wife—investigations, arrests, and whatever else—unlike some husbands who had gotten tight lipped about their work. It made Gwen realize there was no preventing the news about her arrest spreading around Morrissey; there was only controlling the ferocity of the burn, possibly.

"I don't think our boys are in the same class, are they?" Patty asked.

"My son, Nate, has Mrs. Viander."

"Where's your family?" Keller asked.

"They should be here any minute," Gwen said. They were late, typical of Brian, who never hurried the kids along; herding was Gwen's job. She turned to the boy, Andy. "Who do you have as your teacher?"

The kid buried his face in his mother's hip. Had they clued him in, too?

Keller squatted and pulled Andy away from his mother's hip. "Mrs. Raine asked you a question. Look at her and answer."

The boy reluctantly raised his eyes to Gwen. "What?"

"I just wanted to ask who your teacher is," Gwen repeated.

The boy mumbled the name "Miss Amico."

Gwen wasn't going to torture the kid by asking anything else. She looked at the detective and was about to ask for a moment alone when Nate appeared at her side. Nora followed, wearing capris and not the skort she had wanted.

"Sorry we're late," Brian said, bringing up the rear and handing the bag containing their breakfast to Gwen.

"Mom, can I get a doughnut?" Nora asked.

"If you eat your bagel and fruit."

Nora took her bagel from Brian and joined a friend at a nearby table.

Brian held out his hand to the detective. "Brian Raine. We met once before."

Keller shook his hand and introduced his family.

Nate had gotten Andy's attention by showing him his two wristwatches, one of them a SpongeBob and the other a spy watch that toggled through seven different time zones and had a motion sensor that set off a beeping alarm.

"Cool," Andy said. "Can I try it on?"

Patty Keller was not pleased. Her eyes narrowed and the bags stiffened into angry creases. She looked ready to intervene when another mom called her name and she turned away.

Parents and their first graders sat in groups at the cafeteria tables. Nate stood nearby, letting Andy try on his spy watch. Gwen and Brian found themselves alone with the detective. Gwen immediately asked why they hadn't heard about the charges against her being dropped.

Keller said, "That's a question for the DA. I don't know when or if the charges will stick or go away."

"What do you mean, *if*?" Brian said.

"I'm just telling you it's out of my hands. I don't accuse, I investigate."

Gwen said, "I made a deal. Why isn't the district attorney keeping his side of it?"

"I don't make deals, either. You'll have to speak to your lawyer," Keller said. "He's the deal maker."

She had spoken to Roger, twice in the last week, and he told her the DA's office hadn't gotten back to him yet, although he'd put in three calls.

"The outcome might depend on whether or not the name you provided is useful to our investigation."

"Has it been so far?" Brian asked.

Keller shrugged. "I wish I could tell you more, but I can't comment about an ongoing investigation. Although if you have anything else to add that might be of use . . ." He reached into his pocket for cards. "You can call me. I don't know if I gave you a card before." He took out a pen and wrote a number on the back of two cards, then handed one each to Brian and Gwen. "Cell phone, if you need a direct line to me."

"What else can I add?" Gwen said. "Your extortion techniques already extracted everything I know."

"Easy, Mrs. Raine," the detective said. "Let's not say anything you'll wish you could take back."

"I'm beginning to think I already did that," said Gwen.

Brian gave her the *shut up* look.

Patty returned to their circle, ending the conversation. Nate came up and asked if Andy could come over after school for a play date.

No one answered him.

"Pleeeease," said Nate. "Please."

"We have to take Nora to the optometrist after school," Gwen said, sharper than she wanted to, still fuming about the so-called deal she'd made.

"Drat!" said Nate. "I don't want to go to the optimist. Can I go to Andy's instead?"

"Optometrist, not optimist," Gwen said, although a trip to an optimist might serve them better.

Patty Keller kept silent. She wasn't having a drug addict's kid in her house—wasn't giving Nate's suggestion the dignity of a response.

"I have to go," said Brian, kissing Gwen quickly on the cheek.

She looked at him for help but he was bailing. He leaned so only Gwen could hear and said, "Let me talk to Roger. I'll call him from work and get this straightened out."

Gwen went to her weights class and the grocery store, and back at home she looked up New York State real estate licensing on the Internet and weighed the idea of visiting Gull and telling Jude what had happened. How she'd been in an accident, coerced by the police to reveal her source in exchange for dropped charges, and then betrayed by them, just as she'd betrayed Jude. She owed him this much, didn't she?

She rejected the plan. Whether he was a real dealer or not, he'd be angry with her. And if the police were watching him closely, staking him out or something, they'd probably see her, which would escalate her legal problems.

It would be better to call Amy and pursue the real estate licensing.

In the end she did neither. She made sauce for that evening's pasta dinner, dropped off the dry cleaning, went to the bank, and at three o'clock picked up Nora and Nate from school and drove to the optometrist appointment. Nora read the third line on the chart, missed several on the fourth, and burst into tears on the fifth, knowing her fate. Gwen soothed her by promising they'd pick out a cool pair of frames and the three of them tried on almost every pair in the store—forty-four of them, by Nate's count.

"You look so beautiful in those, Nora," Gwen said.

"I do?" She still had tears. Gwen wiped them with her hand.

"My beautiful kids," she said, "both of you." She gathered them into the fold of her arms.

Brian came home late again that night, long after the kids were asleep, although Gwen was up and anxious for Brian to tell her about the conversation he had with Roger today.

But that wasn't the story Brian started to tell.

"I was interviewed by a *Times* reporter today," Brian told her. "I should have passed her on to the PR department but I got talking to her. That was probably a mistake."

"About what?" She wanted to ask about Roger, but held off. If Brian was ready to tell her what was happening at work, she was ready to listen. At least he was opening up to her about what was going on.

He backed up and told her about another call he'd received recently, from Dr. Marta Everson, a publicity hound Brian knew from conferences and whom he had arranged a consulting agreement with to host educational seminars. Everson had been prescribing Zuprone for a dozen patients for weight loss and claimed three were exhibiting symptoms of anorexia. She had called Brian demanding that Caladon do something about it.

"After she called, I spoke to Stephen and he promised to deal with her," Brian said. "Evidently he didn't because she went to the *Times* where she has some chummy relationship with the health beat reporter."

The reporter's name was Tina Soriello. She asked Brian if Caladon promoted the anxiety drug Zuprone for weight loss.

He started by telling her that all media inquiries went through the media relations department and he could transfer her.

But it was after business hours. Ms. Soriello would be dumped in voice mail. Could she ask a few questions? Her deadline was less than an hour away.

So does Caladon promote Zuprone as a weight-loss drug? she asked again.

No, that would entail illegal marketing practices.

Was he aware of any research studies of Zuprone used for weight loss?

He told her that like any other pharmaceutical company, Caladon conducted or sponsored studies for all of its drugs and for almost all uses they were prescribed for, whether FDA approved or not.

What about studies of Zuprone for weight loss?

We have them, but they would only be available to prescribing physicians who ask for them, since Zuprone is an anxiety drug not approved for weight loss.

Brian wasn't entirely sure where the reporter was heading, because the line of questioning seemed rudimentary.

But then she asked if he was aware of a study conducted by Dr. Marta Everson who found that 25 percent of the patients she prescribed Zuprone to for weight loss were experiencing symptoms of anorexia.

So that was it. Brian said he was familiar with Dr. Everson's situation. He explained to the reporter that Dr. Everson was prescribing Zuprone for only twelve patients—all of whom were prescribed higher than recommended dosages and her "study" had no control group, did not account for other medications or health conditions. It was not a study at all. Even Dr. Everson didn't call it a study. You could call it an observation.

So you're disputing her claims.

No. I didn't say that.

Did you warn Dr. Everson that she shouldn't publicize her findings?

No, we discussed the implications of publishing health-care outcome observations that did not follow scientific protocol.

She said you threatened her.

That's absurd.

At this point, Brian realized he'd said too much. Too late. The reporter thanked him and hung up.

"What happens now?" Gwen asked.

"I wait for the *Times* to get delivered in the morning and see what's in it. Hopefully nothing. Reporters write a ton of stories that never make it into the paper—maybe she doesn't have enough of an angle for this one. If she does, then I'll have to deal with the fallout."

"But what about Zuprone? Are there serious problems with it?"

"There are problems with any drug if it's not used appropriately. And when it's off-label, you have to rely on anecdotal evidence, peer reviews, recommendations, and even the manufacturer for guidelines. It's surprisingly chaotic."

"You once said you thought Teresa was taking Zuprone. Has she lost weight?"

"Twenty-five pounds."

"You know the exact number?"

"She told me."

Gwen had met Teresa only once, at the company holiday party just after she and Brian started working together. Gwen remembered the pretty face and beautiful skin as well as the extra weight. Big boobs and butt, several chins, a dress that highlighted her flabby arms and rounded shoulders.

"How does she look?" Gwen asked.

"Better than she did."

"Does she look good?"

Brian hesitated. "She needs to lose a few more."

"But she looks better?"

"She's lost a bunch of weight."

"Did she keep her boobs?"

"What do you mean?"

"You said she lost a bunch of weight and I'm wondering if her boobs shrank."

"I'll have to ask her."

"Does she know you're a married man?"

"You have nothing to be concerned about."

She shouldn't be pursuing this. It was just her own guilt over that kiss from Jude. She let it go and changed the subject. "So what did Roger say?"

Brian stiffened like the kid who'd forgotten to do his homework assignment.

Gwen said, "That's okay, it sounds like you had a tough day." Cutting her husband slack.

"No, no excuse," Brian said. "What time is it? I'll call him now."

"It can wait until morning."

"I'm sorry, Gwen. I got so wrapped up at work. I'm probably assuming they'll drop the charges when they get around to it and this will just go away."

"Detective Keller acted like he didn't know about any deal. I never should have said anything."

"Keller knew about it. It was probably his idea. Roger wouldn't have presented the deal if he hadn't been in discussions with the DA and the police."

"People get stopped every day with a bag of pot and they pay their fine and that's it."

"I guess that guy Anderson dying really complicates it," Brian said. He moved closer and held her.

"Now I have to see that detective at every school function. His wife thinks I'm some dangerous addict—a threat to her son. The way she looked at me. I think she's been spreading the word."

"People will stand by you," Brian reassured her.

She fought the urge to cry. "You could have at least called Roger."

"It's not too late." But the machine picked up at the Fitzgerald household. Brian left a message asking Roger to call him at work the next morning.

The Task at Hand

Past midnight and sleep seemed like an appointment hours away, with nothing for Gwen to do while waiting. She envied Brian's quiet, regular breathing, his body stretched the length of the bed. He never missed out on his sleep, even when tense or worried. He said he couldn't afford to, as if that statement alone allowed him to overcome insomnia. Not Gwen. Tonight would stretch on, no relief until she followed through on the thing eating at her. There was no point wrestling the sheets for two more hours.

She got out of bed and checked on the kids. Both asleep, curled in their blankets. They slept completely, solidly, through the night. Never woke from nightmares. Little Brians in their sleep habits.

She went back to her room and dressed by moonlight. She used the downstairs bathroom to brush her teeth, rinse her face.

Her car was parked in the garage so she took Brian's to avoid the motorized chug of the garage door opener. She drove downtown.

Gull was quiet on a late Tuesday night, the dining room nearly empty, a few patrons staked out at the bar. The cocktail waitress, now off-duty, drink in hand, sat chatting with the bartender. Gwen recognized her, one of the women filling out applications the day she picked up the bag from Jude. The others in the bar— two men with beers, a couple at one of the tables—glanced in her

direction and went back to their conversations. She hadn't registered. No one recognized her. No one looked like law enforce-
ment. That was one of the reasons she hesitated coming here:
What if the police were watching Jude and saw her come in? They
would think she was desperate to have come here to buy more, or
foolish for the reason she'd actually come. She'd end up in more
trouble than she already was.

She sat and ordered a glass of cabernet. "Is Jude here tonight?"
she asked the bartender.

"He's around. You want me to find him?"

"That's okay." She put her money on the bar. She looked
around again. There was the table by the window where she'd had
lunch with Jude in the winter.

"What time do you close?"

"When everyone leaves or two o'clock, whichever comes first."

Every minute was an exercise in working up her nerve. She'd
gotten this far. She left the house while her family slept. She
drove and parked the car. She walked into Gull. She ordered a
glass of wine and quickly finished half of it. She had considered
calling Marlene to come with her, the one person she could
phone at midnight, and construct the ruse of two women out for
a drink to catch up, which would make it easier for Gwen to
explain to anyone who wanted to know why she was out. Anyone except Marlene, that is. For her, Gwen would have to lay
out the story. She'd have to reveal Jude's identity, admit her purpose for visiting him. Marlene would object. Anyone would
object.

She took another sip of her wine. A better idea than this was to
get your priorities in order, return to your life, and let others deal
with the consequences of their own choices.

She swiveled on her stool intending to get up and leave, but there he was. He'd come up behind her while she was talking herself into making an exit.

He said, "I thought you said you were in bed every night by eleven."

He smiled, like he knew something she didn't. Then it vanished. "What happened to your eye?"

There was a pink line above her eyebrow from the healed gash and the first prickly sprouts of her eyebrow growing back in. The bruise lingered greenish yellow. During the day she hid the jaundice with makeup, but it didn't seem right tonight, putting anything on her face that might make her look better, the way she had last time, as if she were trying to make an impression or get noticed or be kissed. That was not the task at hand.

"That's okay, you don't have to tell me."

"No, I'm fine, I was in a car accident, that's all."

"Sorry to hear that." He slid onto the stool next to her. "I hope everyone is okay."

She'd been given the perfect opening: Jude asking about her eye, her responding about the car accident. Now tell him the rest of the story. Get it over with and get out of here.

She busied herself sipping wine.

He leaned closer to her and lowered his voice. There was his cologne. "Don't tell me you've run out already?"

"No, no of course not." Although she had run out—the police had confiscated her bag.

He waited her out.

"I couldn't sleep and wanted to get out for a drink."

"You don't have to be so nervous about it."

"You don't believe me?"

"If you clench the stem of that glass any harder it might break. I'd have to charge you for it."

Gwen looked at her hand, white from her grip. She moved her hand away.

Jude motioned the bartender, who started to pour Gwen another glass of wine.

"I have to drive," Gwen said. "I shouldn't drink another."

Jude waved the bartender away. "I'm not trying to get you in any trouble." He asked how her trip up north had been.

"We had to postpone it," Gwen said. "Things got hectic with our schedules, but maybe this weekend we'll go."

"Does your husband know you're here?"

She didn't respond.

He placed a hand on her knee. She held her breath, aware of her mistake now: a kiss like that is never just a kiss. It's always, always something more, and Gwen knew it the instant he had kissed her, but she wouldn't admit it.

She moved her leg and his hand slipped off, as if he didn't care one way or the other, or maybe hadn't even noticed that his hand had been touching her in the first place.

"That's not why I'm here," she said.

He shrugged, but his eyes locked to hers. "No, you told me. You couldn't sleep."

She tried again, but instead she said, "You must think I lead a pretty dull life."

"Actually, I'd say your life has a little excitement to it if you're slipping out at night to see me. Because I think that's what you're doing."

"I did come to see you, but not for the reason you think."

"Well, you didn't come to ask me to get you another bag."

"Is that what most people come to you for?"

He frowned, as if he didn't understand her question. "Most people come here for a drink or to eat. And there are plenty of other places for that closer to your home. So I'm presuming you have a different reason for coming here tonight." He was smiling at her again, thinking this was a game of sorts.

"Excuse me, Jude?" A waiter in a white waist apron stood next to them. "The deuce at fourteen is insisting on seeing you. I opened a bottle of Cristal and they said it's sour."

Jude shook his head. Gwen let out her breath.

"Tell them I'll be over," he said to the waiter. He turned to Gwen.

"Maybe I will take that glass of wine," she said.

"Excellent idea. I'll be right back."

The bartender returned and filled her glass. Jude excused himself and went into the dining room and beyond a row of booths and half wall. As soon as he was out of Gwen's view, she got up and made for the door.

When Jude returned, he asked the bartender what happened to the woman sitting there.

The bartender shrugged. "I didn't see her leave." She'd left the change from her twenty. "Maybe she's in the restroom."

She wasn't.

Jude couldn't get an accurate reading on her, which troubled him. What had she come here for if not to start something? Why else would she have been so anxious? It puzzled him how Gwen's comment about her "boring" life excited him, drove him to want her even more.

He looked up her number on his phone and called. After five rings, the phone was answered by a groggy male voice. *Hullo?*

He disconnected. There was nothing he could do now, except keep the date he'd already arranged for tonight, the one he'd been ready to abandon for Gwen when he saw her at the bar.

He went upstairs to his office and got the manila envelope he'd prepared earlier. He told Simon to close up tonight and left Gull and drove across the bridge over Oneska Creek, slowing as he entered Morrissey's residential neighborhoods. A cop often waited just over the bridge to catch people coming back from the bars, and, sure enough, Jude passed the cruiser lurking behind the roadside landscaping in front of the dentist's office, lights off, radar gun pointing out the open window.

He turned at the signal on Delaware, then at Brighton, and finally on Van Buren, a long dead end that circled back toward Oneska Creek. Leni's house was the last one on the right, an old farmhouse with several newer gables, a pool and hot tub in the backyard and a fireplace in the master bedroom. He was surprised to see other cars parked out front and in the driveway. Lights flooded the back of the house and music played.

He turned off his engine and sat in the dark for a few minutes, listening to voices and laughter and splashing. Then he called the house. An unfamiliar voice answered, "Party Palace, can I help you?"

He asked for Leni. When she got on the line, he said he was out in front.

"Come in, come in, you're late, I've been dying for you to get here."

"I can't," Jude said. You can't be the guest that arrives ten minutes before the hostess puts out an assortment of drugs on a serving tray.

"Baby, did you bring me what I asked for?"

"I expected you'd be alone."

"It's just a few friends. It came about all of a sudden. Rick and Leslie called . . ."

"Come out and get it if you want it."

"Don't be mad, Judy." She hesitated. "I'll be right out."

A few moments later she appeared from around the side of the house, her sandals snapping with each step. She wore an open cover-up over her bathing suit. She opened the door and got in beside him. He reached across and shut the door. She was wet and smelled of chlorine and alcohol. All smiles and smooches but he knew she'd tumble soon if that blow didn't get up her nose.

"You're pretty hammered," he said.

"You used to find that attractive."

"You used to handle it better."

He handed her the sealed envelope. She didn't open it.

"I'm sorry," she said. "You probably think I'm a complete twit."

This was the type of woman he'd been hanging with. A fading beauty, a homecoming queen, but you'd have to perform an archaeological dig to uncover that now. Today she was an alcoholic, drug hungry, divorced. Lost custody of the two kids who now lived with the former husband and his new wife. Dana had been right: he didn't bring the women he dated around to the house, but not only because she might grow attached to them. Maybe when Dana was younger, yes, attachment might be the issue, but now that she was older she'd be repulsed by some of these women. Imagine telling Dana this was her new mother. Leni was starting to remind Jude of Claire, always jonesing, falling under the spell, too weak to maintain a semblance of control. Maybe that's why he'd been thinking more and more of Gwen, had felt a deep thrill when he saw her in the bar tonight. She was the type of woman, or perhaps *the* woman, he should have been with all along. He wasn't paying close enough attention years ago, and now it was probably too late. But maybe not. Things happen for a reason. She hadn't worked up the nerve yet to take the next step, but by visiting him tonight she showed she was on the path, and it meant more to him than he would have guessed.

Leni shivered in the cool night air. She leaned closer and placed her damp face against his chest, an arm around his waist.

"Let me make it up to you," she said. She began to pull at his belt buckle; he put a hand over hers to make her stop.

"I'll make you forget all your little worries." She tried again, getting his clothes wet.

"Stop it."

"Then why did you come over?"

"You said you were going to be alone."

"We're alone right now, aren't we?"

"Sit up," he told her.

She did. She opened the envelope and took out one of the grams of coke. She unfolded the paper and licked the tip of her pinkie, stuck it in the powder, rubbed her gums. She folded the envelope again.

"Come on, Judy, come in and have some fun."

"Go back to your party."

He reached across and opened her door, wouldn't look at her as she got out.

Noted Physician Raises Alarm

Brian had been in his office less than thirty seconds when Jennifer Stallworth walked in, slapped the *Times* on his desk as if she were swatting a fly, and demanded to know how the heck this happened. An already bad morning was about to turn worse.

"Heck" was Jennifer's choice of words, her way of swearing. A native of Georgia, Jennifer's singsong drawl came off sounding sweet and naive, whether she was chatting about her weekend of waterskiing or preparing to fire your ass for incompetence.

Brian didn't need to look at the newspaper to know what this was about—he'd seen it online first thing this morning—but he picked it up anyway. Jennifer had folded the paper open to page three of the business section. Why in business and not health? Probably because recent drug industry legal woes posed a more significant risk for investors than for the health-care consumers who actually took the drugs.

The headline read:

Noted Physician Raises Alarm
About Drug Used for Weight Loss

How does Marta Everson do it? She even got the *Times* reporter to spin the story around her, referring to Dr. Everson as a "noted physician" in the headline.

When Brian offered no immediate response, Jennifer snatched back the paper and read to him.

> *Everson said she raised her concerns about Zuprone with Brian Raine, a business development and marketing director at Caladon, and was warned by him not to make the results of her study public.*
>
> *Raine denied he'd made any threats and stated that Everson's conclusions were not the result of a scientific study.*

Jennifer read a few more seconds to herself, her lips twitching as she silently formed the words. Then she thrust the newspaper at him, as if parrying with a sword.

Brian scanned the text. It was a short article, focused on Everson's claims, a synopsis of Zuprone, the off-label prescribing for weight loss. General trends in off-label prescribing—on its way up and up. Not enough industry oversight. End.

It struck Brian as a weak article, a favor the reporter or editor did for Everson rather than significant news. A good story would have dug deep into the benefits and dangers of off-label prescribing, exploring on the one side the many consumers who were helped and on the other side the risks of unknown side effects and potential drug interactions. But even that wouldn't be a new story. It had been making the rounds for years, flaring up whenever a big brand drug proved problematic.

"Since when are you a media contact for Caladon?"

Brian had known at the time he shouldn't have been talking to a reporter—but he hadn't been able to stop himself. The questions came and he answered and enjoyed answering until he realized the hole he'd dug.

"She called me and I happened to pick up the phone."

"Who—Everson or the reporter?"

"Both, actually."

"Gosh darn it, Brian," Jennifer said. "This is a real mess. Stephen's waiting for us right now."

Brian hadn't realized Stephen Jeffries was in town. If Stephen had made a special trip for this, then the situation was serious.

They met Stephen in the conference room. He was on the phone when Brian and Jennifer appeared at the door, but looked up and waved them in. Jennifer took a seat at the table across from Stephen. Brian remained standing, waiting for Stephen to finish his call. He was telling the person on the other end of the line—perhaps Hank Cutler, the CEO of Caladon; perhaps a riled FDA official—that a full investigation of the situation had already been launched. The situation being the one that Brian had created.

Stephen ended his call and wrote a few words in his notebook.

"I thought we agreed that I would handle Everson," he said, not looking up.

"You told me I should consider it off my plate," Brian said. "And I haven't spoken to her since then." He didn't ask if Stephen had actually done anything to handle Everson, although clearly he hadn't.

"Then what's all this threat business about?" He lifted his chin to meet Brian's eyes.

"There were no threats. When Everson told me about the anorexic tendencies she observed in her patients, I cautioned her against publishing the information. It hardly qualified as a study and she could damage her own reputation."

"Is that what you told her—she could damage her reputation?"

"I don't know the exact words I used, but something to that effect. I mentioned it. I wasn't telling her she'd better not do it or else."

"Or else what?" Jennifer asked.

"That's just it, I didn't say anything to that effect. I definitely didn't threaten her. It was more like professional counsel."

Stephen shook his head. He took his turn slapping the newspaper on the table. He stared out the window. Heat waves blurred above parked cars.

He turned back and explained the situation. He'd just gotten off the phone with the FDA. They were sending their guy, Marcus Ward, on Tuesday for a preliminary inquiry. They needed to satisfy Ward; if they didn't, the U.S. attorney could begin an investigation.

"And how would that turn out?" Stephen asked.

"A federal investigation?"

Stephen nodded.

Brian measured his answer. "Those often don't turn out very well."

"You get the picture," Stephen said. "But in this case, the FDA would find very little to go on. We're going to satisfy Marcus Ward, and this will come to an end. They will discover that Caladon adhered to standard industry practices and the letter of the law."

"All of our marketing has been approved by legal," Brian said. He looked to Jennifer for agreement.

"Do you have documentation to that effect?" she asked.

An alarm inside him went off, to accompany the headache he was already suffering due to a poor night's sleep. If necessary, he would be sacrificed, no question. If something surfaced that could be construed as illegal or even borderline, Brian would take the fall. He acted independently and inappropriately, they'd say, although it was Wilcox who'd dictated most of the strategies.

"We regularly submit marketing briefs to your department," Brian reminded Jennifer.

"Electronically or print?" she asked.

"That's not the point," Stephen interrupted. "The only documentation you need—print or electronic—is the documentation that shows our ethical marketing and selling operations. You should already have it, Brian. Didn't you just do the business case presentation?"

"That was different. We only included . . ."

"I'll forward you the e-mail from Ward. It has a list of what he wants by Tuesday."

"Can I explain something?" Brian asked.

"Like why you still think it's a good idea to seek FDA approval for Zuprone?"

"In fact, yes. The evidence . . ."

Stephen stood, signaling the meeting had ended.

After he left, Brian turned to Jennifer. "Thanks for throwing me under the bus."

"This is a serious situation, Brian."

"For anyone other than me?"

"For the entire company. Do you know what it means if Zuprone is causing anorexia at those dose levels?"

"It means physicians all over the country are prescribing it incorrectly for the wrong indication."

"And why would they be doing that?"

"Because Caladon implemented an aggressive plan to capture market share, which included stealth publishing a few microtrials, paying doctors to host seminars, and sending reps out to the targeted physician groups."

"Well, there you have it," Jennifer said. "And who conceived and managed those programs?"

"I managed them, but Stephen and John Wilcox set the strategy."

Jennifer folded her notebook and stood to leave. "Like I said, Brian, this is a serious situation for the entire company. I wish you hadn't spoken to that reporter. I have a call into Everson. I'm hoping we can get her to retract her statements."

She left the newspaper behind. Brian took it on his way out. He stopped in his office and checked the stock charts for Caladon to view the insider trading transactions for the past six months. Some options exercised and shares sold by the executive team and board members, which made sense given the stock's rise over the past year. Nothing unusual. No sudden dumping this morning.

He filled out the online form to exercise the fifteen thousand options he had vested so far, face value of eight dollars per. With the stock today around twenty-four dollars he would net $240 thousand. Another five thousand shares bought through the stock purchase plan at various prices would bring another $120 thousand. He put in to sell that as well. Enough for a soft landing if he was going down.

He had been to the Blue Slipper a few times after work with colleagues for drinks, but never alone in the morning with the sun streaming through the front window to reveal the crud in the corners and dust coating the bottles behind the bar. He claimed a middle stool and ordered a vodka and soda. Two other men sat at the bar, one at either end. The old guy watched horse racing on a television mounted to the wall. The other guy was showing the bartender his fake hand, which he had unscrewed from his wrist and held out to the bartender for a look.

He had started a second drink when his phone rang. Teresa.

"Where are you? We're meeting with the Frazier folks now."

"I'm in the Blue Slipper."

"What should I tell Frazier? We're going over the campaign budget."

"Tell them it's on hold."

"Because of the article this morning?"

"I doubt we're going to be seeking a lot of attention for Zuprone right now, even as an antianxiety med."

The *Times* article only nudged open the disclosure door. There would be follow-up reporting. Every researcher or prescribing physician would pay attention to Zuprone. Everson would shout from the mountaintops and Caladon would be forced to play defense, a game for lawyers and the PR department, not marketers. Whether or not the company planned to submit an application to the FDA, they'd have to conduct extensive trials of Zuprone on their own. It would take three years. It would cost millions. They might as well go for the approval, as Brian had recommended in the business case. But the cacophony of panic among the executive team was drowning out his voice.

Eight years of his life thrown to the pharmaceutical business, specifically to a drug called Zuprone, a laggard that couldn't grab share in the antianxiety market, but a real fat burner when prescribed off-label in the weight-loss category. Of course they jumped on the opportunity to grow sales.

He could be fired for speaking with the *Times* reporter. He could be fired if the FDA found anything they didn't like about the marketing of Zuprone. Simply for his association with Zuprone, he could end up leaving Caladon to "pursue other interests."

And on top of it all, he could end up losing his wife.

———

He'd been waiting at the kitchen table last night, lights turned low, when she came home at 1:30 in the morning. She jumped and put her hand to her chest when she saw him. No doubt he scared her, but what a dramatic gesture on her part: as if to still her racing heart.

"What are you doing up?" she asked.

"Your phone rang. You left it on the night table next to the bed."

She came farther into the room. He could see her scrambling for a story. She straightened her shoulders, as if standing up to him, and started talking. She wasn't going to lie to him, she said. She'd gone to Gull to see Jude with the intent of telling him what had happened and warning him that the police could be investigating him. Brian started to respond but she cut him off. She'd been haunted by the fact that she gave Jude to the police, she said, she'd been unable to sleep, she'd betrayed a trust and broken a promise. She owed him this, at the very least, if she could help him stay out of trouble. But in the end, she didn't go through with it, she didn't tell him.

"That's your story?"

"Well, I hope you understand my point of view," Gwen said.

Brian raised his voice. "Here's what I understand: I understand you either want to fuck him or get hurt by him. Which is it?"

"I told you why I went there!"

"Do you realize that you are in trouble with the law, and doing something like this—even being seen with him—is only going to make matters worse? Do you think this is going to help your case?"

"No one else seems to be helping me."

"You're only asking for more trouble. Gwen, you don't owe him a goddamn thing. What you owe is to your family: to me, and to Nora and Nate. That's where your priorities need to be. Not to some drug dealer you fucked in the good old days."

"Fuck you, Brian! I am thinking of my family. Why do you think I walked out?"

It was a phrase he'd never heard her utter to his face: *Fuck you.* It crushed him, as if she'd told him she was in love with Gates, or wanted a divorce, or simply couldn't stand her life with him.

"I don't know why you walked out," he finally said, teeth clenched. "I don't even get why you went there to begin with."

Then she started to cry, not just the modest gasps and tears he was accustomed to when she was upset, but heaving, choking sobs that shook her.

Let her cry. He left her standing in the kitchen. Didn't speak a word or even look at her in the morning.

And now Brian thought he might cry sitting here in the Blue Slipper. He looked up from his drink and glanced around, wondering if he'd made a sound: a moan or whimper. No one had noticed him. He finished his drink and decided to go home and work out what needed working with Gwen.

He was sorting through his money on the bar when the door opened and Teresa walked in.

"I'm glad you're still here." She took the stool next to him.

"I was just leaving."

"I'll have a drink with you." The bartender came over and she ordered a gin and tonic and another for Brian.

He sat back down. What's another ten minutes.

"Cheers." Teresa held up her glass.

They sat quietly for a moment. She looked at him through the mirror behind the bar.

"Marta Everson would have found an outlet whether you spoke to the reporter or not. And if you had sent the reporter to

PR, they would have declined comment on the accusation of threatening her. Is your denying it any worse than that?"

"You don't need to do this."

"I think Everson's full of it, anyway. I think Zuprone is amazing."

"You haven't been taking it for a year."

"By the way, I appreciate what you told me the other day, about noticing me. I like knowing that you've been looking at me."

Jesus, Teresa. Don't go down this road. Not today.

She looked around the bar. The dusty bottles. The smeared windows. She said, "This is no place to be during the middle of the day."

"It's the first place I thought of."

"We could go back to my apartment."

He could feel her staring at him now, waiting for his approval, but he kept his eyes on the bottles lined up behind the bar.

"No one has to know," Teresa said. "I won't be the kind of person who makes it complicated." She put a hand on his arm, her grip unexpectedly firm. "I like you."

Brian tried to move his arm, but he didn't want to force the break. "I thought Zuprone was supposed to dull your libido."

"I happen to tolerate it well. Do you know how long it's been since I've had sex? I mean with someone else."

"I don't need to know."

He moved half off his stool. Her hand dropped. Brian said, "There are other guys around the office to date, single guys."

"I've tried. They're dweebs."

"Online dating services. Get involved with your church. There's other ways to meet men."

"Mr. Advice Columnist," Teresa said. "I know you would like it."

He probably would. He could go back to her place now and fuck another woman for the first time in nine years; and he believed her when she said she'd be a good sport about it. What an opportunity to get back at Gwen—although he wouldn't tell her, he'd just do it, which would make the event an inconclusive "If a tree falls in the forest" situation. Not exactly documented revenge.

He said, "Teresa, I'm married. I love my wife. I have a family."

"Are you going to file a sexual harassment complaint?"

"I'm calling my lawyer right now." He got up and left without looking at her again. In the car driving home, he did call his lawyer—Roger, who had left a message that morning stating that progress had stalled and nothing was going to happen about dropping the charges this week, but next week they should see some action.

"They're more determined than I would have expected," Roger said on the phone. "I guess they want to check out this guy Gates first."

"We saw Detective Keller at school yesterday—we're going to be seeing him for the next five years. He said it was out of his hands, he just does the investigating work and has nothing to do with any deal."

"That's probably true, although he can make recommendations based on what he finds out."

"Do they have anything on Gates?"

"I haven't heard of anything, but they'll keep close to the vest whatever they find."

"It shouldn't make a difference whether or not they get anything on Gates," Brian said. "The agreement wasn't give us the name and if he's a drug dealer we'll drop charges against you. It was just give us the name."

"I'm sure this is frustrating for both you and Gwen and difficult to hear me say be patient, but that's really what's needed. I wouldn't be surprised if this is so minor that the DA's office has put it at the bottom of the pile."

"It's not minor to us. Gwen is very upset."

"I'll tell you what, I'll give Bob a call right now—Judge Donovan. He knows the DA well and can give a nudge. But really, Brian, I'm confident of this just going away in a few days' time."

"That's what you said last time, when Gwen was first arrested."

part 3

Mother's Little Helper

Feeding the Lion

Jude handed over a gym bag containing the cash—Sweet's down payment and most of Jude's own reserves. Gil said, "Back your van near the loading dock but leave room to swing the doors open."

Jude did as instructed and got out and waited by the van with Gil, who smoked and kicked at a broken fist of tar on the ground with his pointy black shoes. A pale maize glow from the sodium lights tinged the night air.

The loading dock door rose on its mechanical chain. A dishwasher in a soiled apron and sporting a flame tattoo curling up one side of his neck wheeled out a hand dolly stacked with cardboard boxes. He bumped the dolly down one stair at a time, crouching to keep the cargo balanced.

Jude climbed in the back of the van and folded down a wire shelving rack lining the passenger side wall. He loosened a panel on either side wall by gripping two plastic extrusions and raising up, then pulling toward him to free the bottom. The side panels slid out with a practiced back-and-forth maneuver. He handed one and then the other out to the dishwasher.

The walls weren't the secret. The floor was. With the side panels removed, Jude reached in and pulled at the floor and Gil wedged his cigarette between his lips and helped on one side. They slid the floor out together to reveal a storage well six inches deep running the length and width of the hold, its interior padded with layers of charcoal scent-lock fabric, cushy as a coffin.

Jude returned to the dolly and opened the top box. He removed packages the size of bread loaves wrapped in white butcher paper and began lining them in the well of the van. Coke and crack, heroin, X, Vicodin, bennies, barbs, HGH, and GHB—the last two new products for Jude to carry because Sweet had been the first to ask.

They finished and Jude reassembled the floor and sides, and it appeared to be an empty van. Gil had gone inside and now came out with Roxanne. She carried an overnight bag on her shoulder and wore a leather jacket with an imitation fur collar. She looked scared until she saw Jude and her face relaxed.

"She have a passport or identification?"

"We didn't discuss anything about a passport," Gil said. "You said it would be easy."

"Easy at the border, but once she's in the States she might need documentation to stay."

Gil shrugged. "I thought you had a place for her all arranged."

"I do." He didn't like this part of the deal but you had to feed the lion guarding the gate and in this case the lion was Leonard Deitch.

"It's okay," Jude said. "I know someone who can fix her up."

Gil turned to Roxanne. "Jude will take you to your new husband. He will take care of you and you will be an American." He repeated himself in French. Jude didn't know if she'd understood either version. She nodded but her expression did not change.

Jude went around to the passenger side and opened the door for her. He shook hands with Gil, got in the driver's side, and started back to the U.S.

While driving he glanced her way for the first good look he'd gotten of her outside of the hotel room. She was young and pretty with dark hooded eyes and a small, flat nose and a scar the size of a staple across her chin.

He crossed the bridge leading out of the city; the lights of a passing freighter steering in from the St. Lawrence Seaway blinked below. Maybe earlier in her adventure Roxanne had gotten into Canada stowed away on one of those ships, and now she's in a van headed for the U.S. and the future husband waiting for her there. He hoped he was taking her to a better place than she'd been, but couldn't be sure.

When he approached customs, there was more traffic than he had expected. A uniformed official directed the cars to various lanes. He pointed his arm for Jude to go left toward lanes six or seven. That wouldn't work. Jude would have to run him over or get into another lane and then steer around the uniform back to Leonard's lane four. Either way he drew unwanted attention.

He hesitated and the official kept motioning him to the left.

"Move, move, move!"

He started left, swung around the official, and steered back into lane four. He caught a glimpse of the uniform in the side mirror, his mouth yelling something Jude couldn't hear. He started toward the van but the traffic behind Jude moved forward with each driver making his own choice about lanes, and the official abandoned Jude and turned back to sort out the oncoming.

Safely in lane four. About eight or ten cars ahead of him. He smiled at Roxanne, who looked nervous again, her worried brow creasing her creamy skin. He turned on the radio to fill the silence.

Finally Jude's turn. He lowered his window and steered up to the booth and Leonard Deitch stared out at him, and then past him to Roxanne in the passenger seat. Deitch got off his stool and leaned closer. His night-shift breath blew in. Jude pressed into his seat.

Deitch made a sucking noise deep in his throat. "Even prettier than in the picture," he said. He waved at Roxanne and said, "Hi, sweetie, I'm Len. I'll be home real soon."

"Your new husband," Jude said.

The flash of dread that swept her face made clear she understood, but she quickly recovered to display a courageous smile, said hello, and bowed her head a touch. A man old enough to be her father or even grandfather, an insistent urge in his eyes.

Deitch stood straight and handed Jude an index card with directions written on it. He looked again at Roxanne. His smile was not unkind. "I'll be home right after my shift, make yourself comfortable."

Deitch stepped back toward the door of his booth and waved them through.

Jude had just erased a debt for his passage across the border and prepaid until Deitch retired or died.

He drove straight onto the Northway. He glanced down at the directions. Route 11 to Malone, left on Chester Road. That was toward Canton. If he weren't carrying the stash in the hold, he'd visit Dana. He hadn't heard from her about the cross-country meet and wondered if she was running. There was still a chance he could see her tomorrow in Plattsburgh. For now, he had to stick to a schedule in order to meet the impatient Mr. Sweet on time.

He drove for twenty minutes, up to and through the town of Malone, and only on the other side when the number of storefronts and houses dwindled did he remember to look for the turn-off on Chester Road. He glanced at the directions again. He had missed the turn. Where was his focus today? He couldn't be careless like this, even if it were only following road directions. He U-turned and headed back through the town. He stopped at a Stewart's and went in for a coffee and bought two and returned to the van and handed one to Roxanne. She took it and said, "I find toilet."

He pointed to the side of the building where the restrooms were. She stayed in the bathroom for a long time and he wondered if she'd tried to run off, whether there was another door into the store and she'd slipped out from there. He got out and knocked on the restroom door and she immediately opened it and came out. The edges of her hair were wet from washing her face. She'd touched up her makeup. She said nothing and got back in the car.

He pulled onto Route 11 tracing the way he'd come, driving slowly, finding Chester Road two miles back and turning onto it. The road bisected fields on either side and they passed a barn and farmhouse and then the road curved and started climbing into hills and became dirt and gravel through a canopy of hardwoods beginning to turn. The next instruction said to turn left at the T.

He came to the T and the road worsened with two narrow tracks for the tires. They bounced along through water-filled ruts. Roxanne held her coffee away from her to keep from spilling. She looked at him doubtfully as if to ask had he made a wrong turn. Jude continued on and branches scraped along the top and sides of the van.

The road dipped and leveled, ending in a packed-dirt clearing. The sun had risen above the treetops now and the leaves shone but the squalor could not be abated by autumn's early color. Junk lay strewn about the yard like the aftermath of a blast. Leaning towers of wheel rims and piles of old tires and faded, cracked lumber of every dimension lying under a tarp half blown away. Mechanical parts and scraps of metal welded together into spidery shapes. A rock pile fireplace with blackened chunks of logs and ashes in its center. Two pairs of buck antlers screwed to the drip edge of a shed stacked with firewood.

The house was worse. Once a single-wide modular, additions now grew from it like tumors. A lopsided porch with a corrugated plastic roof. A room annexed to one end never sided beyond the tar paper, windows left untrimmed. There were no neighbors except trees and beyond the trees more and deeper and thicker woods.

For a moment he considered turning around and taking Roxanne with him. How in his right mind could he leave this poor girl here? But he had no choice, really. If he didn't fulfill this part of the bargain, the supply chain would break and everything would fall apart, he would fail at his goal.

He got out of the van and started toward the house. Roxanne stayed in her seat. Something moved from around the side of the house. A muscular German shepherd loped toward Jude, head pitched down but eyes up and ready. Jude tensed his fists, but the dog just sniffed and stood there.

He went back to the van and escorted Roxanne out. She let him lead her, pliant as tissue. He opened the door to the house and the shepherd stayed back, watching.

More of the same on the inside plus the smell of disinfectant. On a hook near the door was a blackjack and pair of handcuffs hanging with a U.S. Customs hat, a dog collar and leash for the shepherd. He motioned to a ratty couch across from a television the size of a sheet of plywood and he said she should sit and wait, Len would be home soon. She took a seat as she was told, at the edge of the cushion, clutching her bag to her chest. Her lip trembled.

There was a folded note on a chipped coffee table in front of the couch. Jude picked it up. *To my new wife.*

He unfolded the note and read it out loud. *Make yourself at home. I will see you soon. Fondly, Len.*

Jude told her everything would be fine, Leonard was a good man.

He turned and went back to his van without looking at her again. Somewhere on the other side of the world she had dreamed of reaching America and the dream could not have included this place where she ended up. Maybe she would brighten the rooms, add a woman's touch and nice paint, cook meals for Leonard and he would care for her and love her and they would become a family. Maybe he wouldn't cuff her to the table or put that dog collar on her and do what he once did as a conscripted warrior unleashed and unabated in the Vietnamese jungle half a world away. Who was Jude to say there was no hope, although despair hammered him now for leaving Roxanne to an unknown fate.

Jude called Aaron twice from the van. The first time Jude woke him. Twenty minutes later he called again. Write a note to yourself if you have to, he told Aaron. Just don't greet me with a shotgun pointed out the door.

When he arrived, there was an unfamiliar truck parked in front of the cabin. Jude pulled in behind the big silver Tundra, blocking it in. He stayed in the van, waiting.

Aaron came out to greet him.

"That yours?"

"Just got it in Placid."

"All-wheel drive?"

"With the V8."

"You should get a plow put on for winter."

"I'm planning to."

"How many pounds did we get in all?" Jude asked.

"Thirty-two. Got it all ready."

Thirty-two pounds. If he could run this deal every ninety days with Sweet he could clear his goal in less than a year. He used to buy from a guy in Boston, but the quality and source varied. Mexican, skunk weed, hothouse, his Boston guy just another broker taking his cut. The price went up and down, as did Jude's profit. But demand for hay was growing, everyone seemed to be getting high again; there was opportunity he couldn't fulfill using his Boston connection. That's what got him thinking about the old hunting cabin that had been in Claire's family before Jude had known her. When her father died, the place passed to her and by proxy to Jude, although the name on the deed and in the tax rolls was still Claire Dumont. For years the property lay neglected. When he went to check it out, he realized the cabin could make a viable operation; it had good water and a propane tank, although a new generator would need to be installed for electricity. It wasn't hooked to the grid. There were no neighbors in view. He just needed someone to operate it. He met that someone on a flight from Washington, a former soldier returning to his boyhood home in upstate New York, minus part of his face and future prospects. A kid all alone who managed a painkiller habit reasonably well, who might stick around for a year or two, long enough for Jude to fill the treasure chest. Worth a try.

Although recently Jude had begun to question his decision to own the means of production. The last few times Jude had seen him, Aaron seemed to be bolting awake from a bad dream. Lost in space and then suddenly jumpy. Hitting his Vicodin too hard or suffering from traumatic brain injury or both or more. Plus that incident with the shotgun. The kid could be getting too unstable.

But Jude could not deny the quality of Aaron's work. The harvested plants were dried, bagged, and stacked neatly on the kitchen table. The grow room was clean. The new plants aligned beneath the lights. Even the living quarters were clean: Aaron had made his bed, no crusty dishes lined the kitchen sink.

"Looks good," Jude said. "Let's load up."

He disassembled the rear of the van as he had in Montreal. When Aaron saw the packages lining the cargo hold his eyes widened like a kid's in a candy shop.

Jude gave one to Aaron. "For you. A sampler."

He also handed Aaron an envelope containing cash. "There's extra. You did a good job getting this together in a short time."

Aaron brought out the plastic bags of weed and Jude made room for them in the hold, arranging the packages and squeezing the last few bags in. He zipped the filter fabric closed and replaced the floor and panels.

Aaron went back inside and returned with a small stack of mail and handed it to Jude.

"I stopped at the post office in town. Mostly just bills addressed to Claire," Aaron said.

"How's the propane usage?"

"The guy comes every other week and I've been giving him the extra hundred each time."

"He's never been inside?"

"Hell no."

"Up him to two hundred. We need him on our side."

"Those buds could have used more drying," Aaron said. "Some of the weight might shrink out but we ran out of time."

"Not a problem. I'm moving the whole lot tonight. It will be divided and dispersed within a few days."

"You want to taste it?"

"We should."

They went back up on the porch. Aaron produced a joint, lit, and passed to Jude who took one hit and handed it back. "A lot better than what I used to get," he said.

Aaron took a long hit and held it out for Jude, who held up his hand to say no. He had to stay clearheaded.

"How's the pain?" Jude asked.

"Doing better."

"You been in touch with your doctors about the surgery?"

"They haven't called. I don't think I'm at the top of their list. There's all this paperwork I don't have."

"So do they owe you a call or do you owe them paperwork?"

Aaron looked unsure. Jude thought about Alfred Haynes, the congressman who owed Jude a favor.

"You want me to put in a call for you? We could bypass the whole military chain of command, find you the best doctors, and get you fixed up right."

"That would be cool." But no real enthusiasm there.

"I'll pay for it," Jude said. "You shouldn't have to go through this. You've been loyal to me and I repay loyalty." He completed a slow scan of the property, turning three-sixty, nothing but woods all about.

"You get out of here ever? You visit your friends in Glens Falls?"

"I get out enough."

"After I get this run established I'll have you drive and deliver," Jude said.

"Yeah, okay."

Again, the lifeless response.

Jude took a last look around. The mums Aaron had planted radiated with color, casting a brighter outlook on the entire day. His low mood from dropping off Roxanne improved; he chose to believe Leonard would love her. He believed he could help Aaron. He was ahead of schedule and had plenty of time to fuel up and deliver to Sweet.

I Didn't Expect to See You Here

Brian had come home early yesterday and told Gwen he was taking the next day off and the kids could, too, so what if they'd only been in school a few days. They were going to the lake for the long weekend they didn't get to enjoy last time. He needed time with his family, he said. He needed the new scenery. Mostly he needed to get past their argument over Gwen stepping out to see Jude at Gull. He was angry about her decision to go but ultimately she'd done the right thing by not saying anything to Gates about the police. It was time to reconnect with his wife.

Gwen was all for it.

By the time they arrived at the house night had fallen, a web of stars pricking the sky above the tall pines around their house and reflecting on the still surface of the lake. Brian turned on the outdoor lights to illuminate the fire pit and dock, and he sent Nate and Nora out with flashlights to hunt for downed sticks and branches for a fire. Get ones with no leaves, he reminded them.

The kids gathered wood while Brian helped Gwen unload the car. The house smelled musty, and they walked from room to room, turning on lights and opening windows. A kitchen and living area with picture windows dominated the first floor, with a den to one side. Upstairs were two bedrooms and a bath. They had purchased the house furnished, from beds and towels to kitchen utensils and games and books. That helped make the deal more attractive—she and Brian wouldn't have to spend weeks trying to furnish and supply a second house.

To one side of the house a scramble of granite formed a small peninsula into the lake. On the other side stood a boathouse they shared with their neighbor, although Brian and Gwen didn't own a boat. Between the peninsula and boathouse a beach of sandy grass and pebbles lined the water's edge.

Brian built a fire from a tepee of dried sticks and they roasted marshmallows on branches he cut from saplings. A breeze picked up, fanning the flames and heat toward their blanket. Gwen moved the blanket to the other side. Still, they needed sweatshirts because any body part not facing the fire got chilled. When the kids had their fill of marshmallows and started to argue about who had counted more stars, Gwen broke up the party and called bedtime.

Once the kids were down, there was nothing for Gwen and Brian to do except go to bed themselves. There was no television. No picking up to do, no laundry to fold.

"Should I go down and get a bottle of wine?" Brian asked.

"Not if you're going to stay mad at me."

"It's not that."

"You haven't looked at me since we've been here. You're like staring off into space, and I don't mean counting the stars."

"I'm sorry, I'm still at work."

He stood by the open bedroom window. She got up and joined him. A bent tree rooted in moss and granite leaned over the black water.

Brian mentioned there was a possibility he could lose his job. He told her about the story in the *Times,* his confrontational meeting with Stephen and Jennifer, the potential FDA scrutiny of Caladon's marketing practices.

"You haven't been doing anything illegal, have you? I mean, that can get you into trouble."

"Not personally, I don't think. It's such a gray area, there's no way of knowing. It really goes back to the day drug companies won the right to advertise directly to consumers. The industry became a free-for-all, with patients demanding certain drugs for all kinds of conditions. And it's only gotten worse with the Internet."

"What about our stock options?"

"Yesterday I cashed in everything vested and sold the shares we had. I'm not taking chances. The worst case is the whole company takes a hit."

"When I see you unhappy like this I keep thinking I'm the one who made you leave medical school," Gwen said.

"We've been through this many times. You didn't make me do anything. I was looking for an out."

"You wanted to go to Africa to provide medical care to the poor. How noble can you get?"

Brian smirked. "You don't think marketing pharma is a noble calling?" he said. "We made decisions together, Gwen. We chose it all. Together."

"I could get a job to take some of the pressure off. I was speaking with Amy Hellman. She has a real estate business and is looking to bring on another agent. I could take the course and be licensed in like eight weeks."

"What about the kids?"

"A lot of the work is on the weekends and during school hours."

"You've been telling me we already don't have enough time together."

"It feels more like you don't want to make time for me."

He put an arm around her. "Am I not the one who invited you to a glass of wine a short while ago?"

"Yes, that's true."

"I don't want you to work, unless you really want to or have to. For now I'm still employed."

"No wonder you're so stressed. Come here." She held him and kissed his neck and told him she loved him completely. How long had it been since she'd said that to her husband? It felt so good: *Brian, I love you completely.*

"That's mostly what I need to hear," he said.

"I know my situation hasn't made things easier for us."

He nodded, but said, "And I know you've been put in a difficult position. I admire your principles and your wanting to do the right thing."

"Let's not talk about this now. I want to get into bed."

"I'll get that bottle of wine," he said. "I'll be right back."

A car passed on the road, the headlights shining into their bedroom as the vehicle rounded the curve. Brian lowered the shades and went downstairs to get the wine and two glasses. She heard him opening and closing cabinet doors. When he came back up she heard him look in on the kids in the twin beds on either side of a window facing the lake. He came down the hall to their bedroom and stopped in the doorway.

Gwen had changed into a nightshirt, gotten in her side of the bed, put on her reading glasses, and opened her novel.

"Wait a minute—didn't we just agree on a plan that involved wine and kissing?" Brian said.

"We did."

"You'd better set down that book."

She looked at him and turned her book upside down. Finally. A sudden craving for Brian engulfed her, to be held, to be loved—and to give back. Yes, this is how it should feel.

"You'd better take off your glasses."

She set her glasses on the night table.

"You'd better get out of that shirt."

———

"I want to go swimming," Nora said. She was eating pancakes Gwen had made from a mix brought from home.

"Me too," said Nate.

"Mommy, did you bring Nate's floaty vest?" Nora asked.

"Yes I did."

"She brought your vest, Nate."

"I know."

"When can we go swimming?"

"After breakfast. Dad will take you." She turned to Brian. "I should go into town and get some groceries."

"Sure, stick me in the cold water."

"Get your bathing suits on, they're in the suitcase in my bedroom," Gwen said. "And don't forget your water shoes, the bottom isn't smooth."

The kids ran upstairs to get changed.

Brian approached Gwen at the kitchen sink from behind, wrapped his arms around her waist, looked at the rippled surface of the lake.

"Maybe we can have a repeat of last night."

"That would be nice." She turned to kiss him. Amazing what lovemaking could do, when it was the perfect timing, ideal setting, and the right man. It could vanquish all the stress, ease her guilt over the accident, mitigate her legal problems, marginalize her betrayal of Jude. And the aftermath of their love, side by side on the bed and holding hands under the warmed sheets, only the crickets interrupting the silence: it helped you remember who and what were essential in your life.

The kids came down in their swimsuits and water shoes. Nate had his suit on backward and shoes on the wrong feet. Gwen helped him out of his suit and shoes and back on again the right way. She zipped him into his vest.

"Guess how many sharks I have?" A pattern of tiny blue sharks covered his suit.

"How many?"

"Guess."

"Twenty?"

Nate laughed. "Nope. Thirty-seven."

"That's a lot of sharks."

"Come on," said Nora. "Let's go."

Gwen grabbed the camera and walked down to the lake with them. Brian squatted at the water's edge with Nora and Nate on either side and he tickled them just enough to coax big smiles. Gwen snapped two pictures.

"I'll take another of you going in," she said.

Nora waded in, but Nate touched the water and sprang back as if bitten by a fish.

"It's too cold," he said.

"It's great!" said Nora. She dunked under.

"I don't want to."

"Come on, buddy, you just have to get used to it. Take my hand." Brian looked at Gwen and chattered his teeth. He mouthed the words *fucking freezing*. Nora called for him to get in.

"I want to stay with Mommy," Nate said, breaking away from Brian.

"I have to go in town to the store," Gwen said.

"I want to come with you." He clung to her leg at the water's edge.

"Let's swim," Brian said. "It's already feeling warmer." He was midcalf now, Nora still yelling at him to come out farther.

"I want to go with Mommy."

"It's okay with me," Gwen said. "I'll take him, you two swim. Come on, Nate."

She unzipped his vest and got him into a T-shirt. He insisted on keeping his bathing suit and water shoes on.

Gwen could make do with the small market about fifteen minutes away rather than driving the half hour into Saranac Lake. She'd pick up something Brian could grill for dinner, hopefully find fresh produce and get ice cream for dessert. A six of beer. Eggs for breakfast tomorrow.

On the way, she played a CD of kids' songs that Nate liked and was stunned by how beautiful the mountains looked, the bold contours, the leaves starting to change. They hadn't taken advantage of the mountains yet, having owned the house less than a year and hardly coming up. Now, according to Brian, they were at risk of having to sell it. Things could be a lot worse, Gwen knew, and if they had to liquidate, downsize, and live a different lifestyle, she would do whatever it took to make that life successful. The one thing about last night with Brian was she realized they already had everything they needed in each other, as clichéd as that sounded. If finances got strained, they could re-create their early days together, when they were living in a one-bedroom apartment and in debt with school loans. It hadn't been easy, but at least they'd made love a lot.

Although they didn't have two children to worry about then. Having children changed everything.

The market doubled as a gas station. Gwen steered past the two pumps and parked in a space on the side of the building. Nate held her hand walking in. There were no carts to push or ride in, which disappointed Nate, but he bounced back when Gwen asked him to pick out ice cream for dessert.

He asked Gwen to read off all the names and when she got to Cookies & Cream he said that's the one.

"I haven't gone through them all yet."

"Cookies & Cream," he insisted.

Gwen added the ice cream to the basket. She found chicken breasts and drumsticks and a head of lettuce that still looked reasonable, and tomatoes that felt firm and fresh. It wasn't their produce share from the community farm but it would do. She picked out a six-pack of beer. At checkout she divided the items into two bags, giving the lighter one with the ice cream to Nate.

They held hands again on the way out, Nate cradling the bag with the ice cream in his other arm. As they passed the gas pumps, someone called Gwen's name.

She looked up and tugged on Nate's hand, knocking him off balance. He dropped the bag with the ice cream.

"Mom!"

"Hi—wow." She looked down at Nate. "I'm sorry, honey. Just pick it up. Hi."

Nate let go of her hand and reached down.

"Sorry, I surprised you."

"No. No, I'm just. I didn't expect to see you here."

Jude replaced the gas pump and the cap on his tank. He looked as if running into her up here was the most natural event, even planned, unlike the way she reacted, which was more or less as if he'd landed from another planet.

He took a step closer to Gwen. She tried to step back, but her feet wouldn't move.

"You mentioned you had a place here—Tear Lake, right?"

"We're up for the weekend," Gwen said. She feared her heart pumped loud enough for him to hear.

Be normal, she said to herself. Have a regular conversation. "You have a place around here too?"

"Just a cabin that's been in the family for years near Rainbow Lake. I'm going to visit Dana—at St. Lawrence."

Nate recovered the ice cream bag. He stared up at Jude.

"This is my son, Nate," Gwen said. "Nate, say hello to Mr. Gates. You met him at his restaurant once."

Nate didn't say a word.

"Hello, Nate, it's good to see you again." Jude crouched down and held out his hand.

Nate looked at Gwen, then at the hand. "Hi."

"Are you helping your mom do the shopping?"

"Uh-huh."

"That's nice, Mother's little helper. I remember when my daughter was your age. She'd always want to work at my side in the restaurant."

He stood and turned back to Gwen. He spoke so only she could hear. "You left the other night without telling me what you came for."

She lowered her eyes. Nate was picking splattered bugs off the front bumper and headlights of Jude's van.

"Nate, don't do that." She pulled his hand away.

"You walked out."

"Sorry, it's just . . ." She couldn't come up with an excuse. Her throat tightened. "Did you call me? Because Brian answered my phone and . . ."

He whispered in her ear. "You're very beautiful, even more than you were years ago."

She shouldn't blush, but felt the heat rise in her face. She looked down again at Nate. Now he was scratching at the van's license plate and flicking the dead bugs off his fingertips. "Stop that. It's gross." She pulled his wrist.

"Mommy, can we go now?"

"Just a sec, honey. Why don't you get in the car?"

"The ice cream is melting."

"It will be fine. Go ahead, I'll be right there. And use a wipe on your hand."

Nate walked over to their car, tugged open the door, and climbed into his car seat.

Jude said, "We should meet later, when you can get away." He expected her to say yes. He wanted her and he told her, and she understood that with his confidence came control.

No, she was in control. He'd just handed it to her to accept or reject him. Use it.

He stepped closer and she stepped back, and just as she started to speak he leaned and touched her face as he had last time and she realized he was about to kiss her again. She raised a hand between them and held him off, glancing over Jude's shoulder to see if Nate was watching.

"No, don't," she said. Then: "I told the police you sold me pot."

That stopped him. A shadow eclipsed his face; he frowned and his Adam's apple moved.

"I had to," she said.

"You had to what?" he said, backing off.

"That accident I got in, I was arrested. It was either . . ."

"You told the police?"

"That's why I came to see you the other night, to warn you, but I couldn't say it. I thought I'd end up in more trouble, or you'd be angry."

He stared at her, waiting for more. She had no more.

"Gwen, I asked you not to tell anyone."

"I wanted you to know, in case the police ask you questions."

"That's why you came to see me?"

She nodded. "This other thing—I can't do it."

Nate screamed out the open car window. "Mommy, my eye! I got a bug in my eye."

"I'm sorry, I have to go."

"Wait. Gwen."

"Mommy!"

"I need to know when . . ."

"I hope I didn't get you in trouble," she said, already on her way to the car.

She ran to Nate.

She climbed into the backseat with him and shut the door.

Nate cried. She searched for a clean wipe and dabbed at the corner of his eye where a dead bug floated. She looked out the window. Jude stood next to his van, watching, squinting from the sun in his face.

Gone Fishing

Brian estimated the swim across the width of the lake measured close to a quarter mile. He swam by Nora's side the whole way, but they didn't talk. Nora focused on swimming, her freestyle strokes smooth and coordinated.

The cool, clear water calmed him. At work, they'd be looking for Brian, even though he'd left a message for Stephen that he was taking a long weekend, saying nothing about the information he was told to compile for the FDA. There would be messages on his desk phone and cell phone, e-mails, people stopping by his office. The FDA guy was coming. People would be asking: Where is Brian?

He believed that whatever was going to happen had already been set in motion, months or even years ago. The marketing of Zuprone would be labeled unethical or not, illegal or not, regardless of Brian's position and explanation. Not that he wouldn't fight any attempts to use him as a corporate scapegoat. But that was not a battle he would fight today.

Teresa was another story. Maybe the poor woman simply needed to be fucked and he could have done her a favor by obliging, although one sympathy roll when you've had a few drinks can turn into a bad habit. Anyway, that wasn't the reason he'd turned her down. The temptation had not been strong. It was his love for Gwen that was strong, and it had been reaffirmed last night, not only because they'd made love—after nine years they'd had sex plenty of times without the trumpets of affirmation—but also after nine years he knew when their bond was strengthened, their spirits connected.

Although a few loose threads remained to be clipped. For one, Brian planned to visit Jude Gates when they got back to Morrissey. His objective: demand that Gates stay away from his wife. Brian had little experience with violence, and no desire to gain more, but confronting Jude Gates was part of defending his territory, a noble cause, and in that way he looked forward to it.

He and Nora crossed the lake, stopped to catch their breath, and started back at the same steady, controlled pace. Nora alternated sidestroke and breaststroke now. Brian executed a combination crawl and doggy paddle so he could keep his head above water and eyes on his daughter. There was no need; she swam flawlessly. When they reached shallow water again, Brian put his foot down but Nora stroked until her belly rubbed the bottom. They held hands coming out of the water. He wrapped a towel around her and then himself and she sat on his lap in one of the Adirondack chairs by the water. Nora's teeth chattered and her limbs shivered. He held her until she warmed.

"Are you going to try out for the Dolphins this year?" he asked her.

"I can make the team."

"I know you can make the team. Is that something you want to do? They practice twice a week and have a swim meet every weekend."

"Lauren Reed is on the Dolphins."

"Mommy said sign-ups are next week."

"I might take flute lessons instead."

"Since when do you like the flute?"

"I saw a Jethro Tull video and he plays the flute."

"Jethro Tull? Where did you see that?"

"On YouTube. Mommy showed me."

Gwen's watching classic rock videos on YouTube with the kids? Had she scored another bag of pot? No, she would have told him this time.

"I like the way Jethro Tull plays the flute."

"Jethro Tull is the name of the band. The flute player is Ian Anderson."

"Or maybe I'll be on the Dolphins."

"Either one is fine."

"Can we get dressed now? I'm freezing."

They went back to the house and dressed. Nora asked if they could go fishing. In a closet near the back door Brian found the fishing poles and tackle box that also had been part of the house purchase. He took a slice of bread to tear apart and use as bait.

Looking down into the water from the dock, they could see a number of small fish in the shallow water.

"There they are, Daddy. I see them."

"Shhh. You don't want to scare them away." Brian outfitted the pole and handed it to Nora, who let her line drop into the water. He was about to get the other ready for himself when Gwen turned into the driveway. Nate jumped out first and came running toward them, yelling, "I wanna fish! I wanna fish!"

"You have to be quiet!" Nora screamed back at him.

Gwen went into the house with the shopping bags.

"How'd it go at the store, buddy?" Brian asked Nate.

"I got a bug in my eye."

"Did you get it out?"

"Mommy did."

Brian breaded a hook and handed Nate the pole and helped him lower the line on the side of the dock opposite Nora.

"Now you just have to wait," Brian told them. "Be very quiet and still and most of all be very patient. We're counting on you guys to catch our dinner."

"Mommy bought chicken," Nate said.

"That's only for an emergency. We'd rather have fresh fish."

Gwen came outside and halfway down to the water. She called to Brian and motioned for him to come up.

"What's the matter?" he asked, approaching her. She looked worried, face tight, and she jerked when a car passed on the road.

"Are you crying? What happened?" He turned to keep one eye on the kids standing at the dock's edge.

This is what happened: she ran into Jude at the market and told him she'd given his name to the police.

Immediately he slammed her with questions, anger twisting inside him. "What do you mean you ran into him? You told him? Didn't we just go through this?"

He stopped and waited for her to answer.

She'd been surprised to see him and completely caught off guard and felt guilty and . . . You know it's been a struggle for me. I couldn't help it.

Okay, okay. Brian held her to calm her, although he'd rather shake her for being so stupid.

"What did he say?"

"Nothing, really. Nate started screaming about a bug and I left."

"Did he do anything to you? Did he hurt or threaten you?"

"No, no." But she'd gotten scared. A few minutes after driving away she noticed Jude was behind her, and she thought he was following her. After each curve in the road he appeared closer. Then he turned off at Route 186.

"What was he doing up here, did he say?"

"He's got a cabin or something."

"Where—here?"

"No, I can't remember. Another lake. He was going to visit his daughter at St. Lawrence."

"And he just ran into you?" Brian said. That was hard to swallow. "Did you arrange to meet him up here or something?"

Gwen shook her head. "No, no."

"Does he know where we live?"

"I don't know, I don't think so. He knows we're on Tear Lake."

"Jesus, Gwen."

"He won't do anything."

"How do you know what he plans to do? If I was a drug dealer and discovered someone turned me in to the police, I'd be pretty pissed at that person. I might want to do something about it."

Brian tried to think of what was up Route 186. A bunch of small lakes, a lot of wilderness, he wasn't sure what else.

"Where was Nate in all this?"

"He was with me, and then he went to the car."

"I'm calling the police," Brian said.

"No, I don't think we should."

"Better to be safe. We'll just let them know what happened. Let them advise us on what to do."

"I don't want them to know I told Jude. I'm sure I committed another crime doing that. I'm like an accessory or something now."

Brian considered this. Gwen might be right. Maybe he should call Roger first and get his advice. No, not yet. For now, the fewer people who knew, the better. But still, he wasn't sure what to do.

He said, "That's not our biggest concern right now. Safety is. You came home worried and told me about this—he must have done something to scare you."

"Please, Brian, let's just wait," Gwen begged. "I overreacted, that's all. I shouldn't have. He doesn't know where we are, and even if he did . . ."

"I still think we should call the police."

"No, please. He's not going to do anything."

She wiped her eyes with the back of her hand and stood straighter. "It's fine," she said, pulling herself together. "Really."

He gave in. "Okay, if he didn't follow you and he doesn't know where we are, I guess nothing can come of it right now."

Then Nora started yelling that she caught a fish, a big one for dinner: "Daddy come quick, there's a big fish stuck on my hook!"

Gwen went inside and put away the rest of the groceries, her hands trembling on the cabinet knobs. When she shut one of the doors, a mouse darted out from its hiding place and ran across the kitchen floor, disappearing into a crack in the kick plate where two cabinets met in the corner.

A mouse did not frighten her. It just meant more work. She'd have to go through the pantry and examine every box and bag for signs of mouse entry, then seal food into Tupperware containers or tins. Brian would set traps.

Would anyone really stand on a chair and scream hysterically at the sight of a mouse? What is a mouse but a quiet little nuisance. But Jude?

What a mistake. What a series of mistakes. She had wanted to tell Jude about the police because she owed him that much; you don't turn in a friend who does you that kind of favor. But in the end, Jude turned out not to be the friend she thought he was, and she told him about the police to prevent him from kissing her again. She either did the right thing for the wrong reason or the wrong thing for the right reason. She wasn't sure which. At least she told Brian about the encounter, even if she did leave out the part when Jude tried to kiss her. Of course Brian reacted in a protective way; he'd been suspicious of Jude all along.

Now what were they going to do?

Start by putting away the milk. Do normal tasks.

Even muffled inside her handbag, the chime on her cell phone clanged like a tripped alarm. She almost peed when it sounded.

Gwen dug it out, knowing who. Took the call before she could consider ignoring it.

"Please don't call me," she said.

"I should thank you for letting me know."

Footsteps on the porch, Nora at the screen door.

"You need to tell me, when did you speak to the police?"

"I can't talk. I'm hanging up."

"Gwen, it's important. You owe me this one."

Nora coming in the kitchen.

"I'll call back."

She shut off the phone and took a quick breath. Composed her expression and turned to face Nora. "Where's the fish you caught?"

"Daddy said it was a little sunfish and we had to throw it back."

"Well, that's okay. She can swim to her friends and tell about her scary adventure."

"Mr. Garrison is taking us fishing on his boat. He said the big ones are out in the middle of the lake."

Gwen looked out and saw Brian, holding both fishing poles, speaking with Walter Garrison. He owned the house next door and kept a small motorboat in the two-bay boathouse he shared with the Raines.

"Be sure to wear your life vest."

"Mr. Garrison said we had to in the boat."

"He's right, even if you are a good swimmer."

"I swam all the way across the lake and back with Daddy."

"That's pretty amazing."

"Are you coming?" Nora asked.

"No, you go fishing, sweetie. There's no room for me in the boat. I'm going to take a little walk."

"I'm joining the Dolphins." She ran back down to the water.

Gwen waited until the four of them settled into the boat and reversed out from the dock, then took her phone and left through the back door.

She walked along the road on the gravel shoulder a few hundred yards to where an old fire trail she recognized cut into the woods. She and Brian had hiked up here in June with the kids for a picnic lunch but had not gone far before finding a rock ledge and stopping to eat. She started up the trail. She passed the spot where they'd had lunch and she continued on. The trail dwindled from two tracks to one. The forest pressed closer on either side.

She wore her slip-ons, not the best choice for a trail, but she paid attention to where her foot went down and didn't plan to be gone long.

Her phone showed one bar of battery and one bar of signal strength. She retrieved Jude's number and pressed to call him.

No Race for You

When Dana got back to her room Jen wasn't there. She dropped her backpack on the floor, fell onto the bed, and buried her face in her pillow. She wanted someone to come in and notice her shoulders shaking and hear her quiet, muffled sobs—only she wasn't crying, she was gulping air. She was exhausted. Getting up was out of the question, although her stomach echoed with hunger.

At this hour she'd typically sit down to her last big meal the afternoon before a track meet—a meal of high-octane fuel, pasta with fresh veggies or tuna on whole grain. The rest of the day and in the morning she would eat light, several times. Yogurt and fruit, a slice of toast with peanut butter. But it didn't matter what she ate now. She could wolf down a sloppy burger, dive into a bucket of wings, although she'd probably puke from the shock to her system.

Whocares.

She wasn't running tomorrow in Plattsburgh. The cortisone shot had helped a little, but not enough. She'd rested the two days as instructed, then went out for a few easy laps on the track on her own. At first, her knee held up and her spirits rose, and she went with the team for a light run on the grassy trails. Nothing vigorous, a pace where you can carry on a conversation. Dana stayed at the back of the pack and paired up with Marissa Pratt, another freshman, who came from Long Island and would take Dana's place in the meet if Dana couldn't run.

"How's it feeling?" Marissa asked.

"Right now, fine. I think the shot has done the trick."

"I hope so."

She sounded sincere, but if Dana's knee held up then Marissa would be watching the meet, not running in it.

"My boyfriend from home says he wants to drive up for the meet," Marissa said. "But if I'm only going to be an alternate, maybe I should tell him not to come."

Great. So the health of Dana's knee determined whether Marissa got to see her boyfriend this weekend. Marissa's comment also reminded Dana that she had to call her father and tell him whether she'd be running. There would be no reason for him to come if she couldn't compete.

"So you're probably hoping I can't run," Dana said.

Marissa got a stricken look on her face. "Oh, no—I don't mean it that way. What I really mean is, actually, I don't want him to come either way. He seems like part of a previous life, you know? One of the reasons I came here was to get away from my high school life."

"So tell him not to come."

"I might. But it's a hard call to make."

"Text message works."

Marissa laughed, as if Dana had given her a devilish idea. The text message was the same advice she'd given Steve, who on the way to class earlier that morning told Dana that his girlfriend from Syracuse was coming up tonight for the concert, but he kind of wanted to put her off. There seemed to be a lot of that going around. Steve was afraid of a "worlds colliding" situation; his girlfriend wasn't going to college, and Steve planned never to live in his hometown again. When Dana suggested he just tell her on the phone or by text message, he said he could never break up with someone in such an impersonal way, he'd have to do it in person.

Have you ever done that? Steve asked Dana.

If I had someone to break up with I might, she answered.

I'll keep that in mind, he said.

Afterward Dana thought about his response, whether he was implying anything about the two of them in the future, that they might hook up, fall in love—although their relationship wouldn't last and when Dana broke up with Steve via text message he wouldn't be surprised or outraged.

Just then the shout came from up front—*Pace!*—which meant a one-minute interval at race pace.

As soon as Dana lengthened her stride and increased her turnover she felt the stab in her knee, so painful she stumbled and Marissa had to reach out to keep her from falling. She tried to start up again but even a jog delivered the excruciating sting. The cortisone hadn't worked.

She must have fallen asleep because she bolted upright when the door opened.

"Oh, sorry, I thought you were still at practice," Jen said.

"Go away." Dana turned her back, facing the wall. Then she mumbled, "I'm sorry. You can come in."

They were already in. Jen and Mark sat on Jen's bed, Heidi joined Dana on hers, Steve stood in the doorway and introduced his girlfriend, Sarah. So he hadn't texted her after all.

"How's your knee?" Jen asked.

Dana bent her knee and rubbed the cap, as if trying to get information from a crystal ball. "I can't race tomorrow."

Jen groaned in sympathy. The others murmured in assent.

"That's such a drag," Jen said. "I know you really wanted to."

Steve stepped in and put an arm around her shoulder. "On the other hand," he said brightly, "now you can go to the concert tonight."

"What concert?"

"The one we've been talking about all week. Grace Potter—at Clarkson," Heidi said. "We're all going. That's why we're here now. We came to smoke a joint and brainstorm how to get there." She held up a fat joint for Dana to see.

"I've got my car," Steve said, "but it can only fit four. That leaves one of you looking for a ride, now two of you with Dana coming."

"I'm still going with the team to Plattsburgh in the morning," Dana said.

"Don't worry, we'll have you back by then."

Heidi, a lanky girl with hair like a bird's nest who lived in the suite with Dana and Jen, lit the joint and started passing it around. Dana leaned back and let Heidi pass it to Steve. She turned and opened the window over her bed to let the smoke drift out.

"Wait, there's one problem," Jen said. "Dana doesn't have a ticket and the show's sold out."

"I'll probably just stay here," Dana said. "The bus leaves at seven tomorrow."

"No, you're not going to *probably just stay here*," Steve said, mimicking Dana's monotone. His girlfriend looked at him as if he'd said something flirtatious. "There's always people scalping tickets out front."

"It's going to be a great show. Did you see the video of her covering Dylan's 'Tangled Up in Blue' on her website?"

The joint had made the rounds twice, Dana letting it pass both times although she was tempted to try it; she'd never smoked before or even wanted to, and the sudden lure of it puzzled her. But it was too late—Heidi snuffed the roach by licking her fingertips and squeezing off the red end. She turned and flicked it out the window.

Jen said, "So, how are we getting to Potsdam?"

A few minutes of stoned silence passed until Heidi perked up and said, "I know this guy Chuck who lives downstairs who said he was going to Massena this weekend. Maybe he can give us a ride."

Later, Jen and Dana stood side by side at the two sinks in their suite's bathroom. Jen applied mascara and eyeliner, giving life to her somber eyes. "I wish I had a car," Jen said. "You can't get anywhere around here without one. We're out in the middle of nowhere."

Jen had grown up in Boston and had the benefit of the T to get around the city.

"I had a car all summer but my father wouldn't let me bring it here," Dana said. "I didn't even try to argue with him about it. He said if I wanted to go somewhere I could go to the library."

"I'm really sorry you can't be in the race tomorrow," Jen said. "I know how important it is to you."

"Maybe next week," Dana said, although she was afraid that her knee might not be better next week, or all season for that matter. She cast her eyes down, trying to shake that thought. *Whatever.* When she looked up again, Jen was smiling at her in the mirror.

"What?"

Jen lowered her voice. "Can I show you something?"

Dana nodded. "Sure."

Jen was wearing a denim button shirt. She undid the top buttons and lifted her right boob from its bra cup. She had a wide, pillowy breast with a tiny areola and a nipple the size and color of a pencil eraser.

Dana held her breath and felt weakness in her legs, unsure what was transpiring and pretty sure she wouldn't like it.

Then Jen lifted her boob to reveal its underside. There, in dark blue ink, was a tattoo. At first Dana thought it was a teardrop, but then realized it was one half of the yin and yang symbol, the dark half, with a white dot.

"Wow, you got a tattoo," Dana said.

"Mark has the other half," Jen explained. "We got them today. There's a tattoo parlor right in town. The yin and yang represent the two energies of the world coming together to create everything. I know we haven't known each other that long, but it just feels so right to connect ourselves in this way."

"Is it permanent?"

"Of course it's permanent—it's a tattoo."

"I mean, I thought maybe it was one of those that wears off after a while."

"You don't approve?"

"No, it's fine."

Jen put her boob back in her bra and straightened her shirt. "I can see why you might think that a permanent mark on your skin isn't a positive thing," Jen said.

"I have nothing against tattoos," Dana said. "It's really beautiful."

They looked at each other in the mirror. Under the intensity of the bathroom lights, the inky, swollen mark beneath Dana's eye looked anything but beautiful. Of course she'd already clued Jen in on the details, how could she not? When you look like someone punched your face, there's always a story to tell, in this case the story of a venous malformation she'd had since birth. "Venous malformation": sounds like a misshapen planet, an embarrassment to an otherwise balanced solar system.

"So which half do you have?" Dana asked. "The yin or the yang?"

The question caught Jen by surprise, because she laughed and blushed. "I'm not sure."

Heidi entered the bathroom and went in the stall. "I got a ride for Dana and me, we leave at eight. This is so awesome. And I know this guy at Clarkson, I called him and he's going to meet me. He's going to the concert, too."

"I applied to Clarkson but didn't get in," Jen said.

"I didn't get into Brown and, like, two other colleges."

"What about you, Dana?"

The three of them now shared two sinks, Dana in the middle, trying to keep a steady hand with a mascara brush.

"This was my first choice," she said. "I got the scholarship, plus a writer I like went here and that made me want to come."

"Who?"

"Lorrie Moore—you probably haven't heard of her."

"No," Heidi said. Then added, "By the way, the ride is just one way. You'll have to find your own way home. I'll probably stay at Clarkson tonight."

"We'll find you a ride," Jen told Dana. "Even if you have to sit on a lap."

Jen reached for the buttons of her shirt. She said to Heidi, "Can I show you something?"

Just a Friend Doing a Favor

He leaned against his van watching Gwen run to comfort her boy. Moments ago he imagined making love to her; now he wanted to choke her. Anger heated him like a sudden fever. Sweat ran beneath his shirt. He had done her a favor he would not have done for others, getting her that puny fucking bag, a tiny gesture as a means to an end but breaking the rules of how he ran his business. And this is what she does in return.

When she drove out of the parking lot, he followed. He could run her off the road, send her rolling into a ditch, then stop to finish her off. Clamp down on her pretty neck and squeeze the breath from her. He sped up, accelerating out of each curve, closing in.

But then: Who was he kidding? As quickly as his anger had spiked, it died, like a firework banging brilliant trails of color before drifting into smoke. What was he thinking? He wasn't. He was gut reacting, a guaranteed way to make the situation worse, which is what he'd also done in letting his desire for Gwen build unchecked and unexplained. The way he had driven by her house this morning and pulled to the shoulder within sight distance of their property, the van's hold full, no real plan in place, just watching, then blessing his luck when she came out to her car. And then the real kicker: asking her to meet him later. Where exactly were they going to meet? At the cabin where Aaron operated the grow house? At her lake home where she vacationed with her family? Maybe he could bed her down in a mildewed mountain hotel while the biggest business deal of his life slipped away?

The deal. How would he get the deal done now? He'd never been touched by the police before. Never sold to the wrong customer. Never been stopped on the road. Never needed a last minute Plan B.

Now he did.

First order of business: get off the road and figure out his next steps.

He glanced in his side mirror to see who might be tailing him. No one. Not yet.

At the junction of Route 186 he stopped following Gwen's car and turned off. He snaked between Mount Adams and Rainbow Mountain for eight miles and turned again on the dirt road leading back to the cabin he knew to be safe. No one could locate him here, even if Gwen had told the police about him. His name was not associated with this property, never had been. There was no reason for anyone to believe he'd be up here.

Aaron's truck was gone. Good. This gave him time to think. He sat on the porch and willed himself to calm down. A vise clamped his chest. Breathe, he reminded himself. Use your head. Think it through.

Quit acting like a frightened, weak man. Think.

He could reasonably conclude no one had tracked him into the mountains or followed him on the road. You couldn't be tailed on these remote roads and not realize someone was behind you. Plus, no one would be looking for this van; it was registered to the dining company, not to Jude. And any surveillance on him would have taken place back in Morrissey, at Gull. A plainclothes posing as a patron: observing, finding nothing. Or a cornered rat set up to make a buy, wearing a wire. He hadn't been approached by anyone new. But, wait, Gwen had come into the bar a few nights ago, edgy and nervous. He thought it was because she wanted to be with him, didn't know how to express it or get started after being out of the game for so long. Could she have been bugged? But she never asked about getting more—he'd been the one to ask her if she'd run out already. Idiot.

No, she couldn't have been wired. She said she'd come to Gull to tip him about the police.

There was no one setting him up.

There was Sweet.

Of course. Sweet had trapped him. Gwen had told the police where she'd gotten the pot and they set Jude up using Sweet, who was either an informant or a cop himself, all of this put into play because he'd gotten careless and sold Gwen a few buds of weed as a way to see her again. Panic and disgust choked him as he comprehended his situation, realized what a fool he'd been.

If he had not run into Gwen at the gas station, he'd be on his way to rendezvous with Sweet and a police ambush right now, and he didn't have the Jericho with him. Not that he'd instigate a shootout, unless it were to turn the gun inward. That's what he'd always told himself: he'd go out before he'd go down, but who really knew until the moment came.

Yet the only reason he could avoid that moment now is because Gwen had tipped him off.

And then he understood Sweet couldn't be the one. Jude had been negotiating with Sweet before Gwen had come to see him the first time last winter. Sweet was clean. Sweet was his business partner, even though Jude had never trusted him.

No, Jude was scaring himself, still not thinking clearly.

He looked up Gwen's number on his phone and called.

When she answered, he started by thanking her for letting him know, trying to put her at ease.

She whispered something he couldn't hear. There was a voice in the background.

When did you tell the police?

She couldn't talk. She'd call him back.

She cut the connection.

He sat on the stoop of the porch and watched yellow leaves fluttering in a stand of birches. Cloud cover moved in, blocking the sun behind a hazy white blanket. Think. How fucked was he? How much evidence did they have? Sweet had paid him half the money—did the police see that transaction? Were they watching him that night? He'd provided Sweet a sample of product—the sample alone was evidence enough against him. But the police could not have discovered much about him in a few weeks. With Dana preparing to go off to school, Jude had been lying low on the business side while helping her get ready. Focusing on finalizing arrangements with Sweet. Working with Simon to set up the online pharmacies, cultivating clients with that kind of taste. Ritalin instead of coke. Opiates instead of pot. Off the street and online. Not much traffic for an observer to see.

Maybe the situation wasn't so bleak. With no one looking for the van and no need to stop at Gull, he could drive directly to Sweet's location and make the delivery, earn his profit on this deal and get out now. This one deal would be a good nut; there was no need to get greedy.

He walked to the van and opened the back and decided it looked empty. He stood there staring at the hold for a long time, but couldn't get himself back into the driver's seat and on the road. He couldn't put himself out there.

His phone rang. He saw Gwen's number in the display and answered.

"I wanted to explain myself," she said. "I mean—why I did it."

"Go ahead."

She launched into her story: the accident, the police finding the bag of pot in her car, testing her blood in the hospital, the other driver dying. Then came the threat of indictment for vehicular manslaughter if she didn't reveal where she'd gotten the bag—even though the evidence showed she wasn't at fault in the accident.

"I kept telling them it was just a friend doing me a favor. I didn't want to give your name. But they really pushed. It's a big deal because there have been problems with drugs in the schools and the police are following up on every little thing."

"So now they're following me."

"I don't know. That's why I'm telling you."

"Did they ask you to wear a wire and try to make another buy from me?"

"No, nothing like that."

"To record our phone calls, like this one?"

"They didn't ask me to do anything else."

"So the police think I'm selling drugs to schoolchildren in Morrissey," Jude said. An echo followed his voice, as if someone were repeating his words.

"That's what they said they want to find out."

"What do you think, Gwen?"

She paused, then answered. "I think you're a friend who did me a favor."

He said, "I have a daughter, she's just eighteen years old." He was a single parent, he reminded Gwen. He loved his daughter. He tried to raise her well. He read to her, helped her with school work, attended her track meets. He protected her. Sacrificed his personal life. "Do you remember, Gwen—that night when you watched Dana for me and she asked if you were going to be her new mother? I knew how confusing that could be for a young child. That's the last time I let that situation occur."

"We both have families to think of," Gwen said. "Everyone would have known. I'd be barred from volunteering in the school. My kids, they would have been shunned. You don't know what it's like in Morrissey."

"I understand. I know you had no choice."

"Thank you for saying that. I didn't want to get you in any trouble, I never intended to."

"I know that. Forget about this police business, it's just an unfortunate turn for both of us, I'm sure it will blow over."

"That's what I was hoping."

"They'll discover that following me is very dull."

"You mean you're not . . ."

"Let's not talk about it anymore." Instead: Would she come see him when they were back in Morrissey?

She didn't hesitate. "I told you, I can't do that." She sounded strong and definitive, but also stilted, as if she'd expected his question and rehearsed a response.

"We could have been something, Gwen, you and I. That time we spent together, there was something special between us."

"That was years ago. We have different lives now."

"You reached out to me, remember. Just to buy something—was that the only reason you came to see me?"

She hesitated. "No, not just that."

"Then what, Gwen? Tell me."

"You haven't been carrying some kind of torch for me all this time," she said. "I won't believe it. You didn't carry one back then, we didn't have that kind of relationship."

"Let's say I've rediscovered you. I've been imagining you." He clenched the phone in his hand. "Okay, I've said too much." This wasn't turning out the way he wanted, none of it. Why couldn't he control himself? "Actually, if you think about it, you're the one who's said too much."

"That's the reason I called—to apologize," she said.

"So isn't it your turn to do me a favor?"

"I just did you one, telling you about the police."

"You'll come see me?"

"It's flattering, but, I know I might seem ungrateful, and if the situation were different and I were free . . ."

She stopped speaking.

"You want to say yes."

Silence.

"Gwen, are you still there?"

"No. Jude, please."

"Where are you right now?"

I Want Mommy

They fished for over an hour with Walter Garrison, catching nothing despite Mr. Garrison's assurances that any minute now Nate or Nora or both of them would hook a fat, juicy trout. The entire time Brian kept watch on the house and when Walter motored around a dogleg in the lake and beyond the sight line of the house Brian asked him to turn back the other way.

They stayed in the boat until the kids got hungry and Walter headed back to the dock. Brian said there was nothing wrong with having peanut butter and jelly for lunch instead of trout.

Gwen wasn't home.

"Where's Mommy?" Nate asked.

"I'm not sure," Brian said.

"She went for a walk," Nora said. "She said there was no room for her in the boat."

It fit for Brian, at first. He figured she needed alone time to collect herself and expend tension after her encounter with Gates at the market.

"Did she say where she was walking?" Brian asked.

Nora shook her head.

There wasn't anywhere to go except along the road. It curved in and out with the shape of the lake and was pretty and quiet enough for a walk, although you were confined by the waterfront houses on one side and a rugged wooded tract on the other leading up the eastern slope of Mount Adams. She could walk down the road, and then walk back the same way.

Brian made sandwiches for the kids and poured milk. He drank leftover coffee from the morning. He suggested they go for ice cream and Nate said they bought ice cream at the store.

"We can save that for later," Brian said. "I'm in the mood for a cone."

"Me too," said Nora.

"We can have ice cream twice today?" Nate asked.

"Why not?"

The kids cheered and ran out to the car. Brian left a note on the counter for Gwen.

He drove to the market Gwen and Nate had gone to that morning, where they sold soft ice cream from a window at the side of the building. He looked for Gwen along the way but saw only the flattened remains of a raccoon along the side of the road and two bicyclists riding in the other direction.

At the market, they stood in a short line waiting their turn and all three of them ordered a vanilla twist, Nora with a butterscotch dip, Nate with rainbow sprinkles, Brian plain old. They licked their cones at one of the picnic tables set up in a grassy area next to the parking lot. The sun dipped behind a bank of clouds moving in from the west and Nate started complaining he was cold. Brian wanted to ask his son what he saw happen between Gwen and the other man, but Nate would detect something wrong and so Brian kept his thoughts to himself.

He drove back the long way, taking a left instead of a right on the road circumventing the lake to approach their house from the opposite direction. Nate fell asleep. Nora leaned her forehead against the window and stared out. Brian began to worry.

His initial fear was that Jude had indeed followed Gwen back to the house and had picked a spot to wait, then snatched her when he saw her, the drug kingpin motivated by revenge for the ratting out. But the snatch theory was unlikely: Gwen said that at one point Jude had stopped following her and turned off, and Brian hadn't lost sight of the house for more than a few minutes when they were out on Walt Garrison's boat. He would have noticed any vehicles. Plus, Brian doubted Jude was immersed in that way as a drug dealer, although he had pointed out just that possibility whenever Gwen insisted that Jude was only a friend doing her a favor.

The other explanation was that Gwen's involvement with Jude was more than old friends, former lovers, or business. He played this scenario out: she runs into him at the market, is consumed with guilt and remorse at having given his name to the police, not because she broke a promise to him and compromised her own integrity but because she's attracted to him and he to her and they've been planning and hoping for an opportunity together. Her visit to Gull the other night was just a prelude to the main event. At this moment she's tucked away in a mountain hideaway rolling him in the sheets.

Come on. This was even less likely than her being abducted. Not that Gwen or any other adult wasn't capable of carrying on an affair—just look in the mirror, buddy, and think about Teresa, whom you rejected yet knew that if he had been more attracted to her, if he had been a tad weaker, if he had wanted to get back at Gwen, it might have gone the other way. At least it fell within the realm of possibility. And for Gwen? He believed their marriage was strong, but knew the flesh was weak.

But the facts didn't add up. If Gwen had been plotting a liaison with Gates, she would have made up a different story to cover for the other night. She would not have told Brian she ran into Gates at the market or been so tense about it. And she would have planned the deed for back in Morrissey, when the kids were at school and he at work and Gwen had time to herself.

He ran through remaining possibilities: she met a neighbor while walking and stopped to visit, she left the road and walked in the woods, she was hit by a car and tossed into a ditch on the side of the road.

Or the most likely possibility: she'd be at the house when they got back.

Only she wasn't.

The note remained where he'd left it on the counter. Her purse and sweater on a chair. Her hiking boots by the door. Wherever she was going she hadn't planned to be gone for long. He turned on his phone to see if she'd called. He had five messages—all of them from work. He skipped them without listening. Nothing from Gwen. He tried calling her number and got voice mail. He called again. Same thing.

He hid his distress and explained to the kids that Mom wanted some time to herself and went for a long hike. But now the sky had turned uniformly gray and a faint rain began to fall.

The house was well stocked with games and books. Brian occupied the kids playing checkers and Life and cards and reading from a book of fairy tales. He made two bags of popcorn. He mixed lemonade. The rest of the afternoon passed and evening came, and with it a steadier rain. Brian decided to call the county sheriff. He took his phone upstairs so the kids wouldn't hear.

He called directory assistance for the nonemergency number and spoke to a deputy named Clay McAllister. He explained that his wife had been missing since before noon when she went out for a walk and he suspected she might be in trouble.

"What's your wife's name, sir?"

"Gwen Raine."

"What kind of trouble, sir? Do you mean that she's lost?"

"She could be lost, but it could be more than that. She . . ." He started to break down and couldn't get his words out. He began again. "There's a possibility my wife has been abducted," he told the deputy.

"Why do you think that?"

He lowered his voice further and tried to explain. He could see Nora at the bottom of the stairs, looking up at him, her face a replica of Gwen's when stressed.

"I'm sorry, you'll have to speak up, sir. Are you on a cell phone?"

"My children are right here. My wife is missing and may be in danger."

Deputy McAllister told Brian he would send someone out to the house.

Brian started to protest but there was no point. The kids were already spooked. He took the stairs down two at a time and put on a cheerleader face and said, "Hey, we haven't had dinner yet, how about Daddy grills the chicken?"

"I'm not hungry," said Nate.

"Where's Mommy?" Nora asked.

"We have to eat dinner," Brian said.

"I don't want to."

"Who were you talking to?"

"When's Mommy coming home?"

He sat with them on the couch, one in each arm, and explained that, number one, Mommy might have gotten lost on her walk and the police were going to help find her and, two, everything was going to be fine. The police help find lost people all the time.

"Did she walk for twenty miles?" Nate asked.

"I'm not sure how far she walked," Brian said.

"Is she walking in the rain?"

"We don't know, but Mommy is very smart. If she got lost, she'll find a dry place to stay until the rain stops."

As if on cue, the rain intensified at that moment, drumming on the porch roof and gurgling through the gutter and down-spout.

The person Deputy Sheriff Clay McAllister sent over was himself, an officer of the law who looked all of twenty-two years old to Brian and fresh from the academy. Brian wished they had a TV to distract the kids while he spoke with McAllister; instead he gave them each a bowl of Lucky Charms and told them it was very important they play quietly or look at books while he spoke with the police officer.

He stepped out on the porch and the first thing McAllister said was that if Brian wanted to file a missing persons report he would have to wait at least twenty-four hours from the time he'd last seen his wife.

"I just want to tell you what's going on, and maybe you can help me decide what to do," Brian said.

"The sheriff's department is here to help in any way we can, sir," McAllister said. Straight out of a textbook of standard re-sponses.

Brian recounted the story of Gwen buying a small bag of marijuana—he was embarrassed telling it—from this Jude Gates, who his wife claimed was an old friend. She was later arrested with the marijuana in her possession and coerced—not coerced, persuaded—to tell the police where she'd gotten it because the police in Morrissey were motivated to investigate sources. Then, just today, she ran into Jude Gates at the market in Adams Station and admitted to him that she gave the police in Morrissey his name.

McAllister looked surprised at this last detail. "Why would she do that?

"I've been trying to figure that out myself."

"What did she tell you?"

"That it just came out. I think she felt guilty. Like I said, she considers him an old friend."

"But he's a drug dealer?"

All Brian really knew was that his wife had gotten marijuana from him on two occasions, in both cases small amounts. Who knows who deals drugs these days?

"How does your wife know Mr. Gates?"

"She worked in a restaurant he used to manage, years ago, before we were married."

"And they stayed in touch since then?"

"Not that I know of. I think just recently, when she was looking for . . . a place to buy something." Brian leaned against the door and crossed his arms.

"I see. Is she involved with him, on a personal level?"

"No."

"In a romantic way."

"No."

"Are you sure?"

"Yes, I'm sure." Not as sure as he wanted to be, but Brian did not want that line of reasoning pursued; he didn't see the benefit. If the police thought Gwen was having an affair, they'd lose interest, thinking she had run off with Gates, leaving a cuckold to wring his hands and call the police about his missing wife.

McAllister nodded, as if wiser than his years. "Do you have any idea why Mr. Gates would be here in Tear Lake?"

"My wife said he has a place in the mountains somewhere around here. I don't know where. And he knows we have a house on Tear Lake."

"How does he know that?"

Brian stared at the rain dripping from the edge of the porch roof.

McAllister continued. "And you say she left around noon to go for a walk and you haven't seen or heard from her since?"

"That's right."

"If you'll excuse me for a moment, sir."

McAllister stepped down from the porch and walked to his cruiser. He'd left the headlights on and engine running, the wipers slapping back and forth on intermittent setting.

Brian glanced through the door to check on the kids. They had finished their cereal and were sitting together on the floor in front of a bookcase, paging through books together. They looked so sweet right now, close together, bodies touching, and he felt horrible for having exposed them to this. And what had he provided for a healthy dinner to nurture them? Lucky Charms.

McAllister came back to the porch. Raindrops spotted his gray Mountie-style hat and the epaulets on his shoulders. He told Brian that no properties in the county were deeded to the name of Jude Gates.

"Sir, did your wife say anything about Mr. Gates acting aggressive or threatening her?"

"No, nothing. But she did say when she drove away from the market that he was behind her for a while and she thought at first he was following her and she got scared, but then he turned off at 186."

"And your wife was alone all through this?"

"No, my son, Nathaniel, was with her."

"Can I speak to him?"

"Nate? Why?"

"Maybe he heard or noticed something that could be helpful."

Brian opened the door and invited the deputy sheriff in. The kids turned and stared at him. Brian told Nate that Sheriff McAllister would like to ask him a few questions about being with Mommy at the market today.

Nate stood and approached, wary of the uniformed man towering over him. Nora stayed back by the books on the floor. McAllister removed his hat and introduced himself. He asked if Nate had been with his mother when she was talking to a man outside the market today.

Nate nodded that he had.

"Did you hear what they were talking about?"

Nate looked down at the floor.

Brian held his breath. What had Gwen said in front of Nate?

"It's okay, buddy, you can tell us," Brian said.

"Mom yelled at me for picking bugs off the truck."

"Picking bugs?" Brian said.

"Dead ones."

"Which truck?"

"It was a van, but not a minivan like ours," Nate said. "It had a lot of dead bugs on the front."

"What do mean, not like ours? What did it look like?"

"CR74642," Nate said.

"Excuse me?" said McAllister.

Nate repeated the sequence.

"What does that mean?" McAllister asked.

"Is that the license plate number?" Brian asked.

Nate nodded yes.

"He noted the license plate number?" McAllister asked, looking doubtfully from Nate to Brian.

Nora piped in from her spot on the floor. "He's better at math and I'm better at reading."

"Thank you very much," McAllister said. He asked Nate if he'd heard anything else, but the boy shook his head. McAllister motioned for Brian to come back out on the porch.

"I'll be right back," Brian said to the kids.

The rain had stopped, replaced by a mountain night chill. Brian shivered. McAllister said he would run the plate to see if in fact it was a correct number and to find out the name on the vehicle registration, but beyond that there wasn't a lot they could do, at least not until twenty-four hours had passed since Mrs. Raine had been missing, at which time Brian would have the option of filing a missing persons report.

"Can't you look for the van? Put an APB out for it or something?" Brian wondered whether there even was such a thing as an all points bulletin, or was that just from TV.

"If the vehicle does belong to Mr. Gates, I could have it flagged in the state database to alert police departments in the event the van happened to be stopped."

"But you won't proactively search for it?"

McAllister apologized. At this point, no. He suggested Brian call Mercy County Hospital in Tupper Lake and Placid Memorial Hospital to see if any unidentified woman fitting his wife's description had been admitted. You said she doesn't have any identification on her?

She didn't have her wallet, it was right here in her purse. She might have her phone, which he had tried calling.

McAllister said that in these cases the missing person usually wants to be missing, and that Brian would likely hear from her soon enough.

"In these cases?" Brian said. McAllister was playing the runaway/

affair angle again. "Are you speaking from your years of experience?"

"I'm just going by the statistics, sir."

"You're right. I'm sorry."

"Give us a call tomorrow if you want to file a report," McAllister reminded him.

Brian composed himself before going back inside. He put on his brightest face and told the kids that the police were going to help and Mommy should be back very soon.

"But where is she?" Nora asked.

"We don't know exactly."

"I want Mommy."

"I want Mommy too."

And they looked at each other and started to cry and Brian wanted to cry, too, and he wanted to smash something and he wanted to shake Gwen by the shoulders and snuggle against her warm neck. He settled for maintaining his composure and getting the kids ready for bed. He sat on the floor between their beds and read book after book until eventually he heard first Nate breathing heavy and steady and a few minutes after that, Nora.

Ticket to the Concert

Dana took the back while Heidi sat up front with Chuck. It was only a twenty-minute ride to Potsdam. Dana dug out her phone. She called her father, who didn't pick up, because it was Friday night and the bar would be full.

"I'm not racing tomorrow, so don't come to Plattsburgh," she said in her message. She explained her knee hadn't healed and the cortisone helped but not enough and she could miss more than just this week. Dana expected the words to stick in her throat, as if delivering news of death or disaster, but it was easy, almost a relief. She experienced an unexpected sense of freedom and spontaneity. After, she scrolled up and down the contacts listed on her phone. At the beginning of the list she saw Aaron's name. He was the guy she'd met in the kitchen at Gull when she'd gone out back to get her sweater from the car. He'd been standing by the back door, plate in hands near his chin, forking in food like a starving refugee. He hadn't noticed her until she was almost upon him.

Why are you eating back here? she asked him.

He swallowed what was in his mouth. I'm sorry, am I in the way?

Um—no, but the party is out front.

There's a party?

Who are you? she asked.

He was just making a delivery and heading out. Grabbing a bite to eat first. Jude said it was okay.

He looked for a place to set down his plate, and put it on the top of a laundry hamper near the door. He looked out the back again.

What's out there?

Nothing. You want to smoke a bowl?

No thank you.

He wore a baseball cap that cast a shadow across a dent in the top part of his cheek. Some of the bone must have been missing because it looked like an inch of his face had caved in under his eye.

He caught her staring. You must get a lot of that, too, he said.

Sorry. Yeah, I do. All my life I've had this.

I'm still getting used to it.

Where are you from? Dana asked.

And that's when they exchanged numbers: he lived not far from where she was going to school in Canton. It would be cool to get together. Maybe they'd call each other. Neither had.

Until now. Dana pressed his number. He didn't pick up and she was about to hang up but when she heard his message—"Talk"—she started to ramble, Hi, Aaron, this is Dana, we met at Gull and I wanted you to know I'm going to be in Potsdam tonight to see a concert at Clarkson, I don't have a ticket yet but I heard you can get them out front and I thought if you aren't doing anything maybe you can meet me there, if you like music, anyway give me a call if you want, but you're probably not around, so anyway . . .

"Who's that?" Heidi asked from the front seat.

"This guy I know."

"Do you have a boyfriend you've been keeping secret from us?"

"I just met him before I came up. He lives around here."

Chuck dropped them off at the Student Center in Clarkson and they followed the crowd making its way to Fander Hall. The plan was to meet Steve and the others near the front door, once Dana got her ticket.

"Do you see anyone selling tickets?"

"Let's look around," Heidi said. "How much money have you got?"

"Enough." She still had the three one-hundred-dollar bills her father had given her and had brought them along, although she'd never need that much.

At first they mulled around near the front doors and then walked farther out to a plaza of concrete planters and benches. Too bad it was raining now. Dana put up the hood on her jacket and walked with Heidi, waiting for a scalper to announce tickets.

They didn't have to wait long. A guy in a Clarkson jacket walked past, repeating over and over: "Tickets. Who needs tickets. Tickets. Who needs tickets."

"I do," Dana said.

The guy stopped and showed two tickets. "One-fifty for two. Tenth row."

They were better seats than the balcony seats her friends had.

"I only need one."

"You gotta buy both."

"Okay," she said, thinking she'd get one for Aaron, too. If he showed up. If he got her message. If he cared.

After meeting up with Steve and the others, Dana followed them to the bleachers and never went to her ticketed seat. She parked herself in the aisle next to Heidi's seat on the end and once the concert started it didn't matter anyway because everyone got to their feet and danced. Someone passed a leather flask down the line and it ended up with Dana. She smelled the alcohol—some kind of mixed cocktail, she thought—and started to hand it back but remembered she wasn't running tomorrow. She took a small sip that stuck in her throat like a hot ember. No wonder she wasn't much of a drinker. No one would mistake her for a campus party girl, which seemed to be her father's worst fear. She didn't even stay out late; if she were running tomorrow, she'd already be in bed asleep.

The band played for more than two hours. Dana's ears rang from within, setting her head humming, and after a second encore she followed her gang to a bar across the street from campus. They carried fake IDs Steve had made up and sold for fifty dollars each during the first week of the semester. Good thing. A doorman checked everyone coming in and turned away a lot of people from the concert.

"Hey, no fighting in there," the doorman said to Dana as he let her pass.

Another witty comment about her eye. Hands in her jacket pocket, she shot him the finger.

The bar was elbow to elbow, sweaty as a locker room. Her group carved out space in a rear room with a pool table, although there were too many people for anyone to play pool. Steve and Mark headed for the bar and came back ten minutes later with two pitchers of beer and a tray of glasses. Steve poured and Mark handed beers around. Dana tried to strike up a conversation with Steve's girlfriend, Sarah, but all she got were one-word answers. The guy Heidi knew in Potsdam had met her in the bar and now three couples were paired off with Dana solo. She took a sip from her beer and put it on a shelf on the back wall of the bar. She still had songs in her head from the concert and she swayed on her feet. She stifled a yawn. It was after midnight and for the first time she wondered how they were going to get back to the dorm.

"Don't worry about it," Heidi said. "Have some fun."

"I am having fun."

Then someone moved between Dana and Heidi. It was Aaron.

"Hey, you got my message."

"Yeah, but I was late and couldn't get in, so I hung around by the doors thinking I might catch you on the way out."

"You waited the whole concert outside?"

Aaron shrugged. Looked like an aw-shucks gesture to Dana, like it was no big deal waiting two hours, mostly in the rain, just for her.

"I got you a ticket." She pulled the unused ticket out of her purse.

"Oh, cool, sorry. I'll pay you for it."

"No, that's okay. It was part of a package deal."

"Let me buy you a drink then."

She held up her full glass of beer. "I've got one."

He was staring at her and she waited for him to say something. Finally: "So is that a birthmark?"

She hesitated and he plowed on. "Only because, well, I thought I'd ask, you said you had it all your life and . . ."

How dreary to tell the same story over and over—it wasn't really a birthmark, although she'd had it from birth—and so Dana had crafted several variations of the story. For those thinking themselves witty or original when they asked who punched her, she might reply: "My parents beat me" or "I got mugged." One that pinged the moronic boys was "My boyfriend hit me." With that statement she could learn a lot about a boy. The brave ones would puff up thinking they could dispatch the abusive boyfriend and take his place—until realizing they didn't want to take the bad boyfriend's place beside a girl with a smeared face; the gnome boys, on the other hand, would back off, not wanting to mess with a guy willing to pound his girl in such a fashion. She'd already encountered a few of both types of boys this week on campus.

But she didn't use any of these stories on Aaron. Because there was something incongruent about his face, he'd earned the right to the truth, although she wondered if he was talking to her only because of the mark on her face—for the exact opposite reason other boys ignored her.

She told him it was called venous malformation, a collection of extra veins that discolored and swelled beneath her eye. She was supposed to have surgery over winter break. There was nothing that could be done about it while she was a child, but the past year she had been to vascular surgeons, ophthalmologists, and neurologists and undergone numerous scans that indicated the veins were not integrally linked to the ocular veins or vessels connected to the brain. Surgery was the recommended option. Something like a sclerotherapy, which women do to get rid of spider veins, injecting the veins with a solution that would kill them. Scheduled for semester break in January, with a follow-up procedure in June.

"So it will be gone?"

"Hopefully," Dana said. "It might not work a hundred percent but it should get a lot lighter."

He took this news by finishing the rest of his beer—close to half the bottle in one long slurp down his throat—and again asking Dana if he could get her a drink. Again she pointed to her own almost full glass on the shelf and said she was all set. As if to prove she wasn't much of a drinker, she picked up her glass and took a small sip and replaced it.

"I'll be right back," Dana said.

She turned and made her way toward her friends. Heidi took hold of her arm and said, "Is *that* the guy you wanted to meet?"

"He's a nice guy."

"What happened to his face?"

Dana shrugged. "What happened to mine?"

She checked the time and it was going on one o'clock. She asked Heidi again about getting back to the dorm.

"Ask Steve for a ride. I told you I'm staying here tonight." Her friend from Potsdam was a tall jock type, with a shaved head and thick neck. Heidi held a pink drink but not very well. She tipped the glass and some of it sloshed over the rim.

"Just don't ask him now," Heidi added. "Look, he's having the breakup talk with his girlfriend."

Steve was in a back corner of the bar leaning over Sarah and she had tears in her eyes, and Dana thought: he should have taken my advice and used a text message; it would have saved the girlfriend a long trip up.

When she got back to Aaron he was standing exactly as she had left him, leaning back with his elbows on the shelf next to her beer. He looked like he hadn't moved at all.

"You know, I was thinking, you don't need that operation," he said.

"What operation?"

"Your eye. You're already pretty hot."

She reacted as if he'd literally stroked her, arching her back, warmth rippling her spine.

"I'm getting it anyway," she said.

He shifted back and forth on his feet and settled in a stance that listed to one side, as if he were having trouble with balance.

Her mouth was dry and that current she'd felt running down her spine turned out to be a bead of sweat. She took off her jacket and reached for her beer and this time took several sips.

"So I hear you're a produce supplier. Do you work on an organic farm or something?"

"A what?"

"You deliver produce to Gull, right?"

"Where did you hear that?"

She smiled. "Are you going to tell me anything about yourself or not?"

Sense of Direction

Kids finally asleep, Brian alone downstairs. He drank one of the beers Gwen had bought at the market but it did little for his nerves. He didn't dare another. He needed a clear head, although there was nothing to do except wait and pace.

He'd driven the roads. He'd called the sheriff. How else could he help?

He circled the possibilities again: Gwen stalked and caught by Gates as punishment for informing on him, or Gwen having an affair. Neither made sense. Gates hadn't followed her and couldn't have been lurking near their house waiting to find her alone. And Gwen wouldn't run off with him after coming home anxious about seeing him.

Which left getting lost or injured.

He tried her cell phone again. No answer. He tried their home number in Morrissey and got Gwen's voice saying *You've reached the Raine residence,* followed by Nora and Nate chiming in together to please leave a message. His throat tightened and he hung up.

The only other thing he could think to do was call Detective Keller in Morrissey. Maybe he had turned up something in his investigation that might be useful, to either cast hope or deal further despair on the situation.

He still had Keller's card in his wallet with the detective's cell phone number written on the back. He pressed the numbers.

"It's Brian Raine," he announced when Keller answered. "You're handling the case of my wife, Gwen. I think she might be in trouble—with Jude Gates."

"Don't tell me she's dealing with him?" His voice sounded surprised.

"No. He knows Gwen reported him to the police."

Keller sighed into the phone, the long, heavy exhale of the exhausted and exasperated, all surprise gone.

"What did she go and do that for?"

Brian went through the story—the trip to the Adirondacks, Gwen running into Gates at the market, admitting to him what she'd done, coming home and telling Brian about it, then going for a walk and not coming back.

"I called the county sheriff. He thinks she's having an affair and will come home when she's ready to, or not come home at all."

"It is the most likely situation," Keller agreed.

"Jesus Christ, is that all you people think about?"

"Settle down, Mr. Raine, I know this is upsetting. I'm here to help you."

"Gwen wouldn't have told me about meeting him if she was trying to sneak off and have an affair."

"Your wife tells more than she should sometimes, as we've just discovered. This could be another example: she wants to be caught. It's not unusual."

Brian could understand why Keller would see it that way, but the detective was wrong. "What about Gates?" Brian asked. "Does he want to be caught?"

"That's a good question. We're still not sure where he stands in all this."

"You haven't found anything on him?"

"And now we'll find even less. Doesn't your wife know that tipping off a suspect puts a damper on our investigation, let alone that she can be charged as an accomplice?"

"You said you were going to help me."

Keller paused. "I am going to help you. What else can you tell me?"

Brian told Keller about the van Gates was driving and the license plate number his son had memorized, and that the sheriff could not identify any property owned by Jude Gates on the county tax rolls.

"Let me see what I can come up with," Keller said. "Can I reach you at this number?"

"Yes, it's my cell. I'm at our house now in Tear Lake."

"Is it raining up there like it is here?"

"It was," said Brian. "Looks like it's over now."

"I'll get back to you."

So this is helplessness, a condition he knew little about. He'd always been a person of action, a decision maker, and now his only action was to go upstairs and get into bed. When the aloneness and anxiety piled on and tried to suffocate him, he got up and went into the kids.

Nora had kicked away her blanket; he tucked her back in, kissing her forehead. Nate had pushed himself against the wall. Brian climbed in with him, causing his son to stir, and Brian whispered: it's okay, it's okay; and he lay his cheek on a warm downy spot on the nape of his son's neck and tried to be still and silent and strong, but mostly he repeated Gwen's name over and over to himself.

Gwen had walked along the road and cut up the old fire trail she recognized near their house. She climbed beyond the ledge where she and her family had picnicked in June. She returned Jude's call.

After speaking with Jude for a few minutes, she decided that telling him about the police was the right thing to do. He thanked her for explaining the situation: the accident, the arrest, the charges. He told her the police would be bored following him. He told her to forget the whole episode.

She was so relieved by his words that she missed the transition in their conversation when it stopped being about Gwen explaining what she did and Jude understanding 100 percent, and started being about Jude propositioning her again.

When she did notice, when he reminded her about the intensity of their brief relationship years ago, when he asked about her coming to see him again, she still was so grateful he wasn't angry that she relaxed her guard. She protested his advances, but not too much. Rather than ending the call, she allowed herself to listen to what he had to say. Didn't she? She couldn't help wondering what triggered his interest in her. Why her? Why now?

The thing about living in Morrissey is that you can lose your sense of uniqueness. You probably could swap places with almost any other woman you knew and no one would notice. The Morrissey wives. The names and faces and little problems and joys would change, but ultimately it reduced down to kids, school, home, taxi service, and if you were lucky, occasional intimacy with your husband.

You were no more special than your neighbor. No one made passes at you. No men told you how beautiful you looked. And each year the likelihood of being noticed seemed further past, which 90 percent of the time didn't matter because you were already 90 percent fulfilled with your life. You could harbor fantasies to close the small gap, but there really wasn't anyone to be the object of your fantasies. The husbands were as interchangeable as the wives. Those key parties Gwen had heard about taking place in the seventies weren't as daring as they sounded. So you went home with someone else's spouse for a night; you might not even notice.

So she let Jude flatter her. It was hard to resist having her ego stroked this way. And it was only over the phone; she wasn't going to take it any further. She knew she wouldn't see him again. In any event, it was much better than being frightened because he was angry with her over telling the police.

But then he asked where she was at that moment, and she recognized his intent to find her and be with her right now. His question snapped her back to reality, caused her to look up and shift her focus. What she saw was unfamiliar.

And then the line went dead.

She stared at her phone. The battery had drained. No charge, no signal. She studied the blank display a few seconds longer and then looked up again. She took a moment to catch her breath, and then turned and looked behind her, in the direction she'd come from. At least Gwen thought it was the direction she'd come from. She walked a few yards that way. Where was the trail? She stood at the edge of a small meadow, with dense stands of trees on three sides and on the fourth a rocky outpost that grew into an escarpment as it curved out of sight into forested land. A breeze flitted the treetops, but otherwise a silence surrounded her like a solid wall.

A shot of adrenaline surged through her, leaving her stomach queasy and throat hot and dry.

She looked at the sky. When had the sun disappeared behind the clouds? She turned in a circle, trying to decide which way was back down. None of them looked down. There was no horizon, no view. Only trees and boulders.

One skill she had never learned was how to avoid getting lost. She was terrible at following directions and often took wrong turns driving in unfamiliar areas. She didn't remember landmarks.

Once in New York City she'd taken the subway to Brooklyn to visit a friend in Marine Park but turned the wrong way when she emerged from underground and walked for blocks and blocks until she realized she'd ended up in a decrepit neighborhood where no one looked like her and everyone looked at her. Fortunately, she spotted a policeman in a squad car and enlisted his help. Brian wanted to know what it was about women and their sense of direction. She resented his sexist generalization but in her case it was true. One of her earliest memories was being lost. She was three or four and playing outside and was supposed to stay in front of her own house and she always did, but that day she happened to see a beautiful black cat on the lawn next door and she went over to pet it and the cat started to purr but then the cat started to walk away and without thinking, Gwen followed. She followed it down the sidewalk all the way to the corner, which was only three houses away, and then around the corner. When she turned the corner, the cat had disappeared.

Gwen had told this story to the kids once.

Did you go back home? Nora asked.

I tried, Gwen said. But the problem was that a tall hedge bordered the corner house, and as soon as Gwen had turned the corner, the hedge blocked the view of her own house and she no longer knew where she lived. She was lost. And scared. She sat down on the sidewalk right at the base of the hedge and started to cry. She didn't know how long she cried for. Then a lady walking down the sidewalk approached her carrying a shopping bag from the market and she asked why Gwen was crying, and Gwen answered she didn't know. The woman said, I know you, you're Irene Cassert's little girl and I know where you live. She reached into her groceries and came out with a whole bag of Hershey's Kisses which she gave to Gwen, and she walked her home around the corner and back to her mother.

How many Hershey's Kisses did you eat? Nate asked.

I shared them with my brother and sister.

You got lost just around the corner?

I was little.

Now she was grown up. But her sense of direction hadn't gotten much better and so she was lost again, and instead of being just around the corner from home she was in a mountainous wilderness and could see no guardian angel with a bag of Hershey's Kisses who would take her hand and lead her home. If Gwen was going to be saved, she'd have to do it herself.

Okay, then. She'd just have to find her way back to the trail. One thing she remembered from Girl Scouts was how to find a trail you'd lost. You walked in a rectangular pattern, small rectangles, then larger ones, fanning farther and farther out with each pass until you came upon the trail. That's what Gwen would do, although she'd never had to do it before.

A hawk circled overhead, pierced the air with a long screech, then drifted away.

Gwen set out, somewhat confident, but the terrain varied up and down and she had to detour around thick brush and rock formations. It was difficult to know if she'd covered the same territory or was working a proper grid. Her feet grew sore in her thin shoes.

An hour later she'd walked many rectangles. An hour after that the rain started falling.

Out to Catch Bad Guys

After getting off the phone with Mr. Raine, Keller returned to the Yankee game he'd been watching with his son, Andy, and told his wife he had to go out for work. The Yankees were losing, 6–1, to the despised Red Sox, and it was only the fourth inning, their starting pitcher already chased after giving up two home runs, two doubles, and three walks. The team stood four back with three weeks to go, and after tonight would be five back. If he'd been watching alone, Keller would have turned the game off earlier, knowing his team faced a long and painful night, but Andy would stick it out until the end, whatever the score, reminding his dad their team could always come back no matter how far behind, since the clock does not wind down in baseball.

Patty said, "Say good night to your father, Andy." When Bill went out at night for work, he stayed out for a while, sometimes until the next day.

"Are you going out to catch bad guys?" Andy asked.

"That's the plan," Keller told his son.

"Can I come and help?" Andy said hopefully.

"You know the answer to that."

"Good night, Dad." The boy kissed his father.

"You should think about getting ready for bed."

"It's Friday night, Dad. Falcone is pitching now. Is he good?"

Falcone was a young middle reliever just up from the minors. "I guess we'll find out," Keller said.

He kissed Patty, telling her he'd call at some point. She whispered to him to be careful.

Despite his team's poor showing, he listened to the game in the car. By the time he got to Gull, the score was 8–1, the young Falcone getting in trouble right away.

At Gull, he asked the pretty hostess at the front desk if he could speak to Jude Gates. She was short and thin, with small breasts squeezed together to create a narrow canyon of cleavage. She reminded Keller of a girl he dated in high school, back when he played baseball and believed that someday he'd be the second baseman for the Yanks.

The hostess informed him that Mr. Gates wasn't in tonight.

"Do you know where I can find him? At home maybe?"

The hostess shook her head. "I don't know, and I'm not allowed to say. We don't give out that kind of information."

"No, of course not. That's a good policy."

She smiled and tilted her head, as if he'd paid her a personal compliment.

"What about Andrew Cole? Is he here tonight?"

"He's in the kitchen, but he's pretty busy."

"Sure, okay," he said. Probably true. Most of the tables and all of the bar stools were occupied. The staff moved quickly with trays and plates and glasses. He considered trumping the hostess by pulling out his badge, but decided against it. No need to trip the alarm at this point.

He left and walked down the alley to the back of the building. He noticed Gates's Lexus parked there. The van that Brian Raine's son had identified by plate number was not here; it had been here last time Keller poked around this lot, and he'd run the plates afterward and found it registered to the Upstate Dining Company. The kid had gotten his numbers right. He remembered Nate Raine from the first-grade breakfast, a dreamy kid wearing a gadgety spy watch Andy had been begging for ever since. Andy had taken to him right away and told his father he'd been hanging out with Nate at recess all week. Andy wanted a play date, but that wouldn't happen if Patty had any say in the matter, which she did. She would not allow her son to hang around with a boy whose mother smoked pot. On the other hand, if for some reason Gwen Raine's children were taken from her or Gwen taken from them, Patty would be the first to offer a foster home to the boy. That's just the way she worked. Over the past couple of years they'd had two foster children staying with them, temporary placements—a six-year-old girl for two months, followed the next year by a ten-year-old boy for six months— and while it hadn't been easy on the family dynamic, it had been the right thing to do and a good experience for everyone in learning to get along with others from different backgrounds and circumstances.

He looked through the screen door at the back of the restaurant down a hallway leading to the kitchen. The crew passed in and out of his view, waiters and cooks. Orders barked, swearing, plates and pans banging in tuneless percussion. Keller caught a glimpse of Andrew Cole when the chef stepped around the cooking line and checked a plate one of the waiters held, adjusting the arrangement of a garnish.

No point in calling him out. Keller doubted there would be anything to discover from him.

Keller next drove to Gates's house. The windows were dark, at least those that he could see. An eight-foot hedge hid most of the façade of a grand-looking Victorian in the oldest neighborhood in town. Big wraparound porch, fussy moldings and trim over the windows and doors. Exterior lights on the porch and over the garage, likely on timers. So Gates had his van up in the mountains. What was he doing? Cruising the Adirondacks in a love mobile with a married woman from Morrissey? That didn't compute.

He drove to the station to get the file on Gates. The dispatcher, who was the newest member of the Morrissey police department fresh and squeaky from the academy, greeted him as Detective Keller. Williams, the night sergeant, sat at his desk, talking on the phone. He nodded when he saw Keller.

He closed the door to his office and went through Gates's file containing the same shuffled papers he'd been through a dozen times. Nothing added since he'd begun the investigation, except a handwritten note that Gates had dinner with Daryl Sweet, owner of Sweet Fitness, the same night Keller had taken Patty there. After observing Sweet and Gates at dinner that evening, Keller ran a background check on Sweet; nothing unusual came up. Former NFL player, arrested once in his playing days for DUI and speeding (103 mph in his Mercedes), also suspended for two games after having failed a drug test. While that might be a red flag, the substance in Sweet's blood was a steroid, considered standard operating procedure for many football players. Now that he owned a chain of health clubs, Sweet could be hawking steroids, but Jude Gates—a restaurateur—seemed an unlikely source for them. Drugs channeled through restaurants were typically the traditional recreationals: pot, coke, ecstasy. Prescription meds usually involved rogue physicians and pharmacies.

Still, Sweet was worth keeping an eye on. His home address was listed in Chappaqua, well south of Keller's jurisdiction, but he knew someone in the Westchester County sheriff's office he could place a call to if he needed help.

He went through the other information in Gates's file to see if anything stood out. The crossings at the Canadian border had to be significant; Gates was likely getting supplied from up north, at least partially, which was odd because most drugs sold upstate came up from the city, and it didn't make sense to risk a border crossing.

Keller checked his computer. There was an alert that the van had hit U.S. Customs earlier that day. He'd previously put a flag on both the Lexus and the van.

So Gates had gone up to Canada and picked up a supply, but why was he hanging around up in the mountains? Think about that. Mr. Raine had told Keller that his wife had told him that Gates had told her that he had a place up there. Jesus, that's too many he told/she tolds to be credible.

He flipped through more paper in the file; his eye caught a photocopy of Gates's marriage certificate, to a Claire M. Dumont. What the hell ever happened to her? No record of a divorce, no evidence of her at all. That gave him an idea. He went back to the computer, logged in to the Franklin County property database and searched on the name Dumont, Claire M.

Ding. Now here was a useful piece of information. Two acres and a thousand-square-foot dwelling owned by Claire Dumont at 2364 Old Rainbow Lake Road, Township of Tear, Franklin County.

Normal protocol called for Keller to notify the Franklin County sheriff and have them check the situation. But that would ruin it for him. When you're a police detective in Morrissey, you investigated residential burglaries, unattended deaths, vandalism in schools, bad checks passed at Morrissey Square. You submitted to evidence techs the bong found under the school bleachers. There wasn't a lot of opportunity to catch the really bad guys, like his son, Andy, asked if he was going to. There had been that excitement some months back when a perp holding up a Bank of America branch escaped on foot. Security cameras caught the track pants, sweatshirt, brown hair, and long bangs, the thin mustache littering his lip. No visible weapon. They locked down the schools and sent the dogs out. Every squad car on the streets. Then the state helicopters were called in and circled the neighborhood like flying bugs from Mars. Scared the hell out of everyone; the phones at the station lit up like holiday lights. The shithead got away, too, the theory being that he sprinted to nearby St. Thomas Church where he'd parked his getaway car in the rectory lot. That's where the dogs lost the scent. One of the dogs, Sergio, kept sniffing and staring down Delaware Avenue, straining at her leash. She knew which way that fucker had gone.

Driving up the Northway and working undercover off a tip from a five-year-old, Detective Keller wondered if he was going to discover a van of narcotics and Mr. Jude Gates on the mattress with the lovely Mrs. Raine—regrettably the mother of the five-year-old—unless Gates surprised him and went the other way, carving her up to repay her for tattling on him.

Keller didn't have a feeling one way or the other about it. Patty would pick the mattress and passion; she thought that way and usually was right, but it always surprised and disheartened Keller that people with children could behave so despicably, no matter how many times he witnessed it. Gwen Raine—he didn't see it in her. She was attractive enough and he saw a gleam in her eye, but getting messy with a guy like Gates, that kind of gleam was a glare, and Gwen Raine gave off a soft light. Her eyes were calm. Her manner lovely and even. Of course maybe that could be attributed to her being stoned a lot of the time. The mellow mom.

As for the tall, dark, and handsome Gates—Keller wouldn't be surprised if he turned out to be a fag.

What could he say, this was how he classified people. In his line of work, you always had to think in terms of types. Types who would do this, types who would do that, although now they called it profiling. He hated to say it, but that was the main reason he believed Sweet could be involved: he possessed certain attributes of a well-recognized profile. Maybe Keller could catch him, too.

It's Hard to Kiss You While Driving

He began his story three years back, his first semester of college, just like her situation now. St. Lawrence had been on his list, he said, so had Clarkson right here in Potsdam, and Colgate in Hamilton. He'd been angling for a hockey scholarship because he'd been the captain of his high school team and third-leading scorer in the league. A few schools offered aid, but it wasn't nearly enough—you know what it costs a year. At the last minute he registered for community college, and even that was a stretch because he was paying every penny himself, working for a landscaper in summer, plowing snow in winter.

He ended up joining the National Guard, which seemed like a smart move at the time but turned out to be the worst decision he'd ever made. They recruited him harder than any of the hockey schools had. Two weeks a year, one weekend a month—it sounded like a fair deal. He'd get help paying for school. He'd serve his community, like when that ice storm hit two years ago. Remember that? When the whole northern part of the state lost power. He helped transport food and fuel, moved people to emergency shelters. He knew what it felt like to make a difference in people's lives.

He had her attention now. She followed every word, her gaze moving from his mouth to his eyes. Once or twice he caught her checking out his body, a quick scan down and up. He'd taken off his jacket, and his arms and flat stomach showed well in just the black T-shirt. The only problem: she wasn't drinking. That, and he really wanted to touch her, feared his hand might reach out on its own before he could think to stop it. There were parts of his body no longer under his control.

"You don't like your beer. Can I get you something else to drink?"

"No, I like it." And to prove it, she picked up her glass and took a few gulps.

"Keep going," she said. "I'm listening."

You keep going, he thought. Keep drinking.

The rest he didn't have much to say about. The call to duty came. He went, he wasn't scared. In fact, he liked the idea of being a soldier. Someone had to stand up to those chickenshits. He just hated the desert, that's all. Spent forty-six days there, until someone along the roadside tossed a grenade into his Humvee, and Aaron's buddy saved his life. Pounced like it was a fumble in the Super Bowl. He'd never seen someone react so quickly in his life. Or die so instantly.

Aaron: the lucky one. This guy he hardly knew sacrificed himself to save Aaron. He still couldn't get over it. But, Christ, was he grateful. Who wouldn't be. I'm still alive. I keep reminding myself of that. But now he had to do something big and important with his life to make that soldier's selfless act stand up.

"I was supposed to get a titanium plate and plastic surgery, but it never happened and I hated the hospital almost as much as I hated the desert. I was discharged and put on a waiting list. Now I'm missing part of my zygomatic bone."

She giggled when he said *zygomatic,* then covered her mouth and apologized. "It's the name of these obscure body parts," she said. "My problem is with my iliotibial band. See what I mean? One of my problems, I should say."

"Your what?"

"Also known as a pain in my knee. It's a running injury." She picked up her glass again and took another sip. She almost missed the shelf setting it back down and he helped her, guiding her hand, a reason to touch her, a rush when he felt her warm skin, come and gone like an eyeblink.

She told him she ran on the Saints cross-country team but had developed this thing called ITBS and couldn't race this week; in fact, the race was tomorrow; in fact, she really had to get back to campus.

"But you said you're not racing."

"I'm still part of the team and going to Plattsburgh with them."

She looked around for her friends and he quickly pulled her attention back, afraid he might lose her. He risked touching her hand again and she didn't flinch. Like petting an exotic and unfamiliar creature.

She said, "I'm so hot."

"Like I told you earlier."

"That's not what I meant."

But he could see she liked what he said.

"You want to go outside for some air?"

"Definitely. I could use that."

"Drink up," he said, and finished his beer while watching her take another sip of hers. He led her down the hall and out a back door marked emergency exit that was propped open with a brick.

In the parking lot, in the cool night air with the ground and cars still wet from the earlier rain, he told her she had beautiful lips. He asked if he could kiss her.

She let him kiss her and he knew from her reaction—she

tensed and drew back—that he'd started out too hard. He tried again, more gently this time, acting like she did have beautiful lips and he was honoring them. The simple act of kissing this girl weakened his knees. He'd not had that pleasure or comfort in too long.

When he finished, she said, "Wow, I'm feeling a little dizzy, but I didn't drink that much."

"Yeah, I know what you mean."

She looked around. They were alone in the parking lot, leaning against the side of his truck. She kissed him again, then stopped abruptly and said she really had to get back to campus because her team's bus was leaving early in the morning for a meet.

"I'll drive you," Aaron offered.

"That's okay—my friend . . ." She stopped and laughed. Her friend—who said they'd give her a ride?

"I don't mind. It's not far. Come on. You can call your friends on the way and tell them you got a ride with me."

He pulsed from the X he'd popped earlier, although the half life must have spent. Still the glow, but not so radioactive. He'd sorted through the package from Jude and then driven all the way to Glens Falls to check out his buddy Guy who was home with his girlfriend, Rose. They each did one of the X tabs, monogrammed with an exclamation point on one side, yellow as the mums he'd planted. They got wrecked and listened to music and when Guy started making out with Rose, Aaron tried to get in. She pushed him away and made a face and sound like she'd stepped in dog shit. Guy got all puffy and ended up pushing Aaron and so he punched Guy twice, knocking him into an aluminum table that collapsed and Rose yelped. He'd fucked that up but when he got back in his truck he saw his phone on the seat blinking a voice mail, a beacon from a goddess as he discovered when he listened to the message. He couldn't remember what she looked like but thought he could pick her out if he saw her again.

"Come on, get in." He unlocked the door and held it open for her. At first he worried he hadn't used enough—a single squirt into her glass when she went to the bar. Either he hadn't used enough or she hadn't drunk enough of her beer, because when he got her in the truck she spoke clearly and said she appreciated the ride because at least she'd be able to get four or five hours' sleep before meeting the team bus in the morning. She also noticed when he headed out in the opposite direction and she pointed out that Canton was the other way.

"Oops, old habits," he said, and did a U-turn and passed the bar again, which she took a long look at as if trying to place in her memory.

Part of him regretted he'd put the G in her drink. She was being nice to him, he might not have needed it. Too late now. What was done was done. And it turned out he had used enough and even timed it perfectly because once they were turned around and heading toward Canton she opened her window and yelled out "Road trip!" and pulled her head back in and said, "I always wanted to do that." She began to laugh and said she was feeling kinda drunk, at least she thought that's what it was—could he believe she'd never been drunk in her entire life, that's right, not once, even though she practically grew up in a bar or maybe that was the reason why she never got drunk because she's seen a lot of drunk people and witnessed how it can ruin your life or at least make you very stupid and sick for a few hours.

Maybe she wasn't drunk, she said, maybe just feeling good— for once. Maybe not for once, but you know what? Having a damaged knee wasn't the worst thing that had ever happened to her. I mean, she'd be better in a few weeks after another cortisone shot and regular icing and no running, although the fall season was basically shot, but right now there was no pressure on her, she was carefree and could do anything she wanted, no grueling training regimen, none of those prerace jitters which sometimes made her throw up although she was used to the puking, it wasn't so bad, did he know what she meant?

He did.

Here she paused and frowned. Aaron looked at her and wondered if she was about to heave now. Please not on his leather seats. Then her frown passed and she was smiling and giddy again and saying where was I, oh yes . . . Did he know he was like the first person, the first guy, she meant, who hadn't asked first thing how she got her black eye?

Forgetting that he had already asked her about that. It was what made her so special to him.

Well, if he must know it wasn't a black eye, it was like a birthmark but really extra veins just below her skin—did she already tell him about that? And now she had two things, a venous malformation and iliotibial band friction syndrome wow she couldn't believe she pronounced that properly but don't worry they weren't as bad as they sounded, they weren't contagious or anything so when are you going to kiss me again?

He looked at her and smiled and put a hand around the back of her neck. He would have said her name but he'd forgotten it. Instead he said she was beautiful.

She unbuckled her seat belt and leaned over and kissed him. First on the cheek just below the part that was missing and it made him flinch and he felt sad for a few seconds, then she put her face in front of him and kissed his mouth, putting her tongue right in. He swerved and corrected his course and bent his neck to see the road. And all through the kissing she wouldn't shut up; if it was possible to talk while kissing she was doing it, telling him now he was cute and strong and how she'd always wanted a boy-friend.

He reached and grabbed one of her tits through her sweater. Not much there but it still felt like discovered treasure in his hand. She kind of squirmed and moaned.

She'd gone from zero to sixty in about two minutes. He should find a spot to pull over before the magic moment passed or she passed out.

He drove another mile and came upon a turnoff for a parking area. The tires spat gravel when he skidded in. Empty and dark, the one overhead light shot out by jerkoffs playing with their shotguns. He slowed and parked as far from the road as he could, next to a picnic table and garbage can.

"What's the matter?" she asked.

"It's hard to kiss you while I'm driving."

She found this funny enough to start laughing, a horsey twang. At least she'd stopped talking so much.

It would be tough to do her in the truck. He'd have to recline her seat and bend her over the back of it. Not that he couldn't, but he'd pictured going to a hotel and having a regular bed, maybe waking up with her the next morning and having coffee and a conversation, the way other people did it.

She wore a denim skirt and some kind of tights; he could yank them down and go to bat.

That's how he was now—hard as a bat, jittering for a swing. For the contact and her flesh. He reached across her and released the seat and it shot back, giving her a jolt.

"Hey what was that?"

"Nothing, making you more comfortable."

But she was already comfortable, she said, so comfortable, like her body was floating in warm water. Could she be that wasted?

He tried turning her over. She was thin but heavier and more solid than he'd expected and she didn't just roll like a ball. He had to push and she said hey again. "What are you doing?"

He reached up under her skirt and grabbed a fistful of fabric and yanked until it tore and she grunted as if he'd punched her in the stomach.

Wait! Stop!

He held the back of her neck with one hand while the other went at his own pants and zipper. In a hurry now, he could feel it had to be now, fumbling with the button on his jeans, only one hand to work with because he needed the other to keep her down. Come on, come on, and at the same time she protested that he was pressing her head and said she wasn't feeling well.

Let go! Get off me. She twisted wildly under his grip.

He pounded his fist on her back and she fought back. He tried to pin her down with his forearm and knee but she got an arm free and slammed her bony elbow right into his solar plexus.

He punched the back of her head.

She got herself turned and kneed him in the nose. He slammed her against the door and it opened and they tumbled out together onto the gravel and rolled into a puddle. He cocked back to strike her but she wasn't underneath him anymore.

She'd gotten to her feet and was already running, heading toward the road. He had to fix his pants and then started chasing after her but she had a lead and the distance was growing between them. How the hell can she run like that. She was abandoning him, leaving him here alone.

He yelled after her, spitting saliva with his words, "Wait, I'm sorry. I'm sorry! It's okay. Come back!" And he was sorry now. And afraid, too, because he hadn't been able to stop himself, all the time he'd been going after her his conscience was gasping for air against the flood of drugs poisoning his blood, and he knew he was wrong, wrong, wrong and he wanted to stop but he couldn't.

"Come back!" he yelled into the dark night. He stopped and listened and heard nothing. Fuck. He pursued for another fifty yards and stopped again, knowing he'd never catch her on foot, then turned around and went back for the truck.

You Must Keep Moving

Gwen reached out for the trunk of a tree to keep herself from stumbling. She gulped at the air. When she could stand straight again she looked back into the darkness, listening, waiting for the bushes to move. There was nothing. Only gray and black shadows, silence.

It had been a deer. That was the logical explanation. It had come upon her and they scared each other and she bolted in one direction and the deer in the other.

No bear, no madman, was chasing her.

Her hands clung to the clammy tree bark. With each breath she heard wheezing. She began shivering again. She didn't know how far or long she'd run, or which direction, only that when she'd heard the noise she bolted into the dark. She'd tripped and fallen once, staggered a second time and managed to stay up by throwing her arms around the tree.

So much for staying in one place. That had been her plan to get through the night, after facing the reality that she was utterly lost. She had spent the daylight hours walking downhill and then up and then down, hope melting that she'd reach the road if she simply walked downhill. Because every downhill ended and turned into an uphill, she was trapped in a labyrinth of mounds and gullies, unable to determine in the dense forest which direction headed up the mountain and which down. As darkness overcame the day, she found a grove with a few sweeping pines and she tucked under the low hanging boughs of one and scraped up some of the drier pine needles underneath and covered herself with them to stay warm. The rain had ended but clouds still covered the moon and stars. She would stay in this one spot for the night rather than wander without direction, and when the sky began to brighten she'd get a better sense of her bearings and set out again. That was her plan.

But soon she began to shiver. First her teeth and jaw, then her shoulders, soon her entire body shook uncontrollably. Was she having some kind of seizure? No, just cold and wet. And alone and lost. And terrified. She snapped pine boughs to make a better cover for herself and the exertion warmed her up but when she huddled back down she began to shake again so badly she became dizzy and disoriented.

Then she'd heard the noise, like footsteps, only louder. Hooves. Giant clawed paws. Leaves trampled, swishing. A shadow feinting. And she'd sprung from her cover beneath the pines and run blindly through the black forest.

Now she was somewhere else, but it might as well be the same place. Same conditions. Her cotton sweater heavy and wet, flimsy shoes soaked through, jeans sticking to her, skin like chilled dough. She'd ripped her pants and cut her knee on one of her falls, the blood warm and sticky on her cold flesh. What was the temperature—midfifties? Gwen didn't know. Cold enough. It didn't need to be any colder than this for her to die, because wet and cold together created a deadly whole much greater than the sum of its parts. She was no outdoors expert but knew that much. Whatever flush and heat that filled her earlier that day had long dissipated. The skin on her arms and hands had taken on the pale look of a corpse, milky and unnatural in the lightless night. She wouldn't want a glimpse of her face in a mirror right now.

She decided if she stayed in one place hypothermia would set in.

So she'd have to keep walking. And stop crying. And stop feeling sorry for herself.

Keep moving, step slowly, you don't need to cover a lot of ground, just move enough to keep the blood flowing and get through the night.

But that bear could find her again. No, it was a deer. It had to be a deer.

She took a few steps and listened. Nothing but dripping from the trees when the breeze kicked up—and her heart drumming; her rapid, shallow breathing. She started again and stepped into a thicket of thorns that stabbed and scratched. She retreated, extricating her ankle from a noose of ground vines.

She walked with one ghostly arm outstretched in front of her, the other hand gripping her extended forearm so it wouldn't shake so much.

The same thought kept returning to her: she was going to die due to her own selfish stupidity. She would not see her children again, she would not see Brian. She would die out here cold and alone, and now she was crying again.

You must keep moving, she repeated to herself. You will get out of this. Remember what you know about survival in the wilderness. You were a Girl Scout once; you went to camp in these mountains when you were a girl; you learned to make a fire. Although that would require matches or a lighter. You learned to dress appropriately in layers and the importance of keeping your feet dry, although that would require a change of clothes. You learned campfire songs, which she tried singing now to feel less desolate and alone.

In a Spill of Blood

The road curved left and right following the base of the mountain. Every quarter mile or so a narrow dirt driveway cut off and headed uphill. None of the cutoffs were marked with numbers or mailboxes, this area rural enough that people who wanted their mail drove into the post office to pick it up. According to Keller's dashboard navigation map, he'd passed 2364 Old Rainbow Lake Road, then passed it again on the way back. After a third pass he identified the correct driveway by process of elimination. He drove past one more time until he reached the next cutoff, where he pulled to the side of the road and parked.

He checked the clip in his Glock, which was full and shiny. He'd never fired it in the line of duty, only at the practice range, but would not back down from opportunity or obligation if the situation arose.

He secured a blade in an ankle sheath.

It was colder in the mountains than in Morrissey, and he shivered when he first stepped out, but his jacket and cap would keep him warm enough once he got moving. From the puddles spotting the shoulder he concluded the earlier rain had been steady, and now the ground and vegetation along the side of the road were tamped and soggy; he could step silently.

He walked back down the road toward the driveway for Gates's property where he stopped and listened. He peered into the woods looking for any light from a house. Nothing. The building could be another fifty yards or more farther in. He spotted the magnetic detector at the driveway head, most likely wired to a signal inside the house that sounded when a car approached. He stepped over a ditch to avoid it and cut back to the driveway.

He approached quietly along a muddy gravel drive cratered with puddles, taking a few steps at a time and then stopping to listen and look. It was still too dark to see much but the sky would begin to gray within the hour. His plan was to get close enough to the house and find a hiding spot, reconnoiter from there, and go in at first light.

Soon he could make out a clearing ahead and a single light. He left the driveway and went into the woods, stepping into a wet depression ankle high, just over the top of his boot. That was cold. No option except to walk through it, getting both feet soaked. He pushed on and found a good vantage point near the edge of the clearing. A coach light on the cabin's porch provided the only outdoor illumination, the low-wattage bulb putting up meager resistance against the surrounding darkness. A row of yellow flowers glowed like fading solar lanterns along the path to the porch. There was another light from somewhere inside the house. He didn't see any vehicles, which was not a good sign, although the van could be parked around the side. You didn't walk to and from this house, you needed to drive. He had expected to see the van and discover Gates and Mrs. Raine inside the house or at least Gates. If they'd been here and left or had never been here at all, or if Gates had already moved his supply from Canada, then his hunch was shot. Keller didn't have a plan for what would happen if that was the turn of events.

A steady noise came from within, a whirring chug that might be a generator or fan. He hunched down and a willy passed through him. If he were home right now he'd be in a warm bed with Patty spooned next to him, the way she liked to sleep, Andy in his room across the hall or maybe in their bed if he'd woken from a nightmare and came in for comforting.

Keller shrugged off the tingle and readied himself.

The black night faded to a gray, providing just enough light for Keller to move forward without tripping over himself or any obstacle, but not so much light he could be seen. He set out to circle the house and approach the front from the opposite side, providing himself the element of the unexpected and the opportunity to ID any vehicles. He kept looking at the windows as he moved but they were blank as slate slabs. He made out a propane tank secured in a steel cradle on the side of the house. At least 500 gallons, huge for this size structure. Meth factory? Didn't smell like it.

He picked his way through weeds and saplings in the back of the house, came around the far side. He stepped up close to the window but the glass had been covered from the inside. You know what that means: there's a secret in there. When he reached the front corner of the house he noticed on the porch stairs a bulky shape that had been blocked from view when he'd been on the other side.

He moved carefully against the side of the house, ducking low beneath the windows until he recognized the shape as a human body. Facedown, one arm and leg sprawled wide. Pool of darkness from underneath, seeping over the top stair.

Keller drew his Glock, buttoned off the safety. That got his heart pounding. He couldn't check out the body until he'd secured the inside of the house, and he couldn't secure the inside of the house without getting in there. Which meant stepping over that body and entering full frontal.

Decision time. Retreat and call for support or go it alone.

It was first light, this is what he'd been waiting for. This had been his plan.

He approached the body, an adult male lying in a spill of blood, the back of his skull blasted away. No risk of that thing taking a run at him. Then he was on the porch and at the door; it wasn't closed all the way, the humming rumble from inside chugging like a far-off train.

Keller sucked three deep breaths and exploded through the door, staying low, leading with the Glock, straight ahead, left, right.

No movement in the shadows.

He was standing in a combination kitchen-living area with a queen bed—made, covers smooth, pillows undisturbed—in place of a table in the dining area. He approached a door to the right, tried the handle, and pushed through. The light was blinding and he covered his eyes and dove back into the other room, rolling once on the floor and setting himself to empty the Glock. Nothing. Nothing except the smell, pungent and fertile, a pot farm. And the generator idling.

Keller secured the rest of the building, making sure no one hid waiting to ambush him from the bathroom or closets. He found a loaded shotgun leaning on the wall behind the front door and emptied the shells. He pulled the extension cord on the generator and the house went quiet and dark. He plugged the generator back in and the grow room lit up again, bright as a sunny beach, blazing overheads ricocheting heat and light off the glossy white walls. Looked like a new growing season from the appearance of the plant trays, most of them seedlings, just putting out their first set of leaves. Which meant the old growing season recently ended. The trays were lined up in neat, orderly rows on tables, with a complicated network of drip tubes feeding them. There must have been two hundred or more plants. How many pounds of weed did this place put out per cycle? Thirty or more, probably.

He went back out on the porch to check on his dead friend.

Keller was disappointed, overall. Stymied. He hadn't caught a bad guy, only the mess a bad guy had left behind.

He was about to turn over the body with his foot to get a look at the face when a bell sounded inside the cabin, a single ring too high pitched to be the telephone. That could mean only one thing: company's here—someone had just pulled into the driveway.

He went back inside and pulled the generator cord, waited in the gloomy silence.

Putting Your Best Foot Forward

At some point during the night the clouds broke up and moon came out and cast enough light for Gwen to make out her footing. She could distinguish the shapes of trees, choose her next step without stumbling. She followed her strategy of staying on the move, but couldn't travel the dense and rocky terrain fast enough to stay warm. Any heat she generated she lost. Her energy had drained away, even the adrenaline that boosted her early on. She stopped often for her breathing to catch up. Her cut knee throbbed. Her feet were sore and icy. The worst part was she couldn't stop trembling—her jaw and back ached from the spasms.

It didn't seem stupid at the time, what she'd done; it didn't seem lethal. Her behavior still fit within her moral compass: be responsible for your actions, be fair to everyone, keep your word. A compass—what she wouldn't do for one now, not that she'd be able to see the dial, or even know how to read one—but it would be better than not having one at all. It would give her hope.

Officially, Gwen had not been responsible for the accident that took James Anderson's life, yet she had agonized over the details these past few weeks: the curve in the road, the bright sun, and, yes, the fact she had taken a few hits off a joint. But she'd felt fine. She was driving under control. There had been no time to react beyond her wrenching of the wheel. What else could she have done? She didn't know. With Jude, she had more time to deliberate about her actions. Yes, she'd been extorted into giving Jude's name to the police, but because she believed she was betraying a friend or almost friend or at least an icon from her past by breaking her promise not to tell anyone—and ultimately because she had to stop him from kissing her—when she saw Jude at the market she admitted what had happened.

It never should have gotten to that point. After Jude's first kiss at Gull that day, she told herself she could not, would not, see Jude again—for any reason. She knew the nature of his kiss, its intent and invitation. But she didn't adhere to her own rule. Because she owed him this warning about the police? Or because she craved the morsel of thrill delivered with the kiss? Could her life be that devoid of excitement? She never thought about the level of excitement in her life, that's not what motivated her. Gwen believed the thrill in her life was being married to Brian, devoted to her children, a relatively predictable future in front of her as long as nothing dramatic or disastrous happened. Only now it had. Or might have. And only while driving away from the market with Nate in the backseat and Jude following right behind in that van with the big chrome grill like the mouth of a shark did she begin to worry that the drama and disaster were the result of her own mistakes, her disregard for risk.

And still she allowed herself to be drawn further in. She knew he would call later and she answered his call and she dug her hole deeper in hopes of coming out the other side, rather than climbing out while she still could.

She didn't call Jude back because she fantasized about him. She was a mother with two children to care for and a husband she loved. Most nights she was too tired to fantasize. She had not been thinking about Jude, scheming the possibilities. She did not want an affair, not with Jude or any man. Although she did dress for Jude that day she'd met him at Gull to pick up the bag. Hadn't she. She'd chosen her clothes that morning aware he would see her in them. The sleeveless or the T-shirt? The skirt or the slacks? She deliberated even about her underwear, totally unnecessary—the deliberation, not the underwear—while her husband sang in the shower and called out asking what she was doing today. Nora's last day of swim camp, she reminded him; Nate at Nature's Workshop; errands to run before they left for the lake. And one special errand she didn't bother to mention, not to hide from Brian but not to advertise either. Before going into the restaurant to meet Jude, she had checked her face in the car mirror, played with her hair, reapplied her lips. Hadn't she. Why wouldn't she want to look good to him? Why shouldn't she show her best side?

It's called putting your best foot forward. When she was at the gym, she worked out hard. When she took the kids to the museum, she turned the outing into a learning experience. When she managed PTA programs, she integrated new ideas. When she had sex with Brian, she tried to please him. She cooked healthy meals, read acclaimed novels, bought quality furniture. Everyone she knew in Morrissey did the same. You have your life and you're happy with it, as long as you do your best, look your best, perform your best. And for the most part the model worked. She loved her life and wouldn't trade it for any other, but who doesn't sometimes wonder about other paths, other lives you might have led. It doesn't mean you ditch your life; instead you smoke a bowl or have a couple of drinks once in a while and laugh more. You don't run off with Jude; you flirt with him a little.

Gwen had not taken his kiss seriously enough. But she should have, because that kiss nudged open a door a tiny bit, and she glanced inside to discover she had a pulse. Possibility still existed. Not with Jude, or not just Jude. With the future. She wasn't completely invisible. Life could still surprise her, whether she wanted it to or not.

Here you go, Gwen. Here's your surprise: you're lost in the wilderness on a cold, wet night; your life could be in danger. Flirt with that.

You want to put your best foot forward? Okay, get yourself out of this.

She made slow progress but kept moving. When she came across a rocky area that sloped steeply uphill she tucked into a notch between two boulders sandwiching a towering pine tree and found a drier spot on the ground. She pressed against the granite, which still felt faintly warm, radiating solar energy soaked up during the day, but its mass and hardness and silence reminded her of its indifference. The rock did not care one way or the other if she lived or died in this spot. The trees would not stir if she could not go on. Gwen was alone. She pulled off her useless shoes and rubbed her feet between her hands. The motion helped her hands more than her feet, but her skin remained pale and doughy, drained of color. She rocked back and forth, hoping that by moving in a deliberate rhythm she could control her shivering. After a few minutes her body began to settle.

She got her cell phone from her pocket and turned it on. The screen lit up and joy surged in her, then the phone went blank again. Just a twitch from a battery already gone.

She worried about Brian and the kids. What did they think

happened to her? Nothing good. What story would Brian make up for the kids? There was nothing easy. There was only the story of Mommy isn't here and we don't know where she is. Only the story of Gwen's mistakes.

Brian had called the police, no doubt. He had wanted to call them earlier and she'd talked him out of it. He would tell them about her encounter with Jude—he would think she was with him now.

Please don't think that.

Please think how much I want to be home with you and our children.

If only she could be safe again with her family. If only. And so she started bargaining, with whom she wasn't sure but maybe with God or the mountains or Brian—she'd strike a deal with anyone or anything at this point. And here was the deal: if Gwen could get home, she would atone for her mistakes. She would never see or speak to Jude again. She would cooperate with the police investigation in every way possible. She would never get high and get behind the wheel of her car. She would not take unnecessary risks. She would be a better wife, a better mother, a better person—whatever the word *better* entailed. She'd appreciate and be thankful for her life, which Gwen believed she already was, but somehow she'd be more. Was that a deal?

She rocked and waited, rocked and waited. Her goal now was to last until daylight. If she could see where the sky lightened first, which direction was east, then she would know which way to go. Their house on the lake faced east and therefore if she traveled in that direction she would eventually find the road again. Right? Did it work that way? She had started out yesterday by crossing the road behind their house which meant she had walked west; no matter where she was at this point, by walking east she would be heading back.

Yes, that was her plan now: wait for daybreak and identify the direction of the sunrise.

Except some time later when she noticed the first brightening of the sky, the light appeared directly overhead, the darkness in slow motion dissolving to gray. The tree cover took away the horizons and the ability to detect the direction of light.

A setback—but she'd have to overcome it. She would not despair and cry. She just needed to start out and find a better vantage point, maybe by hiking this rocky slope that now sheltered her at its base.

So Gwen began walking, her feet aching and swollen in her sopping, soft shoes, but determined to find her way out. She hiked uphill, one foot and then the other, wincing with each step, while the sky brightened and soon she noticed off to the right a few clouds tinged with a pink glow. That way was east. She turned and picked her way in that direction through thick tree cover and undergrowth.

She hadn't gone a hundred yards when she heard barking. Distant, barely audible, but she'd heard it.

There, she heard it again.

That had to be a dog. Coming from the direction she was heading. Energized, she picked up her pace, walking as fast as the light and her ruined shoes and damaged feet would allow.

She walked and the barking grew louder. Definitely a dog. Four barks, a pause, four more, another pause.

She came to a steep downhill and slipped at the top and slid on her butt in the mud until her feet bumped against a clump of a mountain laurel. She stood and wiped her hands on her pants and this time kept her footing, deliberated over each step, not wanting to risk another fall or injury. She developed a safe pattern: step, secure her footing, step again. When the slope eased and she looked ahead she saw a clearing below with a shed and a house and a dog tied up to a run and the dog was looking up at her and barking, once, twice, three times, four, then pausing and starting up again. A door swung open at the back of the house, a woman's voice shouted at the dog to quiet down. The dog was facing uphill toward Gwen, and the woman turned that way and saw her coming.

His Awful Mistake

Lightning struck his face with each heartbeat. Not his face—the place where his face should have been, the chunk of bone and flesh that had been vaporized and now floated somewhere in the air of the world. That's what hurt. Phantom pain. Ghost pain. The part of his face he couldn't touch. The part of his face they were going to rebuild at Reed but that never happened because he'd been discharged first, which put him on another list, a longer list, and his turn hadn't come yet and never would because he'd left no forwarding address where he could be reached, he'd cut off all contact with that world.

The pain now. And now. And now. And now. In perfect rhythm with his pulse. He couldn't stand it anymore and reached in the center console for his vial of vikes, squeezed the steering wheel with his knees while his hands battled the childproof top. He pried with his thumbs and the top popped off with enough force to send the pills flying on his lap and the floor. He swore and threw the vial out his window. Fuck it. He didn't need them. That's what got him messed up in the first place. He reached behind his seat where a couple beers from a twelve-pack remained. He popped a can top and swallowed half a beer in his first gulp, but he was spluttering, crying now, and he began to cough and choke. The can went out the window too. Stab, stab, stab. The pain, the pain, the pain—and then he sensed it easing up. The beats fading, retreating to their hideout. What a grateful moment, the pain subsiding, draining—a rapture he likened to the love of a merciful God if such a thing existed, only it didn't.

The pain left, and the scent filled its void. The aroma flamed his stomach, watered his mouth. Grandma's pot roast. Gravy-soaked beef falling apart on his fork with carrots and potatoes soft as boiled macaroni. He pictured it on his plate, tasted it in his mouth, although he hadn't eaten his grandma's pot roast since he was twelve years old—the year she died—and then for years afterward never gave it a thought, until half his face had been blasted off. Within seconds of the explosion in the desert he smelled the pot roast, despite the fact he lay in the roadside dust and blood leaked like lava through his nasal passages.

Pot roast. Grandma. Now he was starving. But there would be nothing to eat for Aaron between Canton and Rainbow Lake. He'd spent an hour driving back and forth on the road between Potsdam and Canton searching for that girl, and now when he passed through Potsdam a final time, having given her up, the bars were closed. No one walked the streets. No open signs lit up diners, or fast-food chains, or convenience stores. Might as well be traversing the desert again.

Her purse lay next to him on the seat. He glanced at it once and looked away. When he looked back it was still there. He was afraid of it for a few minutes and then summoned the courage to touch the strap, then put his hand inside. He felt a pack of gum. He unwrapped and put a piece in his mouth, which chased away the smell of pot roast, but a few minutes of chewing made his face hurt again and he spit the gum out.

He shouldn't have done what he did to that girl.

She was nice. She liked him. He didn't even remember her name.

He looked at the purse again. He could go in there and find

her wallet or ID and learn her name, but it was too late for that. What would he do with the name now? It would be the name of the girl he'd done wrong, and if he learned her name now he'd never forget it. Her name would run through his head for the rest of his life, haunting him like a ghost, a constant reminder of his awful mistake.

But then he did it. He took out her wallet and looked at her license and saw her name: Dana Gates. He took his foot off the gas and slowed almost to a stop in the middle of the road. He'd never wondered who she was or why she was in the kitchen of Gull that night or why she'd made that comment about him being a produce supplier. That's what Jude must have told her: he was a produce supplier.

He didn't know Jude had a daughter, but he did know that Jude would kill him, or try to, if she told him what happened.

He lowered his window all the way and threw the purse out, then the wallet.

Then he made a decision. You've got freedom. You've got money. You've got a chance to redeem your life. You don't have part of your face but you've got enough sense to know you fucked up and need to move on.

He used to be a good person. Did that part of him get blown out? Had goodness resided only in one corner of his face?

He'd go back to the cabin and collect his stash of money and hit the road. He knew an army buddy in Nashville; there was no sand in Nashville. No desert. At least he didn't think there was. But first, maybe he would go back to Reed. They could help him, fix his face. They could make the pain go away if only he would give himself over to them. When he was healed, maybe he would call that girl again someday from far away and say he was sorry. Maybe she would forgive him.

He drove for twenty minutes. He hadn't run his truck off the road and congratulated himself for that simple achievement. He felt better now. He'd made a mistake but would put the past behind him by leaving and starting over fresh somewhere else in America where fresh starts were handed out even to people like him.

He slowed down approaching his driveway, turned in. "Who's there?" he said aloud, a funny habit he'd developed knowing he'd hit the sensor and sounded the bell inside and no one was ever there to hear it.

Early Retirement

Sweet already had paid half the money—an arrangement he hadn't liked—with the remainder due COD. When Jude informed him about the glitch in plans and that Sweet would need to pick up the product, Sweet liked this new arrangement even less.

"The 'D' stands for delivery," Sweet said. "Besides which and in addition to, you're already three hours late. That means I don't have my product, but you still got my money."

"Daryl, it's like I just explained to you . . ."

"Who you callin' Daryl."

"Okay, then. Da Da." Jude spoke slowly, to make himself understood. "I just finished explaining to you that I have the entire shipment of product in a secure location. However, I have reason to believe my movements may be tracked, and I can't risk making the delivery. My getting stopped would hurt both of us."

"And I come get it and someone follows me?"

"No, this has nothing to do with you. I'm in a safe location that no one knows about. No one will follow you."

"I told you not to fuck me over."

"Look, everything is going to be fine. There's just been a slight change in plans."

"Smells to me like Jude is a Judas, you already been tapped and now you giving me up to save your white ass."

Jude could hear the self-congratulatory note in Sweet's comment, as if he were the first one to think up the Judas crack. How many ways did he regret getting into business with this fucking juke.

"What do I need to do to convince you?" Jude said. "If I were setting you up, I'd just drive to you like we originally agreed and bring the DEA with me."

Sweet hesitated for a moment. "Shit, I don't know. You're more trouble than you're worth."

"Let's face it, neither of us likes this turn of events, but it's the situation we're in and we have a transaction to complete. And the results will be worth the effort."

"So where do I go get it? Tell me the name and location of your guy."

"You come to me to get it," Jude said. "I'm your guy." He told Sweet he was in Rainbow Lake in the Adirondacks.

"I got to drive all the fuck way up in the mountains to some hideaway?"

"It's not that far. You got a pen, I'll give you directions."

"Just give me the goddamn address. I got navigation."

Jude hated the idea of bringing Sweet to this location and exposing himself that way, but he had no choice except to take the risk. He couldn't go out on the road, not with what he had stashed in the hold and the police potentially watching. That represented the far greater danger.

"I need a discount," Sweet said.

"That's a reasonable request," said Jude. Anything to get this done. "Like what?"

"Hundred."

"Try fifty."

"Try fuck you."

"Let's remember we're both businessmen. That's why we're doing this deal together. We trust each other, we believe in being fair. I'll give you seventy."

"Eighty."

"Eighty off, for your inconvenience, pain, and suffering. One seventy due at pickup. But don't be presenting me your gas receipts as expenses when you get here."

Sweet laughed, and the tension between them broke.

"I don't need no snow tires, do I?"

How does this idiot operate a chain of fitness clubs?

"It's early September. The leaves are on the trees."

He shouldn't have gone for the big payday with Sweet. It was out of his comfort zone, he'd reached too far. He didn't need a new client at this point, especially a big mean motherfucker with city gangbanger roots and stinking with ambition, and he didn't like moving large quantities of product. He had conducted what due diligence he could, but in the end Sweet remained an unknown, and unknown meant risk.

He'd missed a call while on the phone with Sweet and when he checked there was a message from Dana. Her knee hadn't improved and she wouldn't be running in the meet tomorrow so he shouldn't bother coming to Plattsburgh. He felt for her, knowing how important the race was to her. He'd drive to St. Lawrence in the morning and surprise her. Take her out for a nice breakfast, boost her spirits with a pep talk.

It was now after midnight, Daryl Sweet hours late. Maybe he had changed his mind and wouldn't show, which might end up the better turn of events. Jude would be cash-strapped for a long time while slowly selling off the inventory, but he could leave the bulk of it up here and have Aaron shuttle product down to him as needed.

While waiting for Sweet, Jude used the time to plan the next phase of his life: retirement from this business. After this deal with Sweet, he'd stick with the nest egg already collected—there was enough to launch his daughter, but maybe not to keep the place in Florida. That's okay. He'd stay with Gull for a while, and Andrew had been talking about opening a second place. No need to look beyond that.

Then there was Gwen: her grip on him he couldn't explain. For years he had not thought of her, and then one winter day he saw her in his restaurant and it didn't matter that she was with her husband and children, it didn't matter their own relationship had been both intense and meandering, it didn't matter that she rejected his suggestions of getting together. None of it mattered except that he wanted to see her again, experience her again, and he would find a way to do so. There was a reason he wanted her that he probably could uncover if he dug deep and looked at it from every angle. But that would ruin the mystery of it for him, perhaps destroy his desire.

He believed she had no choice except to give his name to the police, and he forgave her for that. He also believed Gwen would be back to see him. She had her own style of saying yes to him. He remembered it from the days at the Patriot. Like the time she tried to distance herself from that cook she had dated a few times who then became obsessed with her and started harassing her. Jude asked Gwen if she wanted him to intervene and she answered by telling him the cook had tried to break into her house. That was a yes. Or that night when Gwen babysat for Dana and Jude came home to find Gwen asleep on the couch—after he shared wine and a few lines of coke with her, he asked if she'd prefer not to drive home and she answered by closing her eyes and leaning her head against the pillow. That was also a yes. And there were other times, after that night, when he mentioned he might come by after work and the only answer he got was an unlocked door when he showed up at her apartment. And more recently, this past winter, when she'd come to see him about getting a bag of weed and he invited her to return sometime for lunch with him, and she answered by showing up weeks later when downtown for jury duty. Gwen had a way of saying yes without saying yes, which is why he was sure she'd be back to see him again. It made him confident—not just about Gwen, but about this deal he had to close with Sweet, about everything.

The bell sounded on the kitchen wall and a moment later Sweet's Navigator appeared around the bend in the driveway, bobbing through the puddles, beams and fog lights turning night into day.

He parked next to Jude's van and shut down. The doors stayed closed.

Jude came out to the porch. Sweet and his passenger opened their doors together and approached the house, stopping at the bottom of the porch steps. The other guy looked like a white version of Sweet: a mountain boy with an iron neck. He carried a backpack over one shoulder, the straps not long enough to let him wear it the regular way.

"Have any trouble finding the place?"

"You know how to hide, I'll give you that," Sweet said. He stared into the forested blackness surrounding the cabin. "There any bears around here?"

"Never seen one, although this is their habitat."

"Mario, here, he's seen a bear."

Mario smiled. Horse teeth and jaw.

"He's wrestled a bear," Sweet said.

"What was it like?"

"Not too bad because this one had a manicure," Mario said. "Otherwise them claws would have got me pretty good. As it is, a bear's got big teeth."

"Is it kind of like dog fighting? With betting and all?"

"No, just for fun. I happen to know somebody with a circus bear and one thing led to another."

"You going to ask him who won?" Sweet said.

"Yeah, sure."

"It was a tie," Mario said. "I can bite, too."

Looked like he could bite Jude's hand off. "What do you say we conduct business," Jude suggested.

Sweet nodded, and Mario pushed the backpack to Jude.

He leaned from the weight of it. He'd been concerned about a tense "you first" "no, you first" game of showing the money and showing the goods, but Sweet hadn't hesitated to make the first gesture.

"You want to count it?"

"Do I need to?"

Sweet snorted. "Always."

Jude set the pack on the ground and opened it, clawed through wrappers of hundred-dollar bills. He opened one of the packets and folded half the bills into his pocket.

"Yours is in the van," Jude said.

Mario went to the van and opened the back. He stuck his head in and then back out, saying, "Ain't shit in here."

Jude left the knapsack on the porch step and came over and switched an overhead light in the back of the van. Sweet and Mario looked on.

Jude disassembled the false walls and floor to reveal the packed cargo bed.

"Whoa, that's tits," Sweet said. "You do all that custom work yourself?"

Mario started transferring the packages from the van to the back of the Navigator, covering the pile with a blanket when he finished.

"Looks like you could use a better transport system," Jude said. "A blanket for camouflage?"

"We weren't counting on arranging our own transportation. Remember, the deal was you deliver."

"And I told you, it wasn't safe for me to be on the road with the cargo. It put the whole thing at risk."

"I think you're in over your head. Is that the case? Why the fuck couldn't you deliver?"

"The police could be looking for me. That's why I wanted to stay off the roads. You wouldn't want me exposing you?"

"Motherfucker, did you say the police are watching you?"

"They don't know about this location."

"They don't know about this location?" Sweet repeated. "This location right here where I'm standing in the middle of bear country?"

"It's safe here. That's the reason why I wanted you to come here and not have me traveling to you."

"So the police are watching and you want me to drive out of here with a fucking blanket as my armor?"

"You can buy the van," Jude said. "I don't need it anymore. Even dogs can't sniff it out."

Sweet laughed, a low baritone chuckle. "Hey, Mario, Judas here wants to get out of this business. He's looking for an early retirement."

Mario looked up from his blanket work at the back of the Navigator and smiled.

Sweet said, "I knew you were too much a pussy. You ain't got what it takes."

"Probably not," Jude agreed.

"Now what happens when I need a refill?"

"I can get you in touch with some people. I even know someone who can drive for you."

"You can tell them where to find me, right?"

"I'll give you a phone number." To show he meant it, Jude unclipped the phone from his belt. "It's right here."

"Mario, we got any extra plates with us?"

"I got some."

"Commercial?"

"Pretty sure."

"Move it all back to the van. And switch the plates." Then to Jude, "How much?"

"Add thirty back on."

"I don't have the extra with me."

"I'm sure you're good for it. I'll come by and pick it up."

Sweet nodded, and shivered. "Fucking cold up here. I hate outdoors. I played a game in Chicago once with the wind chill twenty below. Every time you hit someone it felt like a bone was going to break. The ball was a rock."

Mario finished moving the packages back into the hold of the van. Jude showed him how to zip the scent fabric and put the sides and floor back in.

When the van was packed and secure, Sweet turned to Mario. "You drive the van."

"Let me get a couple CDs to listen to," Mario said. He fished in the front seat of the Navigator. Then he stood up with something in his hand.

That's when Jude knew. He thought he knew from the beginning when they talked about bear wrestling, something ironic in Sweet's voice, and maybe that's why he tried to sell the van to Sweet, a plan that came from nowhere but one that might put distance between him and Sweet, finish their deal and relationship all in one. Although he thought he knew, he pushed the idea down and aside because who can face such a realization, even when you've been moving in that direction for months now, taking wrong turns that head farther into a dark, dead-end alley. You can't go there, even though you are going there.

He thought of Gwen, how he wouldn't be there when she came to see him again. Then Dana. Suddenly he realized he wouldn't be able to visit in the morning and take her out for breakfast, and right now that was the most important thing in the world. Sitting in a diner with his daughter, eating fried eggs and disparaging the weak coffee. What would he say to encourage and comfort her? Quick—what words?

He expected it to come from Mario, the bear wrestler he had pegged as the ax man. But Mario was only holding CDs in his hand. It was Sweet who reached into his jacket and pulled out the gun. Jude stumbled backward against the stairs before righting himself against the railing.

"Here's your early retirement," Sweet said, the steel barrel rising up level with Jude's forehead. Jude leaned back, as if the few inches of space could make any difference in the world.

She Outran Him

Dana opened her eyes to see a single massive cloud, billowed at the edges, gray middle, drifting across a crisp blue background far above her. She lay faceup in a wet ditch, her body embedded in mud. She tried to move and the mud sucked to keep hold of her. A car whooshed past on the road above, a gleam of steel and tires.

She sat up, using her hands for support. Vomit laced the front of her jacket. Her head throbbed. Her ripped tights sagged like soiled rags around her knees. Her knees. She bent one, then the other. She had run, even with her bad knee, she'd run hard and fast and he couldn't catch her. That much she remembered: a sweeter victory than crossing any finish line. She outran him.

But how had she ended up in the ditch? She must have tripped and fallen or rolled and then blacked out. Did she hear him driving up behind her and scamper off the road? Did he pass back and forth slowly along the road searching for her, the engine growling like a hungry animal? Or was that a dream. It was dark then, and now it was light. That was all she knew of time. He had drugged her somehow, she also knew that. No way a half glass of beer rocked her that way. There had been a unit in her health class senior year that covered date rape, and the drug that made it easy. She couldn't remember its name, but she could describe the effects—she'd just experienced them all.

She crawled out of the cold ooze and worked her way up to the cindery shoulder. The road extended long and straight in both directions, with open fields and rolling meadows on either side, the profile of mountains in the distance. She could see a black-and-white road sign ahead with the number eleven on it. She was somewhere between Potsdam and Canton.

Her purse was gone, her wallet and phone. She had nothing. She had herself. She'd gotten away.

She stood and pulled off what remained of her tights. One of her shoes was missing. She looked down into the ditch but didn't see it. She started walking. She kicked the other shoe away and continued barefoot, no idea how far she needed to go, no other cars in sight.

She wished she could call her daddy to come get her. It was crazy, he was hours away in Morrissey, and she was grown up now and in such a hurry to go to college and no longer dependent on him, but he would drop anything he was doing for her and she would stop and sit right where she was and wait for him. If she could.

A car approached from behind her and she turned to look at it but made no motion to flag it down. The driver crossed to the far lane and sped past. Another car came from in front. No, it was a pickup truck. She stopped walking and stared at it. The driver slowed to a stop, shifted into reverse and backed up, stopping alongside her. A man wearing a camouflage hunting cap rolled down his window and asked if she needed a ride.

"No thank you."

"Are you okay?"

She started to run, one foot in front of the other, barefooted on the stones and cinder, stepping on a crushed beer can, splashing in a puddle, stubbing her toe on a rock.

The truck drove off.

She slowed again to a walk. The sun slid out from behind

another cloud. It lay low in the sky, early morning, but already warmer than yesterday and though her ripped clothing hung from her like wet laundry, she was not cold. Would her team be on the bus? Would they think she'd blown them off because she wasn't running? Says who she wasn't running.

She started out again, walking a steady pace. She focused on getting back to the dorm, taking a hot shower, sleeping for six days. She would write about what happened to her, she would fill an entire notebook, someday.

Another ten minutes of trudging and she reached the crest of a long, gentle rise in the road, then started down the other side. She felt strong enough to keep on, for as long as necessary.

She didn't hear the car until it was upon her. It came from behind; the crest of the hill blocked the noise from reaching her. She turned at the sound of tires skidding against the asphalt and saw the back end of the car whip around as it came to a stop and three doors opened at once.

Out of the car jumped Steve and Jen and Mark. Steve reached her first, putting out his arms and hugging her and Jen saying we've been driving around all night looking for you and calling you, thank God we found you. All three of them had hold of her, no one wanted to let go.

part 4

Deal

Seeking Approval

Not until driving back to Morrissey with his family did Brian begin to think about work and remember to check his voice mail: the usual fire drills, new demands, why haven't you called me. He returned one call he hadn't expected, from Dr. Marta Everson, and agreed to fly out to Chicago the next day and meet her at the airport for what Everson called a confidential meeting and potentially career-changing proposal. You would think Everson had done enough to his career already, but Brian decided to explore all possibilities, keep all options open.

They met in the Admiral Club in view of the busy runway. Brian watched jets take off and land and wheel along the taxiway while he listened to Marta explain her idea.

Dr. Everson remained convinced that Zuprone posed a danger when prescribed at high doses for weight loss. Yet its popularity continued to grow due to Caladon's aggressive and stealth marketing of it for such off-label use. The seminars she had participated in on Caladon's behalf could be justified because the presentation included discussion about other drug therapies. But the entire Zuprone sales and marketing strategy, when the programs were examined in the aggregate—now, wouldn't that tell a story of unethical and illegal practices?

No, it was not a rhetorical question. Yes, she wanted Brian to answer.

Does she think she's the first one to pose such a question? Why should he answer her?

Because Everson needed an insider at Caladon willing to blow the whistle, and did Brian know that under the legal concept of *qui tam,* he would be entitled to a percentage of the fines levied by the federal government against Caladon. The amount would likely be in the millions.

Did he know about *qui tam?*

Of course he knew it. Being awarded a slice of the settlement pie motivated many whistle-blowers, who were shunned and pressured by management, often lost their jobs, and were blackballed from their industries.

"You would know whether a case could be made against Caladon," Marta said. "You're the one who implemented the marketing programs for Zuprone."

"And what's in it for you?" Brian asked. "Why do you want to go through all of this?"

"If you could see the condition of some of my patients, you would agree it's the right thing to do. Two of them are quite ill; anorexia can be a life-threatening condition. Other patients could be experiencing similar bad outcomes—someone needs to protect consumers."

The right thing to do, plus the express line to media exposure for a publicity junkie like Everson.

But what about the fact that Dr. Everson had accepted consulting arrangements from Caladon for hosting medical education seminars about weight-loss therapies?

"I was duped, just as you were," Everson said. "I want to right a wrong."

No one had duped Brian. On the other hand, it was never too late to do the right thing. He said he would consider her proposal, knowing he had the upper hand now. Without him to blow the whistle on Caladon, Everson had no substance to her claims. But there might not be any substance, anyway. Brian didn't believe Caladon had crossed the line into illegal off-label marketing. Maybe because the line wasn't a line at all, not in the traditional sense, but a blurry landmined zone you could navigate if you knew where to step and what to avoid—and if you had an army of crack attorneys ready for triage if anything exploded in your face.

He flew back that afternoon and discussed his options with Gwen.

"If you do this, aren't you admitting you were involved in something illegal?" Gwen asked.

"Not necessarily, but I was following orders. I read about some other cases, and the whistle-blower is typically granted immunity."

"That's an awful expression—whistle-blower. It's like being a tattletale."

"You don't approve?"

"I endured my own dark period of tattling recently and it wasn't pleasant."

"That was coerced out of you," Brian pointed out. "This is just one option for me."

"You shouldn't do it for the money," Gwen said. "And it doesn't seem like a good career move, since you'll lose your job and like you said get shut out from the industry. So the only reason to do it is if Caladon is purposely practicing deception or recklessly harming people. If that's the situation, you need to step up and I'll support you all the way."

"I don't know if that's the situation. I'd like to think it wasn't."

And now, heading into Stephen's office, Brian still hadn't made up his mind what to do. With her limited sample of patients,

Marta Everson had a weak basis for a lawsuit against Caladon—unless she allied with Brian as the insider who could expose Caladon's intent. Except Caladon's intent remained murky.

But, as Stephen said, consumer watchdogs and regulators had placed a target on their industry, which is why the *Times* article raised such an uproar and put Brian in peril. If Stephen tried to fire him today, Brian could mention Everson's offer and see how it played.

Teresa caught up with him as he walked toward Stephen's office.

"Everyone's been asking if I knew where you were," she said. "I heard they even sent someone around to your house. People were thinking you committed suicide or something."

"I hope I didn't disappoint anyone."

She tugged his sleeve to stop him, turned so they were face-to-face. "They're sending me back to Jersey. I'm working on a new project to redevelop our sales territories. We've had multiple reps calling on the same doctors, fighting over who has what account, and even complaints from doctors."

"The fighting's going to get worse before you're done realigning the territories," Brian told her.

She shrugged. "I can take it."

"I'm sure you can."

Teresa started to speak, stopped, then started again. "Anyway, I want to apologize for the other day in the bar. You know, the way I threw myself at you. I shouldn't have done it, and you were right to turn me away."

"It wasn't as easy as you might think."

"Thanks, but I know you weren't that interested."

Brian nodded; Teresa was right. "When are you going back?"

"I start tomorrow. Today's my last day here."

"It could be mine, too," Brian said. "I'll stop by and see you before I leave."

No one with Brian's talent or ambition kept the same job or career path for long, and he was prepared to make a move as need or opportunity dictated. What Brian could never prepare for was losing Gwen, because he'd a glimpse of that and the view was bleak. The night Gwen was missing he lay awake for hours stroking his children's cheeks and hair and swallowing back the dread that he'd never see his wife again. He played over and over again the worst-case scenarios. At one point he moved from Nate's bed to Nora's after having been kicked too many times by his sleeping son. He dozed in and out but the dreams were as bad as being awake, and he surfaced from one of the bad ones when his phone rang and woke him, while the kids slept on and morning light filled the windows.

Her voice—quiet, a single note from breaking—telling him she was safe. Like getting a call from God and ever after you are blessed with faith. Later, when Gwen told him how she'd gotten lost—the call with Jude, losing her direction, the horrific and freezing night in the wilderness—he did not chastise her or erupt in anger or jealous conniption. He comforted her and himself by holding her and whispering how she was his one true love, the only one, and please don't ever leave him like that again.

Shelly told Brian to go right in, Stephen was waiting. She kept her face neutral, even though she knew what was about to happen: whether he was a goner or not. The executive assistants, they always knew; they held more inside information than the chairman of the board.

"Brian, sit down." Stephen rose from his chair and shook Brian's hand, as if Brian had come for an interview.

Brian sat in one of two leather chairs facing Stephen.

"We were getting a little worried about you. Thought maybe the FDA had snatched you up." Stephen laughed, making light of his own comment.

"I was away with my family on a trip we'd been planning for some time."

"Well, good, welcome back. I'll get right to the point. We have to do something about Zuprone, and I know you've been working on it for a long time. So you understand the current situation. We're going to make some changes, starting immediately."

Here it comes.

"We're going to issue a statement to the FDA and the media recommending that Zuprone not be prescribed for weight loss except in clinical trials."

"What clinical trials?"

"We've evaluated your business case and conclusions and have decided to apply for FDA approval for Zuprone as a weight-loss drug."

Brian sat speechless.

"That is still your recommendation, isn't it?" Stephen asked.

"Yes, but what about the reports of anorexia?"

"We think those are isolated incidents, but we're going to find out—without putting Caladon at risk."

"Invest that kind of money to find out about a potential side effect?"

"Well, there's more to it than that, Brian. You see, we believe Zuprone is safe and effective, and don't want to subject ourselves to lawsuits, fines, and the like—which might end up costing close to what the clinical trials and FDA application will, according to the numbers you presented."

"We might be able to wrap the further studies the FDA ordered into the new drug application," Brian said. "That would save some money."

Stephen showed his signature move, a nod to his chin while raising the eyebrows. Almost sheepish, yet a conclusive statement: letting you know you've got the picture.

"You've been a huge part of Zuprone's success, although I can see why an outsider looking in, Marcus Ward from the FDA for instance, might question tactics."

So he wasn't out of the woods yet.

"We both know many decisions regarding those tactics came from Wilcox. He was nothing if not opportunistic and aggressive. That's why he was able to build such a strong sales organization. We'll miss him."

"Miss him?"

"Resigned yesterday. We're completely overhauling the sales force and have brought in Blair McFarland from Roche. He'll be heading up sales and marketing for all of North America. You know Blair?"

"I know who he is, but I don't think we've met."

"He's up here today if you get a chance to say hello. Going back to Jersey tomorrow. See what you miss when you're gone for a few days?"

"Sounds like more than a few days in the making," Brian said.

"But you won't be working with Blair. I want you back on the clinical side, coordinating the Zuprone trials. You'll report directly to me."

Brian's eyes widened.

"Who's the MD?"

"Alice Conners."

Brian nodded. Well-respected physician from the California lab.

"This is a promotion," Stephen said. "In retrospect, you handled yourself well with Everson and the *Times* reporter. She could have done a lot more damage. And I admit none of it would have happened if I'd kept up my side of the bargain and dealt with Everson."

"She might be a problem yet," Brian said. He paused for a moment, deciding, then added, "She asked me to initiate a whistle-blower lawsuit against Caladon."

No surprise registered on Stephen; he simply shrugged. "You think that's a good idea?"

"It wouldn't be easy, but with the right people working on her side an effective case could be made."

"But you declined her invitation?"

Brian said nothing.

"Or you'll decline it now?"

Brian nodded.

"The lure of *qui tam*," Stephen said. "Like a siren's song." He stood. Meeting ended.

Returning to his office, Brian saw Teresa outside a conference room, in conversation with Blair McFarland, her new boss. He was about to stop and introduce himself but neither of them noticed Brian. Blair's eyes were locked on Teresa while she spoke, subtly moving up and down to take her in. Brian knew that look: a man with his eyes on a lush prize. Teresa knew it, too. Brian almost felt the heat shimmering off her as he passed. She stood posed like statuary, oblique hip, cocked head, only her hands moving with her words, her fingers fanned out, a gesture away from embracing Blair McFarland. She'd be much happier back in New Jersey.

Quiet and Busy

Gwen didn't plan to attend the memorial service for Jude, not after her experience getting dumped on by daughter Sheila at James Anderson's funeral. She had heard the news of Jude's death from Roger; he called, and the first words out of his mouth were "Jude Gates is dead." She spent the next hour fighting pain in her abdomen, chewing her lower lip, but finally her stomach heaved and she ran to the toilet and vomited, unable to control the convulsive reaction.

Thank God the kids were asleep. But Brian wasn't. He followed her into the bathroom, wet a washcloth, held it to her forehead. She let him comfort her but could not look at him, or at herself. Acid burned her nose and throat. She sobbed and her husband held her. What more could she ask for in a partner? He hadn't thrown a fit that she'd put herself in danger sneaking off to call Jude. He had stood firm when the police suggested Gwen wanted to be missing with Jude Gates; he wouldn't accept that reasoning. He trusted her, even though she had let him down. It was Jude he distrusted, but no matter now.

Although Brian had advised her against going to James Anderson's funeral, he suggested she attend the service for Jude, and went with her.

It was a simple event. There was no casket, no cemetery, no priest. It was held at Gull, presided over by the chef, Andrew

Cole, who spoke quietly of his long friendship and professional relationship with Jude. The tables in the dining room had been pushed to one side and the chairs arranged in rows with an aisle down the middle. Gwen recognized only two people: Dana, who sat in the first row of chairs with a young woman and man about her own age on either side of her, and Detective Keller, who stood scanning the crowd from the back of the room. After Andrew spoke, a woman read a Shakespearean sonnet that Gwen remembered from a college class years back. Someone else played the guitar and sang. One of the waiters got up and said Jude had always shown him respect and given him opportunity. Gwen wasn't surprised—even a man gunned down in a drug deal gone bad can be loved. Even that man can be a father, and terribly missed, as evidenced by Dana's drawn, stunned face. Even that man can hold allure.

When the service ended, waiters walked the room with trays of hors d'oeuvres. A bartender started making drinks, and the music system was turned on. Conversations started. Brian went to the bar while Gwen made her way and waited in line to speak to Dana. When it was her turn, she started by saying "You probably don't remember me . . . ," but Dana interrupted and said she did: "You used to help me with my homework in the restaurant."

She added, "My father mentioned you recently. He said you came here to see him."

"Yes, I did."

She'd grown tall, like her father, and Gwen recognized Jude's eyes and his nose that tipped downward.

Dana introduced her friend, Steve, and her roommate at college, Jen, and Jen's parents, who stood behind them. She explained she was moving some of her things to their house near Boston, which would become her home base now during semester breaks.

"If this happened last year, my legal guardian would have been my dad's sister in Seattle. I would have had to move there. I mean, she's not even here today. His sister. I think my father expected to live forever, although now I have to wonder why."

She clenched her jaw, and her eyes stared hard at Gwen.

"Did you know?" Dana asked.

"I'm sorry?"

"Did you know what my father did for a living? And I don't mean running a restaurant. I'm asking everyone; I need to find out."

Gwen met Dana's gaze and told her the truth. "No, I didn't know." Not for sure.

"Then why did you see him?" Dana demanded.

She answered with more care. "We reestablished our connection. I thought we were becoming friends again, your father and I."

"I've been through a lot this week." The girl's eyes were wet, but no tears spilled out. "I'm so mad at him. How could he have done this?"

Dana looked ready to reach out and hug her, and Gwen braced for it, but nothing happened. Gwen wanted to tell her that the answers were not always easy, things not always black and white, a platitude that wouldn't be helpful now, so she kept it to herself.

While Gwen had experienced an instinctual and physically violent reaction to the news of Jude's death, followed by a sleepless night and a day of fog, after the second day a sense of relief and finality eased her pain, as if a relative suffering a long illness had finally, thankfully, passed. She no longer had to wonder if Jude would continue to pursue her. She didn't have to worry about Jude's response to knowing she had informed the police, or what that might have led to. She didn't need to fulfill her promise of never having contact with Jude again, for any reason.

But now, seeing Dana, grief bloomed once more, a weary ache

spread through her. She felt prematurely old and helpless. Wasn't there something Gwen could do for her? The orphaned daughter. She had an urge to tell Dana how to contact her, if she ever needed anything.

In the end she just told Dana how sorry she was about her father and moved away for the next person waiting to speak.

She found Brian in the bar, drinking a Bloody Mary and speaking with Detective Keller. She helped herself to his drink, sucking through the straw.

"I was just telling your husband how it's the kids who end up suffering the most when the parents go wrong," Detective Keller said.

Gwen measured the comment: Was it meant for her? Did Keller believe she was a parent gone wrong?

Keller sensed her discomfort. "I'm referring to Mr. Gates," he added.

"Do you think she knew?" Brian asked.

"The daughter? Probably not. Kids are so wrapped up in their own lives, how many really pay attention to what their parents do?"

"That's true, although yours does," said Gwen. "Nate tells me that he and Andy are playing police detectives every day at recess."

"I heard they're getting to be good buddies."

"I hope your wife doesn't mind," Gwen said. "Nate's a good kid." But she knew Patty Keller did mind, because one afternoon Nate came home and asked Gwen why she did drugs.

"Where did you hear that?"

"Andy. He said you did drugs. I thought drugs were bad for you and people who do them go to jail or die."

"You're right. They are bad for you. Did you and Andy have an argument? You know how sometimes when people are angry they might say something mean just to be hurtful?"

"We had the fight after he said it."

"Tell him to stop talking that way. If he won't stop, you should find someone else to play with."

"I like playing with him."

So far, Gwen had deflected Nate's requests for an after-school play date with Andy Keller, knowing Patty Keller would not approve.

"Tell Andy he's mistaken in what he said," Gwen told her son.

At least that explained the source of a few looks she'd gotten. Not looks of condemnation, more of curiosity. A parent here and there must have found out from Patty Keller and told someone else, and so on. And so all the worry she'd endured regarding the word getting out about her arrest had amounted to nothing. The word was getting out anyway, slowly, although no one dared open their mouth and accuse her of anything, not with half the town living in some type of glass house. Perhaps people in Morrissey were more compassionate and tolerant than she had given them credit for.

Brian turned to Keller. "Have you found out for sure who shot Jude Gates? The newspaper mentioned it might have been someone from the military who worked for him."

Keller nodded. "At this point, no charges have been filed. We're still looking in to the matter."

"I know—you can't comment about an ongoing investigation."

"That's right," Keller said. "Well, if you'll excuse me, I think I'm done here. If I stay any longer I'll want one of those Bloody Marys." He made a last scan of the room. "I'll see you around school." He shook hands with Brian and then Gwen and walked out.

"He must be looking for Jude's other business associates," Brian said.

"I think they'd be smart enough to stay away."

"Especially with the 'bad guy hunter' on the case."

Thanks to a front page article in the *Morrissey Bee,* Detective Keller had found local fame and earned a reputation as a detective who hunted "bad guys." The reporter wrote about his dozen years of service in the police department, his relentless pursuit of justice, his spearheading of the town's battle against drugs, and—most prominently in the article—his bold foray into the Adirondacks where he'd tracked a local drug dealer, Jude Gates, to his indoor pot farm, only to find him executed gangland style. Not to come away empty-handed, Detective Keller apprehended the dealer's accomplice who was returning to the property unaware that police were on the premises. The suspect, Aaron Capuano, was being held in Franklin County.

There was no mention of Gwen in the article.

When asked by the reporter what he was doing outside of his jurisdiction, Keller responded, "Hunting bad guys."

Despite the hero worship from the weekly paper and a quote praising Keller from the Morrissey chief of police, Gwen had heard from Roger that the detective was under investigation for operating outside his jurisdiction and not contacting the state police or the Franklin County sheriff until after he'd found Jude's body and arrested Aaron Capuano.

As for her own case, the DA had dropped all charges, not just the vehicular manslaughter that Roger promised would never stick, but also the lesser possession and DUI charges. She was cleared, legally, although she continued to replay the accident in her mind, looking for a way to avoid it. She couldn't find one.

With Jude, she understood some degree of accountability came back to her as well. She tried to piece together a cause and effect around the events that led to Jude's death, and what role she played on the cause side. Jude was killed the same day she told him about the police. Did he panic and make a mistake, one that got him murdered in a drug deal? He didn't seem the type that panicked easily. Or had he been shot by the police—Detective Keller was up there; he was the one who found the body. Keller had known about Jude for almost two weeks, maybe he got his chance and let it rip, then framed the young Aaron Capuano, a disabled veteran. She couldn't rule it out.

"There's no way of knowing," Brian told her. "The best thing is to put this behind you." He didn't want to analyze her tipping off Jude about the police. Or calling Jude back on the phone to explain herself. Or getting lost in the wilderness. She had apologized to her husband and he accepted her apology. He didn't ask more questions.

She didn't tell Brian about Jude kissing her the day she picked up the bag, and his attempt at a second kiss the morning she ran into him at the market. The second time would help justify her blurting out the news about the police as a way to fend him off, but the cost of telling Brian outweighed any benefits. What benefits were there, anyway? Confessing the kiss to Brian wouldn't make her feel better, and it wouldn't help Brian, either. Gwen already felt better, confident she wouldn't make a similar mistake again.

She stayed quiet and busy: helping the kids with homework, driving to soccer practice and dance classes, finding volunteers for Helping Hands for the PTA. She didn't get high, because now she had nothing to smoke and nowhere to get it, and she didn't feel like it anyway, although that could change.

Brian spent a week in California in meetings to launch the start of Zuprone's clinical trials. When he returned, he told her there was a possibility they'd need to relocate to Santa Cruz. The company was taking a wait-and-see approach to determine if a transfer was necessary and would make the decision in a few months, by Christmas at the latest. Santa Cruz was situated right on the coast, on the northern curve of Monterey Bay, a beach and tourist town of perfect weather. At first, Gwen had reacted negatively: their entire lives were here. Their friends, the schools, their mountain house. Parents and extended families within driving distance. You can't just abandon your home. But after her initial objection, Gwen realized that moving would not be traumatic. Families moved all the time to other cities and parts of the country. There was no reason they couldn't find their place in another community, start again, make new connections. Whether they relocated or not, Brian was happier on the clinical side at Caladon than he'd been in business development.

Let's just wait and see what happens, Brian said. We don't have to make a decision yet, so let's not tell anyone about this.

Gwen could leave the issue open, along with the unknowns about the accident and Jude. She didn't need to chase closure, as Brian had suggested when she went to James Anderson's funeral, although sometimes closure found her. She heard from Sheila Anderson, through the mail on a personal letter handwritten on the Alzheimer's Association stationery. Sheila apologized for lashing out at Gwen at the funeral and followed her apology with a request for a donation. She wrote that she volunteered for the Alzheimer's Association now and was raising money for families that needed to care for a loved one suffering from the disease. Gwen wrote a check for five hundred dollars, and that closed a door behind her, at least most of the way.

She'd Be More Careful

Hay bales piled two deep and six high shaped a maze of turnbacks and dead ends. Dried stalks of straw shuffled underfoot. The air smelled like a barn. A hand-painted sign on cardboard between two columns of hay said: ENTER HERE.

Gwen followed the kids into the labyrinth.

"Catch us, Mommy, catch us," Nora yelled. They disappeared at the first left turn.

Gwen turned once at the end of a passage, turned again, came to a dead end, backtracked to a T and was lost. Panic jumped her like a mugger in a black alley. Alone in the wilderness again, the shakes about to set in. Please don't let her be doomed to freak out at every wrong turn from here on in.

She called for Brian to retrieve her and let Nora and Nate fend for themselves.

The maze filled the entire greenhouse except for three picnic tables near the front where parents waited while their kids navigated one end to the other and then came running back a long aisle between the glass walls and the hay bales.

Gwen retreated to one of the tables and sat next to Marlene. Roger and Brian went in the maze to chase the kids.

"What's wrong?" Marlene asked.

"I don't like the idea of getting lost in there," Gwen said. "It creeps me out. My heart started racing. I even started to sweat. I mean, it's just a kids' maze."

"I can understand it, given what you've been through. You just need more time. After Roger had his bicycle accident last year, he didn't ride for months, even after his shoulder healed."

She took Gwen's hand. "Come on, let's get some cider."

They left the greenhouse and walked across the yard to where folding tables served as a snack bar. Cider, coffee, and sugar doughnuts lined the tables. Carts of pumpkins and gourds were parked to one side. Price tags hung on Indian corn bundles. Marlene bought two cups of hot cider and gave one to Gwen. They found a spot on a wooden bench. Today was the autumn open house at Helderberg Community Farm, a sixty-acre organic operation that sold seasonal produce shares. Gwen split a share with Marlene each week. All summer they had eaten fresh lettuce, green beans, snow peas, eggplants, peppers, beets, tomatoes, corn, and more. There had been too much parsley, no one liked the lemongrass, but otherwise the farm share had been great and Gwen had even gotten her kids eating more vegetables. That alone made the cost worthwhile.

The owners, Karen and Eric Granger, graduates of the Cornell College of Agriculture, held open houses in spring, summer, and fall. Brian and Gwen had come with the kids for the summer solstice celebration, and Gwen had taken the kids swimming in the pond once over the summer.

When the kids emerged from the maze, they all rode the hay wagon out to the pumpkin patch. They sat on bales on the wagon, pulled by the tractor, bumping along the rutted track. Eric, tanned from a season of farming, drove the tractor. Gwen sat with Brian, across from Marlene and Roger. The kids had paired off by gender. Nora sat with Abby, discussing the merits of fat pumpkins versus tall ones. Nate sat with Josh, who was explaining the differ-ence between batting average and on-base percentage.

The distance from the barnyard to the pumpkin patch covered a few hundred yards, past dried cornstalks, fading raspberry bushes, and harvested vegetable rows on one side and a stretch of hardwoods and a toolshed on the other. The track dipped and pitched, and the tractor labored and fumed. It looked like an old one, painted a few times, the uncovered engine exposed like a beating heart. The hay seats cushioned the bumps but Gwen was sore and felt each one.

They pulled into the pumpkin patch and Eric U-turned in a broad arc and waved and smiled to them as the wagon circled along behind. A baseball cap shadowed his eyes. An educated farmer, he stood out among his customers who also were edu-cated but had chosen to become lawyers, professors, bankers, and business executives. He and his wife had four kids, two girls around the ages of Nate and Nora, twin boys on the cusp of ado-lescence. A fifth was on the way, with Karen displaying a belly that could be hiding a pumpkin.

Eric shut the engine, climbed down, and released the ladder at the back of the wagon. He swung it to the ground and reached a hand to help his passengers down, his stone dry fingers and cal-lused palm like gritty sandpaper in Gwen's hand.

He spoke to each person as he offered help on the stairs. Thanks for coming out today, he said. It's good to see you. Hi, I'm glad you could make it. Welcome.

The kids were already roaming the field, turning over pump-kins, looking for perfect shapes. Roger and Marlene walked off along the edge of the field, heads bowed in intense, whispered discussion. Gwen hoped they were not arguing, at least wished it wouldn't escalate to yelling at each other. She'd witnessed that between them in the past and it was an ugly and embarrassing sight.

She held hands with Brian as they walked the first row.

"We have to go farther back, all the good ones will be picked over here," Brian said.

"That hay wagon is too bumpy, I think I'll be walking back to the car," Gwen said. "I'm a little sore."

"I'm sorry."

"Don't be."

They'd made love last night, which accounted for the achy ride on the hay wagon, but Gwen was happy. They'd both been asleep and she woke from the dream, the one about being lost, twice she's had it now. But it was Brian who was lost, not her. Or missing. He could be missing or have left her, but the setting was forested wilderness and she was looking for him yet there was nothing except trees and tangles of brush and ferns on the ground, and darkness and isolation ahead. She woke and her heart was beating hard and she felt Brian next to her and she scaled him, finding a hold and pulling herself on top, kissing him awake and getting him aroused and inside her before he was fully aware. As soon as they finished Brian fell back asleep, but he had a smile for her this morning and the intimacy had radiated between them all day.

Somehow what had transpired with Jude provided her relationship with Brian a boost of fresh energy that reminded her of their early days together. They'd touched each other a lot this past week. Made love three times already. Rushed the kids to bed so they could spend the evenings together. Brian called her from work several times a day. She didn't know how long the passion could last, but she woke thankful each morning the spell still held.

"What about this one?" Brian said. He held up a pumpkin in two hands, round as a basketball with symmetrical grooves and smooth orange ridges running from a curved green stem.

"It looks perfect."

Nate approached them, lumbering over clods of dirt and withered vines, holding his pumpkin in two hands. If the one Brian had picked was the archetype of a pumpkin, this one was a mutated disaster: oblong in shape with a flattened side where it had lain on the ground, and marred by ghastly bumps like a bad case of acne all over it. Its color ranged from green to orange and on to brown.

"Look at my pumpkin, look at my pumpkin!" Nate called.

"It's unique," Gwen said. "I've never seen one like it."

"It's a monster," said Nate. "See, here are the eyes and this is the mouth and these are the bullets."

"Bullets?"

"Yeah, it shoots bullets."

Nora called to Brian from the far end of the patch. "Dad! Help!" She had her arms around a giant pumpkin, but couldn't lift it off the ground. Brian went back and picked it up and started walking toward the wagon. Twice he stopped to rest and set the pumpkin down. By the time he reached Gwen, sweat sheened his forehead.

"Mom, I found the biggest one," Nora said. "It weighs a hundred pounds, right, Dad?"

"Feels like it."

"Yuck, that's so ugly," Nora said, looking at the pumpkin Nate held.

"I found the scariest one," said Nate.

"We all found good pumpkins," said Gwen.

Brian pulled out his camera and started snapping photos of the kids next to their pumpkins. Then came the requisite goofy faces: Nora's tongue sticking out, Nate staring cross-eyed. Gwen stepped in and posed them with their arms around each other—a regular smile, please—and snapped a half-dozen more pictures, one of which she hoped would turn out well enough for a holiday card.

Then Nora took several pictures of Gwen and Brian. Gwen would never have called herself photogenic, but when she looked at the photos in the camera's tiny viewer the word *radiant* came to mind. Even Brian noticed.

"You look great," he said.

"I feel great, and I love you." She kissed him.

They went back to the hay wagon and climbed up with the pumpkins, Brian heaving Nora's orange boulder onto the wagon floor, then pushing it to a spot in the corner. Roger was on the wagon with Josh and Abby, each holding pumpkins. Other passengers returned with their pumpkins. Marlene still wandered through the field.

"I'm going to walk back," Gwen said.

"You can bring Marlene with you, unless she's staying out there until the Great Pumpkin comes," Roger said.

Gwen heard the edge in his voice. They'd been fighting.

"We'll save you a cider doughnut," Brian told her. "Right, kids?"

"Do we have to?"

"Of course we have to."

"How many can we have?"

This time one of Eric's teenage sons climbed up and started the tractor. The engine coughed, spewed a blast of exhaust, and settled to idle. Eric's son got down again and secured the ladder step to the wagon and got back on the tractor and clutched into gear. Gwen waved to her family. Nora gave a thumbs-up; Nate was looking the other way. Brian blew her a kiss and she laughed—had he ever blown her a kiss before? She couldn't remember.

She waited for Marlene, who walked toward her as soon as the tractor and wagon left. Together they started along the rutted path. There were raspberry bushes to one side, the sagging canes dotted with late, stunted fruit.

"Are you okay?" Gwen asked. "It looked like you and Roger were talking about something pretty serious."

"We pick the worst times to have the baby discussion. All I had to do was mention that Karen looks really good with her pregnancy and that set it off."

"He's still against the idea?"

"Still and always. And you know what the main reason is? He doesn't want to be tied down. He says we're just getting a little freedom—as if raising a family were some kind of jail sentence."

"I'm sure he doesn't mean it that way."

"We've got our two, I should be satisfied, he says. He's probably right." Marlene tripped on a broken stalk of corn at the edge of the track. Gwen reached a hand to help her stay up.

"You and Brian seem so happy, how do you get along so well all the time?"

"We don't want another baby."

"You know what I mean."

"Not all the time, but right now—we feel lucky, like we dodged a bullet. But Brian says we didn't dodge, it just happened to miss us."

"It's even scarier when you put it that way."

They walked a few more steps in silence. "You know what?" Gwen said. "I really need to pee." She'd felt it during the hayride out and while looking for pumpkins. Between the soreness and her bladder she couldn't wait any longer.

They passed a shed that backed against a line of trees separating two fields. There were two bays with sliding wooden doors. "I'm going behind here," she told Marlene.

She stood at the side of the shed and looked back to the pumpkin patch. Marlene watched the tractor in the distance. Gwen undid the snap on her jeans, dropped her panties and squatted. She peed and felt a sting. She looked in her purse for a tissue or napkin to wipe herself. There was nothing. She unzipped an inner pocket and felt around and her hand came up with a crumpled scrap of tissue. When she unfolded it something fell to the ground.

She reached down to pick it up. It was part of a joint, the remaining half from the day she'd gotten high in Thacher Park after buying the bag from Jude. That day. She remembered she had wrapped the half-smoked joint in the tissue and stowed it in here and had worn the string clutch like a long necklace, which never left her until Brian held it for her when they left the hospital, she in the police cruiser. No one had looked in it. Gwen had forgotten anything was there.

"What is it?" Marlene asked.

Gwen pulled her pants and stood up. "Part of a joint."

"Oh my God, do you have any matches?"

Without thinking, Gwen rummaged the inside pocket and found the pack of matches she'd picked up on her way out of Gull. She paused. Wait. How could she, after what happened? But she didn't have to say no, not always, not forever. It was a beautiful day after a rough stretch. Brian was driving—so she wouldn't get in that situation again. And she'd tell him, which is what he asked her to do. She'd be more careful.

They were alone. The hay wagon was back at the yard. Nothing but crisp corn stalks and trampled vines and a background of autumn trees. A breeze blew stray clouds across the sky.

Marlene held the joint; Gwen struck the match. They passed it a couple of times, glancing back toward the group of people near the snack stand and greenhouse, like two teenagers sneaking behind school.

"Tastes sweet," Gwen said.

"It's been too long," added Marlene.

Then the shed door slid open on steel rollers. Eric stepped out holding a bucket of tools. He sniffed the air and found them.

Marlene dropped the joint, which they'd burned down to almost a roach. Gwen mashed it with her shoe.

"Make sure that's out," Eric said. "It's been pretty dry."

"Sorry," Gwen said. "We didn't think anyone was around."

Busted again. The pot was just kicking in, with it the embarrassment.

Eric grinned, not as if he'd caught them, but as if he'd been the one caught. He said, "You know, just between us, this season I set aside a hidden patch and cultivated a few plants—just to see how well it could grow. I got a lot more than I expected. More than I can use."

"You're a natural farmer," Marlene said.

"Oh, yeah—it's all organic." He set down the tool bucket. "But I can't exactly offer it as part of the produce share."

"No, you can't do that," Gwen agreed. "I can tell you right now, you don't want the wrong people knowing."

"Exactly."

"Maybe you can start a new kind of share," Marlene suggested. "Only for a few people."

Eric nodded. "That's the idea I had in mind. But how do I let the right people know about it, without letting the wrong people find out?"

"It's hard," Gwen admitted. "I wouldn't know where to begin."

"Well, for starters, you can count me in," Marlene said.

They both turned to Gwen. She smiled and shrugged and looked back to the farmyard. She saw Brian and the kids at a picnic table, one large and two small figures hunched over a white paper bag. She'd better hurry back if she wanted a doughnut.

Stash

READING GROUP GUIDE

Warning: Some plot points are revealed in the questions below.

1. Gwen believes that in Morrissey, "You have your life and you're happy with it, as long as you do your best, look your best, perform your best." What type of internal or external pressures make Gwen feel this way? What do Gwen's comments indicate about her seemingly ideal suburban life?

2. Gwen feels awful about the death of James Anderson and keeps reliving the accident in her mind. What is her level of responsibility for what happened? Is she unfairly targeted by the police when threatened with charges of vehicular manslaughter?

3. The first time Gwen goes to tell Jude about the police, she changes her mind and leaves, but the next time she sees Jude, she tells him. Why does Gwen warn Jude that she'd given his name to the police? What are the consequences of her telling Jude?

4. Gwen, Brian, and Jude all take significant risks. What are those risks? Why do they take them?

5. On page 27, it is noted that "[P]harmaceutical promotion had more gray than a stormy sky." Consider the moral dilemma that Brian faces while "promoting" Zuprone's off-label use for weight loss. Does he feel responsible for the patients who developed anorexia? Should he?

6. Compare Gwen's flirtations with Jude to Brian's with Teresa. Do either of these flirtations pose a real threat to Brian and Gwen's marriage? Do you agree with Gwen's decision not to tell Brian about her kiss with Jude? Does a marriage need to have full, complete honesty in order for each spouse to maintain trust in the other?

7. What are Jude's feelings about Dana going off to college? Does he always have his daughter's best interests in mind? How would you describe their father/daughter relationship?

8. Jude is portrayed as having been very careful throughout his dealing career. What blinds him to the risks of the deal he is working on now?

9. What is the basis for attraction between Aaron and Dana? Is there anything positive about their brief time together?

10. Is Brian in a difficult situation at work because of his own decisions, or is he simply caught in the wrong place at the wrong time? Did he act in the best interest of his company, himself, or the consumers taking Zuprone?

11. Toward the end of the novel, Gwen reflects: "It didn't seem stupid at the time, what she'd done; it didn't seem lethal. Her behavior still fit within her moral compass: be responsible for

your actions, be fair to everyone, keep your word." Throughout the novel, does she stay true to her moral compass? Are there any times she goes off course?

12. What decision does Gwen make at the end of the novel? Does Gwen undergo any significant change?

13. What does the novel have to say about drug use? Does society view drug use differently, depending on whether the drug is legal or illegal? Do you think the author would support legalizing marijuana? Why or why not?

14. The novel is told from the viewpoints of different characters. What effect does this have on the building of suspense? On the pace of the novel?

15. "Stash" refers to something put away or hidden, often for future use. Could the title of the novel refer to anything other than drugs?